COMING OF AGE
IN BERKELEY

A NOVEL

D1526372

JAKE WARNER

CourtYard Editions
Berkeley

Coming of Age in Berkeley is a work of fiction. Although the physical details of Berkeley, the Bay Area and the book's other settings are as accurate as the author can make them, all characters are the products of the author's imagination. Any resemblance to actual events or persons is coincidental.

ISBN: 978-0-692-10643-3
Copyright © 2018 by Jake Warner
All rights reserved
Published by CourtYard Editions
Berkeley, CA
www.courtyardeditions.net

For Toni,
Love
overflowing

Did my heart love till now?
Forswear it, sight, for I ne'er saw true beauty till this night.
WILLIAM SHAKESPEARE

Soul meets soul on lovers lips.
PERCY BYSSHE SHELLY

MONDAY

AS HE WALKS DOWN THE PATH that traces the south margin of Cal's Memorial Glade, Alec Burns sees a chunky paperback protruding from the bottom of the pack worn by the tall girl just ahead. Although the book, which is more in than out of the torn seam, jiggles with each of the girl's long strides, it somehow hangs on to the frayed fabric. Then, as the book suddenly drops another half inch, Alec, who plans to veer left to grab a latte at Café Milano on Bancroft Avenue, instead picks up his pace. Now only a few steps behind the girl whose baggy jeans do little to conceal her round, upturned bum, he mouths "Fall baby, fall." Seemingly in response the fat book shifts to the right and descends at a 45 degree angle. Although it now can only be a matter of seconds before the book finally respects the law of gravity, Alec nevertheless slows his pace, embarrassed to realize he is in danger of stalking the girl. But before he can turn towards the café, the book hits the ground with a plop, rolls over once and comes to a rest at his feet.

Feeling, or perhaps hearing something, the girl begins to turn back before apparently dismissing her concern and taking several more steps down the path. Then, as if deciding to trust her first instinct, she executes a ballerina spin, long honey blond hair flying, to face Alec, who has picked up the book.

"That's mine," the girl says in a surprisingly musical contralto as she points at the worn copy of *The Brothers Karamzov* in Alec's right hand. Surprised by the girl's intensity, and even more by her almond-shaped blue eyes, Alec—who thinks of himself as something of an expert when it comes to chatting up attractive girls—is tongue-tied.

"That's my *Brothers K* you just picked up," the girl insists, this time louder as if perhaps Alec is hard of hearing.

"It fell out of your backpack," Alec replies, eyes drifting down to see that her over-sized maroon sweatshirt with Tsunami printed on the front in bold yellow letters doesn't completely hide her curves. Jerking his gaze back to the girl's arresting blue eyes he adds, "I'm also reading it for European Lit, but I haven't seen you in class."

"I'm taking Physics this summer. I read it on my own a couple of years ago and I've been just kind of revisiting my favorite parts."

Still holding the paperback in his right hand Alec moves to the girl's right, all but forcing her to fall into step. Then, as if belatedly realizing he's in danger of being impolite he blurts, "What passages do you like best?"

"Above all don't lie to yourself. The man who lies to himself and listens to his own lies comes to a point that he cannot distinguish the truth within him, or around him and so loses respect for himself and for others."

"Do you think that's profound or romantic bullshit?" Alec asks, a grin lighting his angular face.

"I don't really know," the girl replies looking down as if to avoid an invisible stone. Then, after a short pause she adds in a tone that makes it clear she seriously doubts whether he has opened the book, "OK, so why don't you tell me your favorite part?"

"I'm good with Father Zosima's wisdom, but I also like the passage that goes something like this: *"I find to my amazement that the more I love mankind as a whole, the less I love man as an individual."*

"'In particular'."

"Huh?"

"It ends with – *'the less I love man in particular'*, not, *'the less I love man as an individual'*."

"Did you read the book or memorize it?"

"Pretty much both I guess," the girl replies, reaching out her right hand for her book. "It's not hard for me to remember things."

"I'd love to hear more about why you admire the *Brothers K* so much. How about I buy you a coffee?"

"How about you give me my book back?"

"Of course," Alec says extending his hand, "but what about coffee?"

"Sorry, I have to go," the girl replies, snatching the plump paperback before abruptly turning right on an intersecting path and almost loping towards the north side of the campus.

"But, but I don't even know your name," Alec shouts after her retreating back.

"Tamiko," she says over her shoulder, now moving so fast she's almost running.

. . . . .

Twenty minutes later, Tamiko O'Shea Gashkin pushes through the front door of Bay Books, a small publisher located on Ensenada Street in North Berkeley, her face flushed. "Hi dear, did you run all the way from Cal, or did a tornado fly you over?" Meg asks, looking up. As the plump gray-haired receptionist and impresario of the small bookstore Bay maintains at the front of the converted two-story house, Meg routinely acts as surrogate mother for all sixteen employees.

"I walked fast I guess," Tamiko replies, not sure why her heart's racing and she feels so flustered.

Turning towards the now buzzing phone, Meg says, "Your mom went to lunch with the boss, but she wants me to remind you that you have a mailing to get out."

As Meg says "Bay Books how can I help you?" into her headset, Tamiko makes her way to her cubicle. It's in what used to be a laundry room but now houses a superannuated gaggle of copy and fax machines including an Apple computer so old even the student interns disdain to use it. Pulling up a chair, Tamiko accesses Bay's master media list and begins printing out address labels. Because Bay Books can't afford even marginally current mailing equipment she has to paste the labels on the envelopes by hand before stuffing each with a copy of Bay's newest thriller along with a press release.

"Tami, what's going on?" an impatient voice demands. "Are you okay? Did you doze off?"

"I'm fine, Mom," Tamiko replies, shaking her head as she surfaces from her day-dream of walking on and on next to the tall, dark haired boy holding her book. "I guess I was thinking about something while I was waiting for the labels to print."

"It must have been pretty important since you don't seem to have noticed that you printed them on regular paper, not gummed label stock—not to mention that you've knocked over your water bottle."

Standing quickly, Tamiko feels lightheaded and so reaches to hold the back of the wooden chair.

"Tami, are you ill?" Amy Gashkin asks as she places her right hand on Tamiko's brow. "Just sit back down and talk to me."

"Mom, I told you, I'm fine, everything is great, really."

"Tami, what's going on? Did something happen today at your Physics class?"

"You promised to stop calling me Tami."

"Given that it's been less than a month since you switched back to Tamiko, maybe you can cut me some slack. And don't think I haven't noticed that you're trying to change the subject. So please talk to me."

"I met this guy, or maybe he met me, I'm not sure. It was on that path down Faculty Glade. You know, in front of that faux Greek library."

"A student at Cal? I've told you a dozen times college guys are absolutely off-limits."

"A beautiful college boy, tall with this very thick dark hair kinda like over his ears. And, well, you'll laugh, but like he has these amazing soft brown eyes the color of cinnamon," Tamiko adds, now squatting to help her mother wipe up the water.

"Tami, or Tamiko if you prefer, just how old is this tall shaggy boy? And more to the point what did he say when you told him you're only fifteen and not allowed to date college boys, with or without cinnamon eyes?"

"That's two questions, Mom," Tamiko replies smiling slightly as she realizes her mother is now more agitated than she is. "Anyway, it's nothing to worry about, since I'll never see him again."

4

"Good news there, but still, please tell me what happened."

"A book, my big fat *Brothers K* fell out of the rotted-out seam at the bottom of my pack and he picked it up. Oh my god Mom, like that pack is so embarrassing. Not only is it falling apart, but it has a teddy bear on the flap."

"You're the one who has refused to give it up, I guess because your dad gave it to you just before he was killed. But sure, we can stop at REI on the way home to grab a new one."

"Thanks," Tamiko says, standing as she touches her Mom on the arm.

"But back to the subject at hand. What happened after this guy picked up your book and handed it back to you?" Amy demands.

"He didn't."

"He didn't what?"

"Give me back the book, or at least not right away. He just started walking next to me while he asked which parts I like best. Did I already tell you he's way tall? Like, Mom, he makes me feel normal. But so anyway, I told him one of my favorite lines and and he said he liked that part too and then quoted a passage I love. I mean Mom, he even got most of…"

"He may be cute, but his pickup technique isn't very original," Amy interrupts. "Next you're going to tell me he looked into your eyes and told you how expressive they were?"

"Right at the beginning he did look into my eyes and I guess, well, I guess I kinda looked back. Mom, that was when I got this weird feeling all over—kinda like I sometimes do when I'm amped before a big game."

"What happened to reclaiming your book and saying goodbye?"

"That's when he asked me for coffee, I wanted to say yes, but I don't know how to drink coffee, or even order it—latte, cappuccino, au lait, macchiato or whatever—might as well be Swahili as far as I'm concerned."

"Is this story going to end?" Amy asks, not bothering to keep the annoyance out of her voice.

"When I asked for my book back again he gave it to me and I just kind of took off, almost running all the way over here."

"That's a relief. But Tami, to be clear, you've never even been on a date with anyone your own age and you're not going to begin with a college guy who may be three or four years older and light-years more experienced."

"High school boys are just so lame," Tamiko says, wrinkling her face in exaggerated disdain.

"That's an unacceptable word."

"Retarded, then."

"What's gotten into you? Please don't use…"

"Immature, feckless, crude, puerile, ineffectual, useless, hopeless, feeble, callow…"

"That's enough, I'm sure there are exceptions."

"Mom, think about it. I go to college more than high school so even if there are a few half-grown-up high school boys, which I seriously doubt, how would I meet them?"

"To be accurate you take community college courses, you don't go to college—which is a huge difference. And being intellectually precocious doesn't make you a day older." Then, moving towards the door, Amy turns back and adds, "Just so you know, if you want to drink coffee with someone your own age, order a cappuccino and put in two or three sugars. But for now, please put gummed labels on the envelopes, insert a review copy and press release, and have it all ready for the UPS guy by four o'clock."

TUESDAY

CLAD IN JEANS AND A BLACK T-SHIRT, Alec sits in the last row of his European Literature lecture in Evans Hall. A few minutes before the bells at the top of Cal's landmark bell tower chime eleven, he eases out the door and makes his way to the spot where he first saw the tall girl with the other worldly eyes. Having checked a map of the Cal campus to see that the LeConte Hall physics building is several hundred yards northeast, he isn't surprised when, wearing the same baggy jeans and tent-like maroon sweatshirt, she comes into view fifty feet uphill. Spotting him, she stops so abruptly Alec fears she may turn and run back the way she has come.

Apparently unconvinced by his wide smile, the tall girl remains frozen, students streaming around her on both sides as if she were a truck stalled in the middle lane of the interstate. Finally, almost as if willing herself forward she steps briskly down the path towards him. When she is still ten feet away she extends her hand as she says "Hello, I'm Tamiko Gashkin."

Determined not to smile at the girl's awkward formality, Alec takes her strong, long fingers in his even longer ones as he replies, "Alec Burns, and I'm very pleased to see you again. I was worried we might miss one another and not have our chance to talk about Dostoevsky. Do you have time for that coffee today?"

"Okay, but on one condition."

Afraid she's about to say something about her unswerving loyalty to her boyfriend, girlfriend, or God, Alec, nevertheless, says "Sure."

"You have to let go of my hand."

"Right, sorry," Alec says as he frees it. Then, searching for something neutral to say, he adds, "I like your new backpack."

"My dad gave me the old one three years ago. It's been falling apart for a while, but I kept stitching it back together."

7

"You're close to your dad?"

"He was killed, run over by a beer truck on Shattuck Avenue," Tamiko replies, her voice trailing off.

"I'm so sorry."

"One second I had the world's best dad and the next second, I didn't. End of story."

Okay, how can I possibly respond to that Alec thinks as they approach the place where the book had fallen the day before. Worried that the silence has gone on so long that this skittish girl might again veer off on the intersecting path, Alec blurts, "Gashkin, is that Polish? And your first name, Tamiko, I'm guessing Japanese."

"Gashkin's Russian. I'm half Russian, but my family is from the far northwest, so I'm sort of Finnish Russian. That's my dad's side. My mom is half Irish and half Japanese, but looks like she just got off the boat from Yokohama."

"The Irish seems to have lost out when it came to naming you," Alec replies with a chuckle.

"My middle name is O'Shea if you have to know."

"Do you read Dostoyevsky because of your Russian ancestry?"

"I read all sorts of books, not just Russian authors, but you're right in a way since my grandmother Vera probably wouldn't talk to me if I hadn't read every word Gogol, Turgenev, Tolstoy and Dostoyevsky ever wrote."

"What about Pushkin and Chekhov?" Alec asks. "And then of course there's also Pasternak," he adds, hoping Tamiko won't guess that this is his last Russian.

"Them too, and of course you're just getting started, or would be if you could fire up Wikipedia without me seeing you," Tamiko says, turning to address Alec as if daring him to deny it.

"Ha," Alec snorts, all but conceding she's read his mind. Then, in an effort to change the subject he asks, "Is your grandmother actually from Russia?"

"Is she? Oh my god. She and my grandfather were in the Bolshoi. They defected in 1975."

"Ah, now I understand why you stand up so straight. Was it a big deal when they defected?" Alec asks, now genuinely fascinated.

"Huge. They were among the Bolshoi's most popular dancers, which made them like rock stars in the old Soviet Union. When they were performing in Sweden and somehow made it to the U.S. Embassy in Stockholm, it was an international incident."

"Tell me."

"My grandfather says that at the time, the Russians and the Americans were disputing a load of big things, so it was like he and my grandmother were high-profile minnows caught in a shark fight. For several months while they were essentially imprisoned in the Embassy things looked pretty desperate for the minnows. But then, for reasons totally unrelated to them, the sharks declared a temporary truce, and somehow the minnows got tossed into the deal and found themselves dancing in New York City."

As they approach Campanile Way, the esplanade that divides the Cal campus south to north, Alec places his left hand lightly on Tamiko's elbow to steer her towards the Free Speech Movement Café on the ground floor of the concrete and glass student library. As they walk past kiosks displaying the front pages of English-language newspapers from a couple of dozen countries, Alec says, "My idea, so my treat. Just tell me what you want. While I get in line why don't you go out on the terrace and try to score us a place to sit?"

"Can I have a cappuccino with two sugars?"

Surprised that Tamiko expects the barista to dispense the sugar, Alec tries not to smile as he points at the shelf holding plastic cutlery and condiments. "The sugar is in the little brown bags on the left."

Blushing slightly, Tamiko takes three sugars just in case the coffee is truly foul before pushing through the glass door at the far end of the café. Now on a cement patio covered by a translucent plastic top that effectively screens a few dozen tables from the sun's aggressive brightness, she feels so awkward among the older students and faculty types, she glances around hoping to identify an escape route. But the patio is entirely enclosed by a four-foot concrete wall with the only exit leading back the way she came. Because all the shaded tables are occupied she reluctantly makes her way out from under the roof to an unoccupied table in full sun. Placing her backpack at her feet she remembers the breathing instructions her grandmother Vera has taught her to help cope with the bouts of panic she experienced in the months after her dad's death. Put your tongue behind your front teeth and breathe in through your nose for four slow counts. Hold your breath for another five beats. Finally as if you are sighing, breathe out through your nose to a count of six. Repeat for as many times as it takes to feel better.

As Tamiko finally feels her heart begin to slow she also realizes she is in danger of cooking in the eighty-degree sun. Pulling the sweatshirt over her head she tries to will herself smaller so as to better fit the white scoop-necked top she grabbed from her mom's bureau. Taking another deep breath as she closes her eyes against the sun's glare, Tamiko hears a low whistle. Opening them she sees Alec has scored a table in the shade a few feet away. "C'mon over here," he says, "I want to be able to see your eyes."

Staying where she is for an extra long moment, Tamiko slowly stands, drapes her sweatshirt around her shoulders with the sleeves looped across her chest and joins him at the table that just must have been vacated. "Please don't flirt with me if that's what you're doing," she says ripping the top off one of the sugar packets and letting its contents run into her cup.

"It won't be easy, but I'll try," Alec replies, not quite stifling his grin.

"You're off to a terrible start," Tamiko replies trying not to return his smile as she reaches for a hunk of the berry scone Alec has broken in pieces. "But hey, do you want to hear a stupid dog joke? I'm warning you—it's like mega-stupid."

"Sure," Alec replies thinking that if it makes Tamiko O'Shea Gashkin relax he can laugh at anything.

"This dude comes into a bar with his black Labrador. The dog sits on one barstool, the dude on another and the dude orders two martinis. As if this is a routine occurrence, the bartender mixes the drinks and places one in front of the dog and the other in front of the dude. The dog laps, the dude sips and when they're done the dude pays, leaving a nice tip. For the next several days the dude and the dog return at the same time, enjoy their martinis, pay and head out. Finally, after a week, the two show up at their regular time with the only difference being that the dude is carrying a package wrapped in brown paper. After he and the dog finish their drinks, he hands the package to the bartender saying "You've been so nice to us we brought you a present."

"'Really, for me?' the bartender reacts in surprise. 'Thank you, but what is it?'

"'Two lobsters,' replies the dude.

"'Wonderful, my wife loves lobsters, I'll take them home for dinner,' the bartender exclaims with enthusiasm.

"'No, no, they've already had their dinner, they want to go to the movies.'"

Alec, who hates jokes, and has begun to worry that he will spoil the moment by laughing too soon, or not at all, erupts with a sound between a chortle and a snort. Whether he's laughing at the dumb joke, or the almost impossibly lovely girl who just told it, he couldn't have said, but laugh he does, and with honest delight. Then, as he begins to sober up he locks his eyes on Tamiko's and sees that for the first time since she turned to find him holding her book, she's staring back.

We have contact, Alec thinks, continuing to look into Tamiko's almond-shaped blue eyes. Then, feeling as if he's been flipped upside down, he shakes his head slightly to dispel his vertigo. With his eyes still locked on hers Alec hears himself say, "Although we've just met I literally seem to be falling for you. And Tamiko, please believe me, I never say that when I'm flirting—in fact, I've never said it."

"I'm fifteen, well almost sixteen, but still fifteen for another couple of weeks," Tamiko blurts, her light tan skin flushing a dusky pink. "My mom will tie me to a chair if she finds out I'm even here."

"You're kidding, right, I mean you're taking physics at Cal and you look, I don't know, nineteen, maybe twenty."

"I've been taking college classes since I mostly ran out of high school ones a couple of years ago. Most of my credits are from community college, but in the summer I take classes here at Cal."

"Are you really telling me I've fallen for a fifteen-year-old prodigy who maybe has almost as many college credits as I do?"

"Worse than that," Tamiko says ruefully. "I'm officially still in high school so I can play sports and because my mom says I'm not old enough to go to a sleep-away college."

"How did all this skipping ahead come about?" Alec asks, dividing the last crumb of scone neatly in two.

"I guess it started when my second grade teacher called me a bratty know-it-all and succeeded in pushing me up a grade."

"What did you do? I mean, for example."

"One afternoon when Mrs. Stevens was talking about American history she said that Thomas Jefferson was president after George Washington."

"Let me guess: you blurted out, what about John Adams?"

"I think I was waving my hand in the air when I did it, but anyway it started an argument that resulted in my being sent to stand in the hall."

"Really? You were punished for being right. But why am I guessing from your grin that there is more to the story?" Alec says trying unsuccessfully to push back his chair before realizing it was bolted to the cement.

"I was so super mad by then that I opened the door a crack and in a loud voice began reciting all forty-four presidents."

"Now I'm almost feeling sorry for Mrs. Stevens."

"To give her credit, she didn't start yelling 'You worm, you worm,' until I finished and started naming them backwards."

Shaking his head as he laughs so loudly that one of the middle-aged faculty types at a nearby table turns to glare, Alec says "OK, now you're in grade three, but I'm betting that school was still too easy for you."

"My dad thought so, anyway. He started working with the school district to expose me to more advanced material without officially skipping more grades—which my mom was against for social reasons even though I was so tall I liked being around older kids. Anyway, by seventh grade I was taking Spanish three at Berkeley High."

"They let you do that?"

"Dad was a UC Berkeley professor. He knew how to get school administrators to do what he wanted and I guess he had my tests to back him up."

"So how many college credits do you have?"

"At the end of the summer session I'll have two years worth, not counting a couple of weird things like Sanskrit I've taken for fun. But Alec, what year are you in?"

"At the risk of your forever classifying me as an intellectual tortoise, by taking European Lit and Organic Chem this summer, I'll start September as a senior."

"How old does that make you?"

"Well, I took a gap year so…"

"Just tell me."

"Twenty-two."

Feeling as if she's taken an elbow to her chin, Tamiko grabs her pack as she stands and says, "I'm sorry, I have to go to work now. Today especially, Mom will be freaked if I'm late."

"C'mon, talking is just talking, at least let me walk you to the edge of the campus," Alec implores. Taking her silence as a yes, he follows Tamiko back through the glass door and into the indoor café. When they are blocked for a moment by a café employee cleaning up a spill, Alec glances at the oversized photos of the 1964 Free Speech Movement that line the walls, the most prominent of which shows Mario Savio, the protest leader, standing on top of a police car in Sproul Plaza exhorting thousands of students to resist. Searching for something to say that might stop Tamiko from bolting as soon as she reaches the door, Alec asks, "Do you know what Mario Savio actually said—I mean his famous speech to the students?"

Slowing her pace a little to allow Alec to catch up, Tamiko replies, "*There is a time when the operation of the machine becomes so odious, makes you so sick at heart that you can't take part. And you've got to put your bodies upon the gears and upon the wheels, upon all the apparatus, and you've got to make it stop!"*

"Enough, I bet you can recite the whole thing," Alec says, now lengthening his stride so as to keep up with her as they reach Campanile Way and turn north.

"No. I got, like, super bored and never finished reading it."

"Bored? Truly, I'm surprised. It's such an iconic…"

"I can explain if you really care about what I think. But probably you're just trying to keep me talking."

"Both, so go for it," Alec replies, hoping Tamiko is not going to break into a run.

"Living here in Berkeley I've met people—older friends of my parents' who were part of the Free Speech protests in the 1960's—who think Savio chiseled the whole thing on a golden tablet or something," Tamiko replies slowing just a little. "But to me it's mega-dated. Like, I mean, weren't they essentially protesting about the right to hand out a leaflet or stand on a wooden box to make a speech? Honestly, with information flashing around the world in an instant and Big Brother listening in on everything we say, I don't get why anyone still cares. And, like, Alec, did you ever think that even when Savio made that speech it was already at least fifty years behind the times? *I mean, putting your body into the gears, levers and wheels,* sounds like a Communist trying to foment revolution in 1917. But hey, I want to ask you a question."

"Of course—shoot."

"How come you're still a junior? Did you, uh …"

"Flunk out for a while?" Alec cuts her off, laughing. "No, I'm pretty much an A student, at least lately. After my sophomore year I took off to train for an international sports competition. When that was over, I decided to travel for what turned out to be eighteen months."

"What was your sport?"

"Modern Pentathlon. Have you heard of it? It's…"

"Like a bunch of sports put together in one event—fencing, swimming, riding and something else—running maybe?"

"Right, those four plus shooting pistols. It probably wouldn't exist except for the Olympics."

"Were you in the Olympics?" Tamiko asks eagerly as she turns and makes eye contact for the first time since they left the café.

"Not quite. But because of some unusual, almost crazy circumstances with a bunch of older athletes getting hurt or retiring early, I went from being barely ranked in North America to qualifying for the World Championships in Warsaw."

"Wow! How did that go?"

"Sixty-second, which was above the bottom, but not by a lot. But in my partial defense, Pentathlon athletes tend to peak at age twenty-eight and it's a prestige sport in Europe, China and Korea, meaning I was up against lots of older world-class athletes who treat it as a full time job."

"So, why did you quit?" Tamiko asks in a voice that does little to disguise her disappointment.

Now starting to climb the steep steps next to the postmodern box of the Starr East Asian Library on their way to Cal's North Gate, Alec chuckles as he replies, "You sound like my dad."

"Sorry, I don't mean…"

"The answer is that I took a good look at the athletes six, eight, or even ten years older than I was who were still dedicating most of their waking hours to training in five sports, and decided I wanted my life to be more interesting."

"So, OK then, why didn't you come back to Cal right away?"

"Hmm, that's a tougher question. One answer is that I was ready for a big adventure and going off to see the world was the best one going. But honestly, at first at least, I didn't want to confront my dad and my coaches about my decision to quit. Even though I finished in the bottom third at Warsaw, I was pretty competitive in everything save swimming, enough so that they were full of excited talk about the Olympics. So excited in fact, that when I expressed doubts they talked right over me."

"Taking off solved the problem."

"It did. I had my passport and a few thousand dollars my grandparents had given me over the years so I just went to the Warsaw airport and bought a ticket to London where I caught a British Airways flight to New Zealand."

"Your parents must have freaked."

"Possibly, but I'd just turned twenty and I sent them an email from Auckland saying I was fine."

By now Alec and Tamiko who have passed between the twin stone towers topped by pagoda style copper hats that mark Cal's North Gate are standing at the corner of Euclid and Hearst across the street from the Northside Café. Worried that he's about to lose contact with this mesmerizing girl, maybe forever, Alec asks, "How about I walk with you for a few more blocks?"

As the light changes and Tamiko doesn't say no, they continue across Hearst where they turn left and downhill towards San Francisco Bay, now shimmering a couple of miles to the west.

"I do sports too," Tamiko says.

"Not ballet? You move like a dancer—erect and graceful."

Ignoring the compliment, Tamiko replies, "I took classes when I was a kid of course, but I've always liked games better—anything where you keep score."

"Which ones do you play?"

"Water polo, basketball, and softball."

"Not all at Berkeley High, surely."

"Surely."

"J.V.?"

"All varsity."

"But this last year you were a sophomore, age-wise, right?"

"Yes."

"I'm doing my best not to sound racist here, but doesn't Berkeley High have a load of athletic black kids? I mean I'm surprised that a medium-tall white girl could even make the J.V. basketball team."

"For starters, I'm not white," Tamiko replies, exaggerating her annoyance to cover how pleased she is that Alec put medium before tall.

"I'm a quarter Asian which makes me Hapa."

"Hapa?"

"It means half in Japanese—it's slang for anyone with a mixed-race background although a lot of light skinned kids who are part African American insist on being called black. And just so you know Mr. World Class Athlete, I start at point guard and was voted MVP on a team that lost the NorCal Championship in overtime."

"And now I bet that you're going to tell me you're also MVP in water polo and softball."

"Only in softball. In water polo I'm first team all league, but that's it."

"Are you making this up?"

When Tamiko doesn't reply, Alec asks, "Cat got your tongue?"

"I'm good at sports, it's no big deal."

By now Alec and Tamiko have reached the northwest edge of the campus at the corner of Hearst and Oxford streets. As they cross Oxford and start north next to Cal's block-sized agricultural area with its line of 1950's-style greenhouses, Alec again begins to worry that at any moment Tamiko will insist on continuing alone. As he searches for something to say to keep her engaged, she blurts, "Just so you know, this shirt is my mom's. When I grabbed it this morning I didn't realize that, well, it's so…"

"Snug," Alec says, keeping his voice carefully neutral. "You can put your Tsunami sweatshirt back on if you're uncomfortable."

"It's too hot."

"No need to worry, you look lovely."

"Thanks," Tamiko replies in a small voice. "It's, like, I'm planning to get some nice things of my own."

After another lull in the conversation, Alec says, "I want to apologize if I came on too strong back there in the café."

"No need. Whether you meant what you said or not, it made me happy," Tamiko replies, stealing a quick glance at the tall, serious-looking guy whose long easy stride so perfectly matches her own.

Feeling the relief of a prisoner pardoned as he starts his final walk, Alec asks, "Where are you headed?"

"My mom's an editor at Bay Books. It's a small publisher with an office near Solano. I work there in the afternoons."

"Can I walk you over?"

"No way, like, Mom will totally freak if she thinks I've even said hi to you."

"You like to say like."

"Busted in less than an hour," Tamiko says, grinning. "And just in case you're wondering, yes, I know it's hella high school and my summer resolution is to kick the habit, but you make me a little, well, I guess a little…"

"Like, nervous?"

"Maybe a little. But like, Alec, are you ever going to stop teasing me?"

"Promise."

"So OK, then what did you really mean back in the café? Tell me the truth," Tamiko asks as she slows to a stop.

"Do you remember how we were looking into each other's eyes at the time?"

"Just like now," Tamiko says as she turns to face Alec.

"Yes, and just like now I looked into your lovely eyes and said, 'Tamiko, I've fallen for you.'"

"You said falling, not fallen."

"That was then."

Abruptly turning, Tamiko begins walking north so fast Alec realizes he's in danger of talking to her upturned behind. As he quick-steps to catch up he says, "What are you thinking?"

"That I'm miles over my head here and that I want you to go back to your way-cool twenty-two year old life and let me be. But first I want you to kiss me good-bye."

Several possible responses flit through Alec's head before he blurts, "It's hard to kiss a person who's running."

"I don't mean here," Tamiko replies. "There's a park—Live Oak Park, in a few blocks. It has a couple of massive redwoods we can go behind."

Alec, who momentarily considers saying that in his experience, kissing someone you're attracted to is likely to fan the fire not put it out, keeps his mouth shut. They stride past a line of comfortable century-old houses, each one determinedly different from its neighbors in the way of a patchwork quilt. Crossing a stone culvert that carries Walnut Street over Codornices Creek, Tamiko leads the way through a gap in a low hedge and onto an oasis of rolling lawn occupied only by a middle-aged woman dozing on a blanket next to her elderly beagle. Following Tamiko behind a huge tree, Alec sees that with a second to one side and the creek behind them, they are remarkably alone. Admiring Tamiko's quick and effective privacy strategy, he nevertheless worries that he's going along with a game that can only end in grief. But instead of heeding this inner voice he asks, "What's our next step?"

"You're the expert and this is my first time," Tamiko says seriously.

"Kissing goodbye is your idea," Alec replies with a laugh as he decides no harm will be done if he treats this as a lighthearted moment.

"OK then, well, based on the novels I've read we need to do two things. First, since you're a bunch taller than me, I need to stand uphill from you so our faces are more or less even."

"Got it," Alec says as he backs a step down the slope towards the creek to face Tamiko, who has her back to the tree. "Now what?"

"I stand very close to you like this," Tamiko says as she hesitantly takes a half step forward. And when there is still a small gap between them, another—so that now a sheet of paper can barely pass between them.

"And now…?"

"Remember, no teasing," Tamiko continues in a small voice.

"No teasing," Alec murmurs, placing his hands on either side of Tamiko's long strong waist as he cocks his head slightly to the right and places his lips on hers. Then as she presses against him he lets his hands drift up to her shoulders and pulls her closer. Unmoving, they stand locked together for perhaps ten seconds. Then, as if waking from an enchanting dream, Alec opens his eyes and steps back, only belatedly remembering that he's perched on a slope. Managing a couple of quick steps to recover his balance, he sees that Tamiko hasn't moved.

COMING OF AGE IN BERKELEY

"How come you stopped?" Tamiko asks, sounding disappointed.

"Maybe I just wanted to demonstrate how literally I've fallen for you," Alec answers, realizing that his resolution to tread lightly with this mesmerizing young woman has been slain by one short kiss.

"You're teasing."

"Not at all."

"For real?"

"Well, I still think kissing someone goodbye who you are gobsmacked by is a poor strategy, but…"

"I've totally scratched that idea, haven't you?" Tamiko says, taking her phone from her pocket and snapping Alec's picture in one smooth move. "But I have to push this second or there really will be a meltdown in Momsville."

"Will I see you tomorrow morning?"

"You'd better!"

"So, you've decided I'm not too ancient for you?"

"Of course you are, but what does that have to do with anything? I mean, it was hardly even a real kiss, but, oh my god Alec…"

"I'm curious, when did you decide you liked me?"

"From the second I turned and saw you holding my book yesterday morning," Tamiko replies as she begins walking backward across the grass towards the Shattuck Avenue edge of the park.

"Hey wait, I don't even know your phone number or where you live," Alec says taking a couple of steps after her.

"527-1720," Tamiko calls gaily as she hops into the air and clicks her heels together twice before turning and continuing past a huge free standing Monterey cypress.

"Alec Burns, 548-2212," Alec shouts an instant before she reaches the sidewalk, turns right and disappears behind a two-story tan house.

· · · · ·

Glancing at his watch, Alec sees that Tamiko isn't the only one who is running late. His Organic Chemistry lab begins in thirty-seven minutes and he is at least a mile away, much of it uphill. Awkwardly holding his single-strap messenger bag in front of his chest with both hands as if it's a basketball Alec begins jogging as best he can in jeans and sandals. Arriving back at the Free Speech Movement Café at twelve forty-five and seeing only four people in line he decides he has just enough time to grab a sandwich to go and still make his lab on timeish. But, as so often happens when business slows, the counter guys slow with it as they joke and chat with customers. When ostentatiously glancing at his watch several times fails to speed things up, Alec raises his wrist and begins tapping it. Finally able to order a chicken salad on light rye from the slim, boyishly attractive counter guy, whose name tag identifies him as Ahmad, Alec is further annoyed when Ahmad makes no effort to enter the order on his rack-mounted iPad, but instead asks, "Did you misplace Miss Universe?"

"What the hell?"

"That amazing girl you were in here with earlier. If it isn't a big thing with you two, maybe I can get her number."

"Not even in your dreams. And hey, what about my sandwich?"

"OK, OK," Ahmad replies, quickly inputting the order with his right hand while palming Alec's ten dollar bill with his left before adding, "I thought she was probably a keeper, but you also come in here with a foxy Asian, so who knew?"

. . . . .

With his lab finally over at 4:00 p.m., Alec walks a half dozen uphill blocks to the huge brown shingle house on Panoramic Way he shares with eight other students. Climbing to his tiny third-floor room that, a century before, had been occupied by a maid or governess, he changes into his running gear. A few minutes later he jogs up Panoramic's steep ribbon of switchbacks through a half mile corridor of large century-old Craftsman houses—all of which apparently come with a lemon tree and a Mexican gardener. Intersecting a dirt fire road, Alec leaves behind the relentless afternoon sun and begins loping through the half-light created by a grove of hundred foot pines and redwoods. Immediately buoyed by the cathedral-like aura cast by the huge trees, he thinks how pleasant it would be to believe in God. In an effort to outrun the bizarre turn of events his week has taken, Alec begins pushing himself as hard as he can up the steep road. Just thirty-six hours ago, he had been content with his pleasant, productive, and best of all, uncomplicated life. The two summer session courses he was about to complete would put him in position to graduate next spring, while leaving time to exercise and hang out with Teri Kim, his Korean girlfriend who, in her own words, was in Berkeley for a summer of lots of fun and a little art history. Not only was Teri stop-the-trains stunning, but she came with no strings attached, since in several weeks she'd return to Seoul to announce her engagement to a man her wealthy father had selected. But now, with no plan, or even thought as to consequences, he had told a fifteen-year-old he barely knew that he cared for her.

Continuing to pound up the hill, Alec streaks past dozens of joggers and dog walkers before cresting the ridge. Barely glancing to the west at what today looks more like a sun-drenched lake than the typically wind-whipped San Francisco Bay, he nevertheless takes a moment to congratulate himself on coming to Cal, rather than Yale in dismal New Haven. As he continues north towards the Lawrence Berkeley Lab complex, Alec finally begins to slip into the peaceful easy feeling that makes running long distances a pleasure. With his mood now rapidly improving he tells himself that while one silly kiss behind a tree is forgivable, continuing to pursue a fifteen-year-old, no matter how precocious, plainly isn't.

Back on Panoramic fifty minutes later, Alec pulls off his sweaty T-shirt and steps into the tiny half bathroom he shares with the two other third-floor students. Too preoccupied to go down a floor to use a proper shower he wipes his face, neck, and torso with a wet towel before taking the few steps back to his room where he sits on his bed and taps Henry Goldstein's number.

"Alec Burns," Henry says by way of answering. "Tell me you're not trying to borrow money again."

"No, no. I'm back at Cal, and I'm hoping my days of having my wallet stolen in Buenos Aires are far behind me. And, c'mon, I paid you back with enough extra to buy a couple of six-packs."

"Which is why I picked up," Henry says laughing. "But Lec, although it's always great to hear from you, I'm guessing something's on your mind."

"It's about this amazing girl I met yesterday. I try to put her out of my mind, but I can't."

"And you're calling me? You must be kidding. If I have this right I'm the old married guy who has always been a bit of a social bumbler and you're the boy Casanova, whose charm with the ladies is famous, or should I say infamous, from Perth to Puerto Escondido."

"I'll let that bullshit lie. I'm calling because you still work as a high school counselor, right?"

"The Suncliff School is private, but yes, I work primarily with high school juniors and seniors who are trying to cope with all sorts of teenage pressures including their parents' wildly unrealistic expectations that all of them will matriculate at one of about ten colleges, including, at a big stretch, UC Berkeley. But hey, I think the penny just dropped. Since you're calling me, I'm going to guess that the amazing female you're newly enamored with isn't quite eighteen."

"Almost sixteen."

"You're shitting me. Tell me you're not really bird-dogging a fifteen-year-old? What are you now, twenty-one?"

"Twenty-two last month. But, listen, Henry, I knew before I called that you wouldn't approve. I mean I just ran six miles trying to talk myself out of seeing her again. But what can I say, except that Tamiko isn't like any other almost sixteen-year-old. Even the guy behind the counter at the Café on campus called her Miss Universe. But in addition to being attractive she's memorized whole books like *The Brothers Karamazov*, and is taking an upper division physics course at Cal. Sorry, I know I'm babbling, I just don't want you to think this is some kind of Lolita deal. Just think about the kind of person who matriculates at MIT at fifteen and graduates in two years."

"Lec, let me guess that in addition to being intellectually precocious she's tall, blonde and has big cupcakes."

"Not that big really, It's more that she has great posture. And her hair is this amazing caramel color, a sort of golden brown, with a few blonde highlights from the sun."

"Ha! In a world with at least a thousand impolite euphemisms for stacked, I'll at least give you an A for being tactful. But Lec, Lec, Lec, I guess it's been so long since you were in high school that you don't remember that there are a couple of these princesses in every class. In fact, I had a drop dead gorgeous, red headed version in my office this morning who at barely seventeen, could easily pass for twenty-five and has the same kind of poke-you-in-the-eye tits you're being too gentlemanly to describe. As part of her campaign to talk me into letting her skip Calculus, she bent forward to treat me to a close-up. Just so you know, in my business we have a two-word name for these girls and it isn't Miss Universe."

"Tell me you're not going to say jail bait."

"Career killers is what I had in mind, but jail bait, despite being a woeful cliché, is nevertheless accurate."

"You're kidding, right. I mean, really, jail, just for dating a minor?"

"Even when the girl's parents go on the warpath, if the guy's eighteen or nineteen and the girl is sixteen or seventeen it almost always gets worked out short of that. But with older guys—a category, which in case you're in doubt, now includes you—prosecutions happen. It might end up with a guy pleading guilty to a lesser offense in exchange for a suspended sentence, but even that can result in your having to register as a sex offender until you're ninety. So, Lec, my advice is simple—beat off, take a cold shower and then go out and find someone your own age, which given your history, should be as easy as snapping your fingers."

"You're exaggerating."

"I doubt it. Didn't you once tell me that you paid for your travels by teaching pretty rich girls to surf? And I ask that kindly since despite being besotted by my wife, I won't deny that I've envied you a time or two."

"I mostly made money busing tables in restaurants and bars in tourist towns when it was so busy they happily slipped me a few bucks despite my lack of a work permit. And, sure, where I could I gave surf lessons."

"I'm curious, how did that work?"

"I'd talk to the dudes at a local surf shop until I could convince them to lend me their rattiest board in exchange for me directing my students—mostly girls on vacation it's true—to their shop to buy clothes and gear. Then I hang on the beach trying not to get swatted by the local competition until two or three girls came along, at which point I'd offer to teach them for free."

"And they agreed?"

"A girl alone, hardly ever, but two or three friends would often be eager to give surfing a try. And if they had fun they were happy to buy clothing— and sometimes even boards—which meant I'd get a commission."

"And probably drinks, dinner, and a very fun place to sleep."

"Sometimes, sure, but what was the harm in that?"

"None at all, but listen I'm curious, what happened when dinner and drinks were done and there was still just one of you and two or three of them? I mean, how often did you coax all of them…?"

"Just for the record, I was typically the coaxee, but c'mon Henry, you're supposed to be the adult here. Is there any chance we can get back to my question as to whether there is any noncriminal way, Tamiko and I can see each other?"

"You mean after her dad gets wind of what's going on and calls to tell you he's cleaning his Glock," Henry says in a voice serious enough that Alec wonders if his example comes from something that's occurred at Suncliff.

"Her dad's dead, so it would be her mom. Tamiko's her only child."

"This is not getting better."

"I know."

"Alec, I'm not sure why I'm even trying to help you, but if you can get mom to calm down long enough to listen, tell her you understand her reasonable concerns about the age difference. Then promise you won't have intimate contact, or anything even approaching it, with—what's her name again?"

"Tamiko, it's Japanese, although her background is more Russian then Asian. I mean, Henry, she has almond-shaped blue eyes, a dimple in her rounded chin, and when she smiles she lights up from her toes to her ears."

"All that plus admirably erect posture and world class hair. But Alec, back to my point, not only do you need to assure Mom you won't have sex with Tamiko, but also that you won't meet her in private—especially including not going over to her house when Mom isn't there."

"Will that work?"

"Well, I doubt Mom will give you her blessing, but as long as you and Tamiko only see each other in public places, for example, Starbucks, you're not violating any laws so there's not much Mom can do about it save ground her daughter."

"What about the district attorney?"

"Drinking coffee may or may not be good for you, but it's not a crime."

"But, what if she forbids Tamiko from seeing me."

"In my experience, this may work in the short run. But assuming she loves her daughter and doesn't want to alienate her, Mom is going to have a tough time sustaining a take-no-prisoners approach, especially if Tamiko continues to make it abundantly clear she believes she is being treated unfairly."

"It's no fun to live with a martyr," Alec says, chuckling, as he begins to see a path forward for himself and Tamiko.

"Something I try to explain to Suncliff parents on a regular basis. Assuming Tamiko's mom is even a little kid savvy, chances are she'll eventually see that some kind of compromise is her best strategy."

"Makes sense. Big thanks Henry, you've always been my big brother."

· · · · ·

When Tamiko leaves Alec at Live Oak Park, she feels as if her blood is whipping through her body with class five force. When walking fast doesn't begin to contain her energy, she begins to skip. Then, glancing around to see that no one is in sight she sings,

Alec be nimble, Alec be quick
Alec kissed Tamiko
Smack on the lips!
Tamiko be nimble, Tamiko be quick
Tamiko kissed Alec
And her heart went bananas

Embarrassed by her poor imitation of a rhyme-challenged fourth grader, Tamiko settles back into a brisk walk, repeatedly telling herself to chill. Trying to change her mind's groove to how black holes affect gravity she laughs as for the third time in a half block the image of her lips on Alec's overwhelms her best efforts. Although they have only touched for a few seconds, one thing is heart-stoppingly obvious—she has never experienced anything half as hypnotizing.

Now just a couple of minutes from Bay Books, Tamiko stops under a plane tree and fishes a blue bandana and a bottle of water from her backpack. Wetting the cloth, she wipes her face and arms before pulling the Tsunami sweatshirt over her mom's white top. Hypnotized or not, it's not lost on her that showing up at Bay in a clingy top looking as pink as a mouse's tummy is sure to alert her mom that she's disobeyed her injunction not to see Alec.

Entering Bay Books through the bookstore Tamiko is relieved to see that Meg is talking animatedly into her headset. Hoping to slip through the door into the hall before the preoccupied receptionist adjusts her focus, Tamiko is stopped short by the round black woman's peremptorily raised right hand. Grabbing a folded piece of pink paper from between Meg's thumb and forefinger, Tamiko almost bolts the dozen steps to the relative privacy of her copy room cubicle. Unfolding the note she reads:

"Tami—

"I need to help at the library trade show in S.F. so won't be back this afternoon. I've left the final draft of Maben's latest masterpiece for you to check. And, yes, I know that in your view his writing "hella sucks" but it also "hella sells" which helps pay your modest salary, so keep a smile on your face. And please remember, this is the final draft, so DO NOT fix his beloved clichés (or in

Mabenese, 'Sorry Babe, that dog won't hunt'). Just look for typos, misspellings, and so on. Pay particular attention to how he denotes times and numbers since he often ignores Bay's style guide. We require numbers to be written out and appropriately hyphenated through ninety-nine, not 10 as in the Chicago Manual of Style. And for dates we…"

Having inhaled Bay's style guide when she was thirteen, Tamiko scrunches the note before tossing it in a recycling bin. Pushing through the kitchen door to the patio, she adjusts the faded umbrella so that she's mostly in the sun while the manuscript is in the shade. Even though she knows this is one more job her mother has invented to keep her occupied between sports and school, she's so pleased to earn a regular paycheck it makes no sense to complain. Make-work, or not, at 3:15 p.m. as Tamiko speeds through the final page of Sausalito Blues she feels a tingle of pride. In addition to two typos, one of them egregious, she has spotted the fact that a woman who owned a houseboat on one of Sausalito's piers is called Beverly in Chapter Three, but Bethany in Chapter Twenty-three. Or as Tamiko notes to her mom, "even though Beverly had plenty of time to drown three people off the bow of her boat, there is zero evidence she's made it to court to change her name".

· · · · ·

At four o'clock Tamiko comes out of Bay's front door to find her best friend Jasmine Wang, perched on the hood of a fifteen-year-old blue Ford Focus, a big grin on her full moon face. Jazz, who is barely five feet tall and built like a fire plug, has come by to drive Tamiko to softball practice in San Leandro where both play for Tsunami, one of California's most successful summer club teams.

As they crawl uphill on Ashby Avenue past the wedding cake edifice of the Claremont Hotel towards Highway 13, Tamiko is tempted to ask Jazz, who has just turned eighteen, about kissing etiquette. Not only has the older girl been having sex for the last year with Brandon, her cute, but more than a little feckless high school boy friend, she loves to talk about it. But feeling shy about mentioning Alec and her, what was the right word anyway?—intense, intoxicating, over-the-moon—new feelings, Tamiko reclines her seat as far as the seat belt will allow and pretends to listen to Jazz prattle on about a tiff she is having with her next oldest sister. Twenty minutes later when they turn into the driveway that hugs the north side of San Leandro High, Tamiko sits up and waves to LaTasha Higgens and Amber Gonzalez, who are just getting out of Tasha's dad's GMC pick-up. As the youngest player on a team of mostly seventeen- and eighteen- year-olds Tamiko is perpetually annoyed that she's the only one without wheels.

The practice begins with Coach Rodriguez having the team run through the several defensive schemes Tsunami employs when the opposition has runners on first and third with less than two outs, a play they botched in their last tournament. Instead of throwing to Tamiko cutting across behind the pitching rubber from shortstop, where she would be poised to throw back home to catch the runner trying to score from third, Roxy, Tsunami's catcher, had thrown through to second. Although she'd nailed the runner trying to steal, the girl on third had been able to sprint home. Despite Tsunami having won 6 to 1, Coach, ever the perfectionist, is obviously still so annoyed that a run had been foolishly conceded he keeps them at it for half an hour.

When Coach is finally satisfied, they move on to taking turns hitting off live pitching with the girls' bantering back and forth and even Coach momentarily shedding his dour persona to crack a couple of jokes. With only one summer tournament weekend left for a team that has won over ninety percent of its games, there is little to be demanding about, especially since Tsunami won't be traveling half way across the country to play in the national championship tournament. For Coach, giving up going to Nationals after winning the uber competitive Northern California qualifying tournament, is undoubtedly worse than stepping on a rusty nail. But with several girls already headed to college with full scholarships in their pockets, and two more from families who can't afford the airfare, he has reluctantly agreed that playing in front of family and friends at a nearby regional tournament is the right decision. Since this will be the last chance for four players to put on their wine red and black

Tsunami uniforms, no one doubts that a week from Saturday they'll all bring their A game.

After practice Tamiko walks over to Coach Rodriguez and says, "Coach, I've decided not to play water polo at high school this fall. So I'm wondering if you're planning to sign Tsunami up for a few tournaments?"

"No doubt, if I have enough athletes available to compete off season. Since we're losing Amber, Roxy, LaTasha, and Jazz we badly need to audition replacements. Fall ball, where no one much cares about wins and losses, is the best place to do it."

"I'm thinking about getting back to pitching."

"It's a little late maybe to catch up with the girls who've been working hard since you stopped after your dad died. You've always had the velocity and desire, but don't you still have the same problem of who'll catch you five days a week while you work on your accuracy and spins?"

"I haven't nailed anything down yet, but I have a new catcher idea," Tamiko says, dumping a half-dozen bright yellow softballs into a plastic pail.

"Talk to me when you get a little further and we'll see."

. . . . .

"What was all that heavy talk with Coach R about?" Jazz asks a few minutes later as the Focus crabs its way down the onramp and into the slow lane of I-80 heading west towards the Highway 13 cutoff to Berkeley.

"I told him I was planning to quit water polo so I'd be available to play softball this fall."

"There is no way your water polo coach will accept that—I mean, you're the best player on the team. And what about your mom? Isn't she always saying that a girl who plays lots of sports is too tired to get into trouble?"

"For sure it's going to be a little sticky with Mom, but lately I've been thinking that it's time I begin making my own choices. But hey, Jazz, listen up, since I want to ask you about something major."

"OK."

"I got kissed today."

"Finally, that's chill."

"What I want to know is whether it was a real kiss."

"Huh? I don't…"

"He didn't put his tongue in my mouth like in those rap songs, so I guess I'm worried it doesn't count."

"You just might be the most clueless girl in the galaxy."

"If not the universe, but c'mon, are you going to tell me?"

"Where was your body?"

"Pressed against his."

Where was your mind?"

"God, I don't know. Over the rainbow I guess," Tamiko replies, mentally adding one more cliché to the day's lengthening list.

"How long did it last?"

"I lost track. Somewhere between a few seconds and forever."

"It was a real kiss—I'm sure you'll figure out the tongue part next time. But lover girl, have you noticed that we're sitting in front of your house and I'm already way late getting Mom's car back?"

"Right, but about kissing…"

"Tamiko, I really don't want to get my ass fried, so can you call later with all the juicy details?"

. . . . .

Amy Gashkin's heart speeds up when she gets the call from Ed Crane, Bay Books' publisher asking her to BART over to San Francisco to help out at the library trade show. Undoubtedly Ed's request is all about business, but since late spring when their relationship had become anything but businesslike, she feels like a schoolgirl whenever they talk. After being celibate for over three years, Amy's having a sweet, funny, sexy man in her life has assumed jumbo sized importance.

However, as her train speeds under San Francisco Bay it's Tamiko who fills Amy's thoughts. What sin have I committed that is so heinous, she asks herself, that the punishment is to have my sane, sensible, socially naive fifteen-year-old daughter get her first mad crush on a college student? Dating an older guy would be bad enough, if Tami had already had a few boyfriends her own age, but starting her dating career with a far more sophisticated older guy is not going to happen.

Arriving at the Bay booth a little after 1:00 p.m., Amy finds it so full of chatty librarians she barely has time to wink at Ed before joining the sales fray. *Slide Zone*, one of Bay's recently published Northern California-based mystery novels had been unexpectedly, and very positively featured in the previous Sunday's *New York Times Book Review* a few days after receiving a starred review in *Library Journal*. Not only have sales exploded for this quietly eerie thriller about two revenge murders carried out in the desperate hours after a large earthquake, but the halo of establishment approval has revived sales of the author's three previous titles. After eighteen months of business so anemic it resulted in a ten percent pay cut and a couple of lay-offs, Bay Books now has the robust seller that will allow it to slip the bankruptcy noose for at least another year or two. Later, at dinner with Ed and a couple of prospective authors attracted by Bay's recent publicity buzz, there's still no time to share her worries about Tamiko. Finally, at 9:15, riding BART back to North Berkeley, Amy has a chance to tell Ed about how upset she is that a college guy is trying to take advantage of Tami. Listening patiently to what even she realizes is in danger of turning into a rant, Ed finally interrupts.

"Amy, is it OK if I point out that what you don't know about what's going on is way more than what you do know?"

"Meaning?"

"If I understand this correctly what you believe has happened so far is that Tamiko accidentally met an attractive Cal student and talked to him about Dostoyevsky for a few minutes. I'm guessing of course, but isn't it likely that the guy assumed Tamiko is also an undergrad which would hardly be strange since in this last six or eight months your daughter has metamorphosed into a stunning young woman?"

"She's fifteen."

"Sixteen in a week or two, right? Still, point taken, so I'll amend my description to tall, stunning very young woman. But Amy, you'd have to be blind to believe that either stunning or woman is in doubt."

"Tami didn't tell him she's still in high school, and not even a senior."

"How often do you tell people how old you are within ten minutes of meeting? Chances are she'll never see this guy again, and if she does I'm sure she'll explain. Amy, I've told you what an amazing young person Tamiko is and what a fantastic job you are doing as her parent, but she's growing up fast and at some point you are going to have to take a step back and trust her to make good decisions."

"Well, this most certainly isn't that point, or anything in the neighborhood. She's a socially unsophisticated kid who's never been on a date, and for all I know this guy could be twenty."

"She's been taking college classes for a couple of years and intellectually, at least, she's ahead of many adults."

"Do you imagine it's her mastery of Latin guys are interested in? And, anyhoo, I thought you were on my side!"

"Methinks there's a difference between support and agreement. You have my support come what may, but I can only agree with you when I do."

As the train races under San Francisco Bay, its wheels screaming, Amy closes her eyes and tries to let go of her anxiety. As they pull into the West Oakland Station it occurs to her that she's been acting bitchy, so as an olive branch she says, "Well, it's true that recently Tami, who was late going through puberty, maybe because she was exercising so much, has developed some curves."

"Doubtless it's far beyond politically incorrect to comment on your daughter's anatomy but 'developed some curves' doesn't begin to describe the new model Tamiko. And as you should know better than anyone, she has also grown into that lovely face of hers. If she ever decides to dress like a girl and comb that spectacular mane of hers once in a while, well…"

"C'mon Ed, next you'll be telling me I'm living with Helen of Troy."

"The face that launched a thousand ships and toppled the…"

"Stop it. And just so you know, I never liked Marlowe."

"Got it, but just in case you're keeping track, it wasn't my subconscious that produced antiquity's most beautiful woman."

"I was trying to exaggerate so you'd stop with the hyperbole. Keep it up and I'll think you have a crush on my daughter."

"Amy!"

"OK, I apologize. I really do. I know I started the subject and I also know you're not a lecherous old man."

"Well, of course I am—but the object of my lust is thirty-five, not fifteen. And I promise that when I fantasize about taking off someone's pants in the Gashkin family, it's not your daughter's bag-lady jeans."

"Oh Ed, of course I know that. These past couple of months with you have been a miracle. I'd forgotten how wonderful it is to be so, well, to be so physically, um…happy I guess."

"Were you about to say something a bit stronger, aroused, perhaps? Or maybe even transported?"

"I hope you know even ecstatic doesn't come close to describing it. The truth is that at least half my waking hours I feel like an animal in heat."

"I'll take that as a compliment," Ed says with a chuckle as he steps off the train at the North Berkeley station.

"You'd better," Amy replies, pinching Ed on the bum as she moves close behind him on the narrow stairs to street level. Then, as they pass through the barrier and onto the brick plaza facing Sacramento Street, she adds, "Maybe with what's going on with Tami we should put off our plan to go public with our relationship for a week or two. I know it seemed like a great idea to tell people at Bay at the *Slide Zone* celebration on Friday, but…"

"No worries. I get that it's awkward for you to celebrate being in love at the same time you're telling your daughter not to be. Anyway, I'm guessing three quarters of the people at work already know. In fact, last Friday I overheard Meg describing you as 'Little Miss Hottie.'"

"You're kidding. She absolutely did not."

"I'm not, and she did. And, of course she's right. It's only been a few months since you traded in your loosey-goosey pants and baggy sweaters for skinny black jeans, clingy silk tops, and black leather boots. And I am doing my best not to mention the A-line bob, eyeliner, lip gloss, and dare I say it—push-up bra."

"Not your very best, obviously. And just for the record—I don't own a push-up bra. It's true that being small, I didn't used to bother wearing anything underneath, but now, well…"

"No buts, I love everything about your makeover. And just for the record, your breasts may be small, but they're delectable."

"Sure you're not lusting for a C-cup?"

"Never, I've always been a fan of the perky handful."

As soon as Ed's old green Mini Cooper pulls in front of Amy's two bedroom bungalow on Francisco Street in the Berkeley Flats, Amy levers herself out of the little car and heads up the short walk careful to duck under the late summer spider web that stretches from one flanking tan pillar to the other. Waving to Ed as she closes the door, she is surprised to see that although it's barely ten o'clock, no sliver of light shows from under Tamiko's door. Passing through the small half-dining room on the way to the kitchen, Amy spots Tamiko's new backpack lying on the table, its main compartment open and her phone visible. Unable to resist, Amy reaches for the phone reasoning that it's only a minor breach of her daughter's privacy to see if an Alec is listed under Contacts. When the home screen lights up with a picture of a slim, athletic-looking guy with tousled dark hair, high forehead and a slightly cleft chin, she knows she has her answer. "Oh no you don't," she says in a voice so loud she thinks someone else must have spoken.

Striding down the hall Amy raps on her daughter's door before immediately pushing it open, flipping on the overhead light and saying, "Tami, I know you're not asleep and we need to talk, now…"

"Mom, what's happening?" Tamiko replies as she sits up shielding her eyes with her left arm.

Realizing that her daughter really has been asleep, or close to it, Amy toggles off the light as she moves to Tamiko's desk and twists the switch on the less intrusive desk lamp. Perching on the edge of the small room's one straight-backed wooden chair as she tries with only partial success to avoid the wedge of discarded clothes, Amy says, "Tami, when I glanced at your phone just now it was obvious you haven't kept your promise not to see this college guy—what's his name, Alec?"

"Mom, maybe you weren't paying attention but I never promised anything. And if you're going to trample on my privacy, can you please at least call me Tamiko—this is like, maybe, the twentieth time I've asked."

"Don't change the subject and please tell me exactly what happened today."

"Alec was on the path by Evans Hall, you know, that's the ugly gray toad of a building that squats at the top of Memorial Glade. He was waiting for me to come down the hill from Physics like I always do. We talked for a minute and then he asked me to go to that café in the student library for coffee. Just like you suggested, I ordered a cappuccino and added lots of sugar."

"Don't patronize me. You know very well that my advice wasn't meant to be used with this guy. How old is he?"

"Alec's a junior at Cal."

"That's not an answer."

"He took off a year to do sports and travel, so like he's twenty-two. But Mom...."

"This gets worse and worse. I certainly hope that when you told him you were only fifteen, he got up and left."

"I did tell him Mom, really. I mean, like, right after he said he was very attracted to me. It was like we were both mega-surprised. He thought I was a real Cal student, maybe nineteen or twenty and I thought, well I don't know what I thought, but for sure not that..."

"Just in case you haven't heard, it's a crime for an adult to date a minor," Amy says peremptorily as she pulls Tamiko's clothes out from under her. Glancing down she adds, "Tami, please tell me you didn't wear this white top of mine today. It may be a little loose on me but on you it must be..."

"You're the one who has been encouraging me to borrow your clothes and anyway I wore my Tsunami sweatshirt over it," Tamiko replies, trying not to sound defensive.

"All morning?"

"Well, it got mega-hot in the sun on the café terrace so maybe I took it off for a few minutes. I just want to look nice—the way you do."

Ignoring the compliment, Amy stands, looks under the chair, and says, "I don't see a bra."

"I don't need a bra."

"For reasons of basic propriety you absolutely do, especially when you're wearing a clingy shirt two sizes too small. But anyway, what happened next?"

"As part of saying goodbye, Alec walked me over towards Bay. And you know how it is Mom, we just talked, like really talked about his life and my life. He's super smart and I wasn't bored for a second. And Mom, he even laughed at my stupid dog joke."

"I'll just bet he thought those lobsters were hilarious. But Tami, when do we get to the part where you two say sayonara for good?"

"Mom, believe me, from our first step that was totally my plan. When we got to Rose and Oxford I even asked him to kiss me goodbye."

"You have to be kidding, right there on the street corner? Oh my god, Tami, I can't believe…"

"It was so busy we walked up to that little park, you know, Live Oak Park," Tamiko interrupts, unable to contain her excitement.

"And he went along with this? Honestly, I…"

"Mom, do you want me to tell you or not?"

"I'm listening."

"We stood very close and, oh Mom, when he kissed me, well, I just never felt anything even remotely like that. I mean it's like I can't even begin to explain all the colors that flew out of my heart. I mean, Mom…"

"Tami, Tamiko sweetie," Amy interrupts leaning forward. "Let me tell you one thing loud and clear. No matter whether they were aquamarine, magenta, or chartreuse, that was your first and last kiss with this guy. You're a kid, he's an adult, NO, NO, NO. Even if I have to report him to the Dean of Students or District Attorney or whoever, this is over."

"I thought you were my friend," Tamiko replies in a small voice. "I thought friends talked things through."

"Sweetie, you have your dad's talent for arguing and just like him you never give up, but hashtag this, NO ALEC. And I plan to tell him that right now."

"Mom, do you remember when I was in second grade and those two boys began calling me giraffe because I was a head taller?"

"I do. And I also remember that after you knocked one of them down, Dad had to go in for some kind of intervention. But I don't see…"

"Alec is, like, over six-foot-three. When I walk next to him I feel exactly the right size."

Standing, Amy picks her white shirt off the floor, turns off the desk lamp and leaves the room, saying, "Nice try, but since there are plenty of tall sixteen- or seventeen-year-olds in the Bay Area you're not selling this guy as a giraffe cure." Then, after grabbing Tamiko's phone from the dining room table Amy considers where she can go to be sure she isn't overheard. Rejecting the back patio as too close to Tamiko's window, she fishes in her purse for the automatic garage door wand before going out the kitchen door and getting into her faded blue Subaru in the detached garage.

· · · · ·

When Miles Davis's Saeta from "*Sketches of Spain*" begins playing on Alec's phone at ten-thirty Tuesday evening he guesses it's Teri Kim. Having ignored several of her earlier calls he still isn't ready to talk. Before he does, he knows he has to decide whether the fact that he has been bewitched by a precocious teenager it's a crime to touch, means that he is honor bound to break up with Teri. Or, does the fact that she is leaving the U.S. for good in three weeks, mean that short-term girlfriend overlap is forgivable? Extracting his phone from the inside pocket of his shoulder bag Alec sees a local number he doesn't recognize. Hoping that his premonition of trouble is wrong he slides the answer bar to the right as he says, "Hey, it's Alec."

"This is Amy Gashkin, Tamiko's mother."

Not sure how to reply, Alec hesitates, trying without complete success to suppress a sigh.

"Mr. Burns, why don't you start by you telling me why I'm calling?" Amy Gashkin demands.

Taking a big breath Alec replies, "No doubt you're worried that your daughter is in danger of getting involved with an older guy in what you probably see as being an inappropriate relationship," Alec says as politely as he can manage. "And I'm guessing that you also want to tell me to stay away from Tamiko and warn me that if I don't, you'll take steps to be sure I do."

"Succinctly put, which I hope means you're not a complete fool. I can tell you a lot more about how upset I am that you didn't just get up and leave the café when Tami told you she's only fifteen, but all I really want out of this conversation is your promise that you won't see her again."

"I'm guessing there's no chance we can get together for coffee so that hopefully you can see I'm not the ogre you think I am?"

"Not a poodle's chance at a coyote convention. And now I'd like that promise."

"OK, here's the best I can do. I promise that I won't see Tamiko in a non-public place, without your permission."

"My permission? You must be hallucinating if you think that somehow, some day I'm going to say it's dandy for you to sleep with my fifteen-year-old daughter."

"I just said I won't touch Tamiko and just for the record, she's almost sixteen."

"Even if she turned seventeen tomorrow it would make absolutely no difference. She's an inexperienced high school kid who has never even been on a date and you're a...well, I don't exactly know who you are, but since you're more than six years older than Tami it's irrelevant."

. . . . .

After Amy Gashkin abruptly ends the call, Alec sits on his bed, back against the wall, thinking of all the things he wishes he'd said—that physically Tamiko is obviously a woman; that intellectually she is ahead of many college seniors; and that emotionally she is one of the happiest people he has ever met. But, on second thought, maybe he has been wise to follow Henry's advice to keep things simple. Amy, or Mrs. Gashkin—he realizes he doesn't even know what to call her—clearly hadn't been in the mood to listen to even the most cogent argument that her daughter can handle an adult relationship—which in fairness, Alec has to concede, is no sure thing. So maybe, it's a victory of sorts that Amy has heard him say he won't have sex, or anything close to it, with Tamiko. Amy may not believe him, but if Tamiko says the same thing and they live up to the letter of their promises perhaps Amy's fluffed feathers will gradually relax.

Still in his jeans and long-sleeved charcoal henley, Alec turns off his bedside light. As he slides down flat he attempts to inventory his feelings. OK, sure, he has met a beautiful, brainy, funny, sweet, athletic girl who somehow radiates both sex appeal and—what's the word he is searching for—goodness? wellbeing? happiness? But even with all this going for her, it astonishes him that in the barely thirty-six hours since he first looked into this almost sixteen-year-old's almond-shaped blue eyes he isn't willing to give her up, even in the face of fierce parental opposition and his own common sense.

WEDNESDAY

TAMIKO AWAKENS AT 6:30 A.M. Slipping into her clothes and out the front door as silent as a dove leaving its perch, she ducks under the spider web before heading east on Francisco Street. When she reaches Grant she turns south and crosses the narrow grassy strip of Ohlone Park before continuing to University Avenue. Turning east on Berkeley's main east-west arterial, Tamiko begins walking the uphill mile to the UC Berkeley campus. Telling herself that it's sure to be a fabulous day if she spots five Mini Coopers, she is delighted when the fifth—an orange and black two-seater—wheels around the corner at Oxford and Center streets, almost nipping her heels as she quicksteps into Starbucks. Ordering oatmeal with blueberries, orange juice and a cappuccino before grabbing two bags of sugar and heading upstairs to the nearly deserted mezzanine, she pulls out her laptop in order to review her physics homework. But before she can open the flap her phone pings announcing a text.

"Just so we're clear, I heard you slink out this morning without cleaning your teeth (hopefully you still have a toothbrush in your backpack). And just to be even clearer, I meant every word I said last night about your not having a relationship with Alec Burns or any other college guy."

Starting to reply, Tamiko reflects that she has nothing to say that won't risk further annoying her mom, so instead pours one of the sugar bags into her cappuccino, tips the chair back on two legs and takes a sip. When it tastes OK she imagines Alec's smiling face as she murmurs, "See, I'm a fast learner. Just be a little patient while I catch up." After inhaling her oatmeal and skimming her assignment she slips on her pack to begin the long uphill walk through the campus to LeConte Hall.

To avoid spending the next two hours obsessing about whether her mom has scared Alec off for good, Tamiko decides to pay rapt attention to

Professor Spurgeon, a strategy that works for the first hour. But after the short break, time seems to slow so precipitously she becomes convinced that, Eddington's Arrow of Time notwithstanding, the Campanile will never chime eleven. When the high clanging sound finally signals freedom, she leaps out of her chair and all but runs out the front door of LeConte striding rapidly north towards the path next to Evans Hall that will take her downhill to the top of Memorial Glade where Alec waited yesterday. Slowing to a more moderate pace so as not to trample on the heels of the girl walking in front of her, Tamiko wonders whether Alec will give her a quick peck, a proper hug, or just stand there, hands at his sides, a glum signal that her mother really has intimidated him into agreeing to break off their friendship. However, when she arrives at their magic spot, no one is there. Glancing at her phone to see that it is just four minutes past the hour, Tamiko crosses her fingers as she tries to recover the happy feeling that came with having spotted the five Mini Coopers. But as she stares at Evans Hall's deserted steps, the pebble of worry that's been weighing on her all morning morphs into a stone. At 11:16 a.m., the stone, now a boulder so heavy it threatens to crush her heart, Tamiko starts slowly down the familiar path towards Campanile Way, hoping against hope she'll hear Alec's voice calling after her. When all is silent, she quickens her pace, suddenly anxious to get as far away as she can. Then, hearing someone running up behind, her despair flips back to hope as she turns.

"You're giving up on me already?" Alec almost shouts.

"Oh my god Alec, standing there alone I just felt, so, so—I don't even know the right word. It was as if every second seemed like an hour. But, I hadn't given up. I was heading to the café to wait there."

"For how long? How long would you have waited?"

"'Probably 'til closing time, or when I couldn't cry anymore, which ever came first. But where were you? I thought for sure Mom scared you off."

"Tamiko, I'm really, really sorry. Professor Murray stopped me on the way out of class to talk about the paper I wrote on *The Cherry Orchard*."

"*The train's arrived, thank God. What's the time?*"

"Do you memorize everything?"

"Well, it's the first line of Chekhov's play, so how hard is that? What's your paper about?"

"Whether it's a comedy or tragedy—pretty banal I know."

"What did you decide?"

"A comedy on the surface, but a tragedy deep down. What do you think?"

"It's not my favorite play. Too much Russian fatalism. To be fair, I read it a few months after my dad was killed, when it was tempting for Mom and me to go the Ranyevskaya route and spend our lives refusing to get over it. But hey, are we going to get coffee or what?"

"Sure, we absolutely need to talk."

Approaching the counter at the Free Speech Movement Café, Tamiko steps in front of Alec and extends a ten-dollar bill to Ahmad as she orders two cappuccinos and a blueberry scone. Starting to object, Alec glances at the determined look on Tamiko's face and says, "I'll get your sugar and find us a table."

A few minutes later at the table where they had sat the day before, Tamiko says, "Mom is on the warpath for sure. I've hardly ever seen her so upset."

"No doubt, she certainly whooped at me last night. But in fairness, she's got a point. I am way too old for you."

"Oh Alec, don't start," Tamiko says, suddenly worried her mom really has convinced Alec to back off.

"Look at me," Alec says, leaning forward, elbows on the table.

"Hardly a problem," Tamiko replies, also leaning forward.

"What do you see?"

"You looking back at me as if, as if, well, as if, maybe you even meant what you said yesterday," Tamiko says, a feeling of relief beginning to fill her heart.

"About falling for you big time."

"Oh my god Alec, I can't tell you how lovely that sounds, but is it really illegal for us to even be friends like Mom says?"

"According to Henry, this friend I called who works as a high school guidance counselor, as long as we keep things platonic, we should be fine as far as the law goes. But since you're a minor, your mom is basically your boss, so if you don't follow her rules, I guess she can ground you, or whatever," Alec says, withdrawing his hands as he belatedly realizes he's promised not to touch Tamiko.

"Despite her flipping out last night, Mom's usually pretty chill. Occasionally she goes all adult on me, but mostly since Dad was killed, we've been more like best friends. Although I have to say that since she got a boyfriend a couple of months ago, she's been pretty preoccupied. But, listen Alec, are you, like, really sure you want to deal with all this when you can easily find someone who's older?"

"Yes."

"Really yes? Or maybe, yes? Or, let's just wait and see, yes?" Tamiko asks, as this time she grabs Alec's hands.

"With all my heart, yes. But hey, why is this all about how I feel? What about you?"

"When we're apart I think of you every ten seconds, except when it's more often. But did you just say there can be no touching? I mean nada, even like yesterday with no…"

"For sure, no kissing. In the short run at least, it's our only hope. So if you want to experiment, you'll have to find a seventeen-year-old," Alec says, again withdrawing his hands.

"No teasing, remember. But, like, exactly where did you and Mom leave it?"

"As I said she wasn't in a mood to be reasonable. But I'm guessing that my commitment to keeping things strictly platonic will register eventually as long as you say the same thing and we walk our talk."

"I know I shouldn't say this, but it's not what I have in mind."

"I thought you're the girl who's never been kissed."

"Will you be patient and not laugh if I try and explain something sort of personal?"

"Scout's honor."

"This spring, I woke up one day and just totally realized I wasn't a kid anymore. This is beyond embarrassing, but I even stood in front of my mom's full length mirror and thought—my god, I'm a woman now—maybe a young, silly one, but still, well you know. Hey, you promised not to laugh," Tamiko protests, blushing.

"I'm barely smiling. And remember, I never saw you as anything else," Alec replies, thinking that even when she's bright pink, Tamiko is the most beguiling woman he's ever met.

"One thing is sure, from the moment I met you Monday and, well, saw how you looked at me I guess, the woman thing became a lot more real. But don't worry, it's not all on you. Earlier this summer when I began to notice how guys were looking at me—my physics professor even—I kinda decided I was ready for the girl-boy thing."

"So you're saying I came along in the nick of time."

"On time, anyway, which is something Mom doesn't seem to understand. I mean Alec, sorry if I sound like a whiny brat but I am fed uwith her insisting on calling me Tami and reminding me three times a day I'm fifteen."

"Which is maybe her backdoor way of telling you that she sees just how fast you're changing."

"I don't quite follow."

"She loves her kid, sees you fast becoming an adult and wants to stop time. Cut her a little slack and I bet she'll adjust. And, about your name, I love Tami, so is it OK if I use it?"

"No possible way. I'm a hundred and ten percent on the warpath about that."

"How about if I tell you my childhood name?"

"No promises, but as the elephant said to the zebra, I'm all ears."

"When I was tiny and couldn't pronounce Alec, I called myself Lec and it stuck all the way through high school."

"Lec, that's so sweet."

"You're the only person in California who knows it and you can use it if you wish."

"Definitely."

"So I can call you 'Tami'?"

"You're refusing to see my point," Tamiko replies, sticking out her tongue. "Longterm you can call me whatever you want, but not this summer when I've been trying so hard to get Mom to convert, 'Tami' is a nonstarter. But, Lec, what I'm really concerned about, is that no matter what you call me, you won't be patient enough to let me finish growing up. I'm a fast learner, but for real I'll need time to catch up to you socially—or at least catch up enough so that I'm not boring or embarrassing or whatever."

"You're fine the way you are. And even if it turns out you have a little catching up to do there's the fact that I've fallen for you like a bear with his first bottle of peanut butter."

"Ugh, sticky," Tamiko says, wrinkling her nose.

"Which of course is my point. This bear is not going anywhere without his peanut butter!"

Chuckling as she glances at her watch Tamiko says, "Lec, I need to bounce—it obviously won't go well if I'm hella late getting to Bay today."

"You gotta love Berkeley High speak. But hey, my lab doesn't start until one so I have enough time to bounce with you to the edge of the campus and still make it on time. But yesterday after you took me behind that tree, I was hella late, so definitely no kissing."

"Bouncing, but not kissing, I guess half a loaf is better than none," Tamiko says, standing and heading for the exit.

Following University Drive downhill towards Wellman Hall and the northwest corner of the campus, Alec and Tamiko walk in silence for a few hundred feet before Tamiko blurts, "So really Lec, like, how come you didn't kiss me all the way yesterday?"

"I told you, kissing didn't seem like the best way to say goodbye. But what are you worried about?"

"In books and movies, everyone uses their tongues, right? My friend Jazz says that if you really like a person French kissing is like warm-up, well, you know," Tamiko replies, her face again beginning to color.

"Jazz is a girl, I hope?"

"Definitely, Jasmine. She's my best friend even though she's more than two years older. Jazz has been having sex with Brandon, her way cute, way dumb boyfriend, plus a few other one-time experiments—so she's sort of my sex guru—you know, the person I go to when I have questions. Earlier this summer when Tsunami played a tournament up in Reno, we shared a room at a Motel 6 and she even brought out her Frederick's of Hollywood teddy and started dancing around the room."

"I hope she wasn't trying to get you to take Brandon's part?" Alec exclaims, louder than he intends.

"That's nothing to worry about," Tamiko replies, her happy contralto laugh enveloping them both. "I told her I wasn't about to give up my virginity to a girl."

"Cute, but listen, if we are going to stick to our no-intimacy plan I think we need to change the subject. What position does Jazz play? I mean in softball."

"Second base. She's barely five-feet tall and moves like a jet-propelled bug with Velcro hands. She's also our lead-off batter and is so quick that after she slaps the ball into the ground she usually outruns the defense. Next comes Jackie who walks and bunts a lot and then I'm third."

"The power hitter."

"Yup, it's my job to put the ball over the fence, or if we are on a field without one, far enough over an outfielder's head that it amounts to the same thing."

"Sounds like fun. When can I see you play?"

"We're off this weekend because we didn't go to Nationals, even though we qualified, but August twenty-seventh and twenty-eighth we play our last tournament at Twin Creeks, just north of San Jose. The way it works is that there are three games Saturday to establish seeding for Sunday. On Sunday we play until we lose. But, Lec, listen, if we're really gonna, you know...I mean, if we're really going to, like, hang out even though we have to follow Mom's silly rules..."

"Didn't we settle that?"

"It's just all happening so fast—meeting you and, well, falling, you know, falling…"

"No worries, it's obviously been a thunderbolt for both of us."

"Would it ruin the mood if I suggest a mega-selfish plan that involves you and me spending time together in a way that even Mom will have trouble objecting to?"

"As the elephant said to the zebra, I'm all ears."

"Before my dad was killed I was a pitcher. I just loved being in the center of the diamond with the ball in my hand and everyone waiting for me to move."

"Kinda like a singer poised before her first note."

"Exactly."

"So why did you switch to shortstop?"

"A pitcher needs a catcher to practice with, at least three or four times a week. Getting a ball to go sixty-plus miles per hour underhand while making it rise, curve, or drop to exactly the right spot is definitely a counterintuitive skill."

"No dad, no catcher. But what about your mom?"

"We tried once, but she missed a fastball that hit her on the mask and knocked her over, so, well…" Tamiko replies, raising her hands as if in apology.

"I'm beginning to see where this conversation is going."

"Oh Lec, would you think about it? I mean, even two or three days a week would be huge. Coach Rodriguez, my Tsunami coach, also teaches pitching and we could check in now and then. And Lec, I'm not asking for a freebie, I'll trade you."

"Assuming it's an activity your mom approves of, it might be a short list."

By now Tamiko and Alec are standing at the northwest corner of the Cal campus at Hearst and Oxford. Glancing at her watch Tamiko says, "To get to Bay on time I'll need to jog."

"In all those clothes?"

"I've got shorts and a T-shirt underneath. I'll just put my jeans and sweatshirt in my pack, tighten the waist strap and be off."

"OK."

"I hope you don't think I'm going to strip with you standing there inspecting me."

"Given the shirt you had on yesterday I doubt there will be many surprises," Alec says, doing his best to keep a straight face.

"I thought you were trying to break your teasing habit," Tamiko replies, matching Alec's poker face.

"So long then," Alec says, starting to turn.

"So long then," Tamiko replies as she rises to her toes and kisses him lightly on the lips. "I'm not the one who promised," she adds, laughing.

. . . . .

Alec walks south on Oxford Street for about a hundred feet before turning left towards the wide steps that will take him up to the plaza separating Warren and Barker halls. But instead of climbing, he ducks behind a five-foot cement wall and peeks over the top to watch Tamiko stuff her jeans and sweatshirt into her pack. As she begins to jog north, the gold letters spelling Tsunami.com on the back of her T-shirt glitter in the sun. "Tsunami, indeed," Alec murmurs as he turns to take the steps two at a time. Pulling out his phone as he walks he sees that he has three calls, plus a couple of "Call me now" texts from Teri. Glancing at the time to be sure she'll still be in class and unable to pick up, Alec leaves a message explaining his need to study and suggesting they meet for coffee after his lab tomorrow. This, he hopes, will give him enough time to think of a more or less graceful way to end their relationship.

. . . . .

A few minutes before one o'clock, having bent the rules by squeezing through a hedge and slipping into Bay via the back door, Tamiko steps into the rear bathroom to take a fast shower. Five minutes later, still a little damp, she reaches her workspace just as the intercom buzzes.

"Amy is in the monthly editorial meeting until three p.m., but she left a note in your box, something I would have been happy to point out if you'd used the proper entrance," Meg says in a long suffering tone. "And, of course, whenever you use the shower I'm to remind you not to leave the bathroom looking like a swamp."

"I don't know about you, Meg, but I think it's uber-unfair to keep dredging up something that happened once, two years ago."

"Maybe yes, or maybe no, but since Amy also left you a sandwich in the fridge I'm thinking you should cut her some slack."

Retrieving her mom's note and what's at least an eight-inch pile of manuscripts from her cubby, Tamiko grabs the familiar blue bag from the refrigerator and heads to the patio. As she wolfs down the first half of the surprisingly delicious turkey and Swiss sandwich, she unfolds the paper with her name handwritten on the front:

"*Tamiko—As you can see I've left you a pile of mystery submissions. Please read just enough of each so you can separate them into yes, no, and maybe piles. Last time you did this Emily P. said it was a big help, but that you were too soft on the maybes, all of which should have been no's.*

"*Also I called Ruth and made an appointment for you two to talk at four-thirty this afternoon. Let me guess that this will annoy you since our arrangement has always been that your relationship with Ruth is private and that you see her only when you feel the need and I stay out of it. But, Tamiko, this time since I'm convinced that your seeing a much older man is a huge mistake, I'm asking you to make an exception. I'm obviously hoping that Ruth will provide the kind of common sense advice you can't seem to hear from me, but, of course whatever transpires between you two is confidential.*

"*I love you, Mom*"

Closing her eyes, Tamiko does her grandmother Vera's slow breathing exercise until she feels the wave of indignation begin to recede. Then, going to her cubicle she fires up her ancient Mac and types:

"*Dear Mom,*

"*This is going to be a long one, so be patient.*

"*1) Mysteries: Thanks for letting me sort the submissions. Even though most are terrible, it's exciting to pick up a fresh manuscript, and it makes me feel good that you trust me to make adult decisions.*

"2) Ruth: Ever since you suggested that I talk to Ruth after Dad was killed you've left it up to the two of us to schedule appointments. So my first reaction to you contacting her directly, was to be super pissed. But hey, Mom, I really do get that you're worried about me so I'm over it (well mostly, anyway). And then, of course, there is the fact that Ruth is a sweetheart. So yes, I'll make it over there by half past four and hope you'll treat this as one more sign that your only child is now mature enough to make good decisions.

"3) Water Polo: Between work, softball, school and your being over the moon about Ed (see 7 below) we haven't had much time to talk. And, also, I've procrastinated about bringing this one up so as to avoid an argument. But, Mom, here is the headline—I'm Not Playing Water Polo This Fall. I know this may annoy you since you (and Dad) always believed that a girl consumed by sports is a girl too tired to get into trouble. But enough already. Playing three sports in high school is ridiculous, and, as you well know, basketball and softball (especially) are my favorites.

"4) High School: Aside from Latin 4 there is nothing for me to learn at BHS. Yes, I'll also take Advanced French Conversation so I can stay eligible for sports, but it's pretty much a snore. No, No, No, I don't want to take more courses at Berkeley City College or Laney since I still want to go to a four-year college like a normal kid, not skip most of it (see 6 below).

"5) Work: If there is enough for me to do here at Bay this fall without inventing stuff, sign me up. If not, maybe now that I know how to drink coffee, I can learn to be a barista.

"6) College: Mom, I absolutely do not agree that because I'll be barely seventeen next fall I should choose a University close to home. I want to go East and have a bunch of new experiences either at an Ivy or one of the cool small schools in New England. I know I can handle this (really!). But I obviously need to decide which one(s) to apply to PDQ. Just as obviously this means visiting campuses this fall. Because I think most softball coaches will be interested in me, and I've a perfect academic record, it should be easy to arrange invites with the schools paying my air-fare. But if we can afford it, I'd prefer to go with you.

"7) Ed: Mom, even were I blind and deaf (sorry, sight and sound impaired) it would be obvious that you two are almost goofy with loving each

other. Fantastic! Ed is hella cool and I couldn't be happier for both of you. So anytime you guys want to stop with the three-hour lunches and have a sleepover will be fine by me.

"8) Shopping: I hope you'll be pleased that I'm finally tired of being the last dowdy duck on Francisco Street. In short, just in time for my birthday I'm ready for a makeover, possibly even one as sudden and breathtaking as yours last spring. Yes, this probably has something to do with meeting Alec (I call him Lec), but really it's mostly about my finally being ready to grow up. So, are you still willing to help?

"P.S. I have money saved so you don't have to pay for all of it.

"9) Alec (Lec, remember): I saved this one until last for fear if it came earlier you might freak and stop reading. Let me start by saying that in my rational mind I respect what you think about our age gap. And you're right, a smart, beautiful, tall twenty-two year old guy should be way out of my league. But then, well... I look into Lec's eyes and melt into a puddle of technicolor happiness. Since you're also in love at the moment I probably don't need to say more. So, here's the thing—I can't (and won't) promise not to see Lec. But in hopes of keeping the peace, I do agree to follow THE NO INTIMATE CONTACT PROTOCOL Lec committed us to (OK, to be 110% honest, I did give him a quick goodbye peck today at lunch, but it's nothing but handshakes from now on)."

After Tamiko pushes the send button she puts the top two manuscripts into her pack to read at home later before heading out the front door, relieved her mom is still in the editorial meeting. Walking the mile and a half home, she zigzags through the maze of narrow, winding streets that make up Berkeley's Northbrae neighborhood. On Sierra Street, she unconsciously begins registering the makes of the cars she passes, the first step to the car identification game her dad introduced when she was in second grade. With the goal of having her pay attention to her surroundings, her dad challenged her to pick any two brands of cars she wished. Since that year she was in love with the letter V, she often picked Volvo and Volkswagen. Then, after he selected Toyota and Honda, they walked around the neighborhood tallying cars until, before long, she conceded defeat. Even as she got smarter with her picks, her dad would adopt more sophisticated strategies to stay ahead. For example, when they had expanded the game to four or five brands each, he might choose BMW or Lexus as his fifth choice on Sunday when affluent grandparents visited, but Ford or Chevy on Tuesday when the neighborhood was full of the ancient pick-ups of Latino gardeners.

Having deliberately short-circuited her car counting habit by saying a Buddhist prayer for her dad, Tamiko arrives home at 3:15. Going directly to her mom's closet, she grabs a multi-colored wrap-around Indian skirt and a pair of opentoed Mexican sandals that are only a size too small. Opening her mom's middle drawer, Tamiko removes a black cowl necked top loose enough to fit her comfortably. Stripping, Tamiko grimaces slightly as she squeezes her breasts into the bra which fit perfectly when her mom gave it to her the previous Christmas. Then, after slipping into the top and skirt she goes back to her mother's room where she lifts a set of gold hoop earrings from the jewelry tree. Although the holes in Tamiko's lobes have almost closed from lack of use, she is finally able to push the wires through. Then giving her thick unruly mane a half dozen 'please lie down and behave yourself' strokes, Tamiko reaches back and loosely corrals it with a dark purple ribbon.

. . . . .

A bell tinkles as Tamiko lets herself into Ruth Marcus's tiny reception room on the second floor. The square, century-old brown shingled house on Ashby near Alta Bates Hospital has long since been converted to medical offices. "Tamiko dear, is that you? Come right through," Ruth calls.

When Tamiko pushes through the half-open office door, Ruth stands, pauses for several long beats, and then with no sign of recognition says, "Young lady, I think you must be in the wrong place, screen tests are next door on the first floor."

"Come off it, Ruth, you've seen me in a skirt before," Tamiko replies, her happy grin giving the lie to her attempt to sound matter-of-fact.

"Forgive me dear if I can't remember when, but one thing is clear—

right here, right now—you look smashing."

"Thanks, these are all Mom's clothes of course, but my birthday is coming up and I guess I'm finally ready to get some nice things of my own."

"Before we talk about why that's become a priority, I need to be sure you're OK with being here. Our arrangement has always been that you contact me when you want to talk, and that our conversations are just between us. As I told you from the day we met, a month after your dad was killed, I see my role as a cross between a hopefully wise friend and your honorary auntie, not your therapist, although of course I am one."

"It's OK, really. When I learned Mom made this appointment, I was annoyed—well, pissed, actually. But then, I realized I'd been thinking of calling you myself, so it seemed pretty dumb to stay mad."

"Sounds like we're good then, so tell me what's going on," Ruth says as she leads Tamiko to the seating area by the window overlooking a tiny, but impeccably maintained, Japanese-style backyard garden. Sitting in one of the two straight backed, lightly padded wooden chairs as Ruth takes the other, Tamiko says, "I'm sure Mom told you that I've met a guy she disapproves of big time even though she hasn't even met him."

"She also told me that he's twenty-two and still a junior at Cal. But let's put aside Amy's feelings and opinions for a moment while you bring me up-to-date about yours."

And so, starting with the errant copy of *The Brothers Karamazov*, Tamiko leans forward in her chair and talks animatedly for over fifteen minutes, amazed at how much has happened since she met Lec Monday morning. When she finishes, Ruth says, "This is really going to make me sound like a therapist, but how do you feel about all of this, now, this minute?"

"Isn't it obvious? Excited, happy, bubbling over—as if I had just hit a grand slam and was laughing while I did cartwheels around the bases. Monday, when I looked into Lec's eyes that first time everything changed. I don't know how to explain except to say—and Ruth, this is going to sound ridiculously clichéd—but I felt like I'd stepped onto a rainbow. And, oh yes, I've learned to drink coffee with only one sugar, which somehow makes me feel, I don't know, adult, I guess."

"Do you have a picture?"

Tamiko pulls her phone out of the black leather purse she has also borrowed from her mother, presses the power button and hands it to Ruth.

"Well, his ears are in the right place."

"C'mon Ruth, what do you think? I mean, really."

"Obviously he's attractive."

"He's also tall, like over six foot three. And you know, with me being, well, as tall as I am…"

"Honey, I remember you once told me that as a tyke you hated being the tallest kid in your class, but now surely you must see that you're a lovely height. I mean, what I wouldn't give for a couple of your inches."

"All I know is that around most people, Mom for one, I'm still, like, all legs and elbows, but with Lec, it's just amazing how perfect I feel."

"Wasn't your dad also a big guy?"

"Yes, also six-three. But Ruth, don't you have some good advice for me?"

"Not really."

"You're kidding, right? I mean, who else can I count on?"

"Listen dear, for whatever reason, most people never experience head-over-heels love in the way you just described, especially from the first instant. Typically, it's a somewhat slower process with room to think about the pros and cons of fully committing, which means I might even say something that could be helpful. But since you've obviously fallen for this Alec, or Lec if you prefer, as if Thor clobbered you with his hammer, there really is nothing useful I, or anyone else, can tell you. Or maybe it's more accurate to say that even if I'm able to give you good advice you won't hear it unless it supports your intense feelings. But I haven't asked you if you would like tea and a chocolate biscuit," Ruth says, starting to stand.

"No, nothing, Ruth. But are you saying, I'm on my own?" Tamiko wonders, looking deflated as she leans back in her chair for the first time.

"At bottom, we all are."

"C'mon, at least tell me what you think, whether it will do any good or not, after all we're friends, right?" Tamiko asks imploringly. And then, with a grin sits forward again as she adds, "Maybe I will grab a chocolate thingy if you tell me where they are."

"On the first shelf in the cupboard next to my desk—and bring me one as well." Waiting until Tamiko fetches the box of sweets, Ruth continues, "Tamiko, I treat you as an adult because in many ways you are one, despite your chronological age. You take college courses, have a job, play sports with older kids, read adult novels and plays and, of course, you've had to deal with your dad's death. And someplace along the way you've developed a strong sense of empathy, something I'm sad to say many of my much older patients never seem to manage. All that's great and will serve you well down the road, but it's a little worrying that when it comes to coping with a much older guy you have zero experience with any guys."

"Not entirely, like you said I've been taking courses with kids three or four years older than me for years and lots of them are obviously dudes."

"True, but it's my guess that your decision to spend the last couple of years dressed in a modified burka is related to the fact that you've been largely separated from high school boys and haven't been ready to engage with older ones. And, there may be deeper reasons, perhaps having to do with your dad's death and your not wanting anyone to replace him in your affections, something we can talk about another day if you wish. But for now, my point is that you haven't experienced the typical romantic ups-and-downs of adolescence."

"Like Mom, you think I'm a deer caught in headlights," Tamiko says raising her palms in front of her chest in a mock-defensive posture.

"I give you more credit than that and I suspect Amy does too," Ruth replies with a grin. "But to stick with your metaphor, I see you as a young deer who has always lived deep in the forest, suddenly confronted with the need to cross a busy highway before she's learned to negotiate country roads."

"Maybe Lec will help me get across?"

"Fingers crossed you'll be so lucky."

· · · · ·

At four-thirty, Amy Gashkin knocks on Ed Crane's office door. Hearing Ed say "Yep," she enters and hands him a printout of Tamiko's email. Taking a seat across from his work table she says, "Start with number seven."

After glancing at it, Ed looks up as he says, "That's a relief, isn't it?"

"I was pretty sure Tamiko had a good idea about us, but still, I'm relieved to, well, I guess I don't even know how to put it."

"To have her acknowledge our relationship so sweetly and positively?"

"In a word, yes."

"Should I read the rest?" Ed asks, returning his attention to the top of the memo.

"Please."

After taking a couple of minutes to study Tamiko's nine points, Ed says, "It's amazingly generous, or maybe a better word is mature, of her not to try to make you feel guilty for having a romance at the same time you're waving a red flag in front of hers."

"True, but our situations aren't remotely the same."

"I bet she doesn't agree, but stop worrying for a moment," Ed says as he stands, grabs Amy's hand, and leads the the slim, dark haired woman around the table and onto his lap. "God, I'm hot for you," Ed says as he tilts her chin towards his.

Concerned that someone may come in, Amy starts to pull away. But as Ed tightens his grip and deepens his kiss she feels warmth surge through her as if she had slipped into a scalding bath. Now pressing her body hard against his as if trying to climb inside, she says, "Oh Ed, me too."

"Keep rubbing against me like that and I'll take you behind the couch," Ed murmurs. Then, remembering that the door isn't quite closed he leans back slightly, "Does Tamiko's note mean we can go back to our plan to announce our relationship at Friday's book party?"

"Absolutely, I'll tell her what's planned so she can decide if she wants to be part of it. But right now, since she was considerate enough to keep the appointment with Ruth Marcus, I want to hop over to pick her up and maybe take her to Vanessa's Bistro where we can grab an early bite and talk through her list."

"I'll leave the family politics of all that to you, but one thing is sure, her memo is better written and better reasoned than most of what I get from people who consider themselves professional writers."

"That would be my Tami—for better or worse, always three jumps ahead," Amy says as she stands and pulls her white top into a semblance of order.

"Perhaps you mean, that would be your Tamiko," Ed corrects, gently.

"Are you always going to take her side?"

"Only when she's right."

. . . . .

Arriving outside Ruth's office at five-twenty, Amy claims a sunny spot on the front steps to wait. When Tamiko bounces out the front door ten minutes later looking, Amy has to concede, stop-the-trains gorgeous, she stands, gives her daughter a quick hug and says, "Nice outfit."

"You said it was OK to borrow your clothes," Tamiko replies, putting the emphasis on OK. "But Mom, like, how come you're here?"

"To take you out for supper so we can discuss your nine points. But Tami, I mean Tamiko, please just give me a minute to thank Ruth for squeezing you in at the end of her busy day."

When Ruth promptly opens the door at Amy's knock, the two women briefly hug and Ruth exclaims, "You look amazing. I just love the way your hair falls, so perfectly angled above the shoulders. Is it razor cut to get that stacked look in the back?"

"Yes, according to Lida at Salon 1757 over on Solano, it's an A-line bob. And given your sharp powers of observation I'm sure you can guess it's the first stylish cut I've had since Yuri was killed."

"I hope I'm not insulting you by saying you don't look much older than Tamiko. Is there something in the water at your house that makes women beautiful?"

"Well, if there is, Tami has definitely been drinking it by the gallon this week and, as I told you on the phone, I'm seriously worried. I know you can't talk about your conversation, but is there some advice you can give me—anything that will help me calm down?"

"Do you remember the Montagues?"

"If you mean Juliet's family, from *Romeo and Juliet*, of course. I was an English major, remember, so I've probably read every word Shakespeare wrote."

"My point is that the Montague parents had a choice similar to yours."

"Which is?"

"Risk that this Alec guy will break your daughter's heart, or do it yourself. I mean, think about it Amy, Romeo and Juliet were lovely together, it was the older people who screwed things up."

"Really, Ruth, I don't buy your analogy. The Montagues and Capulets were enmeshed in a long-term family feud and Romeo wasn't some much older man. Tami has never even been on a date and she obviously needs to start with someone her own age."

"I would probably agree with you except for three inconvenient facts."

"Which are?"

"First, since Yuri died you've treated Tamiko more as a younger sister than a daughter. And while I confess I had my doubts, she's responded remarkably. In short, I think you need to think twice before all of a sudden overturning all your camaraderie by becoming a dictatorial parent."

"Second, I doubt there is a high school boy on the planet mature enough to cope with the remarkable young woman who just floated out of here."

"She obviously dresses up well, but that doesn't alter the fact that she's still fifteen. But what's number three?"

"The truck you are trying to put yourself in front of is already barreling down the interstate."

"Well, the person who just stepped on the brake would be me. Tami may be the world's most precocious fifteen-year-old, but she's no where near ready to date an adult. But, listen Ruth, thanks for being available at short notice. I'm sure Tami got a lot out of talking to you."

Blinking against the sun as she comes down the front steps, Amy fumbles in her purse for her sunglasses. When they are finally in place she sees Tamiko on the sidewalk talking to a tall, thin young man who has two gold rings through his left nostril and a vivid red and blue tattoo of a snake curling around his skinny right arm.

"Mom, this is Jason," Tamiko says enthusiastically as Amy approaches. "We were in the same advanced calculus course at Berkeley City College last spring."

"The truth is, Mrs. Gashkin, I would have flunked if Tamiko hadn't tutored me before the final," Jason says, all the while keeping his gaze on Tamiko.

"Nice to meet you Jason," Amy responds before turning to Tamiko and saying, "Sorry to interrupt sweetie, but we have to run."

On the way to the car, Amy asks, "What was snake boy being so intense about?"

"He asked me to a concert in the City."

"What did you tell him?" Amy asks, realizing that this is the second boy she's been concerned about in less than twenty-four hours.

"Sorry, Jason, but I already have a boyfriend."

"I don't know whether to be relieved or annoyed. But, out of curiosity, how did he take rejection?"

"Just maybe groaned a little. It's, like, honestly Mom, no big deal. I've turned him down three or four times before, so I doubt he expected me to say yes."

"I guess I've had my head in the sand, so please tell me, do a lot of boys ask you out?"

"Not counting the weird dudes who try and chat me up at the store or on the bus, maybe half a dozen."

"Really? Who, if you don't mind me asking?"

"Well, three, or better make that four counting Jason at community college. And then this summer, a couple of Cal guys, not counting Lec, asked me for coffee."

"But you haven't said yes, right?"

"Chill Mom, until this week I always said, 'I don't drink coffee and I don't go on dates.' Today was the first time I got to say I already have a boyfriend, which by the way felt way cool. But hey, Mom, where are we going for supper?"

"How about Vanessa's Bistro?"

"Yum!"

Stopped at the red light at Dwight Way as she heads north on Shattuck, Amy says, "Tami, Tamiko that is—I really am trying, sweetie, but just so you know, in Japan where lots of girls names end in '-ko', women often drop the '-ko' at around your age because it means girl and they see it as a diminutive."

"Oh my god, Mom, I can't believe we're still talking about this. Not only are you the one who named me Tamiko, but last time I checked we live in Berkeley, not Kyoto."

"Fine, Tamiko it is, now and forever. But, let's go over the items on your list, saving Alec for last. To begin, I'd like to thank you for the generous things you said about Ed and me."

"Ed's cool and you're both lucky to have found each other, so no thanks needed."

"I showed him your memo and he was delighted. Not only does he like you, he knows I can't be happy unless you are. In addition, I think you'll be pleased that I more or less agree with your points three through six."

"Less? Or more?"

"Give me a chance please. For the record, six months ago I would have resisted your dropping water polo and going back East to college next year, but you've grown up a lot since then, so I guess we've reached the point where, even when I have doubts, I need to respect your choices. Well, some of your choices, anyway. And I definitely want the fun of visiting colleges with you. Do you have a list?"

"I totally want your opinion, but tentatively I've narrowed it down to Harvard, Princeton, Brown, Amherst and Williams," Tamiko replies enthusiastically.

"Sweetie, do you really think you can apply to a handful of the most selective schools in the world and waltz right in to your first choice? What about a couple of safety schools?"

"Based on my SAT scores and academic record, I should be pretty competitive anywhere. For sure, I know there are plenty of other kids who also have all A's in hard courses and perfect Board scores so I might not be a lock without sports. But with my background in basketball, and especially softball, I feel pretty confident. Even in the Ivy League, the softball coach gets at least three picks each year, meaning that as long as the recruited athlete is academically eligible, she gets in."

"But is every coach going to want you?"

"Maybe you weren't paying attention when I told you last week that Coach has had calls about me from Texas, Tennessee, Arizona, and a few other power-house programs. I guess someone has ranked me as one of the three best prep shortstops on the West Coast with the other two being seniors who already have full rides this fall."

"But you don't want to go to those schools, right?"

"You're completely missing the point."

"Which is?"

"If the big-time softball schools want me, coaches in the Ivy League will almost surely be super interested."

"OK then, how about I make reservations to fly to J.F.K. the last week in September. I'd like us to spend an evening in New York City and maybe catch a play. Then we could visit Princeton, Brown and Harvard by Amtrak. From Cambridge we can rent a car to cover the other two. I'm sure you don't remember, but when you were tiny, we lived just outside of Amherst while your dad finished his PhD and I completed my BA and started my Master's."

"I thought you guys were at the University of Massachusetts?"

"UMass at Amherst. There are two schools in the same small town," Amy replies, realizing that it's increasingly rare for her to know more than her precocious daughter about almost anything.

"Got it."

"I even took a Shakespeare course over at Amherst College, which you can do because of an exchange program. Want to hear something funny?"

"Definitely."

"The morning I was supposed to take my final, your dad was teaching and our babysitter called in sick."

"Tell me you didn't take the exam with me in a sling across your back."

"That was my plan, but you were eighteen months and already big for your age so it was never going to be easy. Anyhoo, Professor Files took pity on me and let me take the exam in his office so you could toddle around. Halfway through he came in, picked you up, and walked you around the campus, which by the way, is so lovely you expect a camera crew to be hiding behind every two-hundred-year-old tree. When time was up, he came back and looked very carefully at me be-fore saying, 'Did you find blondie here in a pumpkin patch?'"

"He wasn't the last person to ask that. Half my friends think I'm adopted."

"Funny how genes work. I'm half Irish, but look like I was born in Yokohama. But, except for the shape of your eyes, you look like you could have been born in Helsinki."

"So in a way, we've both already been to Amherst College. Do you still know people there?"

"Yes, there are two friends I'd like to see."

"OK then, why don't I see if their softball coach is interested enough in me to arrange an overnight so you'll have time to hang out with your buddies? But first I need to get a video made. Despite my credentials on paper, coaches will want to see me in action."

"Is there enough time?"

"Sure, Coach knows a video guy who does a good job for four hundred dollars which I've saved. I might even manage to get it done this week."

"I'm happy to pay for it."

"I'm counting on you for my new clothes and the trip. I'll handle the video and still have over two thousand in my account."

. . . . .

Seated in the tiny French Vietnamese tapas restaurant a few minutes later, Amy says, "I've been trying to buy you new clothes for at least two years, so let's talk about what you have your eye on."

"Nothing fancy, I just want to look like I fit in at Cal. And, oh yes, I definitely want an Indian skirt just like this one and some Mexican sandals. But, like, Mom, I'll never be a fashionista so if you have suggestions…"

"Is all this about dressing up for Alec Burns?"

"Was your makeover this spring only about dressing up for Ed Crane?"

"I hope I was making the changes for me because I was finally feeling happier about life. But I can't deny that Ed played a part."

"My answer is the same as your answer. For, like, at least the last six months I've felt stuck in an old me that no longer fit, at the same time I didn't have the energy to create a new one. No doubt when I met Lec Monday the dam burst, but like you, the changes were overdue."

"I thought maybe you kept that XL sweatshirt and Farmer John jeans so guys wouldn't bug you."

"That's Ruth's theory. But I think it's more complicated since when I first started dressing like a tent, I didn't have curves to hide. My guess is that it was more about identifying with you. Remember, up until this spring, we were just sort of deliberately dowdy together. But Mom, it's your turn to talk about you and Ed. As I said, he's a sweet guy and I'm totally happy for you—well, for both of you, really."

"I'm curious, when did you figure out that our relationship was serious?"

"In May, the day after you got your slick haircut. We were standing in the Bay conference room when Ed came in, stopped short, and then grinned as if someone had just awarded him a Nobel Prize."

"The penny dropped right then?"

"No, that happened a few seconds later when I saw you grinning back at him in a way I hadn't seen since Dad was killed. But hey, what's the plan? Are we about to move into Ed's house or something?" Tamiko asks, not quite hiding her concern.

"There's no plan beyond talking to you and sharing the news with our friends and colleagues at Bay. I guess I've thought that because our house is so small, it would be fun to spend some weekends at Ed's in Piedmont, but that's up for discussion. After the New Year—and Tami, this really is absolutely confidential for a few more weeks—Ed has been asked to take an important role in developing an exhibit on the history of the American book at the Smithsonian. The project will take six months so he'll be back in D.C. through the end of June."

"No fun for either of you, I'm gonna guess."

"He's arranged to work from California one week per month so sandwiched between a couple of weekends we'll see each other almost a third of the time. And since I have a boatload of vacation stored up, maybe you and I can visit Washington a couple of times. But there's also exciting news for me in all this. Ed met with the Bay Board of Directors last week and while he's gone I'm to be Interim Publisher."

"Fantastic, Mom, really! It's as if you're suddenly getting a whole new life. But isn't the Board going to think it's kinda incestuous when they find out about you and Ed?"

"Ed told them about our relationship and got nothing but congratulations. But here's the waiter. What do you want to share besides the crispy Saigon chicken rolls and the green papaya salad—which, of course, are non-negotiable?"

"How about the salt and pepper prawns?" Tamiko says to their server.

"Got it," the slim young Asian waiter says, not bothering to write down their order. "Anything to drink?"

"I'll have a glass of the prosecco," Amy replies.

"One, or two?," the young man asks, making eye contact with Tamiko.

"My daughter is nowhere near twenty-one," Amy says peremptorily.

"Could have fooled me two ways," the waiter says, still staring at Tamiko, a gap-toothed grin now lighting his face.

"What exactly do you mean?" Amy asks, letting her annoyance show.

"She could easily pass for twenty-one and you don't look nearly old enough to be her mother," he replies as he turns and heads towards the kitchen.

"Lighten up, Mom—at least he didn't think you were my kid. But, hey, wouldn't all this be much less awkward for everyone if you let me start college back East this fall? I know I can handle it and you wouldn't have to worry about what to do with me when you're with Ed."

"There is no way on this green planet that you're going off to college in two weeks even if some desperate coach could twist enough admissions office arms to shoehorn you in. And I'm not abandoning you or even asking you to do anything that makes you uncomfortable. All I'm suggesting is that we stay over at Ed's now and then on weekends. His house is at least twice the size of ours and you'll have a lovely room on a separate floor. No need to commit to anything now, just keep an open mind. And don't worry about Ed, he knows this is a transition year for all of us so he'll be patient and not try to monopolize my time."

"Is it a surprise that I already hate the sound of words like transition and patient? Doesn't it ever occur to you that you're not the only one on this green planet, or even in this family, who's ready for an independent life?"

"Now you've hurt my feelings."

"Sorry, but Mom, if I was ten when all this was coming down maybe we could try to create a new family, but like, oh my god, even the waiter thinks I'm twenty-one."

"But you're fifteen and whether you like the word or not, patient is exactly what you'll have to be. And also remember, you and Ed have always liked each other so please don't overreact."

"Fair enough, and I really am happy for you both, it's just that I feel a tad left out. And for sure Mom, the idea of a transition year will sound much better if you'll trust me to stay at home when you and Ed go off for a day or two."

"We'll see."

"You already have my promise of no fraternizing with Lec without your permission."

"Calling Mr. Burns by a pet name, isn't helping your stay-at-home argument."

"I, for one, believe people should be called what they want to be called."

"Tamiko, I've already committed to doing my best."

"So, when are you and Ed going public with your relationship?" Tamiko asks, grabbing the last prawn and finishing it off in a bite.

"We'd planned to do it at the wine and nibbles party Friday, but then, this week when you…well, we…"

"Felt bad about celebrating right after warning me off Lec? Please Mom, go ahead, everyone has guessed about you guys anyway. But hey, what about dessert?"

"The menu is right here."

"At an Asian restaurant, you're kidding right?"

"Vanessa's has a delicious western dessert menu, but if you prefer we can walk up the street to iScream."

"Yum. Maybe if we take our time we can even get through the rest of my list."

. . . . .

As mother and daughter walk uphill on Solano Avenue past the Oak's Jeweler's, "family-owned since 1948" and Payn's Stationery, which looks unchanged since the Hoover administration, Amy asks, "I know you usually plead terminal boredom to avoid Bay parties, but will you make an exception on Friday?"

"If I do, the moment you and Ed make your announcement everyone is going to turn and stare at me. Better for you guys to enjoy the moment. After, maybe the three of us can get pizza or something, and I can congratulate Ed. Monday I'll bustle into work with a smile on my face and all will be well."

"For sure we'll go out afterwards for a family celebration."

"Mom, can I ask you about something personal that's been bothering me? I mean it's like we've always been close, so we can talk about real stuff, right?"

"I hope so."

"OK, so when you and Ed started getting together did he, like, completely fill up your mind, I mean push everything else out?"

"Is that what's happening to you?"

"I asked first."

"In a word, yes. Starting this spring I did think about Ed a lot and still do."

"Mom, with me on any one day, or hour or even minute, I used to think about all sorts of random stuff, like a stream of consciousness deal, I guess. When is my period starting? Why did Jazz snap at me? How am I going to make time to pick up the groceries for you? And on and on all in kinda like a jumble. But now it's as if my brain is stuck in a Lec loop: Lec smiling, Lec brushing back his hair, Lec and me meeting, Lec putting his hand on…"

"Sweetie, I'd normally be happy to talk about what little I know about how desire can hijack ordinary thoughts, but I'm not going to do it in the context of this off-limits older man. But I can promise you that when you eventually fall for someone your own age, the same thing is going to happen."

. . . . .

As he comes out of his organic chemistry lab at a few minutes after four Wednesday afternoon, Alec turns on his phone to see that he has three more messages from Teri.

"Alec, I need see you. How about 9 t-nite. This important."

"Alec call me. I serious."

"Alec, please."

Toggling his phone back to mute, Alec heads towards the Recreational Sports Facility downhill from the new student center on Sproul Plaza. Knowing that Teri will be occupied with a Tai Chi class from five to six-thirty he plans to wait until then to leave her another voicemail, this time pleading a headache as well as the need to study. Although he feels guilty for continuing to avoid her, he knows he'll feel even worse when he tells her that their summer romance is over. Again, it occurs to him that it would be both easier and more fun to keep seeing her until she returns to Korea in a few weeks. But, even before he can seriously consider this possibility, an inner voice he still barely recognizes whispers, "It's a terrible idea to cheat on Tamiko, so bad, that if you do you'll deserve to lose her."

"Cheat on Tamiko," Alec replies incredulously, only realizing he's spoken when the dark-skinned young woman in bright orange Nikes walking in front of him glances over her shoulder before picking up her pace. Continuing his protest silently, Alec adds, "How can I cheat on a high school girl I can't even legally go out with? Not to mention the fact that I've been seeing Teri all summer and she's leaving so soon that a short transition only makes sense."

When the voice doesn't reply, Alec enters the student workout area and begins alternating sets on a pull-up machine with a plump, but surprisingly strong red-headed sophomore named Trish who looks younger than Tamiko. Only when he switches to pedaling furiously on a stationary bike, does the voice finally say, 'Karma Lec, it's as simple as that. If you're going to have any chance with Tamiko it's because you're willing to bring her your pure heart.'

Coming out of the gym half an hour later still in his dark blue shorts and a gray T-shirt that says "Property of the University of Melbourne," Alec sees he has another text from Teri.

"*I need talk Alec. Take aspirins and call. Please.*"

Hardly hesitating, Alec texts back, "*I absolutely need to cram tonight. Meet me at the Campanile tomorrow at ten after four.*"

THURSDAY

IF POSSIBLE, TAMIKO WAKES UP EVEN HAPPIER THAN USUAL. She knows lots of things still need to be resolved with her mom, but last evening's conversation was a big step in the right direction. And somehow, even after absorbing Ruth's concern, she feels optimistic that somehow, some way, she can pull off her relationship with Lec. If a heart overflowing with love can move mountains, she thinks while cleaning her teeth, Everest better pack its bags.

"Mom, can I wear the cowl-neck top I wore to Ruth's yesterday?" Tamiko shouts at her mother's closed bedroom door. "And just so you know I'm putting on one of my too-tight bras."

"Sure, but not the Indian skirt since I'm already in it," comes the reply. Then, as Amy opens the door she adds in a softer voice, "But I know where I bought it down on Fourth Street so I'll pick one up for you after work. It will be the first installment for your makeover. And if you hurry, I have time to drop you by campus."

"I was going to take my bike, but a ride would be great."

In the faded blue Subaru Forrester on the way up Hearst Street Amy says, "To be absolutely clear, I'm still totally against your having a serious relationship with Alec Burns. But as long as you keep your no-touching promise, I've decided not to try to stop you from seeing him in public, even though I'm afraid even that will end in tears."

· · · · ·

Arriving a few minutes early to her lecture Tamiko hides in the bathroom, worried that Adam Sheib will sit next to her and try to chat her up after class. Although she likes Adam well enough, she wants no delay when it comes to meeting Alec. Then, as Professor Spurgeon drones on and on about the importance of Maxwell's equations, she attempts to sketch Lec's face. When the result looks disconcertingly like a rabbit, she shuts her eyes and lets her imagination produce a more pleasing result. A minute or two before eleven, Tamiko slips out the back door into the sunny morning. Walking purposefully north towards the graceful Beaux Arts facade of the Hearst Memorial Mining Building, she can barely contain her excitement as she looks forward to the moment when she and Lec meet at what she now regards as their magic spot.

"Yes," Tamiko almost shouts when she clears the corner of Campbell Hall to see that Lec is already there. But as she takes several more steps she sees he isn't alone. Instead, a slim long-haired Asian woman with a heart-shaped face under a curtain of black bangs is standing impolitely close to him. As Tamiko's eager steps begin to slow, the girl grabs Alec's shoulders and pulls her body against his. However, it's only when Alec places his hands on the girl's shoulders and returns her kiss that Tamiko feels her breath whoosh out. Now at a full stop, she begins to back awkwardly up the hill in an attempt to regain a place where she can't be seen. Feeling as if her eyes are stapled to the kiss, a kiss that seems to go on and on and on, Tamiko gulps air as she bumps into a guy coming down the hill behind her who is so preoccupied with chatting on his phone he barely notices. Mumbling an apology to the dragon on the back of the guy's black jacket Tamiko turns, and almost runs back the way she came. Passing LeConte Hall she continues south until she reaches Cal's 300-foot Campanile, where she collapses on a stone bench in the obelisk's shadow, feeling utterly deflated.

After ten miserable minutes Tamiko pulls herself together sufficiently to stand. Immediately feeling light-headed, she sits back down, this time lowering her head between her knees. Keeping it there for five long minutes while she again employs her Grandmother Vera's breathing technique, Tamiko is finally able to stand without dizziness. Heading downhill on South Drive she is careful to stay out of sight of the place where, for all she knows, Lec and the beautiful Asian are still embracing. At least the question of whether Lec already has a girlfriend has been answered, she thinks miserably as she turns right on Campanile Way and in less than the length of a football field finds herself in front of the familiar Free Speech Movement Café. Quickening her stride towards the north side of campus, after a few steps she slows to a stop. Maybe, just maybe, she thinks, everything she has just seen had been a crazy mistake and Lec will be waiting for her on the patio with an explanation. Entering the café, Tamiko continues past the counter and the inside seating area before bursting through the patio door with so much force that half a dozen people look up. Seeing that their table is empty and Lec is nowhere in sight she again feels so light-headed she collapses into the nearest empty chair. With her forehead now lowered to the table, Tamiko begins to cry with a desperation she hasn't felt since the morning her dad was killed. Feeling a tap on her shoulder, and when she doesn't respond, another, Tamiko raises her head to see a middle-aged sari-clad woman with salt-and-pepper hair holding out a couple of paper napkins. "Try to remember that in this world, things can change very rapidly, often for the better," the woman says, smiling. Oddly touched, but nevertheless incapable of forming a reply Tamiko grabs the napkins, stands, and still crying, leaves the café.

Feeling an overwhelming desire to reach the sanctuary of her own room, Tamiko somehow finds her way home. As she turns into her front walk, the sound of her phone playing Adele's "Hello" brings her back to herself. Seeing it's Lec she angrily crashes through the spider web, unlocks the front door, and batting at her face to clear the sticky strands charges through the house. Then, after wrenching open the kitchen door, she throws her phone at the back fence as if trying to cut down the opposing team's winning run at the plate. Finally flopping on the bed, Tamiko pulls her patchwork quilt over her head. But instead of finding a moment of respite, the scene of Lec kissing the willowy Asian girl with the heart-shaped face plays over and over in her imagination as her tears again flow like a spring-time river. Then, as her mental movie stutters back a notch or two, she sees herself coming down the path next to Evans Hall, a big goofy smile on her face only to watch as her expression becomes, at first quizzical, then shocked and finally, as her hands fly up as if to block a blow, crushed.

Although Tamiko eventually manages to switch off her brain's replay button, the image of that kiss and her mortified reaction to it defines her miserable, sniffling afternoon. Most embarrassing, is the fact that despite Ruth's gentle caution and her mother's fierce warning, she's been naive enough to believe that a smart, beautiful older guy like Lec really could fall for her. She may no longer be quite the ungainly giraffe of her childhood, but given the choice of a slim coiffed college girl with a heart-shaped face or her, Lec obviously has had no trouble choosing.

At three o'clock Tamiko drags herself out of bed long enough to eat a banana and use the bathroom. Still feeling as if she's been punched in the gut, she crawls back under her quilt, curls into a fetal position and thinks of her dad's ever-encouraging smile. At four-thirty Amy comes through the front door calling, "Tamiko, are you here? Are you OK?" Then coming into Tamiko's room she continues, "Tami, are you napping? Are you ill?"

When Tamiko's response is a loud sniffle, Amy sits on her bed and asks in a worried voice, "Tami, what's going on? Please tell me."

Face to the wall Tamiko curls tighter, but doesn't reply. Contouring her slim body to her daughter's much longer one, Amy wraps her top arm around her daughter and pulls her tight as she says, "I love you, but sweetie, please tell me what's happened?"

Tamiko starts to reply, but her words peter out into another sniffle.

"Is this something to do with Alec? Talk to me please. Whatever happened I promise not to say 'I told you so.' Please Tami…"

"Mom, it's Tamiko now, no more Tami. I know I'm acting like a baby, but I still want you to use my name," Tamiko says in a small voice. "But Mom, on top of everything else I ruined our spiderweb, just walked right through it."

"I saw that, but I also saw that the spider is hard at work on a new one off to the side, where it will be safe from errant humans. So please, Tamiko, tell me what's really up, or should I say down, with you. When you didn't show up for work I called and called. A few minutes ago when you still didn't pick up I became so frantic I came home hoping against hope you were here. Since you were fine this morning I'm going to guess all this is about something that happened after class?"

"I saw him kissing this beautiful Asian girl. Like, not just a little beautiful, but you know, like maybe an inch or two taller than you and gorgeous. And I'm pretty sure he wasn't just kissing her on the lips, the way he kissed me."

"Did you talk to him?"

"No, I ran off. Seeing him like that felt like someone hit me with a bat."

"Has he called?"

"Just as I got home my phone rang," Tamiko replies, her voice still a bit ragged from her hours of crying.

"And?"

"I'm trying to tell you—I was so upset, instead of answering I threw my phone at the back fence."

"Your precious iPhone? You must really have been seeing red. Hang on a second while I get some water and more tissues. Then I'll look for your phone."

"It's probably smashed into a thousand pieces."

Like your schoolgirl crush on Alec Burns, Amy thinks with a feeling of real satisfaction as she puts a tall glass of water and a fresh box of Kleenex on her daughter's nightstand before going into the backyard. Hardly more than a minute later she's back waving the phone in her right hand and saying, "Good news, it seems to be working fine."

"Really?" Tamiko says, almost smiling, as she rolls over to face her mom,.

"You apparently hit the thick foliage of the lemon tree by the back fence. Anyhow, it was underneath there. And I hope I'm not invading your privacy too much, but I can see from your display that you have a bunch of texts and voicemails from Mr. Burns. Would you like me to read the texts?"

"Go ahead," Tamiko says in a small voice as she straightens her legs, squirms towards the headboard until finally, head elevated, she makes eye contact with her mother.

Hesitating for a moment as she regrets her offer, but unable to think of a way to walk it back, Amy clears her throat. "The first one says, '*Tamiko, I love you. Really, definitely, absolutely all the way love you. Please call so I can explain.*' The next one says, '*I love you Tamiko, only you. What you saw today was a crazy accident. Just listen to my voicemails, please.*'"

"Are there more?"

"A bunch, so why don't I just skip to the last one, which says, *Tamiko, I'd camp out in your front yard until you listen to my explanation or your mom shoots me, but I don't know where you live, so please, please call me.*"

Now sitting fully upright with a relieved smile on her face, Tamiko reaches for her phone with her right hand as she blows her nose with her left. "Thanks, Mom. Really, you've been just absolutely super, but I'd like to call Lec now."

"Sweetie, maybe all of this today should be a very clear lesson that you are out of your depth," Amy says as she reluctantly hands over the phone.

After ducking into the bathroom to splash handfuls of cool water on her face and run a brush through her damp hair, Tamiko perches on her desk chair and taps Alec's number.

"Thank god you finally called," Alec says by way of answer. "I've been freaked all afternoon. Did you listen to my endless voicemails?"

"No, Mom just found my phone out in the backyard where I threw it. She read me a few texts so I called."

"But all those hours since this morning. What have you been doing?"

"Mostly crying, I guess."

"Before I try to explain, can I say one short thing?"

"Go ahead."

"I love you, Tamiko O'Shea Gashkin, and no one else. Now will you listen long enough for me to try to straighten things out?"

"Take your time. The moment Mom read me your text about camping out in the front yard I kinda got that you care about me. But still, Lec...."

"Should I explain now or do you want to meet for coffee or something?"

"There's zero chance Mom will let me out of the house, so go ahead, but remember I saw your beautiful friend so don't try to paint her out of the picture."

"OK, but tell me if you start getting bored or upset."

"I'm guessing my chances of being bored are submicroscopic and that I'll only get upset if you sugarcoat things."

"Nothing but the truth, ma'am. When the summer session started I wasn't seeing anyone. The girl I went out with in the spring went off to study in Bologna for a year making it clear that when she kissed me goodbye she meant just that. In short, I decided to spend the summer dating my books…"

"Based on what I saw, that plan didn't last long."

"I met Teri, the girl you saw this morning, at a friend's party in late June. She's Korean, not Korean-American, but a girl from Seoul who talked her father into letting her come to Cal for the summer session with seven or eight other Korean students. In the fall, she's supposed to become engaged to this older guy her affluent parents have picked out so this was her big chance to have an adventure—rebel a little, I guess.'"

"And you were, and obviously still are, her chief rebel."

"I was until Tuesday, when I realized I'd fallen for you. From the moment we kissed I knew it had to be over with Teri, even though she planned to return to Korea for good in a couple of weeks. But since I always hibernate with my books from Monday morning to Thursday afternoon, I put off the confrontation. I knew this was chicken shit, but since Teri is way into drama at the best of times—almost as if she's the star of her own Korean soap—I continued to hide even though by yesterday she was bombarding me with agitated messages."

"I'm almost feeling sorry for her."

"Turns out you would be right. On Tuesday one of her so-called friends ratted her out to her dad who immediately called and ordered her to fly home by Sunday at the latest."

"You mean like someone told her dad back in Korea about her relationship with you?"

"Yes, along with a couple other girls with Cal boyfriends. Anyway, because I didn't respond to her calls and texts, she showed up outside of Evans this morning where she knew I had European Lit."

"I hope you didn't tell her about me in the middle of her meltdown."

"When she first swooped down I actually tried, but she was so wrapped up in relating her drama she paid no attention. Then, as if I was caught in the world's most clichéd movie, she launched herself into my arms, just as I saw you appear up the hill. I looked for a way to reassure you, but with a hysterical girl in my arms telling me she loved me and wanted us to run away together, I didn't know how to do it."

Not to mention she's drop-dead gorgeous, Tamiko thinks as she says, "But does she really want to elope with you, or whatever?"

"Not hardly. Her dad owns several cement factories and a steel mill so she's not about to risk being disowned over a summer romance."

"The way she was kissing you sure looked like the real thing," Tamiko says, in a small voice, again feeling the lash of jealousy.

"Probably you weren't totally objective, but OK, until I met you Monday things had been pretty intense and there is no doubt that our parting was going to be dramatic."

"For you?"

"A little, sure, but since I always knew Teri was passing through— kind of the reverse of what happened when I was traveling, I was OK with moving on. For Teri though, after a summer in Berkeley, going back to her pampered life as daddy's little rich girl was never going to be easy."

"I know this may make me sound like a teenage martyr, but I think you should hang with Teri until she leaves Sunday," Tamiko says, surprised at her own words. "I mean, for the rest of her life she'll remember her magical summer in Berkeley. You simply can't ruin it now. And Lec, since Mom isn't likely to change her mind about us anytime soon you'll still have plenty of time to be faithful to me, that is, if you still want to."

"Count on it, but, c'mon, after today you can't really be telling me it's OK to continue seeing Teri?"

"I was freaked because I thought you didn't care for me, but now that I get that you do, I'm OK. Really, Alec."

"Great speech but I worry that you're being too generous, and that later on, you'll regret it and be seriously unhappy."

"No need, since I'm going on a date too."

"Who's teasing now?"

"Not I, or is 'me', the correct pronoun? Either way, two attractive Cal guys and another from BCC have been asking me out all summer and now that I know how to drink coffee, I plan to say yes to the cutest one. I have a short dating window and I plan to make the most of it."

"Now, I'm feeling a little jealous."

"Good, especially since I'm guessing it's your first time. But I have a gap in my busy schedule Sunday afternoon if you want to sign up to be my catcher?"

"Where and when?"

"How about four o'clock at Martin Luther King Middle School on Rose Street? Do you need directions?"

"I'm already bringing them up on my phone. See you there."

"Wear a cup, I throw hard."

· · · · ·

When Tamiko comes into the kitchen a few minutes later, Amy, who is slicing an English cucumber on the cutting board by the sink, turns to face her daughter and asks, "Is everything OK?"

"Fine. It turns out I saw Lec trying to break up with his old girlfriend, the one he had before me."

"I thought you said they were kissing," Amy says quietly as she turns back to the cucumber.

Ignoring this, Tamiko perches on a three-legged stool at the counter. "Teri's going back to Korea on Sunday to become engaged so it's all going to take care of itself."

"Oh my god, sweetie, this just gets more and more bizarre. You're supposed to be thinking about things like the high school prom, not trying to cope with a guy who is…"

"Mom, will it help us stop arguing if I say that maybe you are right, at least somewhat, but that it doesn't make any difference. It's like, what you don't seem to get is I don't have a choice. From the moment I looked in Lec's eyes, the old Tamiko just kind of went '*poof.*' So the way I see it—this is my first big test—can I be grown up enough to cope with the fact Lec needs to deal with an old lover in a good way, or am I going to collapse in a puddle of misery? I mean Mom, I'm obviously not the first person in this family who has had to deal with jealousy. When you and Ed got together he already had a girlfriend, right?"

"That was different. Neither of us was fifteen and…"

"Oh my god Mom, please don't start with your 'Tami's just a child' speech. The way I see it, you beat me up for being too young to cope with the adult world, then double down when I try. But, hey, what's for dinner?"

"Soup, macaroni and cheese and a salad."

"Perfect, this is definitely the day for comfort food."

"And just so you know, Ed broke up with Emiline before we became intimate. Well, OK, I guess it's true that since her mother was having life-threatening surgery he waited a few days to tell her so maybe there was a little overlap, but it's not remotely the same thing."

"Mom, is this conversation maybe in danger of following Alice down the rabbit hole? You seem to be forgetting that not only am I not having sex with Alec, but that according to you, it's not even on the horizon."

"Will it clear the air, at least a little, if I promise to try not to use your age to automatically dismiss your legitimate concerns?"

"Eliminate the words try, automatically, and legitimate and you have a deal."

"Don't be greedy. But sweetie, I have a favor to ask. Tomorrow, after the Bay party, is it OK if we all stay over at Ed's house until Sunday?"

"I guess, sure, but I may have a date."

"I haven't changed my mind about your not having permission to date Alec."

"Don't worry, that's on hold until pitching on Sunday, which, remember, will put us forty-three feet apart. Saturday I'm hoping to go out with Mark Sullivan, the older brother of Molly who plays second base at BHS. Anyway, Mark's been asking me out this summer so if he's still interested, I'm ready to say yes."

"How old is he?"

"Mom, in case anyone is counting, your resolution not to use my age against me lasted less than a minute. But, for the record, Mark just finished his first year at Cal, so he's eighteen or nineteen."

"But Tami, since you're still fifteen I don't see that..."

"Oh my god, Mom, listen to yourself. If you really want to order me not to hang with Mark for a few hours you could say, 'Tamiko, even though you have two years of college credit, a job, and are starting university back East next year, it's still not OK for you to go out with a guy who is a couple of years older.'"

"Maybe you should think about a career as a lawyer."

"I choose to take that as a compliment."

"Many people wouldn't, but let's see if we can find a compromise. What kind of an outing do you have planned with Mark?"

"Mom, I haven't even called him, so I have no idea. But in case you're worried, I never have sex on a first date."

"That was uncalled for."

"You're right and I apologize. But Mom, I'm betting you had your first real boyfriend sometime in high school so I don't see why you're being so over-the-moon strict."

Amy removes a cardboard container of Italian Wedding soup from the microwave, pours it into two bowls and plunks them down on the dining room table next to mounded plates full of noodles slathered in cheddar. Back in the kitchen to fetch water and the salad bowl, she asks herself how and when her almost trouble-free daughter—who just a few months before had also been her best buddy—had become the next thing to a stranger. Finding no answer, she joins Tamiko and eats her supper in silence. But, as soon as Tamiko clears the table and goes to her room, Amy reaches for her phone to call Ed, still upset.

"Mom," Tamiko says, reappearing before Amy can tap Ed's number, "I almost forgot, but do you remember how Dad and I used to play a game counting different makes and models of cars?"

"How could I not? For a while there, you two were both like hyper kids. And then you even won that science prize for tallying the car brands on a dozen random blocks in Berkeley as part of creating a statistical model to predict car ownership by make for the entire city."

"It was a little more complicated than that, involving census tracts and sampling techniques, but Mom, we're wandering way off the point I'm trying to make."

"Which is?"

"The reason Dad started me on keeping track of different types of cars was to train me to be aware of my surroundings."

"Right, he thought it would help keep you safe. If you saw a strange car in our neighborhood you would know to stay away from it and tell us, especially if you saw it more than once. But for the life of me, Tamiko, I still don't know what this conversation is about."

"Mom, what I'm trying to tell you is that yesterday I saw a 1982 gray Ford parked across the street from our house. Then, this morning I saw it again, this time about six houses up towards McGee. I paid more attention the second time and I'm pretty sure someone was slumped down in the front seat since I saw what looked like the top of a black knit cap."

"Is it unusual to see a strange car on our block?"

"Not really. If it was a garden-variety Japanese or European car I would have barely registered it. But seeing a Ford almost as old as you are on Francisco Street is about as common as seeing a pelican in our bird bath."

"We don't have a bird bath."

"Exactly."

"It could have been someone doing Airbnb or maybe a new tenant in one of the in-law units across the street."

"True, but like Mom, here's the thing that really got my attention. I think maybe I spotted the same car yesterday when I got to Bay, just turning right onto Solano. I only saw the tail lights and bumper so I'm not one hundred percent sure."

"What would Dad have said if you told him all this?"

"You don't have enough data. Keep your eyes open and report back."

"Consider it said."

"Definitely," Tamiko says, and she spins and goes back to her room.

. . . . .

Finally on her own, Amy reaches Ed. "We were just so close," she laments in a low voice, "I know I probably sound like Siri caught in an endless repeat loop, but I don't see why she's determined to pull away."

"Have you considered that it might be you who's doing the pulling?"

"That's just plain not true. Since you and I got serious, I've gone out of my way to be sure Tami's life isn't affected."

"How would you feel if you realized someone was doing that for you?"

"She's already made that point. But I have to say it sure sounds like you and Tamiko are singing out of the same songbook," Amy says, going out to the front porch as she realizes her voice has taken on an angry edge.

"Maybe you need to get a grip and then call me back," Ed says quietly.

"Sorry, I don't mean to be paranoid, I just hope you're not saying that because both Tami and I are changing, our close relationship is a thing of the past?"

"Not if you're smart about it," Ed says more kindly.

"And that would consist of doing exactly what?" Amy asks, trying to keep the exasperation out of her voice.

"Treating her like an adult, much as we already do at Bay and I'm sure her community college professors also do."

"But she's not an adult."

"Not quite, perhaps, but I'm betting that if you treat her like one it won't take long for her to live up to it. For sure, if you two are on good terms, she's a lot more likely to ask for your advice, instead of almost reflexively resisting it."

"You actually think I should let her date whoever she wants, including going out with a twenty-two year old?"

"Let's agree Alec Burns is an extreme case, but as far as Tamiko's dating eighteen or nineteen year old college boys, I can't see why you're opposed. But even when it comes to Alec, why not at least meet him, if only on the theory that it's easier to cope with a devil you know than one you imagine as twelve feet tall and waving a pitchfork."

"That's not going to happen. But Ed, even though I'm sure I sound like the mad woman in the attic tonight, I agree that I need to find better ways to relate to my daughter than just saying no."

"I'll take that as progress. Now if you don't mind a self-interested non sequitur, did you ask Tamiko whether she's OK with spending this weekend at my place? It'll be wonderful if you and I can work out some kind of sensible way to get our paws on each other more often."

"She's willing to give it a try and I have an idea that might even cause her to be enthusiastic about repeats."

"Do tell."

"She's fixated on learning to drive. She's already taken driver's ed online and is in the process of getting her permit."

"Isn't it lucky that I'm one of the world's best driving instructors?"

"I hoped you'd say that and I also hope you know that I'm as anxious for this weekend to work as you are—and for the same reasons. It would be way past embarrassing if I told you how often I think of getting a lot more than my paws on you."

"You're tempting me to have my first phone sex. But to get back to Tamiko, in addition to setting up a driving lesson, how about dedicating this weekend to making her feel truly welcome? We could plan a meal to cook together and then watch a movie she wants to see."

"Good idea."

"But Amy, in addition to dangling carrots to make it fun for her to come to Piedmont, it might make sense to give her the option of staying home occasionally. That is, make the decision to come over voluntary, not a requirement."

"Leaving her home right now with this totally inappropriate man prowling around is not an option."

"C'mon, not only have they promised not to be alone together without your consent, but anyway, what's the worst that could happen?"

"A pregnant fifteen-year-old?"

"So, get her birth control pills."

"And encourage her to have sex with this man?"

"Listen to yourself for a moment and maybe I won't be the only one who thinks this conversation is going in circles?"

"OK, I grant you that no matter how determined I am to protect Tami from Alec Burns, it's time to discuss birth control. As someone who got pregnant before her nineteenth birthday, I don't need to be convinced of that."

"Good. And now since I have an early morning, I'm going to say good night."

"Wait a minute. Since we seem to be tumbling into big decisions about our future, there are a couple of things about my past I want to tell you about."

"Amy, I love you, from toes to nose. Nothing else counts."

"Just the same, it's important to me that you listen. In fact I've been trying to find the right time to talk to you for the last month."

"I'm not the least bit interested in hearing about a parade of former lovers. A mutual policy of 'don't ask, don't tell' suits me fine."

"I'm sure, since I can count the number of men I've had sex with on the fingers of one hand and I'm guessing you'd just be getting started when you finished with your toes. But I'm not interested in any of that either. It's just that I want to tell you about what happened with one scary guy after Yuri's death."

"I thought you spent a few weeks in an ashram in India to get your head together."

"Yes, but first I visited my friend Gretchen in Amsterdam…"

"Do you want to talk about it now?"

"Tomorrow evening in person will be better."

"You mean in between our hours of ecstatic pawing and being nice to Tamiko?"

"To be clear, I'm not proposing we skip either of those."

. . . . .

When Alec finishes talking to Tamiko, he lies back on his bed, draws in his breath and tenses every muscle in his body. Then, after holding himself board stiff for several seconds, he relaxes with a whoosh. With just one short conversation he's gone from being anxious, bordering on miserable, to relaxed, bordering on happy all because a girl he's spent less than five hours with has said she loves him. And, at least as important, she has coped with a situation where many women would be angry, jealous and dismissive. There's no question that this smart, beautiful, big-hearted young woman is a keeper, even if her mother is determined to make him throw her back.

Before Alec can move to his desk to work on his World Lit paper, his phone begins whispering "Saeta". Seeing it's Teri, or Haewon to use her Korean name, he answers saying, "Hey, what's up? How did your group meeting, or maybe I should say confrontation, go? Did Jen or Wendy confess to telling your father?"

"I'm pretty sure they don't do it, since they are also told to go home Sunday because of American boyfriends. Now we think one of the boys, maybe Dennis or Brian, how you say—rat us?"

"Ratted you out."

"Right—we think now they try get even for, for…"

"Hanging with white guys like me?"

"Jen's boyfriend is black, so maybe better say—for screwing around with American guys," Teri replies, chuckling. "We just got a pizza delivery and now we all talk about how to get back at these boys."

"Plot revenge?"

"Yes, revenge is just what we want! We'll be done by nine-thirty, so you come then. OK?"

"Got it, see you later," Alec says as he hangs up and glances at the time to see he has over three hours to make himself a sandwich and study for his organic chem final which is now only a week away. If he is going to get into a good grad school, he knows he has to ace it.

. . . . .

At 9:20, Alec is getting ready to walk the half mile downhill to Teri Kim's shared apartment on College Avenue between Dwight Way and Derby Street, when he receives a text: *My apartment is still full of mad Korean students arguing. Better I come to your place later, maybe midnight.*

Not sure whether he's feeling relieved or disappointed, Alec texts back: *Sorry, but I need to crash by eleven to be awake for my lab tomorrow. Maybe we can meet late in the afternoon?*

Seconds later Alec's phone pings again, and he reads: *Father now coming tomorrow so I leave Saturday afternoon. Only chance to meet is if I sneak out at 2:00 a.m. Saturday morning. You pick me up OK?*

Alec immediately texts back: *I'll be there.* With phone in hand and a free hour to spend, he checks his email. In addition to a "just saying hi" message from his mom, he has a surprise email from his Uncle Charlie who, faced with a cancellation of his flight from Narita Airport in Japan to JFK, is instead hopping on a red-eye to San Francisco. Tomorrow, Charlie proposes to take Alec to an early dinner before continuing on to New York.

Nice, Alec thinks. Charlie is the perfect person to advise me about Tamiko.

FRIDAY

TAMIKO LEAVES BAY JUST AFTER 3:30 P.M., having helped set up for the late afternoon wine and nibbles celebration for *Slide Zone*. After following her mom's request to pick up yogurt at the nearby Safeway—which, like most everyone in North Berkeley, she still insists on calling by it's historical name, Andronico's—she jogs the mile and a half home. She lays out clothes for her dinner date which consist of her one pair of tight jeans, and her mom's dove gray henley with the six little buttons on the placket. Rejecting her regular bras as too tight, and her sports bra as too geeky, she compromises on a maroon leotard. True, it doesn't conceal much, but with the henley on top her mom can't accuse her of going out half-naked. Then, after putting her PJ's and toothbrush in her backpack and placing it on the dining room table, she scribbles a note:

"Mom, I'm meeting Tabitha Anderson from BHS softball two seasons ago for dinner on Piedmont Ave. in Oakland. Please bring this along to Ed's and I'll see you over there when Tabs drops me at 8:00, or 8:30 at the latest. Love, T"

Locking the front door, Tamiko sits on the top step. Closing her eyes against the sun, she smiles as she imagines Lec placing his lips on hers. She is just working up the courage to extend her tongue when two quick toots of a car's horn steps on her fantasy.

"Are you going to wake up, or should I get the hose?" Tabitha asks as she leans out the window of what Tamiko recognizes as a twenty-year-old Toyota Tercel that might once have been light blue.

Determinedly putting Lec out of her mind she opens the dented passenger door and says, "Great to see you Tabs. Like I told you on the phone, I just have so many things to ask you about. Thanks for showing up on such short notice."

"I have a date with Blaine later, but right now letting you buy me a nice supper works perfectly."

"Hey, it's like eighty degrees in here!"

"The car's been sitting in the sun all afternoon. And the only air-conditioning you're going to get is if you open the window and take off your shirt."

"OK," Tamiko says, pulling off the henley, "but don't rat me out to Mom since she claims going out without a bra is beyond tacky even though I don't really need one."

"Maybe, on this subject anyway, you should listen to your mom. It's as if you're advertising to the whole male population when you just told me on the phone you're only interested in one guy. I mean really, Tami, anyone with a body like yours should know better."

"If I say I hear you loud and clear can this lecture stop?"

"Sure, but hey, what's on your mind that's so pressing?" Tabitha asks as she makes a left turn onto University Avenue.

"It's this guy Alec I just met who is a lot older than me."

"How old would that be exactly?"

"Twenty-two."

"I'm guessing your mom is, like, totally up a tree about that?"

"Three hundred feet and still climbing. To try to coax her down a few branches we've promised no 'sex' or anything that comes close to it."

"Good luck on sticking to that, but where do I come in?"

"Before we met last week, Lec, that's what I call Alec, had another girlfriend. She's leaving the country so that's not a problem. But for a moment there I got super jealous—which got me wondering about all the other girlfriends he's had and whether I should, I don't know, ask him to tell me about them or something. But I'm so clueless about the college dating scene and what it means when kids hook up, I thought I'd better do some research first—which is where you come in."

"Tamiko, why am I not surprised that you're approaching the subject of dating as if you're asking a teacher how to conjugate a Latin verb? I guess it will actually work with me, but I have to warn you that most people are not going to tell you all about their sex lives just because you're curious. But what's with this Lec? Isn't he ashamed to be a cradle robber?"

"OMG! You're supposed to be on my side, Tabs. But anyway, it's not like that. We met by accident at Cal where I'm doing a summer physics class and he had no clue I was still in high school when he invited me to coffee."

Coasting to a stop as the light turned red at the corner of Ashby and Adeline, Tabitha gives Tamiko an appraising look and says, "Last year you were still a big, geeky kid, but now I can easily see how he made that mistake. You can not only pass for nineteen, but for Jennifer Lawrence at nineteen, although the comparison does her a favor since you're better looking."

"Stop it," Tamiko says blushing. "But, it's true that guys have started to notice me."

"And you?"

"I was beginning to notice them back when I met Lec and well, I don't know how to…"

"Got your first mad crush, have you?"

"Very mad, I guess."

"Just curious, but how long did it take for him to figure out you haven't made it to Sweet Sixteen?"

"My birthday is only ten days away now, but it was on our first coffee date, the day after we met. By then it was too late. I mean I can hardly believe it, but I actually asked him to kiss me."

"I'm guessing that went well," Tabitha says dryly.

"It was like I was bodysurfing when this humongous wave picked me up, tumbled me over, and slammed me down so hard that I thought my bathing suit would be torn off."

"Been there, my dear, and sad to say when the wave went back out I ended up with my bum in the air and my mouth full of sand," Tabitha says as she maneuvers the Tercel behind a UPS truck to turn left on 57th Street.

"Talking about your love life, are you, like, really still going out with Blaine, your boyfriend from Berkeley High?"

"Since he goes to UCLA I didn't see him all year. But we stayed in loose touch on Facebook and this summer when it turned out we were both doing internships here in Berkeley, we've been hanging out. It's more FWB than boyfriend and girlfriend, if that's not too X-rated for your almost sixteen-year-old ears. His parents are away this weekend so we have his place to ourselves tonight. As long as I get home before one, my parents won't raise an eyebrow."

"Fun, I guess. But although this must sound impossibly naive, I don't know what FWB means."

"Friends with benefits, which at least in theory means you can share a bed, but still be free to go out with others."

"So you're having fun this summer?"

"Definitely. Senior year at high school Blaine and I mostly had sex behind things—bushes, couches, and even once, a compost pile. And since neither of us had any prior experience, it was always way too quick, at least for me if you get my drift. But now, with plenty of time, and how should I say it—a better grasp of the basics maybe—things have heated up nicely. It's never going to be true love, but the other night when he said, 'Tabitha, I really and truly love to fuck you', I laughed and said 'right back at you dude'."

Glancing at her watch as she gets out of the car near the corner of Piedmont and Pleasant Valley, Tamiko says, "We're twenty minutes early. I guess I was allowing for how long it takes on the bus."

"They'll probably seat us now, but before we go in, how about a quick show and tell about Mr. Heartthrob?"

Fishing her phone from her mom's black leather shoulder bag, Tamiko presses the on button as she says, "Here's the show. But I'm afraid there isn't much to tell since, like I said, when my mom got wind of Lec, she threatened to call the cops if he shakes my hand."

"Yo Tami, kidding aside, you hooked a pretty one. It's not hard to see why your mom is following you around with a chastity belt."

"I'm not sure sex is even her big worry. It's more like she's freaked that I'm not going to be her little girl anymore."

"Sweet, especially when you consider that by your age loads of parents are trying to elbow their kids out of the nest. But listen Tami, would it totally amaze you to learn that people call me Tabitha now?"

Sticking out her right hand Tamiko says, "Pleased to meet you Tabitha. My name is Tamiko Gashkin."

"Touché. When did you ditch 'Tami'?" Tabitha asks, laughing.

"In July but it hasn't been easy to enforce."

"Tell me about it. As usual, you're two years ahead. But hey, let's talk while we eat."

A few minutes later, seated at a table by Lo Coco's front window, Tamiko says, "I've never even been on a date. I mean Tabitha, I know I probably sound pathetic, but I'm more than a little lost."

"Tamiko, never sell yourself short. Even when you were thirteen and by far the youngest girl on the BHS team, and probably in the league, you were clutch. True, your body was still geeky and your social skills could be primitive, but deep down you knew your own mind. So let's get to what you're worried about," Tabitha says, reaching for the menu.

"OK, so just tell me about how dating works at college, you know like, hookups or whatever. But, hang on—what do you think, how about splitting the biggest pizza going and loading it up?"

"Anything but pineapple and anchovies."

"Done, so go back to educating this naive virgin."

"Start by remembering that what I know about college dating is based on one year at a small school in Maine that doesn't have fraternities or sororities. Plus, earlier in the summer I traveled to Europe for six weeks with three of my Bowdoin buddies."

"It's still light-years more experience than I have. So first, can you describe the social scene when you got to Bowdoin last fall?"

"Everyone, except maybe the preppies who had already been away from home at places like Andover and Choate, arrived pretty excited about finally being over the parental horizon. I'm gonna guess that except for the few uberreligious kids, at least three-quarters of the class were ready to party. In addition to my dorm, where I met everyone on the first day, all Bowdoin students are assigned to a social house that hold get-to-know-you parties. Anyway, with hormones firing and plenty of alcohol and pot, despite a boatload of rules prohibiting both, it didn't take long for lots of people to shed their panties. And, at least in my circle, the girls were as enthusiastic as the guys. More maybe, since the guys often got so shit-faced they couldn't rise to the occasion if you'll forgive a terrible pun."

"What about hookups? It's like I keep hearing that term, but I guess I don't know why hooking up is different from dating, not that I have much of a clue about that either."

"Especially at small schools like Bowdoin where everyone pretty much knows everyone else, it's impossible to go out with the same person more than a few times unless you want to be treated as a couple. And I don't just mean a 'before all others' deal, more like you're married. A fair number of people do pair up, at least for a year, because in a lot of ways it makes their social lives simpler. But since I was far more interested in the tasting menu, settling for just one entree wasn't remotely interesting."

"Which is where hookups come in, I'm guessing," Tamiko says as she motions to the waiter, and when he comes over, orders.

Pausing until he's stepped away, Tabitha says, "Imagine you go to a party on Friday or Saturday night and drink too much, or in my case, have a couple of beers and pretend I'm a lot more wasted. Then, hopefully, before the guy you're interested in either gets too blotto to care or leaves with someone else, you hang out and maybe dance a little. Assuming you're more-or-less in step it's off to whosever room is most likely to be roommate free. A couple of days later, if you see the guy on campus, all that's expected is to nod and say hi, since the fiction is that since both of you were out-of-it, your hookup, never happened."

"Suppose you like the guy and want to see him again?"

"Well, assuming he feels the same way, of course you can hang out. But like I said, pretty soon you have to decide if you are a couple or not."

"Great info, Tabs, I mean Tabitha. But can I ask why you don't want to be part of a couple?"

"Eventually I do, but that will come soon enough, probably too soon. For now at least, I want to run a little wild. You know my Grandma June was a 1960's hippie type—an early feminist really—who was into sexual freedom. My mom is quieter about it, but still I was brought up to believe that it's just as legit for women to initiate sex as it is for men. Oops, I hope I'm not shocking your virginal ears," Tabitha says, coloring slightly.

"No worries, but what about girls getting raped at college. I mean, the news is full of it, right?" Tamiko says, glancing at the kitchen door in hopes their pizza is about to appear.

"Bowdoin is a small school with no Greek life and I'm obviously a big girl who knows her own mind and doesn't get drunk, so I haven't had any trouble. But I'm the last one to deny that the American culture that enables rape exists on college campuses. Growing up here in Berkeley you've surely learned many stay safe rules. And next summer before you take off I'll give you my alcohol talk which mostly consists of not letting any guy talk you into mixing booze with soda pop."

"I barely know how to drink coffee."

"Then you'll need to take notes, won't you? If you don't mind a brief change of subject, my mom saw your mom looking beyond fabulous at Zut on Fourth Street having lunch with a very attractive guy."

"That was probably Ed Crane, her new boyfriend, who's also her boss at Bay. Mine too, actually, since I work there part-time."

"Mom said that compared to six months ago your mom has done a complete makeover."

"Yup, it happened in just a few weeks this spring. I would have put the odds of Mom falling in love below those of Israel making peace with the Palestinians, but then, like overnight, it was a done deal. She and Ed tried to keep it secret but I finally blew their cover. The best part is Ed is a great guy."

"So this is double good news for you, right? I mean, not only has your mom caught a cool dude, but it puts her in a poor position to come down hard on you."

"Unfortunately, she hasn't noticed part two."

. . . . .

Alec ducks out of Organic Chemistry twenty minutes early. Since he knows his uncle will plan an upscale meal he walks quickly back to Panoramic Street, where he changes into a pair of black jeans, a white dress shirt, and a charcoal blazer. Borrowing his vacationing friend Ethan's ancient Nissan Altima, Alec points it downhill towards the Ashby BART station where he pulls into a close parking space just as a black Tesla backs out.

Finding a seat in the corner of the last car of the 4:48 San Francisco-bound train, Alec takes off his blazer and drapes it over his head. Thirty minutes of restorative shuteye will be just what he needs to prepare for what is sure to be a high-energy evening. But instead of shutting down, Alec's imagination turns to its Tamiko channel and begins looping.

Tamiko's light-up-the-world smile.

Tamiko's deep, resonant voice.

Tamiko's almond-shaped blue eyes.

Tamiko's erect and graceful way of standing.

Tamiko's Tsunami.com-imprinted bum bobbing jauntily as she ran along Oxford Street.

Tamiko's joy-filled laugh.

Tamiko's long, strong legs.

Tamiko's gravity-defying breasts.

Tamiko's tiny chin dimple.

Tamiko standing shyly behind the big redwood for their first kiss.

Tamiko's husky voice on the phone Thursday afternoon telling him to be nice to Teri.

"Tamiko, Tamiko, Tamiko, just what am I going to do with you?" Alec asks himself for at least the twenty-seventh time as the train's mechanical voice announces, "We are arriving at the Powell Street Station, please stand clear of the doors."

Climbing the two sets of steep steps to the corner of Market and Powell, where the cable car turns around to head back over Nob Hill on its return journey to Fisherman's Wharf, Alec glances at his watch. Seeing he's early, he browses the windows of the upscale shops on

Powell as he thinks about his upcoming dinner with Charlie. Excited as he is at the prospect of seeing his favorite uncle, he is anxious about what he should say about the death of Charlie's much beloved wife, Claire. When Claire died from an invasive brain tumor almost two years earlier, Alec—who was in Goa, and only intermittently in touch with his family—had been reduced to awkwardly expressing his condolences by email. Especially given that Claire had been dear to him, he still feels embarrassed that he has somehow let Charlie down by not being more present for his grief.

Turning left on Stockton, Alec spots the Taj Campton Place Hotel across the street in the middle of the block. Waiting for a break in the traffic he jaywalks across Stockton at an angle that takes him through the hotel's door into its jewel-like lobby just as his uncle steps out of the elevator. Tall, and almost indecently fit for a man in his mid-50's, Charlie brushes aside Alec's outstretched hand and grabs him in a bear hug.

"We have a dinner reservation in forty-five minutes at an Italian place called Ristorante Venticello just over the crest of Nob Hill. I'm guessing you'd rather walk than have a drink here and try to elbow our way onto a cable car."

When Alec nods, his uncle leads him out the door. At the corner they turn left on Sutter, and continue past the Marriott Hotel to Powell where they follow the cable car tracks steeply up Nob Hill towards the iconic views of the city, bay and Golden Gate. Although the temperature is in the low 60's, Charlie takes off his blazer and slings it over his left shoulder. By the time they reach the corner of Bush, Alec does the same.

"How's Japan?" Alec asks, not quite ready to broach the subject of Claire's death. "I'm bummed I didn't get there on my trip, but it was one expensive plane flight too many. But I really appreciate your stopping over in S.F. It's been such a long time since we talked. Growing up, you and Claire were like second parents to my sister and me, but in the last two years I've only seen you once, for a few minutes last Christmas. It's as if growing up we were becoming real friends and then…"

"I feel the same way. The broken plane was a good excuse to drop in, but I was already planning to visit you on my next trip out to Japan."

"I hope you know that I often think of Aunt Claire," Alec blurts as the two men tackle the ski slope-like incline rising precipitously to California Street. "I mean, she was just such a happy, lovable person, so filled with light and life. Being on the road, I was out of touch when she first got sick. Learning that she was terminally ill was easily the biggest shock of my life."

"Invasive brain tumors move fast," Charlie says as he steps aside to make way for a family of German tourists streaming down the hill.

"Is it OK to ask how you're doing?"

"Sure, but it's easier to keep my emotions in check while I'm moving, so let's attack the rest of the hill."

As Alec quickens his pace to keep up, Charlie says, "Probably I'm being more frank than I should be, but the truth is I was so bonded with Claire that for many months after she died, and especially at night when I couldn't sleep, I wondered if it wouldn't be simpler to give up on life and join her."

"But what about now? I hope..."

"Yes, things are better. But even so, getting off the plane this morning here in San Francisco where we had several wonderful visits, was tough. Even though Claire and I were together for just fourteen years, it felt as if she had always been part of my life and always would be. When she died, it was as if I'd forgotten how to be in the world by myself," Charlie says, his breathing now shallower as both men lean into the last sharp ascent to California Street. Continuing more gradually uphill past the kitsch-laden Tonga Room, where somehow campy umbrella drinks have remained popular since the Second World War, they crest Nob Hill in front of the Mark Hopkins Hotel. "Late last year," Charlie continues, "I realized that I was making progress getting my life under control when I no longer became upset when friends and relatives introduced me to single women."

"So, you've been dating?"

"Not in the traditional sense."

OK, Alec thinks, trying to parse this equivocal answer before tentatively saying, "So if dating is still a nonstarter, maybe, well..."

"To be totally frank, intimate contact isn't," Charlie interrupts.

As they pass the crouching brownstone bulk of a nineteenth century silver mogul's hotel-sized mansion, now the male-only Pacific Union Club, Charlie adds, "When you're in your twenties, sex is always on your mind. Fortunately, at fifty-four, it's a little less front and center, but even so, in less than thirty seconds I can go from desperately missing Claire to fantasizing about having it on with the waitress refilling my coffee."

"I have no trouble understanding that one."

"Fortunately my partner Phil understands as well, but Alec, is it OK if I ask you to keep what I'm about to tell you absolutely confidential? And I apologize if I'm burdening you, but it's just that after so many years cocooning with Claire, I don't have many people I can talk to about personal issues and…"

"I don't gossip, especially to my parents. And, Charlie, I also have something private I want your feedback on."

"Trading secrets, what fun. Well, as I said, by late last fall I was missing the physical part of my relationship with Claire in a big way. At first this wasn't even a conscious thing, just my body signaling it was horny. The problem was, I couldn't seem to figure how to do anything about it. Every time I met an attractive woman in New York, she would immediately trigger memories of Claire. Once, in the middle of a pleasant conversation, this woman whom I guess I was beginning to flirt with actually started to look like Claire."

"Sounds borderline scary."

"Not really since I only needed to shake my head a couple of times to be safely back in the present. But it did put a kibosh on dating since if I was going to spend the evening with my imagination, why bother leaving my condo?"

"I'd be surprised if staying home with a book was of much help dealing with your lack of intimate contact issue."

"True, and I still might be trying to finish *War and Peace* if Phil hadn't recognized what a muddle I was in and unbeknownst to me, talked to a friend in Japan. The result was that, voilà, I had a date with Emiko, an attractive thirty-seven-year-old widow who needed to raise money to support her two kids. Since her former husband Tash Masamoto had worked for one of our client companies before he committed suicide, I'd already met Emiko once or twice at company parties."

"So this wasn't a date in the normal sense of the word."

"Out of necessity Emiko had become what we might describe in the West as a low-mileage courtesan."

"Whoa—exciting! Was it a success?"

"Surprisingly, yes. Somehow because of her cultural and physical differences, Emiko passed through my Claire screen and into my bed. In fact, it was so much fun that I've spent considerable time with her on several subsequent trips to Japan, this last one which I had no real business reason to make. I let her know at least a week in advance when I'll be in Tokyo and she arranges for her parents to take care of her kids and moves into my suite at the Imperial Hotel or sometimes we take a short trip."

"So you two raced right passed the dating phase to where she is more or less living with you when you're in Japan. I mean Charlie, is there any chance your relationship has a future?" Alec asks, staying in step with his uncle as he turns right in front of Grace Cathedral.

"History is full of foolish old men who fall for the younger woman they pay to be with, so I try to stay in the present."

"You're neither old nor foolish, and at the very least it sounds as if you've come to appreciate Emiko."

"Fair enough, but remember she's seventeen years younger than I am, speaks little English, has kids and has never been outside of Japan except for one package holiday in Bali."

Entering Venticello's bar, the two men detour to the restroom to towel off the light film of sweat that has accumulated on their climb. Back in their jackets they descend the half dozen steps to the richly intimate dining room where they are shown to a table next to the brick wall. "Can I tempt you with a glass of Sangiovese?" Charlie asks, signaling to the waiter.

"Sure, but don't let me get enthusiastic and drink half the bottle," Alec replies with a chuckle. Finals are only a few days away and I need to dig into my notes later."

With their drinks almost immediately in hand, Alec raises his and says, "To Claire."

"To Claire," Charlie responds, raising his glass and smiling so warmly Alec almost turns to see if she's walking across the room.

"So Lec, it's your turn to catch me up and talk about what's on your mind. Before you tell me I guess I should ask if it's OK to use your old nickname?"

"Lec is definitely good. Everyone back East still calls me that and in truth I miss it out here where I'm Alec to everyone save one very recent exception. Which brings me to what I want your advice about."

"In my experience advice is rarely worth the breath used to deliver it, but I can be a good listener and, if needed, a good sounding board. Hold on a second though, the waiter is hovering."

Alec, who hasn't opened the menu, says, "I'll have whatever you're having."

"Since Venticello's wood-fired pizza oven is at least half the reason I proposed the long walk, I'm going with the fennel sausage pizza and a salad."

"Make that two of both."

"With food on the way you have my full attention," Charlie says, as he breaks a roll in half and dabs on a whole pat of butter.

Leaning forward in his chair far enough to pull his phone from his left pants pocket, Alec pushes the power button and hands it to Charlie.

After putting on his reading glasses, Charlie says, "I'm only stating the obvious when I say she's lovely. But where oh where did this fair haired girl come by almond eyes and Asiatic cheek bones?"

"Her name is Tamiko O'Shea Gashkin."

"Tamiko is Japanese of course, so there's my answer."

"Yes, well spotted. She's a quarter Japanese, a quarter Irish, and Russian from up around the Finnish border. Her dad was a Cal professor who died in a freak traffic accident a few years ago. You might have heard of him, Yuri Gashkin. He wrote a famous book—well, famous in academic circles anyway—about race in twentieth-century American Literature called

Black and White in Black and White."

"Catchy, but no, I'm not familiar with it. But I do recognize the name Gashkin from the Soviet-era Bolshoi dancers who defected to the U.S. They were both very special, especially Vera, who had a smile as heart-stopping as your friend here."

"Tamiko is her granddaughter. Did you ever see the Gashkins perform?"

"Absolutely. Only a few months after Phil and I started our business in 1986 we were trying to sign a contract with a division of one of the major Japanese electronics companies. The boss, who we knew loved ballet, was coming to New York, so we splurged half of the year's entertainment budget on tickets to the New York City Ballet at Lincoln Center. Your grandfather Burns, who knew lots of people in the arts, got us invited to the after party where I briefly met Vera Gashkin, who had just lit up the house in the Balanchine version of Swan Lake."

"What did you think of her in person?"

"I was too awestruck to think much of anything. But getting back to Tamiko. What happened just before this picture was taken to make her look so radiant?"

"She kissed me."

"I assume you kissed her back," Charlie says with a wide grin.

"A quick one."

"Why so reticent?" the older man asks in surprise, as he leans back slightly to allow the waiter space to deliver their food.

"She's not quite sixteen and it was her first kiss," Alec replies, picking up his fork and spearing a tomato.

"Ain't it too bad that life is so rarely simple. When did you meet?"

"Monday, as in four days ago."

"And the momentous kiss?"

"Tuesday," Alec replies, amazed to realize how much has happened in a few days.

"So, poleaxed at first sight, or I doubt you'd be telling me all this," Charlie says, as he goes to work on his salad.

"Great word, and yes, we both got hit hard."

"When will Tamiko be sixteen?"

"In ten days. I met her at Cal, where she's taking Physics in the summer session. I naturally assumed she was a college student, maybe nineteen or twenty."

"She could certainly pass for that."

"Charlie, here's the thing, Tamiko's so intellectually precocious she essentially finished high school at fourteen. Now she's marking time by taking mostly community college courses and working until her mom agrees she's old enough to start college back East, which I gather will be next fall. In the meantime, she has almost as many credits as I do. And you'll probably think I'm blowing smoke, but she's also a killer athlete, good enough that several Division One schools are sniffing around."

"Lovely, smart, and athletic, I guess once in a while even God bats a thousand," Charlie says, as he pours each of them a second glass of wine.

"You left out happy, sweet, self-deprecating, funny, and empathetic," Alec replies, pouring half of his wine into the older man's glass.

"It was a giant poleax, obviously. But Lec, even given all she's got going for her, you obviously have a huge problem," Charlie says, finishing off his pizza and starting on his salad.

"I already know it's a crime to date her."

"I'm not only thinking about the legal aspect. Ethically I think you have to ask yourself if a kid in her mid-teens is really mature enough to cope with someone six years older and a pile more sophisticated."

"I'm not sure I'm going to find out," Alec replies, going on to tell Charlie in some detail about Amy Gashkin's diatribe and Henry Goldstein's advice to stay far away.

"Got the picture, I think," Charlie says, as Alec begins listing Tamiko's virtues for the third time.

"Sorry, I've obviously been going on and on," Alec says as he belatedly realizes that he's been neglecting his dinner.

"No worries, but you need to eat up if you're going to have time to study."

As the two men walk back down Nob Hill towards Market Street,

Charlie asks, "Is it fair to sum up that you're now in a holding pattern with the hope that given a little time plus your noble intentions and impeccable behavior, and despite her reasonable objections, Mrs. Gashkin will come around to accepting your relationship with her only child?"

"Put like that it seems pretty remote, doesn't it? But, c'mon Charlie, despite your determination not to give advice, can you make an exception?"

"OK then. Is Vera Gashkin in the picture? Is she close to Tamiko and maybe Amy?"

"Tamiko for sure, they play this incredible memory game focused on the writings of the iconic Russian writers," Alec replies, wondering what Charlie's getting at.

"In the Soviet Union when Vera was coming up, young dancers who were marked for success, went to ballet schools so intensive that they all but replaced their families."

"I'm sorry, you lost me," Alec says, as he speeds up to try to catch Charlie, who has ignored the red light at Geary Street.

"I'm betting Vera was on her own by the time she was Tamiko's age," Charlie says, slowing slightly.

"You're suggesting she could be an ally?" Alec asks, finally grasping his uncle's point.

"Just a thought."

"If you have any more, will you let me know?"

"Count on it, but the BART stairs are just ahead, so this is where we say good-night."

. . . . .

At 7:20 p.m. Amy arrives at Ed's traditional Spanish style house in Piedmont, an upscale, mostly residential enclave surrounded by far grittier Oakland. Not seeing Ed as she comes through the front door, she calls out, "Hey you, I'm here."

"I'm upstairs, stretched out. Want to join me?" Ed yells.

"I hope you mean that literally," Amy replies as she climbs the red carpeted stairs two at a time. "But we need to be quick as Tamiko will be here soon."

Draped across an oversized pillow on top of a red spread and wearing only a gray terry cloth robe, Ed grins as he says, "I can be as quick as you can. And didn't Tamiko's note say she won't be here until eightish?"

"I'm already halfway to the shower," Amy says with a laugh, as she sheds her white linen top and enters the large bathroom with its deep tub and walk-in shower. Twisting the shower dial just short of scalding, Amy brushes her teeth while the water warms up. Then stepping into the stall she backs into the hot spray as she soaps her wiry body. Feeling desire spread from brain to toes, Amy steps out onto the mat, water running down her legs. Still toweling as she enters the large sunny bedroom, she's briefly tempted to do an erotic dance by the foot of the bed. But seeing from the size of Ed's erection that this would be entirely superfluous, she kneels between his outspread legs and mumbles, "You beautiful man."

After a short minute of room-filling groans, Ed manages to gasp, "Are you almost ready?"

"Oh yes," Amy replies, pulling her head back just enough to speak.

"Better climb on before I imitate Vesuvius."

Moving forward half a body length, Amy takes Ed's shaft in her left hand and guides it into her wet center with a groan of pleasure so deep she could have been conjuring the divine. Urgently rocking her pelvis back and forth she almost immediately explodes with a long juddering orgasm. Then, just as her excruciating pleasure begins to recede, Ed begins to move so forcefully within her that in just a few seconds she's pleading, "Oh god, Ed...fill me, so good, so good, oh my god, fill me...my god I'm coming..., keep me there, keep me there...oh my god, don't stop...please..."

"No one this side of heaven deserves to feel this good," Ed says a few minutes later.

"Really Ed, there are no words to describe what just happened. It felt like that infinitesimal dot inside me began to exponentially expand until it exploded in what I can only describe as my own big bang."

"I'm not sure how accurate your cosmology is, but for sure, big bang is an apt description," Ed chuckles. "I do love you Amy, totally and absolutely."

"Music to my ears, but, like I've said before, when we have a chance for more time together, I really can slow down. I know that I'm often wound so tight that I blow right through the lovely slow parts."

"When I'm lucky enough to climb onto a race horse, there's no sense in taking her for a trot. But, as fascinated as I am by this conversation, I think we need to hustle into some clothes and get ourselves downstairs so that we can appear respectably serene when Tamiko shows up. Given all the delicate author egos I knew we'd have to stroke at the party I guessed we wouldn't have time to eat so I slipped out at lunch and picked up some deli treats."

"Perfect, although when it comes to seconds, I hope you know it's not food I'll be thinking of."

. . . . .

Downstairs, a few minutes later, as they nibble on pasta salad and focaccia bread while sipping Ed's favorite "chewy" Zinfandel, Amy says, "Ed, remember last night I told you there are some things I need to open up about? It's never going to be the perfect time, but I hope you're ready to listen."

"Of course."

"Can you just let me blurt it all out, and spare your sympathy until the end?"

"I'll try."

"When I took off to Amsterdam a few weeks after Yuri died, my main goal was to get an abortion."

"Really! Oh Amy," Ed says, reaching out his hand to cover hers.

"Remember your promise."

"Right, but in what I'm guessing is a new record for bad timing, I just heard a car door slam out front."

"My fault, I should have picked a better time to tell my story, but for now just know that while I didn't have the abortion, what actually happened to me in Amsterdam was at least as traumatic."

· · · · ·

Tamiko walks up the sickle shaped flagstone path towards Ed's square white house, as the setting sun lights its tile roof like a crimson candle. Knowing she's expected to put on a happy face to greet her mother and new lover in their suburban villa, Tamiko slows to a stop ten feet from the massive, iron-studded door suddenly unable to take another step. She is looking around for a way to retreat when the door opens and her mom and Ed pull her inside. Telling herself she'll be off to college in a year so there's no need to take any of this too seriously, Tamiko does her best to smile as she trails them from one large room to the next. Picking up on her downbeat mood, Ed says, "Let's take a quick look back here," as he leads the way through the kitchen and along a short hall to a light-filled room with yellow walls and a queen-sized bed facing a glass door that opens to the backyard. Waiting for a moment for Tamiko to take a peek into the connecting bathroom, Ed says, "Do you think a girl might like to hang out here for the occasional weekend?"

Suddenly understanding that Ed honestly wants her friendship and approval, Tamiko feels a real smile begin to tease the corners of her lips as she replies, "If that bed is half as comfy as it looks, it might be tough to pry a girl out."

"Ed got a movie he's excited about," Amy says. "It's a surprise but the music that's playing, which is new to me, is a hint."

"Rodriguez," Tamiko replies, beginning to sing along. "*Sugarman, won't you hurry, 'cause I'm tired of these dreams.*" Stopping abruptly, she says to Ed, "Sometimes I forget I sing like a frog with laryngitis, so I hereby give you permission to remind me."

"It runs in the family unfortunately, but Tami, how did you know all that—the singer and the song, I mean?" Amy asks.

"A few years ago when a movie about Rodriguez's life came out, his album, *Cold Fact* from, like, about forty years ago, became kind of an underground hit, especially 'Sugarman.' I haven't seen the film but I've heard it's a way cool story—how a singer songwriter who never made it in the U.S. became a big deal..."

"Don't say another plot-spoiling word," Amy interrupts with mock indignation. "I want to be surprised."

A few moments later after Ed disappears upstairs, Tamiko asks, "Mom, does Ed own all of this?"

"Unfortunately no, the bank owns half and Ed's ex-wife Cissy owns half of the other half. After they split four years ago during the recession, she moved to the city with her new boyfriend and Ed stayed here making the mortgage payments in lieu of rent and waiting until the real estate market recovered. Now, of course, prices are over the moon so they plan to sell in the spring while Ed is in D.C."

"Mom, I really do get that Ed's a sweet guy and I totally get why you two want to spend weekends here. I'll try to fit in although it will be a lot easier if someone teaches me to drive so I don't have to spend forty-five minutes on the bus every time I want to go back to Berkeley."

· · · · ·

Two hours later, after *Searching for Sugarman* finishes to the enthusiastic cheers of all, and Amy heads to the kitchen for ice cream, Ed says, "Amy tells me you had dinner with an old friend."

"Tabitha Anderson. She played third base for Berkeley High—a ninja defender, and she can hit too. She just finished her first year at Bowdoin College in Maine and I wanted to ask her about how dating college guys works."

"I hope I'm not invading your privacy when I say that Amy mentioned that you met a Cal guy who she thinks is too old."

"That's Alec Burns, or Lec as I call him. And since I'm pretty clueless on the whole guy subject, Mom is probably right about my being out of my depth. Of course that doesn't change how I feel about him. But here she comes with the raspberry ice cream, which I'm happy to see is slathered in yummy chocolate sauce. Are we still on for shopping tomorrow Mom?"

"Stores open at ten a.m.," Amy says, placing the three bowls on the coffee table, "and we can be the first ones through the door. I'm thinking to start in Emeryville at H&M, the Gap and maybe Urban Outfitters. But it depends on what you want."

"I've been paying attention to what girls are wearing at Cal and also talking to Tabitha—who, by the way, has given up Tabs, a name change she says her family supports a hundred and ten percent." When Amy doesn't reply, but simply takes another bite of ice cream, Tamiko continues, "Most important, I need a couple of tank tops with spaghetti straps, some fitted T's in different colors and some pants including black tights like Tabitha's. Also, for a change of pace, I've been admiring the tops that have a high neck in front, but leave your shoulders and the top of your back mostly bare."

"They're called racer backs, but I hope you haven't forgotten the bras."

"Actually, both Lec and Tabitha agree with you about the bra deal so I'm fully on board with being buckled up. And if anyone wants to jot that down in the column marked 'Tamiko's New Maturity' please feel free."

"I'm curious, what did Tabitha say to convince you?"

"I'll spare Ed her exact language, but it came down to her belief that a girl should point her assets towards the guy she, um, well…wants to share them with, I guess, and not bother to advertise to all those she's not interested in."

Not even trying to suppress his grin Ed stands as he says, "I think I'll get some more ice cream. Give me a shout when this conversation is fit for a gentleman's ears."

SATURDAY

AT 1:58 A.M. ALEC CRUISES SLOWLY down College Avenue half a dozen blocks south of the Cal campus. Since returning home from his dinner with Charlie, he's cleaned his room, put in two hours redrafting his paper on Thomas Mann's *Doctor Faustus* for World Lit and grabbed a ninety minute nap. Now, passing Teri's three-story apartment house, he continues to the corner of Parker Street, where he pulls to the curb and douses his lights. In an excited heartbeat, Teri appears from where she was concealed by an overgrown vine in front of the derelict car repair shop across the street. "I worry you not come," she says as she climbs in and kisses Alec.

"Here I am."

"You good friend. I very excited. I also full of things to tell you, but first we go to your room and …"

"Make love first and talk second," Alec interrupts with a chuckle.

"You always smart man."

In less than five minutes Alec pilots Ethan's Nissan back to Panoramic Street, relieved that the parking space he just vacated in front of his house is still empty. Almost before he sets the parking brake, Teri is out and climbing the dimly lit stone steps, her straight black hair falling almost to her round bum, which is provocatively outlined by black pants so tight they look as if they were sprayed on. Wondering if she is wearing anything underneath, Alec follows, taking the steps two at a time so they arrive at the front door together. After unlocking it, he again follows the slim girl upstairs, this time two flights to the third floor. Because the light is better here, he can see the outlines of her bikini bottoms.

As he trails Teri into his tiny bedroom, Alec thinks of Tamiko. But before he can feel guilty, Teri turns and presses her body against his with an enthusiasm that yanks him back to the present. Returning her embrace as he begins to fumble for the buttons on her blouse, he is surprised when she pulls away, saying, "Wait."

Turning to the desk, Teri pulls a red candle, complete with holder from her over-size raffia bag and lights it with a disposable lighter. Then, fishing out a bottle of Mumm's champagne and two glass flutes, she flips off the overhead light and says, "Open bubbly and get into bed, I be just a little time down hall."

Alone now, Alec takes off the rest of his clothes and pulls on a pair of gray cotton drawstring pants. Knowing that the champagne had been on a bumpy ride, he eases out the cork a millimeter at a time. Taking a guilty gulp directly from the bottle he fills the flutes before leaning back against the bunched pillows at the head of his bed.

When a couple of minutes pass with no Teri, Alec, who is naked to the waist, begins to feel chilly. Tempted to get up to close the window, he decides to stay put, not wanting to be awkwardly out of position when Teri makes her entrance. Now beginning to shiver for real, Alec is just reaching for the covers when the door opens to reveal Teri in a black teddy with red laces criss-crossing the front. His cock springing to attention, Alec forgets his goosebumps as he watches Teri glide over to the desk and pick up the two champagne glasses. Handing one to Alec, she says "To us," as they clink glasses. But when Alec moves over to make room for her on the bed, Teri instead two-steps to the center of the little room and begins moving her round bum up, down and around. Just as Alec feels he's about to burst, she turns to face him and pulls on the teddy's red laces so that it falls open to reveal her small, delicate breasts that somehow always put him in mind of his grandmother's china tea cups. Now urgently reaching for her, Alec is again thwarted as Teri moves away, continuing her dance, now fully naked. "C'mon girl, bring your fabulous body over here before I have a stroke," Alec croaks.

"How much you want me?" Teri laughs, throwing up her arms as if offering herself to Eros, the Greek god of love. By way of answer, Alec wriggles out of his loose pants and begins running his right forefinger up and down his long, thin super erect cock.

"That my job," Teri says as she flings herself into Alec's embrace.

Earlier that evening Alec worried that because he was so besotted with Tamiko this last night with Teri might be disappointing. Instead, it's their most exciting love making of the summer. Whether this stems from the drama of Teri's being yanked back to Korea, the fact that this will be their last night together, or Teri's triple-X dance, is of little moment. What Alec does know is that while in the past, making love with Teri could be compared to floating down a sinuous stream, tonight all lightness and grace are gone. Instead, it's as if he's been seized by a gut-grabbing class five rapids. Immediately lifted by waves of pleasure Alec spins round and round, all but losing track of who he is until Teri cries, "Harder Alec, fuck me harder" as she begins beating his ass with her small fists. Pulled back to himself by Teri's need, Alec begins pounding her into the mattress, aroused even further when she wraps her legs around his torso and squeezes. Then, when Teri's insistent pushing makes it clear she wants a turn on top Alec obligingly rolls them both over. Liberated from his weight, the slim young woman makes a high keening noise as she again flings her arms over her head, literally rising to an orgasm so intense Alec thinks she may take off.

"Yikes," Alec whispers a few moments later, his body now spooned around Teri's. "We saved the best for last."

"Like most wonderful dream ever," she replies, pushing against him as if daring the universe to try to pull them apart. "Now hold me so tight maybe clock stop."

A few minutes later, just beginning to doze, Alec is awakened by Teri turning in his arms just enough so that her mouth reaches his right nipple. As she begins to tongue it up and down, he feels a lazy wave of warmth begin to spread from chest to groin. It occurs to him that it's almost time for seconds when Teri's insistent nibbling makes him realize that time is now. "Can I have this dance please?" he whispers as lifting Teri on top, he reaches down to guide himself inside only to realize that her slim hand is already on the job. Feeling his cock sink into her warm welcoming center Alec is surprised that instead of surrendering to Teri's sensual flow, he thinks about Tamiko. As if sensing his lack of presence, Teri begins moving more urgently. Doing his best to respond, Alec realizes his erection is in danger of wandering off with his thoughts. Worried that he'll spoil Teri's fun, he attempts to grab back his mojo by imagining Tamiko wading top-less out of a warm sea. Now fully aroused, he rolls Teri over and still pretending she is Tamiko, begins an urgent series of thrusts only to have Teri whisper, "Alec, open your eyes, I'm here too." Chagrined at being caught fucking the wrong girl, Alec locks his eyes on Teri's as he wills his body to slow down and sync with hers—which, to his relief, it finally does.

In the car a few moments later, the quarter-light of first dawn giving fuzzy definition to the twisting corridor of Panoramic Way, Teri says, "Alec, I never forget you, never. You always be my lovely American, beautiful man."

. . . . .

In the Subaru on the way to the Bay Street shopping area in Emeryville, Tamiko wishes she could sing. Not only did she sleep deeply in the comfy queen-sized bed but she enjoyed Ed's indulging her at breakfast with eggs and bacon made to order. Even assuming all this pampering is part of a charm campaign to get her used to her mom and Ed's being a couple, all she can think is, 'Good job.' Looking over to see that her mom also appears relaxed and cheerful, Tamiko is tempted to broach the subject of whether she might be willing to meet Lec. But concluding that if she's going to pull this one off she needs to hone her arguments, Tamiko instead asks, "Mom, do you remember what I was telling you about the gray car?"

"Sure."

"I saw it again yesterday when Tabitha picked me up, and I swear, the big dude behind the wheel didn't slump down until I looked his way."

"Alec Burns is pretty big, right?"

"Don't be silly. If Lec had been out front, how long do you think it would have taken me to be sitting next to him? And anyway, Lec is built like a swimmer, not thick like this guy."

"Short of knocking on every door on the block to try to find out who he is, I'm not sure what you want me to do."

"Pay attention, I guess. Remember, Dad would have wanted us to get to the bottom of this."

"Will you relax if I promise to keep my eyes open?"

"Only if you really do. We had this conversation on Thursday and I doubt you've given it a minute's thought since."

"Fair point, but I'm on it now."

· · · · ·

The shopping trip is a success with the exception of a few tense moments at Victoria's Secret when Tamiko tries to choose two bras and bikini-style panties that Amy considers R-rated. Briefly considering digging in her heels and offering to pay for them herself, Tamiko decides that agreeing to more utilitarian styles is a small price to pay to maintain peace in the valley. And, hey, she thinks, given Mom's hostility to Lec, I'll have time to get the hot versions long before I'll need them.

After stopping on College Avenue for yoga pants and huarache sandals, Amy and Tamiko return to Piedmont in the early afternoon, loaded with bags and boxes. Presiding over the late lunch he's put together, Ed says, "When my Uncle Henry back in Wisconsin shot a deer each fall and came home with it tied to the top of the car he had exactly the same kind of delighted glow you two do now."

"Only a barely civilized male would make that comparison," Amy replies as she stands on tiptoe to give him a kiss.

"Who made breakfast and lunch?" Ed rejoins. Then looking at Tamiko to see that she is wearing form-fitting black yoga pants, a dark blue spaghetti strap tank and Mexican sandals, he says, "Young lady, you look almost as devastating as your mom."

"A diplomatic savage at least," Amy says with a chuckle.

After lunch, holed up in what she had already begun to think of as her room, Tamiko flops down on the bed and taps Vera's number. Picking up on the first ring her grandmother says, "*Oh, I lost as usual. My luck is abominable. No matter how cool I keep, I never win.*"

"Pushkin, *The Queen of Spades*," Tamiko replies. "The next line goes something like, '*Herman, why is it that you don't play cards?*'"

"My translation says, '*How is it Herman that you never touch a card?*'"

"So I guess I only get an A, not an A plus," Tamiko says, rolling onto her back. "Now it's my turn, '*Beneath the willow round with ivy we take cover from the worst storm with a great coat around your waist.*'"

"Romantic."

"Obviously, but no stalling while you fire up your laptop," Tamiko insists.

"Pasternak."

"Of course, but what's the next line?"

"*I'm wrong. It isn't ivy entwined in the bushes round the woods but hops. You intoxicate me. Let's spread ourselves on the ground.*"

"Cheater, you googled that, messing up just enough to try to fool me," Tamiko says as she thinks how much fun it is to spar with her grandmother.

"What else can an elderly, forgetful Russian do?"

"The only accurate word in that sentence is Russian and given that you've lived in the U.S. for forty years even that's doubtful. But listen, Vera, I have a lot I need to talk to you about," Tamiko says, now sitting on the edge of the bed.

"Your mother already tells me you're infatuated with an unsuitable older man, which, I'm guessing, is what put Pasternak into your head."

"She called you?" Tamiko asks with genuine indignation as she stands and barely restrains herself from stamping her foot.

"Emailed."

"To say what exactly?"

"That's private of course, since Amy is also my friend. But I guess I'm not revealing any secrets by saying she wants me to discourage you," Vera replies calmly.

"What did you say?" Tamiko asks, resuming her seat on the bed, this time with her back against the wall.

"Love is love no matter what the age, so what can an elderly forgetful Russian do?"

"Grandma, I love you."

"Grandma is a condition, not a name."

"Got it. But tell me, Vera, how old were you when you fell in love for the first time?" Tamiko asks as she reaches to put a pillow behind her back, "I mean like really with your whole world turning upside down."

"Sixteen. I had just been promoted from ballet school to the corps de ballet at the Bolshoi. He was six years older and also a principal dancer. Very beautiful, elegant, and graceful. Too bad I only later figured out that he had no real strength inside. But at the time he only had to glance at me with his lazy green cats eyes and I leapt into his bed. No doubt I should have thought twice, but, as you are learning, patience has never run in our family."

"How long did it last?"

"Barely ten days before he pushed me out and substituted my best friend Klara, also sixteen," Vera replies in a voice that tells Tamiko she's long since come to regard this ancient history as being hilarious.

"Then you met granddad. I mean you were still sixteen, right?"

"Like me, he has a name."

"Stepan. Sorry, it's just that my other grandparents would flip if I used their first names. I'm curious, was it love at first sight with you two?" Tamiko asks, impressed with her own bravery in asking her grandmother for intimate details about her life.

"Ha! I didn't even like him. He was so big and how do you say it—ferocious like a wild dog. Very graceful of course, but still, I was terrified when they paired us in a pas de deux. And I hated it when the audience seemed to like us together and someone at *Pravda* wrote, 'blestyashchiy.'"

"Translation please," Tamiko says, resolving not for the first time to learn Russian.

"Brilliant."

"What a cool story, but Vera, by now you must have been getting to like him," Tamiko says, now moving to sit on the edge of the bed.

"Nyet. All I could think was how to keep away from this scary wild animal man."

"You obviously didn't."

"For many weeks I did, but then I began every night having these dreams of Stepan and me dancing so beautifully that angels sang. I would wake up and shake myself, since in the real world I was still very much afraid of him. But when I went back to sleep, the dream would come again, Stepan and me, dancing in the most beautiful personal way, as if we were about to, well…"

"So what happened?" Tamiko demands, too curious to wait for her grandmother to get to the point. "I mean like, you were still performing together a lot, right?"

"All the time. The critics just couldn't seem to get enough of seeing us together. Beauty and the Beast, they must have written fifty times."

"They were watching you two fall in love. How exciting."

"To you maybe, but I was now hardly sleeping, losing weight, crying, but also thinking very much of when we would next dance again."

"And Stepan?"

"He was calm and quiet, hardly even speaking to me at rehearsal. But when we were dancing, his passion poured over me like a river."

"Vera, my palms are damp. Is this story ever going to end?" Tamiko asks, back on her feet and after looking in vain for room to pace, opening the door to the patio.

"One day after a performance, he put his hand on my arm and asked, 'Are you ready?'"

"And you replied?" Tamiko asks, now outside in the warm afternoon.

"Nothing. I just took his big hand and we went."

"And never looked back," Tamiko says, collapsing onto a green patio chair.

"No need. From that day I walked in the light. And God be praised, I hope to walk there for a few more years. So, milaya moya, I am an almost impossibly rare creature—a Russian woman born in the nineteen-fifties who has lived mostly a lucky life—or, I guess I should say, a lucky life until your father died..."

"Thank you for telling me. But Vera, is there any advice you have for me?"

"When it comes to matters of the heart, everyone is on their own."

"Always?" Tamiko asks, sounding disappointed even to herself.

"Yes, but can you send me picture of this boy?"

"OK, it should be there."

"Even prettier than Amy said, especially dimple in center of chin. But maybe also a man who thinks with head, not just heart."

"So Vera, c'mon, tell me what you think about me and him? I mean, do you..."

"Maybe try to slow things down as much as you are able."

"How do I do that when he pops into my head three times a minute?" Tamiko replies, annoyed that Vera seems to be channeling her mother.

After a long pause Vera answers in an uncharacteristically gentle voice, "For that I have no answer. But try to remember that a tall, beautiful man like this always has choices with women. Having the patience to commit to a very young girl with a watchful mother may be too much for even nice guy."

"I'm trying to grow up as fast as I can. I mean, I know in lots of ways I'm a silly girl, but if Lec will just..."

"Not to hurry please. But lyubov moya, even though I know it is mostly impossible for you right now, I am changing the subject. Amy says you two will be this way in a few weeks looking at colleges. So how about Stepan and I come to Boston to celebrate your special birthday a few weeks late when you are visiting Harvard? Email me your sizes, including bust and I'll buy some grown-up things for under your clothes."

"Oh my god Vera, I'd love that, I really would, but Mom will have a tantrum."

"How about one part of present will be for Amy to see and other part, our secret. Please tell Amy that the hotel in Boston and birthday dinner to celebrate you being new woman is our treat."

"You really believe that? The woman part, I mean," Tamiko trails off as she wonders if her grandmother is humoring her.

"Truly. And when you also believe, it will be so."

. . . . .

After late lunch with Tamiko and Ed, Amy heads to Berkeley for a quiet afternoon of editing *Murder on Holy Mountain*, a savagely frightening mystery Bay Books plans to publish on its spring list. She loves the author's relaxed, almost delicate way of fitting the plot elements together so, at almost the instant she concludes the book is a bore, she begins turning the pages in an almost frantic effort to find out who has been killing Marin County religious leaders and dumping their bodies on Mount Tamalpais.

But the stomach-clenching plot doesn't mean that the manuscript is free of broken sentences, repeated phrases, and forced metaphors—all of which are in Amy's job description to flag, or in the case of this author, to "just fix it babe, so we can get this puppy into the stores." After slaying a particularly cloying cliché a little before four, Amy makes herself a cup of tea and takes a break on the patio. As she puts her feet up on a weathered Adirondack chair and takes a sip of Darjeeling, Amy makes a conscious effort to take stock of her life. The first thing that pops into her head is the surprising wave of disappointment that had hit her the previous evening when she and Ed told their Bay colleagues about their relationship. Why, she asks herself, had what should have been a happy moment left her blinking back tears? The best answer she can come up with is that instead of feeling like a celebration of her new life with Ed it had seemed as if, without fully realizing it, she'd fallen into a long term commitment for which she was unprepared.

But why not couple up with Ed, she asks herself? Hadn't she been so unreasonably happy with Yuri that she'd seldom regretted the sacrifice of her independence at age eighteen? And isn't sweet, smart, caring Ed, another winner? Or, she wonders, does it come down to the fact that at thirty-five with her daughter mostly grown, she's not sure she's ready to make another lifetime vow. Isn't she entitled to at least a short walk on the wild side before putting on another ring?

. . . . .

Wearing her fresh out of the Gap bag blue tank over cream shorts and her 'way chill' Mexican sandals, Tamiko perches by a front window. At 4:30 p.m. when Mark pulls up in a ten-year-old Jeep Cherokee, she calls goodbye to Ed, hefts a bulging backpack, and strides down the crescent-shaped walk.

"Looks like you packed the piano, as my grandmother likes to say," Mark chuckles as he opens the hatch and helps Tamiko unload. Just over six feet, with a sturdy build, and an exuberant shock of dirty blond hair that falls in bangs half-way to his hazel eyes, Tamiko realizes that Mark is even more attractive than she's remembered.

Making eye contact as Mark closes the door, Tamiko replies, "I don't know how much your grandmother eats, but since you're a big guy I got plenty. Plus I slipped in a couple of beers I borrowed from my mom's boyfriend's fridge."

"Hope he doesn't count."

"Even if he does I trust him to be chill as far as Mom goes."

"So he's OK?"

"Definitely, Mom scored a perfect ten. But, listen Mark, it's hella sweet of you to agree to hang with me on such short notice. And I apologize again if I wasn't polite when you asked me out in July."

"Twice."

"I would have said yes the next time."

"My bad, I guess," Mark replies with sarcasm.

"Not at all. But, like, really Mark, it's only been this year that guys have started noticing me and asking me to do things. At first, all I could think of was 'oh my god, what's happening?' By this summer, I was coming around to the idea of saying yes."

"And then this way older dude you mentioned on the phone cut in line ahead of me."

"I met Lec by accident and then suddenly..."

"I get the drift. I hope I'm still in second place."

"Totally, but the thing is I'm really kind of..."

"I said I get the drift. Hey, which way do I turn? I've never been to the Oakland Rose Garden."

Ten minutes later as Tamiko leads the way to a bench on the south side of the garden, she says almost apologetically, "I guess it's the midsummer lull since the roses aren't nearly as spectacular as in spring, but the upside is we have the place almost to ourselves."

"Sweet, but Tamiko, since you've already made your boyfriend decision, I'm still hazy as to why we're here," Mark says, perching on the edge of the bench as if he's about to leave.

"Like I was trying to explain on the phone, I've never been on a real date and haven't even kissed anyone except Lec and even that was hardly more than a peck, so, I'm hoping you can kind of be my big brother," Tamiko replies, trying to be reassuring.

"But why not ask the guy you're hot for, not the guy you passed over?" Mark asks, sounding even more annoyed.

"Lec is off with his other girlfriend—this Korean girl he met before me—and I thought…"

"Really, you mean this is a revenge date?"

"Oh my god, no," Tamiko blurts, her face going pink. Not knowing what to say that won't make things worse she looks at her feet and hopes Mark will come to her rescue. When he doesn't she finally looks up and says, "Mark, I'm sorry I seem so clueless and even sorrier if I've hurt your feelings."

"Fine, but what do you want pointers on? Spit it out," Mark replies, now standing over Tamiko.

Doing her best to ignore Mark's angry tone, Tamiko also stands as she replies, "I can see know that it's a mega-stupid idea, but I was actually thinking maybe you could show me how to kiss—you know, kiss me like you mean it, but not really."

Starting to say something and then thinking better of it, Mark abruptly grips Tamiko by her shoulders and pulls her close as he touches his lips to hers.

After a few surprisingly pleasant seconds Tamiko feels Mark's tongue push against her lips. Keeping them closed at first, she tells herself that it's only polite to respond. And so, tentatively, their tongues begin to dance, at first, in a decorous fox-trot, then an almost lyrical waltz and finally a mesmerizing tango. When Mark moves his hand to her right breast and begins to caress her nipple, Tamiko feels the wave of pleasure that's already coursing through her body begin to surge. Frightened by the intensity of her response, she abruptly pulls back, all but collapsing on the far end of the bench. Flushed, and light-headed, Tamiko lowers her head to her knees so that her long thick hair tumbles in honey-colored waves to the ground. After taking several slow deep breaths she rights herself as she mumbles, "I feel like such a fool. I wanted a beginner's lesson, not to be, well, not to be.... Maybe we should just go..."

"Fool probably doesn't do it justice," Mark interrupts caustically as he too sits. "I'm even going to guess you thought a kissing lesson wouldn't be much different from an AP biology lab where you gather information, memorize it, and then ace the final, which in this case would be kissing this Alec guy with surprising expertise."

"Something like that, I guess—oh, Mark..."

"Shut up, I'm not finished. I also think another part of your brain, a part that hopefully you're barely aware of, wanted to get even with Alec. If he can have sex with his hot Asian, you can at least play around with your backup boyfriend and maybe even tell him about it."

"Will it make you feel better if I admit that you're at least partially right," Tamiko says, meeting Mark's angry gaze. "But, oh my god Mark, in my head at least, flirting was supposed to be just a little part of today. Honestly, I didn't plan to be a pricktease if that's even the right word. Mostly I wanted to ask you about dating, like what college kids do so I could understand how guys think."

"All of which amounts to questions about my sex life, right? Honestly Tamiko, I don't know whether to be flattered, mad or just burst out laughing."

"Mark, will it make you feel better if I admit that when you kissed me, the truth is my body began to get warm all over. Or, maybe hot, is a better description."

"It's hard to believe that anyone, even a virgin princess like you, could think that making out with a person you are attracted to would produce any other result. But I'm also remembering my sister telling me that your social skills are stuck somewhere in middle school, so…"

"Obviously Molly has a point," Tamiko interrupts. "I mean, if you want, we can just call off the whole picnic. It's…"

"No possible way," Mark says, as he nods at the pack. "I'm super hungry."

"Definitely," Tamiko replies with relief as she opens her backpack and takes out a baguette, three kinds of cheese, a tomato, and kosher pickles. By the time Mark reaches for the potato salad and salami she feels a measure of calm return. For better or worse, the kiss and her surprisingly strong reaction to it can't be called back. And fortunately Mark, who's found the condiments and applied a big dollop of hot brown mustard to the huge sandwich he is constructing, now seems more amused than angry. Maybe something still can be saved from this embarrassing afternoon.

"Here's a confession," Mark says, after taking a few sips from his paper bag covered beer. "Since my social life at Cal last year was marginal, in June I asked Molly for a tip on the coolest girls at BHS."

"And she suggested me? C'mon, like now I know you're kidding."

"Well, you were third on her list, but she said that if you ever took off your red shroud and brushed your hair…"

"I can't believe you were having trouble finding girls. I mean, you're good looking, play lacrosse, and you must be smart to be at Cal. I mean…"

"Now that I'm a sophomore maybe things will be easier. But the truth is Tamiko, I didn't really connect with anyone last year. I mean with my girlfriend Sam at Berkeley High junior and senior year, I felt really happy, but once she went back east to Brown and immediately found a new dude I had to start over at Cal. I mean, sure, I had desperate sex a few times, but, that's never going to make anyone feel better. So while I guess I know more about dating than you do, I'm…"

"Remember, I'm Miss Clueless. Are you saying you don't enjoy hookups?"

"I probably would like them fine with the right person at the right time, but for the most part that's not what happened to me. And I'm not even that fussy—there are lots of girls with the potential to turn me on. But what I learned this year is that without at least a little passion, sex is kind of lonely. Also…"

"So women, or girls, or whatever you call us, fall into two categories—the ones who turn you on and the ones that don't," Tamiko interrupts. "And if they do, they're more or less interchangeable. But if they don't, no amount of sex is going to make things less boring."

"Tamiko, you're exaggerating so much you've totally trampled my point."

"But the desire to have sex with a person comes first as far as you're concerned? C'mon Mark, I'm really trying to figure this out so stop making faces and tell the truth."

"Tamiko, if your new friend Alec wasn't in the picture, I'm guessing you and I would be behind those bushes over there by now and it wouldn't be to discuss existentialism."

Pausing for a moment while she tries to figure out how to respond, Tamiko smiles as she says, "Based on what just happened I can't disagree except to say I never have sex on a first date."

"Virgins always say that until the day they don't," Mark replies now also grinning. "But in case you missed it, my point is that just because your heart, my heart or, for that matter, your grandmother's heart, is pledged to one person doesn't mean our bodies won't happily accept substitutes. Or, as my Cal Bio prof puts it, from a species perspective, our only purpose on earth is to reproduce—which incidentally explains why every part of the process is so much fun."

"Do you want my beer? I don't even like it," Tamiko asks, realizing that although it's been an awkward afternoon, she's learned something.

"One's enough, especially since I have to push."

"Already? But I thought now that we're friends we could hang for a while."

"I have a real date later and I need to change."

"Really? How come you didn't…"

"Tamiko, I asked you out in July. A couple of weeks ago I met a girl I like a lot, and who—surprise, surprise—is also hot for me."

"But, then why did you kiss me like that?"

"Unless I've lost my mind in the last few minutes, because you asked me to."

"OK, then, so tell me about your new friend."

"Carlotta Ruiz, she's an exchange student from Spain who just arrived for her junior year. She asked me for directions and well…"

"She must have been on your to do list."

"I'll put your cattiness down to mild jealousy, which truth be told, I appreciate. But, did I see some cookies at the bottom of your backpack?"

Pulling them out, Tamiko says, "Let's change the subject."

"Not quite yet, if that's OK. I guess I want to say that you aren't the only idiot on this bench. Since I like Carlotta a lot and want our relationship to work, kissing a person I've had a crush on was stupid no matter the provocation. Although no one is entitled to be as naive as you pretend to be, I'm the one who should have known better."

"Could it be that we've both learned something?" Tamiko says starting to gather up the leftover food.

"I hope so."

. . . . .

Leaving Bay just a little after six, and knowing that I-80 is sure to be choked with San Francisco-bound traffic, Amy instead chooses to wind her way to Piedmont via city streets. Turning her radio dial to an oldies station, she happily begins singing along to Carole King's version of "Will You Love Me Tomorrow?" with James Taylor and Joni Mitchell singing backup. Momentarily lost in the story about a woman who gives in to a lover's charms even though she knows he will likely abandon her in the morning, she is surprised when, at the corner of Alcatraz and Adeline, the late model BMW behind her sounds its horn as it pulls peremptorily around her. Realizing she's spaced out the light having changed, Amy checks the rear view mirror to be sure that the next car back isn't in the middle of a similar maneuver. Seeing that an old, gray American car is just sitting there, she steps on the accelerator. Ten minutes later, finding Ed perched on one of the kitchen counter stools reading the *New Yorker* and drinking an Anchor Steam from the bottle, Amy gives him a long fervent kiss.

"Tamiko left for a picnic two plus hours ago with a guy named Mark Sullivan whose sister, Molly, you apparently know from Berkeley High Softball," Ed says, after eventually breaking off the surprising kiss. "If you look worried, I'm instructed to tell you...wait a second, I made a note. OK, and I quote, "Mom, this is an information gathering session, not a date with a college guy so no rules are being broken.""

"I hope Mark is in on her 'no romance' plan," Amy says ruefully.

"I'm afraid the way he looked at her in that skin tight tank and those micro shorts you bought her this morning provides reason for doubt. But perhaps you'll be somewhat reassured that she was wearing a bra. But listen, I was wondering," Ed says quietly, "if this would be a good time for you to tell me what happened after Yuri died. I mean, I've been thinking about what it must have been like to lose him in that awful way— apparently right after you learned you were pregnant. It just seems..."

"Thanks for asking, but I have something I'd rather do first," Amy says, determined to banish her afternoon doubts.

"I hope you're thinking what I'm thinking."

"Race you," Amy says darting up the stairs, discarding her top as she reaches the first landing, her bra at the top of the stairs and her tights and panties a few steps inside the bedroom. By the time Ed catches up she is lying back against an oversized purple pillow, her legs spread and her left hand covering her mound.

"Eager girl," Ed chortles delightedly.

"Guilty as charged. No matter how often we do this I just can't get enough," Amy replies, extending her arms towards Ed who is rapidly shedding his clothes by the foot of the bed.

"Oh my god, Amy, you shaved."

"Just the sides, but still I'm a little embarrassed. Do you like it?"

Kneeling on the foot of his bed, Ed replies, "I guess I won't know until my tongue gives it a test drive."

"How about later when I have a chance to shower? Right now I'm sweaty, dirty, and eager to be fucked. No need for preliminaries."

"OK then, I'm all in, or about to be," Ed says, happily.

A few minutes later, curling against Ed, Amy says, "Can we talk about sex?"

"Only if you have nice things to say."

"After that mutual explosion you know I do. But Ed, as I was saying last night, I worry that you are being too nice to me, or maybe I should say, too considerate. I mean, I love to be on top and to come over and over while you wait—I mean what woman wouldn't, but you don't have to spoil me, we could just..."

"Start together and finish PDQ as if we were chasing the horizontal speed record?" Ed asks, his chuckle enveloping both of them.

"Precisely," Amy replies seriously.

"Amy, you're the first woman I've known who can have multiple orgasms apparently on demand so you're in danger of creating a problem that doesn't exist. Your riding me while you come makes me crazy with excitement so I absolutely have no problem with letting you gallop for as long as you like before we eventually cross the finish line together."

"Positive?"

"Not the smallest gasping shudder of a doubt. But hey, what's up with you? I mean, yesterday when we made our announcement you looked like you'd been hit by a bus."

"Ed, what would happen if we broke up?" Amy asks, looking at the ceiling. "What would you do?"

"Amy, aren't you projecting? Isn't the real question what would you do? I've been single for a bunch of years and have it out of my system, but maybe you don't. Truth be told, if I'd been married all these years I might freak at the prospect of immediately settling down."

"OK then, to be honest, I did have a moment at the Bay party when I wondered if once again I was grabbing the first great guy who walked by instead of, well…"

"Was that all? Or were you also worried I might not be Mr. Right long term?"

"Ed, it was just one of those down moods that attack me once in a while. Now, here, in this moment I have no doubts about us shouting to the world that we love each other."

"I appreciate that. But tell me, if I wasn't in the picture, what would you be fantasizing about once Tamiko is off to college?"

"Well, last Christmas when I realized that I was finally done mourning Yuri twenty-four/seven, my friend Jen and I thought that we might each take a six month sabbatical and go to Barcelona to learn Spanish and well…"

"Meet a few cute Spanish guys to help you with your accent."

"Don't mock me. I haven't been on a date in seventeen years."

"Don't I count?"

"Is it a date when you skip out half way through a business lunch to have sex?"

"Best one I ever had, but Amy, how about this? We resist moving in together this year and when Tamiko goes off to some impossibly selective college, you and Jen take off too."

"Go have our trip, really? You'd be OK with that? But what will you be doing while I'm gone?"

"Maybe I'll brush up on my meditation or perhaps I'll go off with my friend Donna to one of those swinger parties she likes so much."

"Do you mean a group sex party? You're making that up. I don't even believe that Donna exists."

"I introduced you to her at the Peet's on Fourth Street a couple of weeks ago."

"Really, that cute kid with the red streak in her hair?" Amy asks, sitting up in bed.

"She's twenty-eight," Ed replies, his eyes still shut.

"I might surprise you and want to go to the swinger party too," Amy says as she pokes Ed to be sure she has his attention.

"Too bad you'll be in Barcelona," Ed replies as he rolls towards the far edge of the bed in what even he recognizes as a vain hope of getting five minutes of post-coital shuteye.

"Oh Ed, I do love you. But just so you know, I've done a threesome, twice actually."

"I'm betting Yuri was the man in the middle," Ed says, finally accepting that the conversation is too interesting to sleep through.

"But it still counts, right, even though it was me, Yuri and Danielle, a friend from New York who was staying with us for a few days."

"Sure," Ed says, standing up and looking for his clothes. "But tell me, did you wish there had been another guy?"

"Later, maybe. At the time Yuri was so excited about sharing our bed with another woman he went into full stallion mode so I had no time to think about much of anything."

"Point taken. How about I color you adventurous from here on in."

"Thank you," Amy replies, "but in the short run it's more accurate to color me hungry so how about I make an omelette and salad? Is there bread?"

"Sure, but if you can forgive me a major nonsequitur, I've always wondered why you got married so young. I mean, didn't you tell me once you had a couple of boyfriends before Yuri, so you must have known about birth control."

"Mom, who doesn't miss much, made sure I had a pill prescription in high school, at least six months before I needed them," Amy says as she heads for the stairs.

"Which was?" Ed asks, still buttoning his shirt as he follows her down.

"In the fall of senior year. By then, I was extremely curious as to what it would feel like to have someone inside me so I coaxed Alan, my endearingly nerdy longtime boyfriend, to finally move past third base."

"But Alan didn't get you pregnant?"

"He didn't even last until prom. I met Yuri a year later in November of my first year at Cal. He looked at me as if I was a piece of chocolate cake and I looked back as if he was two scoops of vanilla ice cream. But hey, I can't find any eggs."

"Under the lettuce in the veggie drawer I think. So, how long did it take to get in bed with him?"

"Your prurient side is showing."

"C'mon…"

"He asked me the day after we met."

"And you replied?"

"I don't remember exactly."

"You don't forget something like that."

"Something like, 'What took you so long to ask?'"

"The exact words you used with me, which explains why you were laughing."

"Busted, but in fairness I didn't realize I'd said the same thing until the words popped out. But, when they did I was delighted since I knew I was as hot for you as I'd been for Yuri. But in the here and now, if you focus on the salad, we'll eat five minutes sooner."

"Sure, but I still don't understand how you got pregnant if you were taking the pill?"

"Because I was stupid. I forgot my pills when we took off to Mexico at spring break. I went on an Internet chat room and someone told me that I should still be protected for at least ten days, especially since I'd just finished my period. Yuri was doubtful so he used a condom most of the time, but obviously not every time."

"Can I ask why you didn't get an abortion—I mean, you were eighteen and Yuri was what, twenty-two?"

"You're right, having Tamiko made no logical sense, especially since I didn't have religious objections to abortion. It just turned out I couldn't do it. But more to the point right now, where do you keep your cheese grater?"

"Second drawer down on the far right. But what about Yuri, you were obviously making a decision for both of you."

"He was disappointed, even angry for a while. I know I thought there was no way he would stick by me. But then he said, 'Amy, I love all of you, so maybe this is the hand of God.'"

"I thought you said he wasn't religious?"

"He used the terms 'God' and 'fate' interchangeably, as only Russians can."

"Sort of like believing in the fickle finger of God even though there is no God?"

"Yes, and after enough vodka it can almost make sense."

"So you two got married, Tamiko was born and all was well," Ed says, putting the salad on the table and opening a bottle of Beaujolais.

"Not even close," Amy replies from the stove, where she's drizzling cheddar onto the slowly congealing eggs. "After Tami was born I became acutely depressed, lost weight, lost my temper, lost my interest in sex, and on some days had difficulty getting out of bed."

"This lasted?"

"Almost a year. It didn't help that by then we were in Amherst, Mass where we knew almost no one. Yuri was starting his PhD at U Mass and I was a second-year undergraduate until I became so miserable I dropped out."

"When did things start to get better?"

"You're probably not going to believe this, but I remember the exact moment. I was in the bathroom after a shower looking at my skinny depressed self in the mirror and feeling so miserable that I called out to Yuri who was in the next room something like 'I hate you! Please just leave, I'll be better off alone,'" Amy says as she flips the omelette into the air, catching it deftly after it turns over.

"Nice hands. But what did Yuri say?"

"Amy, get used to it. I'm here for as long as it takes."

"Sweet."

"Yes, but as miserable as I felt standing there naked in front of the mirror, I was also curious as to why he would continue to put up with me. So I put my nose around the door and asked."

"And?"

"He replied, 'Because I'm so hot for your body.'"

"That's when I stepped into the bedroom crying hysterically and said,

'You fucking liar! No one can want me looking like a starving refugee!'"

"You were naked?"

"Yes, and Yuri kept saying how beautiful I was and how much he loved my body. Anyway, we somehow ended up in bed and for the first time since Tamiko was born, sex was good."

"It was as simple as that?"

"I wish. But it did move things back from the brink. The next big step was my finally being able to talk about how guilty I felt for what I saw as ruining Yuri's life by having a child."

"He didn't see it that way."

"I finally realized that he honestly didn't. I was so dug in to my depression mentality that I'd overlooked how intensely he loved Tamiko and, as a result, how grateful he was to me for insisting on having her. Anyway, when I finally started to hear him, he said he had a big favor to ask," Amy says, slicing the omelette before tipping the pan so that half ends up on each of their plates.

"Which was?"

"That I should throw out the antidepressants, and start jogging or swimming, anything to pump good chemicals into my brain."

"Easier said than done when you're depressed," Ed says, "but, please bring over the salt and pepper before you sit down."

"It helped that we were having sex again. But even so, the first couple of weeks felt like I was walking in ankle-deep mud wearing lead boots. Then, remarkably, I began to feel a lot better."

"Your postpartum depression, or whatever it was, finally lifted?" Ed asks, taking an appreciative bite.

"Yes, and what a relief. We were still starving students with a fussy toddler surviving on handouts from our parents, but I was back in school and Yuri was powering through his PhD in record time, so we were remarkably OK."

"All this was in Amherst, Massachusetts?"

"Right. By the time Yuri finished his PhD in 2005, I had started my Masters. That's when he got a low-end lecturing job at Michigan and off we went. But of course the exciting news was that his dissertation had been accepted for publication."

"*Black and White in Black and White?*"

"Right. And somehow when it came out the next year, it got into the hands of the right people, which in a few months resulted in a great review in an influential journal followed in a few months by several more. That's when the phone began to ring. Yuri was debating a couple of tenure-track offers from very decent midwestern schools when the New York Times published an enthusiastic review and the New Yorker agreed to a chunky excerpt—which was of course what eventually made Yuri a household word in academic circles. Anyway, we suddenly had the choice of a couple of Ivy's and Cal, which of course was easy since we didn't care about the big bucks."

"What I don't know is whether you're going to eat the rest of your salad, or share a couple of bites?"

"Only if it will butter you up for later," Amy says, leaning over to give Ed a long passionate kiss on the mouth.

"Just curious, are you the same woman who was fantasizing about being single in Barcelona half an hour ago?"

"Ha! By your talking about sex parties with Donna, it took you less than a minute to sober me up on that one."

"How long would it have taken Yuri?"

"About the same. Obviously I'm attracted to men who can't be bullied."

"My goal is to encourage you to have some adventures, not talk you out of them, but since the door that just slammed out front is probably Tamiko being dropped off, I'm thinking we better finish this conversation later."

SUNDAY

AMY SLIPS OUT OF BED AT SEVEN-THIRTY and pads silently to the large light-filled living room where she pushes back the two blimp-like armchairs Ed insists represent his former wife's taste, not his. After forty-five minutes of yoga, she hears Tamiko turn on her shower. Suspecting that Ed won't be far behind, Amy puts the living room back in order before going to the kitchen. When Tamiko appears a few minutes later wearing the dove gray kimono with an embroidered red dragon that was the cherry on top of yesterday's shopping spree the two of them set to work. Fifteen minutes later yelling, "Ed, breakfast in five minutes," Amy puts the bacon on a plate and surrenders the frying pan to Tamiko who has five pieces of over-sized sourdough ready to go. Amy is just drawing the big breath needed to shout out a second breakfast call, when Ed comes through the kitchen door holding the Sunday *New York Times* in one hand and a bottle of maple syrup in the other. "Timing is everything with French toast," he says, grinning widely, "So I hope I have permission to eat mine before making the coffee."

"I'm guessing that was a statement, not a question," Amy replies, reaching for the maple syrup as she takes her place at the round, glass-topped table.

"This is just the world's best breakfast—even if I made it myself," Tamiko says after a couple of minutes of companionable chewing. "Who wants another piece of toast? Although, I have to warn you that all the raspberries you're going to get are already in your tummy."

"Silly question, of course I want one," Ed replies. But then rubbing his just slightly rounded stomach, he amends, "How about half?"

"I'll eat his other half and you, my obviously ravenous daughter, can have a second one all to yourself. But Ed, my love, how about firing up your little machine so we can finally have our coffee."

"Cappuccino, latte, espresso, or Americano?" Ed says as he stands and takes a step towards the kitchen.

"Surprise me," Amy replies, turning her palms up.

"Give me a hint, milk or no milk?"

"Milk."

"Tamiko, I know you don't drink coffee, so would you like…"

"Last week I didn't hang with guys or drink coffee, but now I do both," Tamiko says with a pleased chuckle. "But since I guess you can say I'm still at the training wheel stage on both, I better say milk." Then as Ed disappears into the kitchen Tamiko turns to her mom and says, "Mom I have a huge favor to ask—I don't mean to be birthday greedy but maybe we can even call it a bonus present. It's just that Lec, Alec that is, offered to be my catcher at four p.m. today over at MLK Middle School and since it's just a few blocks from home I wondered if after I could invite him over to meet you—to meet both of you that is—and maybe have pizza."

"Whoa Nelly! Exactly when did you hear me change my mind about your dating this man?"

"Like I've said maybe a dozen times, Lec and I both agreed we're not dating—that is not, well, you know, not touching each other type dating, until you say it's OK. But I didn't agree not to see him. And you know I've always dreamed about being a pitcher, especially in college. So can't you see what a great plan it is to have Lec be my catcher since he'll mostly be forty-three feet away? And really Mom, aren't you at least a little bit curious to meet him?"

"You don't think that your getting a crush on an older man who you immediately put in your dad's catcher role might be something to worry about?"

"Dad was a great guy and Lec is a great guy, so where's the problem?"

"I don't mean to interrupt," Ed says, returning with three mugs on a tray. "Or come to think of it, maybe I do, but Tamiko, if you need more help it would be fun to be your catcher a couple of times a week. I played baseball in high school and even caught a few games when the regular guy was hurt, so I'm pretty sure I can handle it—except maybe for having to squat for an hour."

"Wow, Ed! Like that would be chill," Tamiko says happily as she perches on the edge of a chair. "And don't worry about your legs since kids squat, while coaches sit on plastic pails. If you and Lec can each catch me twice a week I'll be legit in no time, especially if I can get to San Leandro now and then to work with Coach on my mechanics. Mom says you might even come to a game next weekend—which would be super since you'll meet Coach and see the pitching level I'll need to get to."

"I'm looking forward to it."

"Fabulous, and hey, I'm in such a good mood I'm going to clean the kitchen to celebrate. And then I want to blast through a bunch of early Pushkin since Vera plans to quiz me later. But, around threeish I need to be back in Berkeley so I'm wondering if I should take the bus or might a ride be on offer?"

"How about two-thirty?" Ed asks, "I need to pick something up at Bay to work on tonight."

"Just for the record, I'm thinking about your pizza proposal," Amy says.

When Tamiko disappears into the house, this time shutting the kitchen door behind her, Ed asks, "If you do decide to meet Alec later, do you want me to be there?"

"Absolutely, but give me a couple more hours to mull."

"While you're at it can you also think about how you want to handle things with me and you this week? I guess I still feel a little nervous about sleeping at your house."

"Let's get over it. This weekend worked beautifully and since Tami doesn't seem to be worried about our relationship, why should we?"

. . . . .

A few minutes after three Alec puts on a pair of dark blue cargo shorts and a faded red T-shirt with Kiwi Power written across the chest. Knocking on the door next to his and receiving no answer, he opens it and examines himself in the full-length mirror. As he suspects, the shorts look baggy, so humming the first few bars of Carly Simon's "You're So Vain" he returns to his room and switches them out for a pair of tighter black ones. Glancing at his watch to see that he's still ridiculously early, he thinks about opening his organic chemistry text. But having slept half of Saturday and studied the rest, he feels sufficiently caught up that instead, he goes down to the backyard where one of his housemates had left some dumbbells on the patio. Alternating stretching with lifting, Alec tries to focus on his workout, only to peek at his watch after his second set of curls. Seeing that barely ten minutes have passed, he flops down and pounds out fifty hyperbolic push-ups before wandering back into the kitchen. After eating a tub of yogurt only a week past its pull date, he again looks at his watch to see that only six more minutes have passed. "Good thing you're not anxious," he says to himself as he heads out the front door, resolving to drive slowly.

· · · · ·

After Ed drops Tamiko off at home at 2:40 p.m., she pulls a dust encrusted blue sports bag with Wilson printed boldly on the side from the back corner of the garage where she'd deposited it the afternoon before her dad died. Sniffling a little as she dumps out her dad's shin guards, catcher's mask, and chest protector, she gets a sponge and a bucket of soapy water from the kitchen and begins wiping them down. Then spreading everything out to dry in the sun, Tamiko goes to her room, where she puts on her maroon Tsunami shorts, a black sports bra, and a gray T-shirt with "Hella Legit" written diagonally across the front. Looking at herself in the small mirror over the bathroom sink, she thinks the girl—well, make that the young woman—who stares back is as excited as she's ever seen her.

Dressed and ready to go at three-thirty Tamiko faces a dilemma. Should she assert her independence by walking the ten blocks to the field lugging the blue bag plus a pail of acid-yellow balls? Or should she wait for her mom to show up to chauffeur her—something she worries will underline her youth? Hearing Ed bang in the front door on his return from Bay, the solution comes to her. "Hey Ed," she says, "I'll tell you where we hide the cookies if you'll drive me and all my gear over to MLK Middle School."

"Do I look that hungry?"

"We'll see, I guess," Tamiko replies, opening the small cupboard over the fridge, standing on tip-toe and extracting a ziploc bag stuffed with chocolate chip cookies.

"Homemade?"

"By me, Thursday evening. Mom and I take turns and always put them up there so we have to notice when we eat one."

"You'll have to put them up higher than that to slow me down," Ed says as he stuffs most of a huge cookie in his mouth. "Delicious," he mumbles as he reaches for a second.

"I guess I have a ride."

"Sure, but no bribes are ever needed—although I might move a step or two quicker when a cookie as good as this is on offer. But I thought you were meeting Alec at four."

"I'd like to stretch first, so is it OK if we go now?"

"Feeling a tad anxious?"

"Excited for sure."

"What's up for later? Has Amy said yes or no to pizza with Alec?"

"She's just texted '*OK for pizza, but don't expect me to be a charming hostess.*'"

. . . . .

When Ed pulls his green Mini to the curb on Rose Street in front of the Middle School ten minutes before four Tamiko sees Alec sitting on a patch of lawn. "Wow, Lec's here already," she exclaims with delight. "C'mon Ed, get out and meet him."

"How about we do the meet and greet later at your place when Amy is there too? For now, just grab your stuff and enjoy the moment."

"Hey you," Alec says, walking to the curb with a big grin on his face as Ed pulls away.

"Hey you back," Tamiko replies, looking at the ground as she hefts the blue Wilson bag over her shoulder.

"How about you stand still for a second so I can look at you?"

"How about you grab the balls," Tamiko says raising her eyes to look at Alec's. At a loss for something to say, she blurts out, "Is that your favorite T-shirt?"

"Of course," he answers as he stares back. After a long minute he says, "Do we need to talk?"

"Not if you're half as glad to see me as I am you."

"Who was here first?"

"Right," Tamiko replies with a grin as she picks up the blue bag. "But before we start I need to ask you if you'll come over for pizza after?"

"To your house? With your mom?"

"Yes and yes. She's not about to give in on the no-dating rule, but since she's not forbidding me from seeing you platonically, I guess she figures she may as well check you out."

"To size up the enemy?"

"Maybe a little. But she'll be polite and Ed, her boyfriend who just dropped me off, will be there. He won't contradict Mom, but I'm hoping he's more open-minded."

"OK, I guess, but I'll want to stop home to change."

"*Pizza at six*," Tamiko texts her mom as she leads the way around the west side of the building to the field behind where she drops the blue bag near the first baseline and retrieves her glove and a catcher's mitt, tossing the mitt to Alec.

"Was this your dad's?"

"Yes, but remember, we're not talking until later. Let's warm up by throwing overhand for a few minutes."

"Got it," Alec says, backing thirty feet towards second base.

Tamiko grins as she cocks her wrist, turns sideways, and effortlessly flips the plump yellow ball towards Alec. When it hits his glove with a firecracker-like pop, he chuckles appreciatively before taking half a dozen long strides towards center field. Now fifty feet apart, the ball flies back and forth with Alec's throws occasionally wandering a few feet high, low or wide right, while all of Tamiko's would have pulverized Alec's right shoulder if his glove hadn't intervened.

"What's next?" Alec asks, still standing ten feet behind second base.

"You set up behind home plate, but since this is a baseball field—and in softball we don't pitch from a mound—I'll walk off forty-three feet towards shortstop," Tamiko says, pulling out an eighteen-inch strip of dirty white rubber. "But first you need to put on the tools of ignorance," she adds as she pulls a mask and shin guards from the bag.

"Forget it. There's no batter and I can catch fine," Alec protests, raising his right hand as if to fend off the equipment Tamiko holds out. "I mean, c'mon, I'm wearing a cup like you suggested."

"The chest protector is still in the bag and the shin guards are optional, although if I bounce one off your leg bone at sixty miles per hour, I bet you'll wish you weren't acting so macho. But Lec, the mask is a hundred and ten percent mandatory," Tamiko says as she uses a scrunchie to corral her flyaway mane at the nape of her neck.

"Who's going to make me wear it?" Alec says, trying to sound like Al Pacino playing a mafia soldier.

"That would be me," Tamiko replies doubling down on the faux Sicilian accent, "I'll be a wild child today and probably for a few weeks. If a ball hits a pebble right in front of you it can go anyplace. A kid I know knocked out six of her dad's teeth that way."

"Maybe I'm quicker than the dad," Alec replies, still refusing to take the mask.

"He played tight end in the NFL for seven years."

"What years were those?" Alec asks, irrationally determined not to be intimidated.

Shaking her head, Tamiko tosses the mask towards Alec's feet as she says, "I've only known your stubborn face for six days and it would break my heart to damage it."

Hearing the slight quaver in her voice, Alec picks up the mask and puts it on as he squats behind home plate and says, "Let's pitch, boss."

"Don't you want to sit on a bucket?"

"Don't you want to pitch?"

"Sure, I'll throw a few easy ones then go for it. It'll be quicker if you drop each ball in a bucket after you catch it and also the easiest way to count pitches."

"You don't want me to throw the balls back?" Alec asks as if his status as an athlete is again being questioned.

"You can if you want to waste time. But if you do it my way, I'll have another ball out of my bucket almost before you drop the one you just caught in yours."

"Got it."

"I'll start with fast balls. Your job is to move your mitt up, down, in and out to give me a changing target always on the edge of the strike zone. I'll be all over the place today, but eventually I'll need to hit your mitt as predictably as if I were dropping an egg into a tea cup from a height of six inches."

Tamiko stands motionless with both feet on the rubber her hands together in front of her chest as if in prayer. Then, as her right arm drops to begin its windmill motion, she slowly pivots to face third base before, in a blur of arms and legs, she turns back towards home plate, her left leg kicking towards Alec's chin like a snake's tongue. When the foot finally pounds the ground at the instant Tamiko's forearm snaps up towards her shoulder, the ball rockets towards Alec. Captivated by the tall girl's fluid athleticism he doesn't raise his glove as the eleven-inch yellow orb flies a few feet over his head to hit the chain-link backstop with a thwack.

"You're supposed to watch the ball, not me," Tamiko says as she reaches into the pail and immediately swings into her windup.

Not an easy assignment, Alec thinks, as, just in time, he adjusts his focus to scoop her errant second pitch out of the dirt. Looking up in the expectation that Tamiko will acknowledge his deft pickup, he sees that she is already starting her third windup. Placing his mitt to the low outside corner for a right-handed batter, he is absurdly pleased when a second later the ball finds the pocket with an elbow-jamming thump.

Throwing all fastballs Tamiko empties her bucket in less than ten minutes, hitting the strike zone with barely a third of her pitches. Trotting in to help Alec pick up the balls that have flown wildly to the backstop, she says, "Hang in there, it will get better."

"I don't need convincing. The ball is exploding out of your hand. How fast can you throw, anyway?"

"Today, best case probably fifty-seven or fifty-eight miles per hour, but when my mechanics improve I'm hoping I can ramp it up well over sixty, maybe even sixty-five. That's my goal anyway."

"But since you're throwing from hardly more than two-thirds of the baseball distance, a batter's time to react must be similar to a baseball pitcher throwing something like eighty-five miles per hour. Assuming your accuracy improves, why isn't that already good enough to make you a killer pitcher?"

"The bat is faster than the ball."

"Huh? Are you saying high school girls can catch up to what is close to a major league fastball? I mean granted a softball is a little bigger, but still..."

"It's true that playing our weaker high school opponents, I can dominate with just a high fifties fastball, but against even an average summer club team, I'd be lucky to make it through the second inning."

"So how can you beat them?"

"In six words—'change speeds and move the ball.' But hey, if you stop asking me questions and go squat, I'll try to demonstrate with my rise ball and then later I'll move on to the drop and screw."

On his way back to home plate, Alec detours towards the first base line where he picks up the third bucket. Back at homeplate, he upends it and sits with a feeling of relief. Tamiko is right, squatting for an hour is something he'll have to work up to.

"You'll be putting on the shin guards next," Tamiko observes dryly as she swings into motion and delivers the pitch ten feet over Alec's head. The dozen or so rise balls that follow are little better, although by standing up and extending his long left arm Alec is able to snag a few.

Then, somewhere around pitch fifteen, after the long-legged girl recorrals her honey colored mane, she begins to bring the ball down towards the top of the strike zone. Still, Alec isn't impressed—a high ball hitter when he played Little League before Modern Pentathlon took over his life, he thinks she'll be more effective keeping her fast ball down. Then, with her next pitch, Tamiko whips the ball in belt high only to have it suddenly hop an inch just before it reaches the plate. The move is so surprising that the ball smacks the top of Alec's mitt before, most of its force spent, it glances off his shoulder.

"You OK?" Tamiko asks, taking a step towards Alec.

"Only my pride is hurt. Now that I know what a rise ball is supposed to do, I'll be fine."

When Tamiko tosses another hopping pitch, Alec deftly raises his glove to catch it.

"Next up I'll throw some drop balls, and then maybe a few screws," Tamiko says.

"OK, but wait a minute while I grab the shin guards. I'm beginning to see that in fastpitch softball, nothing is soft, especially not the ball."

Ten minutes later, with her pitches flying everywhere but over the plate, Tamiko picks up the pitching rubber and says, "Enough, nothing's working and I'm about to get grumpy."

"I'm good to hang in."

"I need to check with Coach about my grips and mechanics before more practice makes sense."

Sitting on a bench in the small first base dugout as Alec takes off the shin guards, he says, "Do we need to talk about your mom before I drop you and go change? I'm more than a little intimidated by the prospect of meeting her. I mean, do I call her Amy or Mrs. Gashkin or what?"

"You're the experienced older guy so you'll have to figure that one out. But, remember, since she already one hundred and ten percent disapproves of my dating you we have nothing to lose. And Lec, don't try to charm her, or she'll just add phony to the long list of the negative things she already thinks about you."

"Sounds like a fun evening."

"Be polite, eat your pizza and chat with Ed and hopefully Mom will see that you're not an ogre. And just so you know, Ed's like seven or eight years older than Mom, has been divorced for a bunch of years, and I'm sure has had a variety of girlfriends. So I'm guessing that if he likes you, he won't see our age difference or my lack of dating experience as deal breakers."

"In fairness to your mom, a six-year age difference amounts to a lot more at sixteen than it does twenty years later. Sometimes, I do worry…"

"Lec, c'mon, I thought we were all in on the idea that love is love, no matter the details," Tamiko says in a small voice.

"I wouldn't be here if I didn't believe that," Alec replies, deciding this is not the moment to add 'most of the time.'

. . . . .

Opening the Nissan's trunk to pull out her gear while Alec idles in front of her house, Tamiko sees Ed washing her mom's Subaru in the driveway. Then, as she glances up Francisco Street, she notices an ancient American car pull slowly away from the curb. "Lec, Lec," she almost shouts as she slams down the trunk lid, "See that old gray car? Try to get close enough to get the license number. Go quick, I'll explain later."

"What was that all about?" Ed asks as he watches the Nissan lumber east on Francisco Street.

"Probably nothing, but I've seen that old Ford hanging around here for a few days, and my dad always taught me to be wary of strange cars."

"With everyone doing Airbnb, I'm sure it's nothing to worry about."

"Probably not, but still it gives me the creeps. Hey, let me help you wash Bessie. Since Mom only gets around to cleaning her twice a year, there's sure to be plenty of scrubbing for two."

"No doubt, since the inside took me the whole time you were pitching. And it's true—if you hold the hose while I scrub, it'll take half the time. Is Alec coming back for pizza?"

"Yes, but he's almost as skittish as Mom so it'll probably be an edgy supper," Tamiko says, picking up a headsized sponge.

"You seem relaxed."

"Pumped is more like it. Even though I pretty much sucked, pitching again was way cool and then there's the bonus that Mom is actually letting Lec in the house."

"There's nothing quite like being in love," Ed says with a grin. Then, glancing at his watch, he asks, "What time is supper?"

"Six."

"Working together, this should take less than twenty minutes, which will give us enough time to clean up."

. . . . .

As Tamiko and Ed take off their shoes by the back door at 5:35, Tamiko says, "While it may be hard for a rich suburban guy to wrap his mind around, we have only one bathroom so as the guest you get the first shower."

"I'll be quick. Amy is picking up munchies as well as a half-baked Zachary's pizza and should be back anytime. In case you're wondering, I think you can color her determined to make the best of tonight."

"Ed, like I totally get you can't take sides, but thanks for being here and trying to keep Mom and me from losing it."

By the time the salad is made and the table is set in the backyard, the bathroom is free and Tamiko sees that she has only a skinny fifteen minutes to clean up and plan her presentation. After her shower she is about to make her usual naked dash to her room when she remembers Ed and wraps herself in a red towel. With her door safely closed, she lets the towel drop as she considers which of her new clothes to embrace. Deciding that she's dressing as much for her mom, as for Lec, she slips into her least tight black pants, before rummaging in her top drawer for her new, admittedly comfortable, white bra. Reaching behind her back in an effort to secure the unfamiliar clasp, it occurs to her with annoyance that being a woman, even a young one, means doing this for the rest of her life. Successful at last, Tamiko turns her mind to Lec as she reaches for the shimmering silver top that is an exception to yesterday's mostly utilitarian purchases.

. . . . .

Pizza tucked into the oven, Amy is about to join Ed in the backyard, when at 6:03, the doorbell sounds. Knowing that Tamiko is barely out of the shower, her heart sinks as she realizes that greeting Alec is up to her. Doing her best to wipe the scowl from her face she opens the door, only to have the tall, dark-haired young man on the doormat step back, his face registering surprise.

"It's OK, you have the right house. I'm Amy Gashkin," Amy says extending her hand.

Shaking hands with the thin, almost elfin-looking woman, who at first glance he thinks might be a college student, Alec sees now that she's older. But with her surprisingly large greenish eyes, high, almost flat cheekbones, and Tamiko's full lips over a strong chin, he also realizes that if he had met this woman at a party, he might have tried to chat her up. At a loss as to what to say, Alec feels vastly relieved when Amy says, "Come in, please. Despite my performance on the phone the other night, I promise not to bite. Tamiko will be ready in a moment so in the meantime, come on through to the backyard where my friend Ed is holed up with today's *Times*."

Sitting on a green plastic chair holding a bottle of Anchor Steam as he reads the *New York Times* Magazine, Ed looks up to see a tall, serious-looking young man trailing Amy in the manner of a well-bred German Shepherd trying not to trample a terrier. Standing, he sticks out his hand as he says, "Ed Crane."

"Alec Burns," the young man replies as he gracefully slides around Amy to take Ed's hand in a relaxed, I don't need to prove anything grip.

Motioning just a little apologetically to the chair he has just taken his feet off, Ed asks, "How about a brew? We also have Corona?"

"Well, maybe I better…"

"You won't score points with Amy by drinking water," Ed says with a chuckle.

"OK, well a Corona then. But I need to study organic chemistry later so one will be plenty."

"I'll get it," Amy says, trying not to show her resentment at Ed's welcoming manner. "You two relax."

As Alec says "Thanks" to Amy's retreating back, Ed chuckles as he says, "It's hard to believe they're mother and daughter, isn't it?"

"Was I thinking out loud?" Alec replies with a smile. "But Tamiko did say she's a quarter Asian and of course there are her eyes, but still…"

"Amy's ancestry is half Japanese and half Irish, but except for her hazel eyes and a few red tints in her hair, you'd never suspect the Irish. If you don't mind me changing the subject, Tamiko tells me you do the Modern Pentathlon at the highest level."

"Did, not do. I represented the U.S. at the World Championships in Warsaw a couple of years ago, but it was something of a fluke since at the last moment several older, more experienced athletes had to withdraw. Right after that I decided I didn't want to spend every free hour training so I quit."

"Twenty-plus years ago I was on the fencing team at Brown doing épée. Saying that I was barely adequate would be charitable, but I enjoyed it. Obviously, this was far from your level."

"Have you fenced lately?"

"In grad school at Madison I joined a club and kept it up for a few years, but it's been what, fifteen, or maybe more like seventeen years since I've picked up an épée."

"Maybe we can give it a go one day. I haven't had my gear out from under the bed since I got back to Berkeley last January."

"I'd like to think I can do well enough to make it fun for you, but I'm afraid I'd embarrass myself."

Before Alec can reply, Tamiko pushes through the kitchen door carrying a large wooden salad bowl in one hand and two beer bottles in the other. "Hey," she says with a wide grin as both men look up.

The word 'stunning', Ed thinks, doesn't come close to describing how the high necked, bare-shouldered, silver top, shimmers waterfall-like over Tamiko's high round breasts. With her thick, caramel hair gathered at the nape of her neck by a purple ribbon and wearing Amy's pinprick diamond earrings, she looks simultaneously demure, sophisticated and dare he admit it even to himself, sizzling. As Tamiko asks if either of them would like water, Ed glances at Alec to see that his look of wary politeness has been replaced by a radiant grin. Wondering if Alec may be the more smitten of the two, Ed stands and says, "Relax, Tamiko, while I help Amy and in the process get us all some water."

. . . . .

After greeting Alec and delivering him to Ed, Amy steps into the bathroom to run a brush through her hair. Momentarily tempted to change into the slippery black top Ed admires, she rejects the idea. This is not going to turn into a party if I have anything to do with it, she thinks as she strides resolutely towards the backyard.

. . . . .

As soon as the kitchen door bangs behind Ed, Alec says, "You look brilliant. It's as if every day I know you, you manage to look more beautiful."

"Thanks," Tamiko replies, coloring slightly. "You're not so bad yourself."

"Talking about attractive people in the Gashkin family, I was blown away by your mom. I mean, despite dropping you out front earlier, when she opened the door I thought I'd come to the wrong house."

"My bad, I should have warned you. For obvious reasons, no one ever thinks we're related."

"It wasn't just the Asian thing. At first I thought she was a teenager."

"The other day at Vanessa's Bistro I thought the waiter was going to card her and let me pass. Remember I told you she was only nineteen when I was born. But what did she say?" Tamiko asks, anxiety creeping into her voice.

"Nothing, beyond introducing herself and inviting me in. Polite, but cool. I'm hoping I came across as being less of a child molester than she fears, but I don't know," Alec says, taking a small sip of his beer.

"Mom makes up her mind quickly and changes it slowly so let's not expect too much. But hey, did you get the license number on the old Ford?"

"Not all of it anyway, since I was pretty far back and the plate was dirty. I think it started 6RT with maybe the next letter being X. But I wouldn't bet much on any of it. As maybe you saw, he ran the stop sign at McGee and then turned left two blocks up at Grant. By the time I got there he was already turning on Delaware. If there hadn't been an older gentleman in the street with a walker slowing him down, I wouldn't have seen anything. What's this about anyway?"

Before Tamiko can answer, Ed backs through the screen door carrying a tray. As Tamiko helps him unload four glasses of sparkling water, Amy appears carrying a steaming deepdish Zachary's Chicago style spinach and mushroom pizza.

The conversation that follows is more relaxed than Tamiko has dared anticipate. A schedule for her pitching practices is agreed to with both Ed and Alec volunteering for two afternoons per week. Alec then asks Ed about Bay Books, saying that he owns an excellent East Bay trail guide Bay published years ago. In reply, Ed, with occasional help from Tamiko, explains Bay's odd mix of West Coast-centric titles, including trail guides, recipe books authored by locally prominent chefs, and mysteries. By the time ice cream is served, Amy has been coaxed into briefly describing the plot of *Murder on Holy Mountain*, and explaining why she thinks it will be a strong seller.

Hoping he's dented Amy's wall of opposition to his friendship with Tamiko, and not wanting to jeopardize it by overstaying his welcome, Alec eats his olallieberry pie, stands and, pleading the need to study, makes a quick exit.

. . . . .

Accepting Tamiko's offer to clean up, Amy goes to her room, closes the door, and begins to cry. While she isn't nearly ready to give Tamiko and Alec her blessing, watching her daughter almost effortlessly shed her adolescent cocoon makes it obvious that the days of their 'us against the world' bond will never be repeated. Ten minutes later, tears blotted, she does her best to smile when Ed appears and wraps her in his arms.

"Tonight, looking at the two of them look at each other, I felt like I'm a mad woman trying to hold up a stop sign in front of a tornado," Amy says.

"Nice metaphor, but as the bumper sticker says, 'Don't believe everything you think.'"

"I don't follow."

"Alec and Tamiko are both smart enough to realize that their mad mutual crush pushes the boundaries of common sense. Your stop sign gives them a welcome chance to pause and think twice."

"I hope so, but oh my god Ed, to see my daughter look…I don't even know how to describe it."

"Stunning, sophisticated and adult, not to mention almost levitating with happiness?"

"I hardly recognized her."

MONDAY 2

WHEN TAMIKO ARRIVES AT THEIR MEETING SPOT wearing black pants and a sky blue leotard, Alec whistles before asking, "How did I do last night?"

"How about starting with 'Good morning, you look nice.'"

"I thought I just did. So c'mon, tell me."

"A journey of a thousand miles begins with a single step."

"That's as far as I got?"

"Since Mom didn't say anything negative, I'm guessing that she might just think you'd be OK if it wasn't for the old man thing. But, hey, let's get coffee and a muffin. And thanks for putting up with last night. I bet it's been a while since you had to be inspected by parents, or in this case, parent."

"Not since Suzy Shearing when I was sixteen."

"What happened with her?"

"She was the first girl I was excited about in a big way so I went along with her three-martini dad quizzing me every time I picked her up."

"Was she your first real girlfriend?"

"If you mean real as in the first girl I had sex with, I thought we agreed that…"

"You must have already figured out I was born curious."

"The truth is I didn't hang in there with Suzy long enough to share the big event, which turned out to be my mistake. In addition to her difficult dad, she had this 'I want to be a virgin when I get married' rap going and we had several half-naked tiffs about it. But c'mon, this ancient history must be a bore."

"About as boring as the Oakland A's winning the World Series."

"OK, so after a final awkward brouhaha with Suzy I moved on to

Kelly Douglas. Kelly was always smiling in my direction, and whenever I smiled back, she'd run her tongue over her lips...."

"Yuck! Finish the story before I hit you."

"Kelly and I got over being virgins in record time and although that part was a huge relief, the truth was I still had a major crush on Suzy. But by the time I figured out how to semi-diplomatically break up with Kelly, Suzy was going out with this Yale freshman, a guy who obviously had little difficulty talking her past her celibacy issues."

"Ha, if you'd just been a little more patient," Tamiko chuckles, as she steps forward on her left foot while flicking her right behind her back so it taps Alec on his butt as if to emphasize her point.

"Hey, you just broke the no-touching rule again," Alec objects in mock indignation.

"Kicking you in the ass is probably the one kind Mom would approve of," Tamiko replies, pushing through the café door a step ahead of Alec.

After collecting their drinks from the barista who mercifully is not Ahmad and finding their favorite table empty, Alec asks, "Why did you ask me to chase that old car? You never had a chance to finish explaining."

"No big deal probably, but I've seen it hanging around our block the last few days and was beginning to get this creepy feeling that it has something to do with us."

"You're kidding, right? There could be a hundred explanations," Alec says, breaking off a chunk of the scone.

"That's what Mom and Ed think and I kinda agreed until yesterday when there it was again," Tamiko replies, dividing the remainder of the scone in two and moving her half next to her coffee.

"It's a public street. That's not proof of anything," Alec says, finishing his last big crumb and eying Tamiko's.

"True, but my dad trained me to watch for strangers, especially strangers in strange cars who keep showing up. Dad was a big-time skeptic when it came to coincidences. And just so you know, if you make a move on my food I'll bite you."

"If kissing is a no-no, biting might have to do. By the way, have I told you how gobsmacked I am about you this morning?"

"Never enough. But, Lec, just being with you is all I need to feel amazing. The truth is I can't remember ever being this happy."

"As far as I can see, you were born with a smile on your face."

"Not this big."

"So tell me, how did your weekend dates go?" Alec asks, pretending to be barely interested in the answer.

"What happened to 'don't ask, don't tell'?"

"I just told you about Suzy?"

"But not Teri," Tamiko says, wrinkling her nose. "But, OK, so I got together with Tabitha Anderson, who I told you goes to Bowdoin back in Maine. Like you predicted, she explained the hookup culture at school in a way that convinced me it's silly to quiz you about names and dates."

"All good, but what about the dude?" Alec persists.

"To get right to the point, Mark kissed me like he meant it, which was a very good thing for both of us—us being me and you, in case you're in doubt," Tamiko says, looking into Alec's large brown eyes.

"Hmm," Alec replies, breaking eye contact as he leans back in his chair in an effort to deflect the feeling that he'd been kicked in the gut. "Why am I skeptical about buying that story?"

"I found myself kissing him back and enjoying it until I thought about you and stopped," Tamiko says seriously.

"I'm supposed to think that was a good thing?"

"Absolutely. In a flash I understood that sexual desire can exist in its own universe, and how you could want to screw Teri and still be in love with me," Tamiko says, halving her last bite of scone and feeding one piece to Alec.

"That's a lot to understand. But just in case you're in any doubt, I don't plan to have other girlfriends going forward."

"Nice to know. And just in case you're even a little jealous, I solemnly swear to have my first sexual experience with you and no one but you, and to be ready the moment Mom gets over the idea that she's the only one in the Gashkin family who gets to have a real boyfriend."

"Oops! I hope I'm not going to be a pawn in your power struggle with your mom?"

"Sorry for the bitchy moment. I hope you know I'm happy for Mom and Ed. It's just that I think I'm old enough to make my own choices."

"In a funny sort of way, I sympathize with your mom."

"So do I, although I sympathize with me and you more. But now this annoying virgin needs to get to work and you have exams to study for."

"World Lit has a paper instead of an exam, which I've mostly done, so it's down to Organic Chemistry, which is a good thing since getting an A on the final isn't going to be trivial. What about your Physics final?"

"It's not until Wednesday and anyway, it's like, basically a snore."

"I've always wanted to have a girlfriend smarter than me."

TUESDAY 2

AMY WAKES UP GRINNING AT 6:15 A.M. Ed's at home in Piedmont and Tamiko isn't up, so there's no one to slow her down as she heads into the kitchen and pours boiling water through finely ground coffee nested in a paper-lined ceramic cone. Sipping her coffee in the car on the way to the downtown Berkeley Y, she's running on a treadmill by 7:10. Feeling a tiny pang of guilt for not waking Tamiko and coaxing her to come along, Amy ramps up the pace to speed through an eight-minute mile. Some mornings, she reflects, the pleasure of moving quickly and alone is just too appealing to be sacrificed on the altar of mother-daughter bonding.

Amy showers before heading south on Harold Way past the Buddhist bookstore towards her car, which is parked across from Berkeley's 1930's era art deco library. Fishing in her purse for her keys as she turns left on Kittredge, she looks up to see an old gray car rumble past. Could this possibly be the one Tamiko has been so concerned about? Although it seems highly unlikely, Amy nevertheless feels a small cloud of foreboding drift across the clear sky of her morning.

Arriving at Bay Books at 8:28, Amy hangs her 'Hibernating Now' sign on her doorknob, mutes her cell and focuses her attention on chapter eighteen of *Murder on Holy Mountain*. She's less than half an hour into rewriting a gaggle of awkward sentences concerning the postmortem of the Russian Orthodox priest when her intercom buzzes. When she doesn't pick up, it sounds again. Scowling, Amy takes the receiver off the hook as she reflects that no one she wants to talk to would use the land line. A few seconds later when she hears an insistent rapping on her door she takes an exasperated breath before saying, "OK Meg, but this better be life threatening."

Looking flustered, Meg opens the door a crack and says, "Amy, I really am sorry to interrupt, but there's this weird guy with a strong accent on the phone demanding to talk to you."

"Just like the sign says, I'm alone in my cave this morning, " Amy replies looking down at the manuscript with a determination she hopes will shame Meg into prompt retreat.

"I know, I know, but when I told him you weren't available, he laughed and told me to cut the bullshit and get my fat black ass in gear. Naturally I started to object, but he cut me off and said, 'If you don't put me through, I'll take up my business with Amy's daughter with the porn star boobies.' And since I had no clue how to respond to that, here I am."

"I'm so sorry, Meg. I have no idea who it could be, but I'll deal with it. I'm sure it's nothing."

Fearing that this is a lie even as the words come out of her mouth, Amy berates herself for not heeding Tamiko's warning about the gray car as she picks up the receiver and pushes the blinking button.

"This is Amy Gashkin," she says as neutrally as possible.

"Bitch, it's been over three years, but I finally find you," the deep, harsh voice says in the accent she still occasionally hears in nightmares.

"I don't..."

"No bullshit, you know who this be. Now use mobile to call me back at 549-1976."

"What do you want? I don't..."

"Call me now, 549-1976. If you don't I bust in there and scare the hell out of darky on my way to..."

"OK, OK, I'm hanging up and calling."

Hand shaking, Amy fumbles her iPhone out of her purse and taps in the number. When, by way of answer she hears a grunt, she again demands in a voice she hopes doesn't quaver, "What do you want?"

"You know because you want it too. But, what I need now is even more important. To get out of this asshole country today I need five thousand and I need it this minute."

"I don't have that. And anyway, why..."

"Maybe your daughter with nipples showing has it, or maybe she gives me something else."

"Where are you?"

"Across street."

"I don't…"

"Listen up *puta*, I give you this one chance to get out of this easy way. So easy no one is hurt and fancy boyfriend with big house and tiny car never find out how in Amsterdam you beg for my big boy. So stand up now. Don't think, just do it."

Amy finds herself pushing back her chair, even as she tries to think of a plan to resist. "Now take mobile, go out front door, walk three blocks to bank and get me five thousand dollars," the voice barks. "Start now, I need to see you in ten seconds or I go get blondie."

"Wait, please, I don't even…I don't even know how to give you the money. And I…"

"No worry, I be there when you come out of bank. And no tricks since I be behind you every second, even in bank. Now start walking and be out of front door in ten seconds. Ten, nine…"

Even as she almost sprints past Meg at the reception desk, Amy knows she is acting foolishly. Breathless and perspiring she hesitates as she reaches the sidewalk trying to think of the best way to protect Tamiko. Just as she decides to turn back and call the police her phone sounds. Sliding the green button to the right, she tries to find the words to explain that she's changed her mind when the voice demands, "Turn right, go to corner, and then uphill to Mechanic's Bank and I never touch sexy girl over at California University. Go now."

Cursing under her breath as she heads east on Solano Avenue past a row of small shops, Amy tries as unobtrusively as possible to spot the old gray car that she now knows is driven by the huge man who'd almost killed her in Amsterdam three years before. Seeing nothing out of the ordinary, she waits in front of the Starbuck's at the corner of Colusa for the light to change. With only a few steps before she reaches the bank she tries to school her jangled brain to come up with a plan to alert the teller to her plight in a way that will result in the police responding fast enough to catch Max. Then, just as the light flashes green her phone rings again.

"Listen up, *puttana*, no games in bank. Just ask for money and get out. I be right behind you."

"But I'll have to fill out a withdrawal slip at the counter before I go to the teller."

"Bank almost empty, so this take maybe fifteen seconds. Don't try to write note or I see. Ask for fifty hundred-dollar bills. Take twenties if not enough hundreds. She have that much in drawer so no problem."

Stopping just outside the southwest door of the Mechanic's Bank as she wipes her sleeve across her sweaty brow, Amy hears herself ask, "What if Jenny or Petra asks why I need so much? It's a small branch and both tellers know me."

"When you hand over slip, smile and say you need it to buy used car for your daughter from old guy who say 'no checks.'"

Feeling as conspicuous as if she were rushing naked through an airline terminal, Amy pushes through the glass door and proceeds briskly to the four-sided kiosk at the center of the room. Seeing, to her distress, that the slot with the withdrawal slips is empty, she steps to the next bay where, to her relief, the slots are full. By the time she has scribbled down her name, account number and the amount of the withdrawal, one of the two customers at the teller's windows finishes his transaction, allowing Amy to step directly to the counter. Not sure whether Max is actually in the bank behind her, or perhaps looking through a front window, she hesitates only for a moment before placing the slip on the counter as she says, "Hi Petra, this is a big one, but I'm buying a used car for Tamiko's sixteenth from a codger who doesn't do checks."

"Not even a cashier's check?"

"I guess he thinks the bank might fail before he can cash it, but listen Petra, I'm kinda in a hurry."

"No problem. But I only have two thousand in hundreds in the drawer and maybe another thousand in twenties so I'll have to go to the safe."

"Sure, but I'm already running late."

As Amy steps away from the counter four minutes later, the bills in a business sized envelope, her phone sounds. Answering, she hears the voice growl, "Go out uphill door, I parked right there. Hurry, this be taking too long."

Desperate now to get this scary man out of her life, hopefully forever, Amy exits the bank and almost runs the twenty steps up Solano to where a gray Ford with two square headlights on each side of a massive checkerboard grill is parked diagonally in front of the beauty supply store. Thrusting the envelope into the huge beefy hand extending from the driver's side window, Amy tries to stay out of reach. But she miscalculates, allowing Max's arm to dart out and grab and twist her wrist. Feeling an electric bolt of pain shoot up her arm, Amy opens her mouth to scream.

"Act normal and you not be hurt," the huge man commands easing up on her wrist as he reaches across and takes the envelope with his other hand. Still holding Amy as if she's a tethered sparrow, he adds, "Now listen up *cipa*, and listen good. Just like Amsterdam, I need one more thing from you, which I know you excited to give me. But just in case you not ready to spread legs, I take same thing from blondie. Now walk away slow and tell nobody. I be in touch. Go."

Suddenly free, Amy lurches back so quickly she stumbles on the curb. Struggling to keep her balance, she feels a hand under her elbow. "Whoa there Miss," a wiry older man holding a Peet's coffee cup says kindly. Regaining her balance as she fumbles out her thanks, Amy turns just in time to see the Reagan-era car lumber through a yellow light at Colusa before disappearing behind a FedEx truck.

Holding her still throbbing right wrist in her left hand as if it might otherwise fall off, Amy jaywalks across Solano, unaccountably thinking that the summer sun has indeed turned the tips of Tamiko's golden brown hair blonde. Scurrying past the Wells Fargo Bank and Shoes on Solano, which she somehow registers is already displaying a variety of ankle high leather boots for the fall, she reflexively looks over her shoulder to be sure she isn't being pursued. Almost colliding with a homeless person dressed like a cabaret performer who sings out, "Get a grip lady," she finally reaches

Ensenada Street where she turns left. Running the last hundred feet to Bay's front door she bursts past an astonished Meg and down the short hall. After slamming the door to her office as if it's the entrance to hell, she collapses on the brown leather love seat in the guest corner.

A moment later when Amy hears a knock, the only response she can muster is to fumble in her purse for a tissue. She is still trying to form the words to say, 'Come in' when Ed opens the door. Seeing her crumpled on the small couch, he takes two quick steps, leans over and awkwardly tries to wrap her in his arms.

"Meg says all sorts of scary things have been going on around here today. I gather she's not exaggerating."

"Oh my god, Ed, I'm such a fool," Amy says, half sitting up. "I gave him money because he promised to use it to leave the country and not hurt Tami even though I know he's a liar. But listen, I have to find Tami right now. She could be in danger. We need to get over to Cal."

"Got it, and of course we'll deal with Tamiko first thing. But Amy, before I can help, you need to tell me what's happening. Just a one-paragraph plot summary, not the novel. And what about your arm? Are you OK?"

"I'm so embarrassed. I went to the bank and gave Max five thousand dollars. I can't believe I was so stupid."

"It's just money. If Tamiko really is in danger, you need to focus. Here, blow your nose," he adds, thrusting a rumpled handkerchief at her.

"You know Friday, when I was trying to tell you what happened in Amsterdam, about this guy in my past?" Amy asks, still breathless from crying.

"Sure, when Tamiko came home early and interrupted us."

"Somehow I just knew I needed to tell you…."

"OK, but let's not worry about that," Ed interrupts, pulling Amy all the way upright. "It's what's happening today that's important."

"Ed, what I'm trying to tell you is it's the same man. He calls himself Max and I met him when I was desperate and alone in Amsterdam. I'm very ashamed to say that I got drunk and we had sex. There's a lot more to the story including my losing my baby on the flight to India, but the important part is that he tried to kill me. And just five minutes ago he threatened to rape Tami and..."

"Let me guess, Max is the guy in the gray car who Tamiko spotted last week," Ed interrupts.

"Yes, which means he's been following me at least since then. For sure he knows all about Tamiko and you, even where you live. Fuck. Ed, what am I going to do?" Amy asks, disentangling herself from Ed as she stands.

"I hope you mean what are we going to do, because for starters, you're not in this alone. If I'm remembering right, Tamiko is at Cal doing Physics so she should be safe for now. But we obviously can't cope with this on our own. So, let's head to the police station downtown, which will be quicker than asking them to come here. I'll drive while you call ahead."

Even though Ed's car is parked in the small back lot, he steers Amy out through the front entrance, where he tells Meg and several others who are clustered in an anxious pod by her desk that Amy has received a scary threat and they are on the way to the Berkeley Police building to report it. Using his most emphatic voice, he adds that any danger is not remotely work-related and there should be no peril to Bay employees. But just to be extra safe, the doors should be kept locked and the police called immediately should anyone spot a large thirty-year-old American car in the neighborhood.

Five minutes later as Ed turns left on Marin and then in two blocks, right on Martin Luther King to head south a mile to the Berkeley Police headquarters, Amy finds their number and presses the call icon. As they wait for the light at Rose Street, she's relieved when a live person answers. Breathlessly reporting that she was attacked, and that her daughter may be in immediate danger of being abducted and raped, she's told to park in the white zone in front of the police building where they will be expecting her at the main entrance. A minute later while waiting impatiently for the long signal at University Avenue to change, Amy texts Tamiko.

"*Scary gray car emergency. Serious. Don't leave class alone. Ed & I are heading to the police station. All safe. Will call soon.*"

When Amy and Ed come through the front door of the Berkeley Police station's two-story glass lobby, they are met by a tall woman in her early 30's with short brown hair. Wearing gray slacks and an ice blue long sleeved blouse that echoes her light blue eyes, she extends her hand as she says, "Ms. Gashkin, I'm Sergeant Dana Helickson. I doubt you'll remember, but we met briefly a couple of times as part of the investigation into the tragic death of your husband."

Still experiencing too much discomfort in her right wrist to shake the officer's extended hand, Amy instead clutches it with the fingers of her left hand as she replies, "This is Ed Crane, the publisher of Bay Books and I guess you would also say, my um, well, my friend."

"I hope so," Ed says with a grin as he shakes hands with the sergeant.

Taking the steps from the lobby to the second floor two at a time, the sergeant waits at the top until Amy and Ed catch up. Then leading them into a small, spare interview room she motions to two straight-backed metal chairs at the near side of the oblong table. "Ms. Gashkin and her friend, Mr. Crane, are here," she says after pushing a button on the desk phone.

Within a few seconds an ebony-skinned man of about forty, with a shaved head enters and introduces himself as Lieutenant Melvin Ramsey. Taking a seat next to Sergeant Helickson on the other side of the table from Amy and Ed, he holds his body almost ostentatiously erect as he says, "Ms. Gashkin, I understand you've had a bad fright this morning and that you believe your daughter may be in danger. To save time, please start with the end of the story—that is, what happened this morning and why you think your daughter may be in harm's way. You can fill in the background later. Also, I need to tell you this conversation is being recorded."

"I'll try," Amy says as she takes in the Lieutenant's starched white shirt and lemon yellow tie with black spots, which on closer inspection turn out to be tiny anchors. Guessing that he came by his exaggerated military bearing in the navy, Amy squares her shoulders and begins, "At a few minutes after nine o'clock this morning I got a call from a very scary, very large, European man who three-plus years ago, tried to kill me in Amsterdam. Max, as he calls himself, told me he needed five thousand dollars to leave the country. If I didn't get it for him immediately he threatened to either harm me or my teenage daughter, Tamiko. But if I walked to the bank and got him the money it would be the last I would hear of him."

"I hope you're not going tell us you gave him the money?" Lieutenant Ramsey asks, not bothering to disguise his displeasure.

"It was obviously a stupid decision. But, yes, I was so frightened he would harm my daughter that I walked, almost ran I guess, from Bay Books on Ensenada to the Mechanics Bank on Solano where I withdrew five thousand in hundreds and twenties. Max was waiting for me out front in what my daughter says is an old Ford, anyway a big American car from thirty or forty years ago, parked diagonally in front of the beauty supply store between iScream and Peets. But listen, I'm worried about Tamiko, who's at a class at Cal. When I handed Max the money he twisted my wrist, this one obviously," Amy says, wincing slightly as she raises her right hand. "That's when he said he needed just one more thing from me and if I didn't give it to him, he would take it from my daughter. And since he's been stalking us…"

"Sorry to interrupt, Ms. Gashkin. Although it may seem obvious to you, we need to ask what you think the words, 'one more thing' meant?" Sergeant Helickson asks as she glances at her watch.

"Sex, obviously, and just as obviously Max threatened to rape my daughter."

"Did you have a consensual sexual relationship with this man Max in Amsterdam?" Lieutenant Ramsey asks, still sitting so erect that Ed wonders if it hurts.

"We can't be wasting time on this," Amy says, beginning to stand, "If you aren't going to help, I'll go up to Cal myself."

As Ed starts to say, "Lieutenant, I don't think…" Sergeant Helickson interrupts in a surprisingly authoritative voice, "Lieutenant, we know Ms. Gashkin, from when her husband, Yuri Gashkin, a Cal professor, was killed by that truck three Aprils ago on Shattuck. In addition, she and Mr. Crane work at a respected local publishing company, so…"

"Please sit down," Lieutenant Ramsey says, motioning peremptorily at Amy. "Have you contacted your daughter? And how do you spell her first name?"

Still standing, Amy replies, "Although it's pronounced as if it starts like the boy's name TOM, it's spelled T-A-M-I-K-O. I texted, but I haven't heard back so I'm guessing her phone is muted. After class I think she plans to meet her friend Alec Burns, who also has a class that ends at eleven, at which point…"

"Alec might even know the license number of the car," Ed interrupts. "And, also, Lieutenant, I think we'll get further, faster if you take us seriously and protect Tamiko."

"Fine. Ms. Gashkin, will you please sit down and try to call your daughter again and if you have his number, this Burns guy too," Lieutenant Ramsey says, leaning into the word 'please' as if it were two feet long.

"Fine," Amy says, doing her best imitation of the Lieutenant's annoyed tone as she perches on the edge of her chair and taps Tamiko's number. When, after a few rings, she's sent to voicemail, she holds the phone out so all can hear.

"What class is she in?" Lieutenant Ramsey asks.

"Physics with Professor Spurgeon. I don't know the building or room," Amy replies quickly. Then, as if surprised her attempt to jog her memory actually succeeds she adds, "LeConte Hall. I think she told me the lecture is in LeConte up near the Campanile."

Moving towards the door, Sergeant Helickson says, If I remember right, she has the same last name as you?"

"Yes."

"OK, I'll contact the campus force and ask them to pull her out of class. What about her friend, where is he?"

"I have no idea," Amy replies, relaxing slightly now that things are in motion. "But I have his cell," she continues as she locates Alec's number under 'Recents' and enters a text that says, *"Call me ASAP—gray car emergency."*

"Just so you know," Ed says, "Amy thinks Alec, who Tamiko just met, is too old for her daughter, so there's a little tension."

Amy is just starting to react to this when her phone rings. Glancing at the display to see it's Alec, she puts the phone on speaker as she says, "Alec, Ed and I are at the Berkeley Police station downtown. It turns out Tami was right about the man in the gray car following us. I'll explain later, but the important thing now is whether you got the plate number?"

"Hang on, I'm still walking out of class," Alec murmurs. Then, after a short pause, "OK, I'm in the hall. But, sorry, I only got the first part, which I think is 6RT and then maybe X. But since I was pretty far back I'm not positive about any of it. Or, I guess I should say that I'm reasonably sure about the 6RT, but a lot less so about the X."

Scribbling the number in a small notebook, Lieutenant Ramsey picks up the receiver on the interview room phone, pushes a button, and begins speaking in a low voice. Switching off the speaker on her iPhone just as Sergeant Helickson steps back into the small room, Amy says, "Alec, hold on a second, things are a little upside down here."

"A Cal officer is already on the way to LeConte to pick up your daughter and bring her over," Sergeant Helickson says. "Now what about her friend? Do we need him down here? And what's his name again?"

"Burns, Alec Burns. Amy's talking to him now and yes, we do," Ed answers firmly, giving Amy a 'don't argue' look.

"OK then, tell Mr. Burns to go to the basement at the back side of Sproul Hall where the Cal force is located. We'll ask them to pick him up after they collect Tamiko," the Sergeant says, reclaiming her chair.

As Amy starts to relay these instructions, Alec says, "I heard that. I'll be at Sproul in three minutes."

No sooner has Amy ended the call than her phone rings. "Tell me you're safe," she says by way of answer.

"Fine, but Mom, what's going on? Are you and Ed OK? And what happened with the man in the LTD? There's a policewoman here, but she won't tell me anything."

"I'm OK and so is Ed. But it turns out you were very right about the guy in the car being dangerous. We're at the Berkeley Police Department on MLK and the Cal officer is going to bring you here, picking up Alec on the way."

"Lec, really? Does he know what's going on? I mean how come no one tells..."

"Your phone was off, but listen sweetie, Lieutenant Ramsey, who's here with Ed and me, wants to ask you a quick question so I'm putting him on."

"Hello, Ms. Gashkin. Mr. Burns gave us a partial license number for the car in question. Can you describe it, the car that is?"

"1982 Ford LTD, gunmetal gray with four doors and these weird double headlights. The paint is so oxidized it looks kinda like an old tank. And, the front right fender is dented pretty noticeably over the wheel."

After again picking up the office phone and relaying this information, Lieutenant Ramsey turns back to Amy. Before he can say anything, Ed says, "Lieutenant, Sergeant, before Tamiko and Alec get here, can we clear the air a little? I'm guessing that Amy and I showing up here with what probably seems like a wild story has not inspired confidence, especially given that Amy tried to cope with Max herself instead of calling you immediately. But as Sergeant Helickson said, Amy and I are, for lack of a better term, reputable citizens and we would like to be taken seriously until it's shown that we're flakes, which is not going to happen."

Sitting impassively for a long moment Lieutenant Ramsey finally says, "Agreed." Then turning back to Amy he asks, "Ms. Gashkin, now that your daughter is safe, can you please fill in some background? Who is this man you say extorted five thousand dollars from you this morning and attacked you several years ago?"

"Neither my daughter, nor certainly Alec Burns who I've only met once, knows anything about what I'm about to tell you and I'd like to keep it that way until I have a chance to tell Tamiko in my own way," Amy says, doing her best to mimic Lieutenant Ramsey's inquisitorial stare.

"Agreed, a second time."

"OK, then I'll try to shorten a much longer story, but it won't make sense unless I go back to spring 2013."

"Do your best to get to the point," Lieutenant Ramsey replies with a sigh that makes it clear that from long experience he doubts this will be anytime soon.

"After my husband Yuri was killed I was in a bad way. With the help of family and my closest friends, I hung in for the few weeks it took to arrange a memorial service, but I wasn't really coping. Because of Yuri's famous book and the awful way he died the media was all over the story, which just made things more difficult for Tami and me. I became fearful about even going to go to the market for fear of running into a chorus line of people, many of them perfect strangers, telling me how sorry they were. Finally Yuri's parents, who'd come out to help with the memorial service, suggested that I go stay with my best friend Gretchen in Amsterdam for ten days while they cared for Tamiko in Connecticut. Since Yuri and I already had tickets to go to Europe that next July, and despite worrying that I was abandoning my daughter, I moved up the date on my ticket and went. My friend Gretchen had just gone through a miserable divorce so the idea was that we could be, I don't know how to say it, except maybe, two damaged birds trying to...to..."

"Help each other through a difficult time," Sergeant Helickson offers, kindly.

"Yes, but unfortunately it didn't work out that way, since I'd barely arrived when Gretchen got a call more or less ordering her to attend a meeting in Frankfurt. Of course she was upset about abandoning me, but by then I'd figured out there was more to her job at the embassy than cultural affairs, so there was nothing to be done. I tried to fill in the time doing touristy things until Gretchen returned, but I was so miserable that, well, I drank too much, which isn't hard for me since I turn pink after half a glass of chardonnay. And that's when I met this guy who called himself Max—the man who just hurt me—in a bar. I'm afraid the rest is beyond embarrassing, but Max, who is the size of an NFL linebacker gone slightly to seed, bought me drinks, pretended to care about my tale of woe and just sort of, well, enveloped me. This would be just one more sad story of a foolish woman being swept off her feet by a good-looking loser except for the fact that he tried to kill me."

"No hurry now, Amy," Sergeant Helickson says as she gives Lieutenant Ramsey a stare that dares him to disagree. "Would you be more comfortable if Lieutenant Ramsey and Mr. Crane stepped out of the room?"

"No, no, it's OK, really," Amy says, cradling her right wrist in her left hand. "As you have probably guessed, the night we met in the bar ended with us going back to my hotel room where we eventually had brief, awkward sex."

"So far all of this was consensual, right?" Lieutenant Ramsey asks.

"Yes, but the thing is that we didn't immediately have sex when we got to my room. Things got weird when Max insisted that..."

"We don't need every detail, Amy," Lieutenant Ramsey interrupts, tapping the fingers of his right hand on the table. "Especially since you already indicated that you were not forced into..."

"Let's be a little patient Lieutenant," Sergeant Helickson injects, "Ms. Gashkin has had a tough morning."

Registering the lieutenant's dismissive shrug, Amy continues. "The next morning when Gretchen called to say that instead of returning to Amsterdam she'd been ordered to Rome, I felt totally lost. I wandered aimlessly around Amsterdam hating myself and for a moment, even considered jumping off a bridge until I immediately thought about what that would do to my daughter." Pausing for a moment, Amy takes a few quick breaths. "So anyway, I continued to self-medicate with Xanax and a couple of glasses of wine until late in the afternoon when I crashed in my hotel room. For reasons I'll never be able to explain, except maybe as a form of self-flagellation, that evening at about eleven, I went back to the bar. Sure enough, Max was there, sitting on a barstool not far from the door. Just as on the previous night he bought me a drink and we went back to my room. And so to finally answer your question, Lieutenant, this is when and where he went berserk, put his huge hands around my neck, and began to choke me. I'm certain I would have died right then if I hadn't been able to knee him in the balls with enough force so he loosened his grip just long enough to allow me to scream. Apparently I sounded so desperate that someone in the next room not only yelled something in Dutch but also opened their door and called down to the desk. Anyway, that's when Max let go of me and pulled up his pants before running out of the room, grabbing my purse as he went."

"I'm guessing your ID was in there, which would explain how he found you over three years later," Sergeant Helickson says kindly, looking up from her notepad to make eye contact with Amy.

"Fortunately my passport and most of my cash along with my credit cards were in the room safe, but he did get my driver's license and about eighty euros."

"Was any of this reported?" Lieutenant Ramsey asks skeptically.

"Absolutely, I called the police, or I guess technically the hotel guy did. Not long after, two officers showed up and I went with them to the main police headquarters building, which was nearby. Given the whole sleazy story and how dumb I'd been, they were polite and even kind. As soon as they were done interviewing me I went back to the hotel, packed up my stuff, and took a taxi to the airport where I got on the first plane to New Delhi."

"As in India?" Sergeant Helickson says, not bothering to hide her surprise. "Really? Why there?"

"After Yuri was killed, Millie, a close friend whose partner Wendy had died very suddenly from a stroke told me that she might not have gotten through it if she hadn't gone to this amazing ashram in India. I had looked into it and even got a visa and shots before deciding to go to Amsterdam to be with Gretchen. After the police were finished with me I knew there was no way I was going to stay in that hotel room by myself. Undoubtedly I wasn't thinking very clearly, but in the middle of that terrible night the ashram seemed like my only refuge."

. . . . .

As the recent-model Toyota Prius with the California State Seal on it's door pulls up to the southeast corner of Sproul Hall, Tamiko spots Lec standing near the gate marked 'Police Personnel Only'. Almost leaping out of the car, she runs towards him as if they are lovers who have been separated by a war. Briefly returning her enthusiastic hug, Alec steps back to hold Tamiko at arms length, "What's going on? Tell me," he asks impatiently.

"Hugging me isn't good enough?" Tamiko asks, a grin lighting her face.

Ignoring this, Alec says, "When your mom called me she was upset. All I really understood is that something scary happened earlier this morning involving the driver of the old gray car and that she and Ed are at the city police station."

"I barely talked to Mom so I'm in the dark except that whatever went down she and Ed are fine. So let's get over there and find out what the fuss is about."

. . . . .

"How should we handle things when Tamiko and Alec arrive?" Ed asks, looking at Amy as he extends his hands, palms up.

"Since Alec Burns and my daughter hardly know each other and I'm determined to keep it that way," Amy says, looking from one officer to the other, "I don't want to discuss what I just told you in front of him. Also, I wonder if either of you has a few aspirin or Tylenol?"

"I have a bottle of ibuprofen in my desk, if that works," Sergeant Helickson replies.

When Amy nods, the tall, pale woman stands. "When they arrive we'll focus on what they might know about the car and driver," Lieutenant Ramsey says. "But Ms. Gashkin, I think you'll have to sketch in a little background about Amsterdam or they'll have no context. In the meantime, who is this Alec Burns?"

"He and Tamiko met a week ago at Cal where they're both taking summer classes. She's going on sixteen and he's a twenty-two-year-old Cal junior—which is the end of the story as far as I'm concerned."

"But Penal Code Section 261-5 notwithstanding, perhaps not as far as they are concerned," Lieutenant Ramsey says dryly just as Sergeant

Helickson returns with a glass of water and a bottle of pills.

After fumbling her attempt to open it with her left hand, Amy hands the bottle to Ed, who twists off the cap and shakes two round orange pills into Amy's extended hand. Then, when she doesn't close it, two more. As Amy reaches for the water, the intercom buzzes. Picking up, Lieutenant Ramsey listens for a moment before saying, "Wait three minutes and bring them in."

Hanging up, he turns to Amy and says, "Ms. Gashkin, to understand what we are dealing with we'll need to look into this further, but in the meantime, it seems obvious your wrist needs attention."

"No bones are sticking out, so let's do the important things first," Amy replies. "When we're done I can can get my wrist looked at. But since I only had a coffee this morning I'm going to need to eat something soon or I'm likely to tip over."

"When we've talked with Mr. Burns why don't we break for an early lunch," Sergeant Helickson says, "that way you can talk to your daughter while we check on a few things."

. . . . .

When Tamiko, followed closely by Alec, enters the interview room, she goes immediately to her mom and leans over to give her a hug. Twisting in her seat to return the hug, Amy flinches when she bumps her right wrist on Tamiko's shoulder.

"Oh my god, Mom. Is your arm OK? What happened?"

Not giving Amy a chance to answer, Lieutenant Ramsey pulls his eyes away from Tamiko's long shapely legs as he says, "Your mother's wrist will be looked at soon, but in the meantime we need your help. This is Sergeant Helickson and I'm Lieutenant Ramsey. Please take a seat, both of you. This morning a man allegedly attacked Ms. Gashkin, after extorting a considerable sum of money and threatening her. Ms. Gashkin tells us that he's someone she met briefly when she was in Europe several years ago. Right now we are focusing on apprehending the suspect who apparently calls himself Max. We've put out an alert for a 1982 Ford LTD with a tag that begins 6RTX, or anything close. Now is there something else either of you can tell us? For example, Tamiko, when did you see this car and why did you notice it?"

"The first time was last Wednesday afternoon near where we live on Francisco Street, west of McGee. When I saw it again, in our neighborhood and maybe also once over by Bay Books on Ensenada, I told Mom. That would have been Thursday. Then, when I spotted it again I…"

"I'm still not quite following," Sergeant Helickson interrupts as she looks up from a pad where she's been scribbling a note. "Like every block in Berkeley, yours is over-stuffed with cars, some quite old, so why did you focus on this one?"

"To keep me safe when I was small, Dad trained me to pay attention to the vehicles around me, especially odd or out-of-place ones. I have a good memory so it became a habit. But in this situation it wasn't hard since in our neighborhood, seeing a thirty-four-year-old Ford is a once-in-a-decade experience."

"Did you see the driver?"

"Not really. The first time I noticed the Ford and before I was really paying close attention, I think someone was slumped down in the driver's seat wearing a black knit cap. Friday when I saw it for the third time, I could see the driver was big, but I couldn't see his face. Sunday, when the car took off just as Alec and I returned from pitching it was obvious that the driver was large, probably very large, and wearing something blue."

After getting Alec's full name, contact information, and glancing at his student I.D., Lieutenant Ramsey stares at him for a long moment before asking what he has to add.

"Not much, since I'm not a car guy. All I can tell you is that after pitching practice when we got back to Tamiko's house on Sunday a little after five, she asked me, insisted really, that I try to get the license plate of this old car that had just pulled away from the curb a few houses up the street. Although I felt a little foolish I did as she asked. But before I really got going the car had already crossed McGee heading east towards Grant where it turned left. I doubt I would have seen anything if there hadn't been an older person slowly crossing the street near the corner of Delaware, which forced it to slow down before again turning left. That allowed me to get close enough to see the first three or four digits."

"And the driver?"

"I sort of saw him from the side when the car turned left on Delaware, but, remember I was pretty far back and concentrating on the plate. So, I'd be in danger of making it up, if I tried to say anything more specific than Tamiko just did about his being big and wearing a bright blue shirt. Except for one more thing that is—he had an oversized watch on his left wrist, you know, one of those bling metal things they sell at flea markets or on the streets of…"

"Actually, from this morning I can confirm that the watch was huge and mostly silver with a gold-colored dial," Amy interrupts.

Lieutenant Ramsey leans forward to speak when the phone buzzes. This time Sergeant Helickson picks up, listens for a minute and says, "Thanks, good job." Hanging up she says, "The headline is we've got the car. It was abandoned in that lot at the Marina across from Skates restaurant. You were only one year off, Tamiko, it's a 1983 Ford LTD Crown Victoria that was reported stolen from a used car dealer, slash junk yard, in Hayward early last week. We found it because of a call from a guy who was making a sales call at Skates. When he returned to the parking lot twenty minutes ago he saw that his 2011 white Toyota Camry was gone. The officer who responded to the stolen car call spotted the Ford a few spaces down."

"I wonder if this guy—did someone call him Max?—I wonder if he switched the plates? That is, put the 6RTX plates on the Toyota," Tamiko says. "I mean he wouldn't know that Alec had seen them, would he?"

"That was my thought as well," Lieutenant Ramsey said looking at Tamiko and smiling for the first time that morning. "Since he would guess that the theft of the Toyota would be reported quickly he'd want to dump those plates pronto."

"Sorry to rain on you guys' parade," Sergeant Helickson says with a smile, "but I was just told that the 6RT plates are still on the Ford, so apparently Max was in too much of a hurry to make the switch."

"Which means you just have to find the stolen Toyota with its original plates," Ed says, as if this is as easily done as spoken.

"Mr. Crane, perhaps you should leave the policing to us," Sergeant Helickson says gently. "But just so you know, unlike the old Crown Vic, Berkeley is dripping with five-year-old Japanese sedans. Also, remember that over any five year period, all Toyotas, and for that matter, most sedans look pretty similar at a distance. So even though the owner said that there was a piece of silver duct tape covering a crack in the right headlight, this amounts to trying to spot one car out of at least several thousand. And of course, even that assumes that Max is still in Berkeley, which I'd bet against."

Waiting a beat to see if Ed will reply, Lieutenant Ramsey says, "There you have it. Before we break for lunch, is there anything else useful anyone wants to tell us? Tamiko? Mr. Burns?"

As Tamiko shrugs, Alec asks, "I wonder if you'll need me much longer? I have a lab at one o'clock and I'd hate to miss it since the final is Friday."

"Not a problem, you and Tamiko are free to go. And Mr. Crane, the same applies to you. But Ms. Gashkin, if you are up to it, we'd like to finish this interview immediately after lunch including possibly having you work with one of our people to develop a sketch."

"What about safety in the meantime? Max is obviously dangerous," Ed asks, real concern in his voice.

"Mr. Crane, based on what we know so far, that may be more obvious to you than it is to us. He may have been boasting more than threatening this morning and already be heading out of town with the money Ms. Gashkin foolishly handed over."

"Or, he may be sitting across the street in his stolen car waiting to attack Amy or Tamiko, whoever comes out of this building first," Ed replies, not trying to hide his annoyance.

"Tamiko, what are your plans for the rest of the afternoon?" Sergeant Helickson inquires.

"Hopefully getting something to eat with Mom. Then I'd planned to work at Bay until four or five before pitching with Ed." Seeing that Lieutenant Ramsey looks quizzical, she adds, "I play fastpitch softball at Berkeley High and on a club team in the summer."

"Ed, if you need to catch up on work this afternoon, I can hang with Tamiko after my lab," Alec says.

"That would be great Alec, thanks. To say the least, this has turned out to be an overfilled day," Ed says, glancing at his watch.

"Fine, we'll have someone drive Tamiko to Bay Books after lunch unless she has an Uber account," Lieutenant Ramsey says. "Then, Ms. Gashkin, when we finish with you, we'll send you wherever you want to go to get your wrist looked at. Tamiko, what time will you be done pitching?" he asks, as he grips the sides of his chair with both hands and slides it back eight inches.

"If we start at five I should be home around six-fifteen assuming Alec drives me."

"And can you also be available at that time, Mr. Crane?" Lieutenant Ramsey asks, standing.

"Sure."

"Fine, either Sergeant Helickson or I will stop by Francisco Street at six-fifteen to update you. By then, perhaps, we'll have a better idea as to how serious a threat this Max is."

. . . . .

At eleven forty-five Amy and Tamiko walk east on Allston Way along the busy north side of Berkeley High, which, with its 3,500 students is larger than many boutique colleges. Continuing across Milvia in front of Berkeley's graceful post office, its facade noteworthy for being influenced by Brunelleschi's fifteenth-century Florentine Foundling Hospital, they soon reach Shattuck Avenue. Turning right on Berkeley's busiest commercial thoroughfare, they continue a block to Bancroft. It was here that three years and almost five months ago, Yuri Gaskin died early on a Saturday morning while listening to *The Goldfinch* by Donna Tartt on his iPhone. Apparently Yuri was crossing the four-lane street on his way to the Berkeley Y, when the light changed against him and he stopped on the median strip next to a light pole. A few seconds later for reasons that have never been officially determined he stepped backwards into the northbound traffic lane immediately in front of a beer truck going about 25 miles per hour and died instantly.

Because it was 7:03 a.m., except for the traumatized truck driver, only an elderly, nearsighted woman heading for the bus stop at Shattuck and Allston, witnessed the accident. She reported that a large black SUV speeding south in Shattuck's center lane suddenly veered into the turn lane that bordered the spot where Yuri was standing, before swerving back into the through lane and disappearing towards Oakland. The BPD theorized that, caught up as he was in listening to his story, Yuri had instinctively stepped back when he looked up to see the SUV bearing down on him.

"I never come here," Amy says quietly.

"I do. Sometimes I even go out on the median by the pole and say a prayer for Dad."

"Sweetie, that scares me," Amy says, turning to look up at her much taller daughter. "Please tell me you won't do that anymore. And anyway, aren't you the one who's always going on about Christianity being a medieval superstition?"

"Mom, it's not like I'm praying to some old dude behind a cloud," Tamiko replies impatiently. "Just a few words to whatever—the universe maybe—to wish Dad well. And hey, it isn't really dangerous. Like, it's such a wide street, when the light changes people stop on the median all the time."

"Well, it gives me the creeps. Can't you pray to the cosmos at the lovely spot up in Tilden where we spread his ashes? But we need to get a move on, the lights green."

"Mom, it's not a big deal," Tamiko says, following her mom across Shattuck. "How about I just promise not to stop out there any more?"

"Thank you. I don't think I could stand it if…"

"Mom, I get it," Tamiko interrupts, touching her mom on the elbow.

A few minutes later, mother and daughter are seated in Gather at the corner of Oxford and Allston where, to keep their focus on the matter at hand, Tamiko decides not to point out that she's sitting on a way cool bench made of recycled leather belts. After they each order a cup of butternut squash soup plus a grilled cheese sandwich to split, Tamiko notices that her mom is again cradling her right wrist with her left hand. "Shouldn't we save this talk until after we get you to the emergency room?"

"Tami, I'm fine, or at least fine enough to make it another hour or two. Right now I need to explain some important things before I lose my courage."

Resisting the urge to correct her name, Tamiko nods.

"When your dad was killed I was pregnant."

"Really? Oh my god, Mom, no," Tamiko says, her hands flying up in front of her face as if trying to fend off an attack.

"When I missed my period I got a drugstore pregnancy test and tested positive. I told your dad the night before he died. That next Monday I planned to go to my gynecologist to confirm the good news and then we were going to tell you."

"Oh Mom, I don't…"

"Let me finish before I start bawling. Anyway, I'm sure you remember how awful the next few weeks were with our pictures in the newspapers, on TV and everywhere online and all those people calling, texting, and someone even leaving flowers in the front yard. In life your dad never seemed that famous, but given his New Yorker piece, and the great success of his book, I guess that…"

"At school, at sports, every place really," Tamiko interrupts, "I mean, it was like I was living in the world's most transparent fishbowl, not to mention having to sit there and listen to all those crying people I didn't even know go on and on for the memorial service." Leaning back to give the waiter more room to serve the soup, she is about to continue when Amy says, "Your dad was such a charming, sweet, talented guy that much of it was genuine, which of course didn't make coping any easier. Anyway, that week and the next, all I could think about was that if I told people I was pregnant, it would multiply the wall of grief we faced by a factor of ten."

"Probably more like a hundred. Oh Mom, I get it. I…"

"Tami, Tamiko, unfortunately there's a lot more, so please let me get to it. I need to start by apologizing for not telling you all this sooner, but at the time you were too young and, in the last year when you weren't, I just never got up the courage. Not to sugarcoat anything, after the memorial service I decided I had to end my pregnancy and somehow get away from Berkeley to do it. So when Vera and Stepan volunteered to care for you, I grabbed at the chance to visit my friend Gretchen in Amsterdam and find a clinic over there. But on the long overnight flight I changed my mind. Although I knew that having the baby on my own would probably be the most difficult thing I'd ever do in this life, I also realized that I owed it to your dad to see it through."

"And you had already gone through something similar having me at nineteen."

"When you were born Yuri and I were together so there was really no comparison. But for sure, the thought that you would be there to support me every step of the way, helped me make the right decision," Amy says with a smile so genuine that Tamiko knows that her mom is speaking from the heart.

"But there was never a baby, so…"

"Have a little patience, and I'll tell you the whole miserable story right down to how it connects to what happened today. When I arrived in Amsterdam Gretchen picked me up and took me back to the world's smallest studio apartment, hardly bigger than a closet really. She'd grabbed it a few months after she split from Frank and was waiting to start her lease on a real apartment. To give me a place to sleep she had bought this cute futon that pretty much covered her whole floor so you had to walk over it to go to the mini-bathroom. We ate take-out pizza, and despite my being pregnant, drank a little wine while I cried on her shoulder. Gretchen was just telling me for at least the tenth time how relieved she was that I was going to keep the baby when her phone rang. She listened for a moment and then insisted to whoever was calling that someone else would have to go since she was caring for a friend who had just lost her husband. But, apparently, no excuse was good enough and when she hung up she turned to me and said, 'Amy, I hate myself but I have to go to Frankfurt right now as in I need to throw some things in my roller bag and be out front in fifteen minutes.'

"I was so staggered by this that I actually said, 'Gretchen you can't abandon me!'"

"Oh my god, Mom, what did she say?"

"That although her office was at the embassy she didn't really work there. But due to the bible's worth of secrecy pledges she'd signed she couldn't tell me more except that the safety of many people could be involved. So of course the first thing I blurted out was 'Jesus Gretchen, do you work for the CIA or something like that?' After a long pause she replied, 'Let's leave it at something like that.'"

"Oh Mom, things weren't getting easier were they? So what happened?"

"Well, in the short term there was no problem since I was so tired I slept until ten a.m. the next day. Because Gretchen's place really was too tiny for two, I bustled around and found a budget hotel nearby and then pulled my roller bag over there. In the afternoon, like any conscientious tourist, I went to the Van Gogh Museum and even kind of enjoyed it. In short I was coping reasonably well until late that afternoon when Gretchen called from Frankfurt to say that the threat had escalated and that she had to go to Rome. Of course she was extremely upset to be gone another day, but was at least happy I was in her cozy place."

"You didn't tell her that you had moved to the hotel? Or had you decided to move back?" Tamiko asks, realizing she hasn't touched her soup and taking a spoonful.

"No, and no. Since I'd paid in advance for two nights at the hotel and had already dragged my stuff over there, I decided to stay, which as it turned out, was the first of a series of bad mistakes in judgment. At this point it was around five-thirty in the middle of May and it wasn't going to get dark for a few more hours, so I decided to try to walk off my disappointment. I wandered around at random—along canals, over bridges, past hundreds of prosperous Dutch shops and through crowds of people until I was thoroughly tired, hungry and disoriented. Hoping to get something to eat, I made a second bad decision and went into a bar."

"Mom, I hate to interrupt, but how about making a good decision and eating a few bites of your lunch. You're the one who's starving."

"OK, got it," Amy says, finishing her soup and taking two bits of the sandwich. "So anyway, when it turned out the bar didn't serve food I sat down and ordered a couple of bags of pretzels and a glass of wine. And then, pregnancy be damned, I ordered a second glass. You know how little I can drink at the best of times and, of course, this was far from that, so the upshot was that I started crying. The bartender, who spoke English, was kind and offered to get me a cab. But when it turned out my hotel was only a few blocks away he gave me directions and I decided to walk."

Pausing to eat the last few bites of the cheese slathered bread, Amy continues, "Not taking the cab turned out to be yet another bad decision since by now it was dark and I somehow made a wrong turn and got even more lost. That's when I went into this second bar called the Hollywood of all things, which was full of guys, some of them at the back wearing leather outfits."

"Yowser, things weren't looking up."

"No."

"Wouldn't anyone help you?"

"I stood at the end of the bar hoping that the bartender would come over and do just that. But almost immediately this huge, relatively attractive guy of about forty moved over next to me, introduced himself, and asked me where I was from and whether he could help. Before I had a chance to object, he ordered me a vodka tonic and some chips, and got me talking about Yuri's death and how depressed I was. Maybe because of his big-guy way of taking charge, or perhaps because I was two-thirds drunk he reminded me a little of your dad, even though he was considerably heavier. Eventually I accepted his invitation to walk me back to my hotel, which it turned out was only two blocks away. Sweetie, I'm afraid there is no way to sugarcoat this next part. When we got there I had this moment of panic about being alone so invited him up to my room.

Even before we got out of the tiny old-fashioned elevator I realized that this was a terrible idea. Not only was I pregnant and inebriated, but it was also beginning to dawn on me that Max, as he called himself, was a pretty strange character. To save you the weird preliminaries, we eventually had what I can only describe as fairly brutish, but thankfully brief sex, after which he immediately left."

"Is this where I get to hug you?" Tamiko asks, sliding along the bench as if to stand.

"Not for quite a while yet I'm afraid, since my avalanche of mistakes is just beginning to roll down the mountain," Amy says, placing two twenties on the table as she adds, "Let's head back while I try to explain."

Leaving Gather, Amy and Tamiko cross Allston Way and fall into step heading north on Oxford Street. Waiting for a noisy truck to pass, Amy says, "In hindsight I should have left Amsterdam that next morning but Gretchen called first thing from Rome saying she hoped to fly back that evening. So, instead I went to the Rijksmuseum—basically the Dutch National Gallery—and after lunch even tried to buy you a sweater. Eventually, I went back to the hotel, took half a Xanax and half an Ambien and fell asleep. The phone call that woke me at about nine-thirty was a distraught Gretchen saying that she had been ordered to stay in Rome for at least another day. I hung in there by my miserable self until about eleven, when I made my biggest mistake by going back to the Hollywood."

"Oh Mom, I wish…"

"Sweetie, let me finish OK? Anyway, Max, who was sitting just inside the door, jumped up like an eager elephant, even introducing me to several people as if we were on a date. When I asked if we could go to a restaurant, he said they were all closed and bought me a glass of wine and a couple more bags of those dreadful chips, which I nevertheless gorged on since again I hadn't eaten since lunch. Max was again full of boisterous charm and what can I say except that on that particular evening bad company seemed better than being alone, so eventually we went back to my room. But this time instead of having sex Max tried to choke me. I was very lucky that I was able to scream."

"But how could you scream if someone that big was choking you? And then what happened?"

"My only good decision of the night was to raise my knee as hard as I could. Luckily, I caught him in the balls, which made him loosen his grip. When I screamed someone in the next room opened the door and shouted for help. At that point Max ran out grabbing my purse."

"Now I get how all of this connects to today. He got our address from your purse. Hey Mom, we turn here on Addison Street."

"Right you are as usual. Anyway, Max called this morning and demanded five thousand dollars to leave the country, the implication being that he was in some sort of criminal trouble. He threatened that if I didn't give it to him immediately, he would attack you."

"Attack me? Really?"

"Yes, and since he's apparently been following both of us he knew all about your going to Cal and even where Ed lives. Anyway, instead of calling the police I foolishly believed he'd leave if he got the money so I went over to the Mechanics Bank and withdrew it. When I handed it over he grabbed my wrist and twisted it."

"Oh my god, Mom, this is unreal—or does surreal describe it better?"

"I also need to tell you that as he held my wrist, right there in front of that beauty store next to iScream, he said, 'Now I need just one more thing. And if you don't give it to me I get it from your daughter with nipples showing.'"

"Oh my god Mom, for sure you'll never have to ask me to wear a bra again."

"I'm sorry to scare you, but I really need you to take this seriously," Amy says as the two cross to the west side of Shattuck.

"No worries there. But, like, Mom, in Amsterdam, what happened after he ran out of the hotel? I'm guessing that's when you somehow lost the baby, but..."

"Because the hotel called them, two policemen arrived and took me to their nearby headquarters where I made a statement. But I don't really know whether or how hard they looked for Max because as soon as I got back to my room, I grabbed my stuff and took a cab to the airport where I got on the first plane to India. On the flight I had terrible cramps and quite a lot of bleeding, so much that I monopolized a bathroom for half of the flight. By the time we landed in New Delhi, I was no longer pregnant."

"Oh Mom, I'm so sorry," Tamiko says putting a hand on Amy's elbow to stop her walking into the side of a silver Audi exiting the garage next to the Freight and Salvage folk club. "So I guess that's when you went to that ashram that your friend Millie talks about."

"Right. Of course I also thought about picking you up and going home, but I felt too defeated to face people. Unfortunately, when I finally dragged myself to the entrance of the ashram after that awful flight and a miserable day on the train they turned me away. In addition to not having a reservation I'm sure I looked so deranged, not to mention babbling and filthy, that they weren't being altogether unreasonable."

"Oh my god! They turned you away at the ashram? When is this story ever going to get better? What did you do?"

"Went out front on a hot and dirty street surrounded by hundreds, if not thousands of mostly desperately poor people, and began to cry. Fortunately Guru Chandra, the ashram's spiritual leader, came along and brought me back in. After asking me a few basic questions about who I was and why I was there, he turned me over to a kind woman who helped me wash, gave me something to eat and unrolled a sleeping mat for me. When I woke up, she gave me a long handled brush and a pail of water and told me that Guru wanted me to scrub the large entry hall, paying close attention to cleaning each tile perfectly."

"You're kidding? Really? I mean it sounds like something out of a hippie-dippy novel. Did any of this work?"

"Remarkably well, actually. Cliché or not, it turns out that when you fully concentrate on scrubbing a tile so it's spotless, you don't have time to think about anything else. After two days, Guru Chandra sat down on the floor beside me to ask what was really going on. I guess I started to babble because he raised a hand and told me he had all the time in the world and to start at the beginning and leave nothing out. When I finished he thanked me and assigned me to peel, slice, and chop veggies before each meal and to wash and scrub when it was over. Again, I was to pay close attention to what I was doing, and do it impeccably."

"Was this guy for real? I mean…"

"Very real. After another three days he called me into his little room, sort of a study I guess. This time he asked me what I thought I needed to do. 'Go home and do a very good job of taking care of my child one day at a time,' I immediately replied. Then he smiled as he said, 'It would be nice for you and for us if you could spend more time here, but for now you have more important tiles to scrub. Talk to our receptionist and she'll help you make reservations for tomorrow.'"

"I remember that before we met you at SFO, Vera warned me that you might still be so upset she would stay with us for a little while. Instead you thanked her and then politely suggested it would be best if she went back to Connecticut to be with Stepan. When Vera sounded surprised, you said, 'It's back to normal now, one minute, one hour, and one day at a time.'"

"Do you always remember every word?"

"I don't try to."

"The important thing is that three-plus years later we've not only survived, but are doing well."

"It seems so unfair that after all this time and when, like you say, things are great, this crazy dude Max shows up."

"Life is never fair. We both learned that the hard way and I think it's made us tougher. But, here we are back at the headquarters of the skeptical Lieutenant Ramsey and the supportive Sergeant Helickson. Before I go in I should tell you that while I fully explained my encounters with Max in Amsterdam, I didn't mention being pregnant. Call an Uber and I'll wait with you until it shows up."

Back in the interview room with Lieutenant Ramsey and Sergeant Helickson, the Lieutenant says, "Amy, I hope it's OK to drop a level of formality and call you by your first name, while on our side of the table we'll answer to Melvin and Dana." Then, as if sensing Amy's surprise at his more cordial tone, he continues, "While you were at lunch we side-stepped international protocol and called the Amsterdam Police direct. Very fortunately our call was taken by a Sergeant Toors who doesn't like red tape any better than we do. To be sure we were legit, Toors simply googled the BPD and called us back. He speaks excellent English and had a free moment so pulled up the report of what happened the night you were attacked and was able to translate it on the fly adding his own comments where context was needed."

"They were very decent to me especially since until they tracked down Gretchen, they probably thought I was a nutcase."

"I doubt that," Sergeant Helickson says, "but since time is short, let me read the fairly detailed notes I took while Melvin and I talked to Sergeant Toors. I don't know formal shorthand but my own version is accurate enough for these purposes. If there are important things you want to add or correct, please wait until I'm done."

"Fine."

"On May 8th, 2013, at 12:37 a.m., a call came from the night clerk Hendrik Dekker at the Zeeburg Hotel, a hotel catering to budget tourists and the occasional working girl a few blocks from the red light district. The clerk reported that a minute or two after hearing loud screams and some shouts coming from the second or third floor, a very large dark-haired man ran down the stairs, through the lobby, and out the door. When Dekker went upstairs to investigate, the attractive Chinese female in her mid-20's who occupied room 311 hysterically claimed that the man had tried to strangle her showing him red marks on her neck to prove it."

"So far, he's wrong about my age and nationality."

"I thought you were going to save your comments until the end," Lieutenant Ramsey says, sounding annoyed.

"Right, got it, please go on," Amy replies, raising her palms slightly in an effort to appear contrite.

Looking down at her notes Sergeant Helickson takes a moment to find her place. "Two officers on patrol nearby were immediately sent to

COMING OF AGE IN BERKELEY

the hotel where they escorted the alleged victim, a Mrs. Amy Gashkin of Berkeley, California, USA to our central station. Mrs. Gashkin reported that a consensual sexual encounter with a man named Max turned ugly when he tried to strangle her. Mrs. Gashkin also told us she was visiting a friend in Amsterdam who worked at the American Embassy as a cultural attaché who was currently out of town. When, despite the late hour, we got in touch with Ms. Gretchen Symes in Rome, she assured us that Mrs. Gashkin was a reliable person who she was sure had given us a trustworthy report. As a result, at 1:45 a.m. we issued an alert to pick up the man identified as Max for questioning.

To explain why there is now a substantial time gap in the report, Lieutenant Toors explained that by the next day, when no one fitting Max's description had been apprehended, the incident would normally have dropped from their priority list, replaced by more pressing police concerns including the misadventures of that day's tourists. But because of the embassy connection a decision was made to learn more about Max, which meant that Officer Dijkstra was dispatched to the Hollywood Bar the next evening to talk to the bartender and any regulars who might have encountered Max. What follows is my version of Sergeant Toors reading Dijkstra's report.

"May 8, 8:00 p.m.: I interviewed three regulars (names and addresses attached) plus the bartender, Marten Hoff, at the Hollywood Bar just off Leidseplein Square. They reported that a man matching Mrs. Gashkin's description of Max had begun coming into the bar about ten days previously. Speaking broken, but effective Dutch he claimed to be Francisco from Lisbon. Then after a few days, he told people to call him Max and that he was from the Calabria region of Southern Italy. Because the man was huge and frequently talked about the many fights he had been in, people were wary, probably even a little afraid, of him. Max also frequently bragged about being a killer ladies' man, usually accompanied by lurid details about one or another of his conquests. As it happened, all four men were present on May 6th, about 10 p.m., when a slim, attractive Asian female, maybe a grad student, Bartender Hoff thought, entered the bar alone looking a little 'out of it' or 'stoned' or 'lost' depending on the observer. Max immediately moved to the next stool and began to chat her up in surprisingly decent English. Although no one was close enough to hear this conversation, all claim they were concerned that somehow Max seemed to be using his good looks, fake charm, and vodka to seduce her. Concern turned to worry when, after forty-five minutes, Max followed the attractive woman out the door, turning back at the last moment to lewdly pump his fist.

"Fast forward now to the next evening. Again according to Hoff, at around 11:00 o'clock, Max was in the process of bragging about what an unbelievable fuck the little slant-eyed bitch from the night before had been for at least the fourth time, when in she walks, looking, if anything, more out of it than the night before. Max immediately jumps up and hugs her as if they have a date and even politely introduces her to a couple of people. They hang out for a while, but after she says no to a second drink, they again take off. But here the story takes a big turn. Less than an hour later Max comes charging back into the Hollywood and demands that bartender Hoff hand over the gym bag he's stashed behind the bar. When Hoff does Max runs out without another word to anyone."

"OK Amy, that's the meat of it," Lieutenant Ramsey says. "Our new friend Sergeant Toors adds that because the Amsterdam Police are pretty good at turning up people like Max, the fact that they didn't likely means that he left the Netherlands soon after attacking Mrs. Gashkin, perhaps by walking the relatively short distance to the main railway station and hopping onto an international train. It would have been possible to examine all the video shot by surveillance cameras in the station, but by this time Mrs. Gashkin had left the country and the embassy connection notwithstanding, interest in Max petered out."

When Lieutenant Ramsey finishes, Amy smiles and says, "Does the fact that this report backs up my version of events have something to do with why the three of us are on a firstname basis?"

Waiting a few beats to see if Lieutenant Ramsey is going to respond, Sergeant Helickson replies, "Amy, in the course of a week—sometimes even in one day—we hear some pretty outlandish stories. A very few turn out to be one hundred percent true, but many more are in varying degrees bogus. So when someone bursts in like you and Ed Crane did this morning, we need to take sensible steps to mitigate any immediate danger while we try to independently verify what's going on. In the meantime, experience has taught us to maintain an arms length relationship. However, when the facts do check out there is no longer any need to address each other as if we're characters in a Jane Austen novel."

For the next half-hour Amy sits with John Flores, a freelance forensic artist that the Berkeley police have called in, preferring his results to what a computer is likely to produce. Although Amy fears that her description of Max is disorganized, disjointed and vague, Flores soon produces a sketch that remarkably resembles the huge man she has encountered again that morning. When Flores finishes, Sergeant Helickson returns to say she's talked to the emergency room director at nearby Alta Bates hospital who has promised to see Amy as expeditiously as possible. "But, Amy," Sergeant Helickson adds, "there's one more thing I want to raise. While you were with John Flores, Melvin put the Chief in the picture. She pointed out that we simply don't know enough about what we're up against in this situation, or even if there's an ongoing threat to you and your daughter."

"Max is a violent criminal who tried to strangle me three years ago and has just threatened Tamiko and me, not to mention breaking my wrist a few minutes after nine this morning. Isn't that plenty to get started?"

"Amy, this guy is obviously not one of your run-of-the-mill American screwups we're used to coping with. Not only did he carefully stalk you and your daughter before extorting money, he also meticulously wiped down the Ford, so..."

"I'm not sure where this conversation is going."

"In addition to circulating Max's photo around your neighborhood, meeting later to coach you and your family about how we can help you stay safe and alerting all East Bay departments to try to apprehend him, the Chief wants to bring in a psychologist to help us better understand who we're dealing with."

"You mean profile Max? You're kidding. What good can that possibly do?"

"That term 'profile' is too dramatic for what we have in mind, but on occasion we do work with a local psychologist, Malcolm Frank, who studied forensic psychology as a kind of avocation. His insights have helped us before."

"Sorry, but I'm still not sure I follow."

"For one thing, we're trying to figure out why Max showed up here in Berkeley after all these years. Is it just about the money he extorted from you today, or is some deeper obsession somehow driving this whole drama? Even if we guess that Max came to California for some reason unrelated to you, perhaps as part of a failed criminal enterprise, and if we also assume he really does need money to leave, why not just grab the cash and go? Why put himself at risk by demanding sex?"

"So you want me to talk to this psychologist about Max's, well his weird sexual behavior, I guess."

"In a word, yes. If Max is already gone it'll be irrelevant, but if he's still around it might be important."

"I don't know. I'm suddenly exhausted. I mean I've told you everything that happened in Amsterdam and I really don't see how a psychologist can add anything."

"Maybe he can't, but we'd like to give it a try."

"OK, I guess as long as I have a chance to lie down for an hour before we meet."

"Would four-thirty work if we can get Dr. Frank to drop by your house?"

"Fine, but what if Max shows up in the meantime?"

"Amy, we don't have the resources to provide you and Tamiko twenty-four-hour protection, but if you call me when you leave the hospital I'll have an officer meet you at your home to check all is secure. Beyond that we suggest you and your daughter arrange not to be on your own until we know any danger has passed."

. . . . .

When Tamiko gets back to her corner at Bay Books a little after one, she's too agitated to concentrate on the mailing she's supposed to get out. Although she did her best to be cool with her mom earlier, the tale of what happened in Amsterdam has shocked her right down to her toenails. If the fabric of her life was ripped apart three years ago by her dad's sudden death, her mom's had been shredded. Standing, as if changing altitude might make her feel better, she wonders if she should give up pretending to work and walk home. Before she can decide, her phone sounds and Ed asks her if she can join him for a cup of tea. "Be right up," she replies, happy for the distraction.

Ed stands in a corner of his office pouring boiling water from his electric kettle into brown mugs, as Tamiko comes through the open door. Thinking again how radiantly beautiful she's looked since meeting Alec Burns he wonders if their budding romance has had the same affect on Alec. And for that matter, do Amy and I look more attractive since we fell in love six months ago. Deciding to ask Amy whether she thinks falling in love improves a person's looks, Ed kicks the door closed with his left foot as he hands Tamiko the less chipped cup. Then, motioning to one of the chairs by the small circular table, Ed says, "I won't pretend to be wise enough to say anything helpful about what happened this morning. But because we're both upset and worried, I thought it might help to hang out for a few minutes. Later I'll call a brief all-hands meeting to give everyone a very edited version of what's going on so they can take sensible safety precautions."

"I've been sitting in my cubby trying to wrap my head around what Mom went through in Amsterdam. Then, after all this time, to have this horrible guy show up like Banquo's ghost."

"If memory serves, Banquo's ghost was trying to make Macbeth feel guilty, not attack him, but I get your point. Having Max reappear must be a nightmare for Amy—for all of us, really. But even so I've been doing my best to keep today's key stories, or maybe I should say plots, separate."

"I don't follow."

"At the risk of going over-the-top editor on you, I think the most important back story is your dad's tragic death and the effect it's had on you and Amy. Learning that Amy was pregnant when your dad was killed and that she lost the baby adds a mind-bending element to this fundamental plot. But, it doesn't change the fact that you and Amy have very successfully put your lives back together, perhaps even becoming stronger and more compassionate people in the process."

"Sounds good, but you left out all of what happened to Mom in Amsterdam, not to mention this morning."

"Deliberately, because the way I see it, none of that is really part of the important story, but more like an accidental subplot Amy stumbled into. True, what happened in Amsterdam was awful and it's taken plenty of guts for Amy to put it behind her, but, once she did, it's become almost irrelevant to the arc of her life."

"Until Max showed back up. Or, is your point that what happened today is primarily about the screwed-up life story of a dangerous sociopath, and not fundamentally about Mom and me at all?"

"Exactly. And even your mom's voluntary participation in Max's plot early on, doesn't change that. Maybe it'll help you see my point if I tell you that at a weak and vulnerable moment many people, myself included, have engaged in a regrettable sexual encounter in an attempt to feel better. Normally, this is no big deal, you shrug your shoulders, resolve to be smarter next time, and move on. What you don't bargain for is that the person will try to kill you and failing that, to show up three years later to menace you and your child."

"Mom doesn't let anything or anyone get her down for long."

"Bingo! So it follows that if we can keep both of you safe until the cops catch Max, or he disappears, this won't be a big deal and we can all get on with the important plots in our lives. Incidentally, I hope you're planning to follow the BPD's advice to not go any place by yourself until we know more."

"Definitely, and thanks Ed, Mom always says that before you became the boss, you were a pretty good editor."

A few minutes after four as his review session winds down Alec texts Tamiko to confirm that he'll pick her up at Bay at four-thirty. Arriving just three minutes late, he double-parks on the quiet street, wondering if it's too rude to honk. Before he can decide, Tamiko emerges from the front door wearing her wine red Tsunami shorts and a clashing red T-shirt with an angry-looking yellow jacket over the words BHS Softball. Lugging the blue Wilson sports bag and a plastic pail filled above the brim with acid yellow softballs, she flings them into the back seat as she says, "I thought about trying to look nice for you, but this pissed-off wasp pretty much sums up how I feel."

"Did anyone ever tell you that you're way cute when you're mad?"

"Did anyone ever tell you to shut up and drive?" Tamiko replies, trying to hide her pleased grin as she settles into the passenger seat.

"Usually they tell me which way to go first."

"Let's try Codornices Park up on Euclid. Go right on Solano, and then right again at the second light on the Alameda."

"What's the word about your mom's wrist?"

"She called to say a bone is cracked, but not out of place. They gave her some painkillers and a soft cast, mostly I think to remind her to take it easy for a few weeks."

"I'm still not sure what happened this morning except that somehow a big guy named Max who your mom met in Europe a few years ago showed up, scared her into giving him a bunch of money, and hurt her in the process," Alec says as he makes a right turn at the Alameda.

"When he called this morning he threatened to rape me if Mom didn't hand over five thousand bucks. When she gave it to him he twisted her wrist and said he wouldn't leave until she gave him one more thing, or he'd take it from me."

"Nasty! No wonder the police are involved."

"Turn left at the light. Then go up Marin two blocks and take the second traffic circle spoke onto Los Angeles. At Spruce, turn right."

"Got it. You OK?"

"Mostly I feel bad for Mom. Just when everything's been going great, here comes another bean ball. The only silver lining is that she's slightly more willing to have you hang around. Like when she called from the E.R. earlier and I reminded her that I was going pitching with you, she actually said 'good'. Take the next left on Eunice, go a couple of blocks to where it T's into Euclid, turn right, then park."

When Tamiko and Alec lug the equipment across Euclid Street and up a small rise to the ball field, they're pleased to find it deserted save for several dog walkers chatting in center field while their charges dash in happy circles. Depositing the blue bag on the first-base side of the wire backstop, Tamiko turns to Alec behind her and says, "Lec, how about the day's second hug?"

"Sounds sweet, but what about…"

"C'mon, those terriers aren't going to rat us out. And today, I don't even think Mom would object."

"Somehow I doubt that," Alec replies as he tentatively puts his arms around Tamiko's strong back.

"My god Lec, I'm not your grandma," Tamiko says, wrapping her arms tightly around him as she wriggles her torso against his. Then, after thirty seconds of what Alec experiences as a surge of enveloping warmth quickly centering on his groin, she pulls back saying, "OK, I'm ready to pitch if you are."

Hmm, Alec thinks as, feeling his incipient erection gradually relax, he straps on the shin guards. "What happened to warming up?" he asks as he watches Tamiko drop the pitching rubber in the middle of the diamond and place the pail full of balls next to it.

Am I the only one who's already hot, Tamiko wonders as she says, "Put your ass on the pail and let's go."

Alec has barely positioned his glove on the outside corner when Tamiko's first pitch knocks it back a couple of inches. With his hand still stinging, he sets up on the inside corner an instant before another rocket pounds it.

"Your velocity is up today."

"I'm so amped I bet I can throw through a wall. Fastballs up, down, in and out. Your job is to move the glove, mine is to hit it."

"Riser coming," Tamiko announces halfway through the second pail. Expecting at least the first few to fly over his head as they had Sunday, Alec tenses his leg muscles, ready to leap with arm extended. Instead, Tamiko's first attempt approaches like a belt-high fastball begging to be hit, before, at the last possible second, hopping to the letters.

"First time lucky," Tamiko says, a huge smile lighting her face.

"You're beginning to find your rhythm," Alec says, the mask hiding his equally wide grin.

"I called Coach last night and he talked me through the riser delivery."

"Some coach who can figure that out on the phone."

"After twenty years working with kids who throw balls over the backstops, he only had to ask me a few questions to zero in on the problem."

After tossing fifteen mostly successful riseballs Tamiko turns to the screwball, muttering "Merde, and more merde," when her next few pitches veer so far off the plate they would have been behind a right-handed batter.

"Please note that your catcher isn't complaining about chasing a few balls while you work to get it right."

"Thanks, but trying to fix the problem is pointless since I've forgotten the screwball grip. When your mechanics are way off, it doesn't help to practice."

"My fencing coach used to say that practice makes permanent, not perfect."

"Let's take a look at my two-seam fastball," Tamiko says, bending to take a ball from the pail. "The idea is for it to come in straight like a regular four-seam fastball, but then break sharply left at the last moment. Give me a low, outside target to a right-handed batter."

When Alec sets up as instructed, Tamiko does a decent job of putting the ball close to his mitt, but with no break. "I know my grip along the seams is OK, so the problem must be that I'm not getting my finger pressure right," she says disgustedly after tossing another half dozen with no improvement.

"Maybe you're trying to throw it too hard."

"Good point," Tamiko says as she attempts to brush a thick strand of damp hair off her sweaty cheek. Giving up, she drops her glove, gathers her flyaway caramel mane with both hands, and reinserts it in it's scrunchie. Then swinging easily into her windup she lets the ball fly.

"You did it," Alec almost shouts after moving his glove an inch off the corner to catch the darting ball. "Must have been the hair."

"Definitely," Tamiko says delightedly as she throws back her head, arches her back, and raises both arms to the heavens.

Pushing the catcher's mask up on top of his head as he watches Tamiko's breasts lift the angry yellow jacket towards the sky, Alec wonders if anywhere on the planet there is a girl as lovely as this.

"Lec, joking aside, it's like I totally appreciate your help," Tamiko says a few minutes later as they stuff the gear into the blue bag. "Coach said he'd work with me at practice Thursday and if things go OK might even find me an inning or two on Saturday. But, I hope you know I also want to do stuff you enjoy. Like, maybe you could teach me to surf."

"Sure, but when school is on I barely have time to get out to the ocean a couple of times per week and even then it's usually at six a.m."

"If it means I get to see you with your shirt off I can be ready to go at five."

"Now who's teasing?"

"I may be a silly teenager but I've never been more serious."

"Your wish is my command," Alec says as he lifts his Cal T-shirt to reveal a slim, but chiseled chest. Executing a quick spin, he let's the blue fabric drop as he adds, "Curtain's down, show's over."

Freezing like a deer who hears a twig snap, Tamiko stands mute. "Thank you," she finally manages in a tone halfway between a whisper and a croak.

. . . . .

At 4:20 p.m. Amy's alarm wakes her from a restless doze. After a scalding shower followed by a big mug of black coffee, she feels remarkably better when twenty minutes later the doorbell rings. The thin pleasant man with short gray hair on her front porch is dressed in black yoga pants and a T-shirt that says, Forgive. When introductions are complete and Amy has made Malcolm Frank a cup of Earl Grey tea, they sit at the table in the backyard. After taking an appreciative sip the psychologist says, "I understand that you edit many of Bay Books' excellent crime titles including *Slide Zone*, which I just read."

"Yes, a few years ago Andrea Kitness, the editor who had done it for twenty years retired and I got the chance. I'd always had a soft spot for 'whodunnits' so I grabbed it."

"In a way that describes how I got involved with helping the police. Since I was a tadpole and fell in love with Sir Arthur and Agatha, I've loved a good mystery. So ten years ago when I began to get a little bored with the more predictable concerns of my patients, I took a few courses in criminal psychology and offered my help gratis to East Bay departments."

"Sergeant Helickson says your suggestions have helped more than once."

"I'm serious about trying, anyway."

"I'm sold, so where do we start?"

"I've listened to the recording of your interview this morning so I think I have the background about the unhappy chain of events that brought you to Amsterdam," Malcolm says, pausing to take a second sip of tea. "Today I see my job as focusing on what makes Max tick, with the hope that something helpful will emerge as to why he's here in the Bay Area stalking you over three years after you met. Can we begin with exactly what happened, from the moment you walked into the Hollywood Bar?"

"As I said earlier, I was already tipsy from a couple of glasses of wine and not enough food when I went in there," Amy says with a grimace. "And then I foolishly accepted something with vodka in it that immediately had me seeing double. But for all of that, I think I have pretty good recall as to what happened, probably because casual sex was so new to me and…"

"Are we getting a little ahead of the story?" Malcolm asks.

"No doubt, because when I accepted this big guy's invitation to have a drink, I wasn't thinking about anything except maybe how nice it would be able to talk to a sympathetic person, especially someone who reminded me a little of Yuri."

"So to start he was polite and friendly."

"Exaggeratedly so, really. For example, when I began crying he gave me his handkerchief, which was wrinkled but clean. But since I did almost all the talking in the bar I don't think there is much more I can tell you about that part," Amy says earnestly, as she hopes Malcolm understands just how miserable she'd been that spring night.

"Eventually, after he walked you back to your hotel you invited him up to your room," Malcolm continues, matter-of-factly.

"I'm not sure I invited him, exactly. He was just so big and, I don't know, in control I guess, he just came."

"Amy, just to be clear, I'm not here to judge or second-guess you. As far as I can gather, you're a strong person who for reasons largely beyond your control experienced a huge load of trouble in a very short period of time. If you ever want to delve deeper into any of this I'd be happy to make a recommendation, but…"

"Not so short, apparently," Amy says, pouring more tea into both their cups.

"Huh?"

"My time of trouble appears to have been extended."

"Oh right, I don't know if I can help remedy that, but I'm obviously here to try. So let's get back to what happened when you and Max got to your room," Malcolm says in a kind, but firm voice Amy thinks must be a key tool to keep his patients on point.

"Since I had zero experience with this kind of thing, I had no idea if he would expect to kiss me and make a pretense of romance, or if I was expected to unzip his fly, and well…. Anyway, as is not uncommon in my life, it turned out I was worrying about the wrong thing because as soon as we got to the room, Max disappeared into the bathroom mumbling something unintelligible as he closed the door. I assumed he needed the toilet so I perched on the edge of the bed trying to keep the room from spinning. But when he didn't come out for maybe ten minutes, I kind of collapsed back against the pillows and maybe even dozed."

"Eventually he reappeared?"

"Yes, looking and sounding annoyed and I don't know, uptight, I guess. Certainly he was no longer the confident, sweet-talking king of the jungle type I'd met at the Hollywood. By then, since all my bodily systems were crashing, my greatest wish was for him to leave. Instead he started making demands, telling me to take my clothes off and act sexy. I'm afraid the rest is acutely embarrassing," Amy says, pursing her lips as she blows out an audible stream of air.

"After twenty-five years as a shrink I don't embarrass easily, so take it as slowly as you wish," Malcolm says, leaning back in his chair as if he has all day.

"He kept saying he needed me to tell him how much I wanted his big boy inside me. When I couldn't fumble out the correct words he became so frustrated I thought he might hit me. Eventually, I took off my clothes and did my best to pretend I was in an adult movie by leaning back and well…well, playing with myself. None of this made me feel the least bit aroused, but somehow—maybe because I was so abjectly in his power—it turned Max on. Anyway, without further ceremony, he literally jumped on top of me."

"I don't mean to be prurient, Amy, but did he enter you immediately?" Malcolm asks.

"I don't mean to be prissy, Malcolm, but do you really need every detail? I mean…"

"Amy, in this situation, yes," Malcolm replies, making eye contact.

Amy pauses for the dog in the next yard to stop barking before saying, "He clumsily and I guess you could say forcefully, pushed into me with no preliminaries and zero finesse, kind of like ramming my vagina with the handle of a tennis racket. Once he succeeded he was all manic energy, a huge man poking me like a piñata. But despite all that, and I hate to admit this, by fantasizing that I was with Yuri I was just starting to get into it when he climaxed. I don't know for sure, but I'd bet the whole thing lasted no more than ninety seconds, probably less."

"And afterwards?"

"In a maudlin sort of way, he was sweet, or at least tried to be. He kept repeating how mind-blowing our sex had been and asking whether it had been great for me too. Because it was so obvious what he needed to hear, and because I so badly wanted him to leave, I said that yes, it had been special. And when this seemed to disappoint, I told him he was an absolutely fabulous lover. The moment he heard that, he pulled up his pants, kissed me, and left," Amy finishes, taking a deep breath and expelling it slowly.

"Again, sorry to drag you through more of this, but can we move on to the next evening when you saw him again?" Malcolm asks, raising his hands with fingers spread as if to reassure Amy that she's doing well.

"You mean when I stupidly went back to the Hollywood, hating myself every step of the way? Anyhoo, as soon as I walked in, Max, who was sitting near the door, jumped up, spread his arms and called out my name. Then he draped his huge right arm around me and, using a combination of Dutch and English, introduced me as his new girlfriend."

"That's what he called you? Really? His girlfriend?"

"Well, to be precise he called me something in Dutch I didn't understand and then in English, his 'smoking hot lady friend'. And here's the sad part—for a moment, leaning against this mountain of a man I felt better. Not good really, but since my grief for Yuri had been driving me nuts all day it was a relief to change the narrative."

"I gather from the tape that in the Hollywood things went pretty much as the night before?"

"Yes. And like the first night I was hungry. When it became clear there was no place to go to eat real food at that hour, it was right back to chips and alcohol, in my case white wine. But since I had already told Max my sad story, this time I mentioned that I'd gone to the Rijksmuseum earlier in the day. He immediately said that this was an amazing coincidence, because he was an international art dealer who was in Amsterdam because he had just outsmarted a big collector and made a huge profit. He added that he was relaxing for a few days before going back to his place in the south of France."

"He was bragging?"

"Boorishly. He went on and on about his successes in a loud voice, even bizarrely claiming that people said he looked like the young Cezanne."

"Did you believe any of it?"

"I had no idea what Cezanne looked like, but I was pretty sure it wasn't like a heavyweight boxer who drank too much beer. But, remember, I was so obsessed with my own drama I didn't really care. Also, as absurd as it sounds, at that point Max, and even the people in the bar, seemed almost like friends. Someone even bought us a second round of drinks, although I didn't finish mine."

"So again you headed back to the hotel."

"Yes, but this time Max announced it to the whole place. He was speaking at least half in Dutch, but the gist seemed to be that although we were heading off to my bed, he didn't expect to get any sleep, wink, wink," Amy says, wrinkling her nose in disgust.

"When we got back to my room Max again headed for the bathroom and stayed there for an extended period. Anticipating the next step, I removed my clothes and propped myself against the pillows. When Max finally appeared, at first he seemed pleased that I was ready. And in truth, I was less out of it than the night before and at least part of me wanted the release of orgasm. In short, I did my naive best to play the vamp, even trying to grab his arm and pull him onto the bed."

"How did he react?" Malcolm asks quickly, as if this could be a key interaction.

"He pulled away, even moving his chair further from the bed. And that's also when he began to get angry, calling me puta, cunt, cipa, and a bunch more things in a language I didn't understand, something Eastern European I think."

"Do you think he was truly upset, just trying to arouse himself, or…?"

"Malcolm," Amy interrupts impatiently, "All this happened in a very few minutes over three-plus years ago when I was not only tipsy, but half nuts with loneliness and grief. In short, I wouldn't bet a dime on my opinion."

"Even so," Malcolm says, reassuringly.

"Both, probably. I think now that when he came out of the bathroom he was expecting to order me around much as he had the night before. But when I appeared to be ready, if not eager to have sex something changed."

"Got it, so what happened next?"

"He lurched himself on top of me using his big body to press me down as he began squeezing my neck with his huge hands."

"Still calling you names?"

"Yes, and as I told Melvin and Dana he was so angry and out of control that I'm convinced he would have killed me if I hadn't kneed him in the crotch so hard he loosened his grip enough that I could scream."

"Was he wearing his pants when he moved on top of you?"

"They were down around his ankles I think. But he was still wearing some type of boxers which he'd had his hand inside of when he was sitting on the chair."

"Trying to get an erection?"

"Probably, I don't know for sure. But, Malcolm, what difference does any of this make?" Amy asks, pushing back her chair."

"Bear with me another minute, Amy. Before he ran out with your purse, did he say anything?"

"'This isn't over, putana,' which, in case your Italian is rusty, means whore."

"Thanks Amy, I know this hasn't been easy. I only have one more question if that's OK."

"Ha! Do I really get a choice?" Amy asks, grinning for the first time since Malcolm's arrival.

Smiling in return, the psychologist says, "Describe the Hollywood Bar in more detail. When you were talking to Melvin and Dana you said some customers wore leather outfits."

"Yes, but mostly in the back where the relatively narrow bar area kind of bellied into a room with a bunch of tables."

"Do you think it was a gay bar?"

"Malcolm, as an editor I can't help but note that this is your last question plus one. But, OK then, remember, I was in a city I'd never visited and in a place I wouldn't normally go. Add to that the fact that in that neighborhood prostitution and soft drugs were all around so I don't honestly know."

"But what do you think?"

"The mostly middle-aged guys on the barstools seemed more or less straight, like the Hollywood was their social club. There were a few younger women mixed in but I have no idea if they were professionals or not. To the extent I could see, the vibe seemed different at the back—as if gay guys had staked out their own territory. But Malcolm, do you think any of this can possibly help find Max?"

"I have a yoga class at six-thirty, but first I'll chat with Lieutenant Ramsey. It seems obvious that in addition to any other personality disorders Max is at least to some degree sexually dysfunctional and, in common with most bullies and braggarts, has a weak ego. My hunch is that the first night when he left the bar with you it was mostly to show off to the guys. In the bathroom it seems likely he was trying, but failing to sustain an erection. Then—and this is a wild surmise—because you were small, vulnerable, and seemed to believe his boasts, he somehow convinced himself he could pull off having sex with you, which, in a weird fashion, he did."

"But the next night he tried to kill me," Amy says, now standing behind her chair and gripping it with white knuckles.

"We'll never really know why of course. But possibly because he was so disappointed he couldn't repeat what he obviously regarded as his virile success of the first night, he blamed it on you. From your description you went from being scared and cringing the first night to acting the coquette the second, so maybe it's as simple as the fact his fragile ego couldn't cope with a woman asserting her sexual need, or perhaps power is a better word. But of more relevance to what happened this morning, I'm guessing it's his success the first night that's stuck with him."

"C'mon, really, are you saying he showed up after all of this time because he's hot for me. I don't see…"

"Probably he did need money at the start. Again I'm guessing of course, but it may be that shadowing you for a few days and especially getting his hands on you this morning, changed his dynamic. Especially if impotence has continued to plague him, he may now imagine that getting you into bed will somehow cure him."

"Even if you're right about some of this, how does knowing that Max is an impotent nutcase help find him?"

"Habits die hard. I'm guessing he functions best, feels most secure and powerful, in venues like the Hollywood. That is, places where sexual roles are fluid and no one will challenge a big guy who now and then buys a few drinks while bragging about his sexual conquests. So for starters, I'm going to suggest that our friends at the BPD enlist their colleagues in the cities around the Bay with low end bars and clubs to make a real effort to show Max's sketch around."

"Does this mean you believe I'm Max's only target and Tamiko is safe?" Amy asks, pretty sure she already knows the answer.

"Transference can happen, I'm afraid, and given what Max said about your daughter this morning I wouldn't take anything for granted."

. . . . .

At exactly 6:15 Amy opens the door as Lieutenant Ramsey comes up the three steps onto the porch, still looking like he's stepped out of a bespoke tailor's. "Melvin, can I get you a coffee or perhaps tea or water? I also have a SodaStream gizmo so I can easily do a bubbly water with a twist of lime.

"Or if you're off duty, we have plenty of beer," Ed calls from the kitchen.

"Just tap water, maybe with some ice, will be fine. But where is Tamiko and her, um…Mr. Burns?"

Glancing out the front window, Amy replies, "Pulling up now."

Coming through the front door a step behind Tamiko, Alec nods hello and asks Lieutenant Ramsey, "I don't know if you want me to be part of this conversation?"

"For sure," Ed replies promptly, making eye contact with Lieutenant Ramsey. "Didn't we agree that she's far less vulnerable when she's not alone."

"We did," Lieutenant Ramsey says, shifting his gaze from Ed to Amy. "And now if everyone will sit, I'll update you on what little we know and then discuss strategies to keep you safe. This afternoon we put a couple of extra cars on the street in hopes of spotting the stolen Camry. We had a flutter of excitement when a patrol officer radioed that he had spotted a white Japanese car driven by a huge man in a blue shirt with the correct license tag."

"Really?" Tamiko exclaims, excitedly.

"Unfortunately, not. When the officer made a U-turn and pulled the car over, it turned out to be a 2010 Honda, driven by an obese woman wearing what Officer Wang described as a blue tent."

"What about the plate?" Alec asks as if this is somehow still relevant.

"The first two digits were the same as the stolen Toyota's, but I'm afraid that's where the similarity ended."

"Anything more relevant?" Ed asks.

"No. It's our guess that after this morning's drama Max has gone to ground. Of course he could also have left the area, but since he took the trouble to steal the Toyota, it seems more likely he's still around. So in the last two hours, we've circulated the sketch Amy helped John Flores create to every house within a three-block radius of where we sit. And tonight we've suggested that everyone in the area leave on as many lights as possible and call us pronto if they see or hear anything even a little bit out of the ordinary. Finally, we've added a car to our night patrol that will cruise Francisco Street at least every hour."

"Do you think it's safe to remain here?" Ed asks.

"It's probably safer than your place in Piedmont, where the houses are farther apart and farther from the street. Assuming your neighbors light their front rooms and leave their porch lights on, Francisco Street should be pretty bright."

"That doesn't answer my question."

"Safety is obviously a relative concept," Lieutenant Ramsey replies in the long-suffering tone he might use when answering questions at a middle school assembly. "If Amy and Tamiko were in Idaho right now, they'd doubtless be safer. But at least for the next day or two, while everyone is on high alert, I don't think the difference is big enough to fly to Boise. That said, Amy, and you too, Tamiko, let me emphasize again that it's a poor idea for you two to wander around Berkeley alone. As Amy found out this morning, if Max gets you in his grasp it won't be easy to get out. Bay Books with all its employees, should be safe enough, especially if the doors are kept locked during working hours. And Tamiko, you should be fine at Cal where the campus force is on alert and Max would anyway stand out like a chicken in a duck convention. Just the…"

"Malcolm Frank thinks you should be looking for Max in sleazy bars in places like East Oakland," Amy interrupts.

"I've spoken with Doctor Frank. A lot of what he says had already occurred to us, so let's just say that his opinion has been a valuable addition."

"At some point, Max will give up and leave the area, right?" Ed says.

"Logically, sure, but both Amy and I have just been told by Dr. Frank, that given Max's personality issues, logic may not be the biggest element in his decision-making."

"Alec is a world class marksman," Tamiko says impulsively.

"That's an exaggeration," Alec replies, "but I do own a target pistol I used competitively."

"I think it's best if you leave any shooting to us," Lieutenant Ramsey says peremptorily as he stands and straightens his tie.

WEDNESDAY 2

THE DREAM, LIKE A GRAINY SILENT FILM in three-quarter time, begins with Tamiko standing on the pitcher's rubber of a softball diamond surrounded by tall trees, a little like Codornices Park.

She is the only player visible, her shorts and T-shirt bluntly colored in as if by an unskilled artist who only had red and blue crayons. As the invisible camera slowly zooms in, Tamiko, now holding an electric yellow ball in her right hand, windmills her arm, kicks out her left leg and rockets the ball towards an unseen batter. Poker-faced, she then raises her glove to catch the ball presumably tossed back by the catcher. When Tamiko again places both feet on the rubber, she seems smaller and farther away as does the field itself, which is now more tightly encircled by darker, taller and altogether more menacing trees. Not seeming to notice, Tamiko, whose clothes have now lost most of their color, again executes her windup and releases the still-vivid ball before grimacing slightly as if the umpire has missed the call. The third time the camera focuses on Tamiko, she has become a tiny gray figure almost completely enveloped by dead trees, their twisted black branches all but blotting out the field. And when she begins her windup, what little is left of her begins to fade so that only a pinprick of yellow is visible in what must be her upward-flung right hand.

Sitting up sweaty and dry-mouthed, Alec raises his arms as if to fend off an attack. Rarely experiencing a scary dream, to say nothing of a grimly foreboding nightmare, it takes him a few seconds to understand that he's safe in his own bed and, more important, Tamiko hasn't been enveloped by killer trees. Glancing at his watch to see that it is 2:05 a.m., Alec pads to the bathroom for a drink of water as he thinks about trying to study at least until the nightmare's oppressive hangover lifts. Then, thinking about Tamiko and recalling the rush of emotion he had felt the previous afternoon when he had hugged her at Codornices Park, Alec realizes that trying to get back to sleep in his own bed isn't an option. If there is one chance in a thousand that camping out in the car in front of Tamiko's house will make her safer, he needs to be there.

Despite his fierce resolve, Alec begins to have doubts when, fifteen minutes later he turns onto Francisco Street two blocks from the Gashkin residence to see that the neighborhood looks almost as bright as a county fair midway. Feeling far too conspicuous to park on Francisco he turns onto McGee and heads south to where the lights peter out just before the street deadends at Ohlone Park. Fearful that a neighbor will spot him and call the police if he approaches the Gashkin house on foot, Alec considers aborting his plan. Then, remembering how the dead trees with their twisted black limbs crowded in as if to consume Tamiko, he grabs his sleeping bag, slides out of the Altima and, literally on tiptoe, walks north.

When Alec gets back to the empty brightness of Francisco Street he feels as if he's caught up in another nightmare, this one where all the people have been atomized, perhaps at the moment they'd flicked on all those lights. Barely breathing, he continues his stealthy progress towards the Gashkin bungalow, scanning the houses for a raised blind or twitching curtain. Now just two houses from his destination, he begins to relax. Then, from a gap in the hedge in front of a two-story house to his left something large and fast emerges heading right at him. Dropping his sleeping bag as he turns and brings up his fists, Alec watches as a yearling deer lopes across the street a few steps in front of him and disappears into the shadows.

Chuckling as he realizes that despite the lights he is as effectively invisible as the raccoons, skunks, and other critters that patrol every Berkeley neighborhood at night, Alec continues another fifty feet to the Gashkin driveway where he turns right. When he reaches the back corner of the house, Alec uses the flashlight on his phone to locate the gate in the waist-high wooden fence. Lifting the latch as noiselessly as possible, he eases the gate open enough to slip through and onto the patio where he has so recently been on his best behavior for the pizza supper.

Like so many bungalow-style houses built on the Berkeley Flats in the first third of the previous century, the Gashkins' hugs the street. The result is a deep, narrow backyard with a detached single-car garage forming a wall on its east side. A huge tree spreads a dark canopy over the wild blackberry bushes that choke the rear third of the yard with the result that the kitchen light only dimly illuminates the patio and the small square of bedraggled lawn immediately beyond.

Again, using his iPhone flashlight, Alec spots the pile of lumber Tamiko had wistfully explained her dad bought a few days before he died intending to construct a raised vegetable bed. Within the skinny three feet between the boards and the fence that marks the west side of the yard, Alec shakes out his mummy bag. Wriggling his long body inside, he checks his phone to see that it's 2:45 a.m. With Tamiko now less than twenty-five feet away, he can finally get some rest.

Awakening from a doze so shallow he hadn't realized he was asleep, Alec hears what sounds like a branch rubbing against the side of the garage. Telling himself this is surely just another innocent nighttime sound, produced either by the breeze or a nocturnal animal, he adjusts his position slightly and begins drifting back to sleep. But wait, the still-awake part of his brain interjects—there's no wind and like the deer he had encountered earlier, animals that move at night don't bump into garages. Now wide-awake, Alec glances at his watch to see that it's 5:05, as he raises his head to peek over the lumber. Trying to make out what is happening across the yard, he again hears the rubbing noise. As his eyes adjust to the predawn glow, Alec can see that a very large man is using some sort of metal bar to slowly and carefully pry out the garage window, frame and all.

Barely twenty feet behind the man who he guesses must be Max, Alec realizes he is helpless inside the tight confines of his mummy bag. Sitting up, he wriggles his shoulders until the down-filled nylon tube falls to his waist. Then crossing his ankles, he tips his weight forward and stands allowing the bag to fall to the ground. The whole operation would have been a soundless success if Alec hadn't snagged his left foot on the drawstring resulting in his taking an awkward hop to avoid falling.

Spinning towards the sound, Max hardly hesitates before he takes several quick steps towards Alec. Grabbing the patio table as he comes he sends it flying towards the younger man. Alec, his foot still snagged, and surprised by the speed of Max's attack, is half a second late in moving out of the way so that the table hits his left shoulder and knocks him to the ground. With Max now raising the bar for a crippling blow, Alec rolls over twice and staggers to his feet just in time to hobble clear. Continuing to scuttle to his left, as he desperately tries to free his foot, Alec barely ducks under Max's lightening slash. Knowing that as long as he's encumbered by the bag, Max is sure to maim him sooner or later, Alec stops trying to scrabble away. Instead, standing tall, he kicks out at Max with his free foot as if in a martial-arts movie. Surprised, the huge man stumbles as he takes several steps back allowing Alec a couple of precious seconds to drop to a knee, feel for the cord, and with a savage pull, break it. Thank God I bought the bargain bag, he thinks as he turns and grabs a three-foot-long two-by-four from the top of the lumber pile. With a derisive snort at Alec's puny weapon, Max again presses forward, swinging the iron bar back and forth so quickly that Alec can't follow it in the dim light. But what he can't see, he can hear. So when the swooshing sound tells him the bar has passed center, he steps forward and uses every one of his 178 pounds to drive the two-by-four into Max's gut. As the big man folds at the waist literally gasping for breath, Alec shouts, "Help! Call 911, Help!"

Still doubled over, Max backs away from the house along the side of the garage somehow managing to keep his head up and his weapon extended. Shadowing him, Alec looks for an opportunity to deliver a knockout blow. Just as he steps forward to make his move, Alec is brought up short when the Gashkins' east side neighbor opens a second floor window and shines the beam of an industrial-strength flashlight into his eyes. Momentarily blinded, Alec throws up a light-screening arm in time to see Max turn, and still gasping, move crab-like towards the blackberry bushes at the end of the yard. Ducking under the light beam, Alec starts after him when a hand grabs him roughly by his painful left shoulder. "No Alec, no," Ed says. "The police are on their way. This is their job now."

The first patrol car arrives in three minutes with a second trailing in another four. Alec promptly explains what happened including the escape route Max has taken. But with only those two cars on the Berkeley streets in the predawn hour, Max is almost surely gone even before the officers can organize an efficient pursuit. Indeed, according to the dawn jogger interviewed twenty minutes later, a big man matching Max's description ran out between two houses on Delaware St. at about 5:15, before hurriedly getting into a light-colored car and taking off. Double checking to be sure that Max isn't still hiding in a neighboring backyard, an officer reports that some kind of a cutting tool had been used to slice through the wire fence at the rear of the Gashkin yard, as well as another fence in a backyard on Virginia Street. With his escape route prepared in advance, Max likely reached his vehicle even before the first BPD car rolled up to the Gashkin front door.

By the time Sergeant Helickson, who lives just over the Berkeley line in north Oakland, arrives at the Gashkins' at 5:43 a.m., a wide band of light has appeared in the eastern sky. As Ed makes coffee Lieutenant Ramsey—en route from his home in El Sobrante, thirty minutes to the north—talks to Amy via his blue tooth connection. In the meantime, the iron bar that Max dropped on his way through the blackberry bushes is on its way to the lab to be checked for fingerprints, and the police in neighboring cities as well as the California Highway Patrol have been alerted.

When Lieutenant Ramsey appears ten minutes later wearing jeans, blue Crocs with no socks, and a white T-shirt that he must have slept in, Sergeant Helickson can't disguise her smile. "Well, Sergeant, at least you can see that I didn't waste any time getting out my door," the lieutenant says wryly. Then as he settles into the empty chair at the head of the dining room table, he adds, "In the interest of time, let me summarize what I think I learned on the phone driving in. You're all welcome to make needed additions or corrections."

Looking around the table to make sure he has everyone's assent he continues, "Alec, I gather you woke up in the middle of the night with a premonition that Tamiko was in danger. You arrived here a little before three a.m., lay down behind a pile of lumber next to the west side fence and woke up a little after five a.m. when you first heard, and then saw, a big man trying to break into the locked garage. You fought what amounts to a brief duel, which you got the best of. At this point lights came on, people started yelling and Max escaped in the confusion."

"I'm going to guess he didn't head onto I-80, since the CHP had two cars with license plate readers near Berkeley, and freeway traffic is still fairly sparse at five-fifteen," Sergeant Helickson says.

"I wouldn't turn your guess into a bet," Lieutenant Ramsey says, making no effort to hide his sarcasm. "Instead I'd put my money on Max having switched out the Toyota's tags last night before he attacked. As we've just seen again, although he may be a nutcase, he's also cunning and dangerous."

"No argument there," Ed says. "We're obviously up against an ingenious monster. If he'd broken the window to get into the garage, Amy probably would have noticed and stayed out. But by prying out the whole semi-rotten frame before climbing in and then reaching out to pull it back into place, she would never have known that anything was amiss until he attacked her when she unlocked the door. Given his size advantage, it would have been a simple matter for him to drive off with her in the car with no one suspecting anything was amiss. I don't mean to be critical, or maybe I do, but it's like you guys seem to be out of your depth here."

Pouring himself another half-cup from the chrome carafe Amy has placed on the table, Lieutenant Ramsey takes a sip of the black beverage before saying, "Stripped of the hyperbole I can't disagree with any of that. Even at a time when we were all hyper vigilant Max came up with a plan to abduct Amy from her own home without anyone even realizing he'd done it. And if it hadn't been for Alec's bad dream and quick action, well…"

"I'd likely be dead, or close to it," Amy says.

"Alec, you obviously dispatched Max quickly, but I don't quite understand how you did it, since Max had a tire iron and you only had a wooden stick," Sergeant Helickson interjects.

"Alec's a world-class athlete," Tamiko says, not trying to disguise her pride.

"Still, I don't quite see how…"

"I participated in the Modern Pentathlon which consists of five different sports, fencing being one. If Max had been able to get his arms around me I'm sure he'd have broken me in half, but at what amounts to sword's length, I had thousands of hours of training to rely on."

"But it was almost dark," Lieutenant Ramsey muses, leaning forward. "How could you see a thin, fast-moving bar?"

"Fortunately, sir, I didn't need to. When Max slashed the iron bar back and forth it made a swooshing sound kind of like a golf club does if you swing it from the wrong end."

"You mean when you heard the bar move from left to right you knew Max was momentarily unprotected? But wasn't he swinging it back and forth at warp speed?"

"Melvin, if an old, and at my best, barely competent fencer can put in a word, Alec is undoubtedly quick enough that the time it took Max to swing the bar from one side to the other seemed like ten seconds to him."

"Long enough, anyway," Alec says with a smile.

"If I can bring the conversation back to the present," Ed says, "it's obvious that no matter how many precautions we take, Amy and Tamiko aren't safe in this house, at my house, or for that matter, in the East Bay. So Melvin, not to tempt fate any further, we've decided to leave the Bay Area late this morning and stay away until the nightmare ends."

"I can't argue with that," Lieutenant Ramsey replies. "But where will you go?"

"We'll tell the folks at Bay, our friends, and anyone else who cares, that we're off to L.A., where Amy and I both often frequently travel on business," Ed says as he reaches for the coffee carafe. "But in truth, we'll go to Washington, D.C. where I have business anyway. Since no one outside the people in this room will know where we are, we should be safe. In the meantime, since I don't want anyone at Bay to be in the remotest danger, we'll close the office for the rest of the week and delight folks with an end-of-the-summer holiday."

Exhaling so loudly that everyone glances her way, Tamiko says, "Ed,

Mom, I know I'm only borderline sixteen and so maybe don't get a vote, but I haven't agreed to this. Like, sure, I can probably get my Physics exam rescheduled to whenever, but this weekend is Tsunami's final tournament. That means for Amber, Roxy, Tasha, and Jazz, this is it—their last games. Maybe it sounds silly, but since most of us have been together for three summers, Sunday especially is a way big deal. C'mon Mom, like you know how it is, all the families will be there for pictures and flowers, and even a few tears. Then we'll go out for pizza for the presentation of the plaques. Plus Coach has said that I can probably pitch Saturday. And I…"

"None of which is remotely worth risking your safety for," Amy interrupts.

"What risk?" Tamiko says leaning forward, her elbows on the table. "If I stay with Auntie Les and Uncle Dan in Palo Alto I should be just as safe as in D.C. It's like they don't even have the same last names as we do so how can Max possibly find me?"

"What do you think Melvin? Dana?" Ed asks, "What would you two do if your families were in danger?"

"I gather Tamiko is talking about your sister?" Lieutenant Ramsey asks Amy.

"Yes, Leslie works at SRI International in Menlo Park and her husband, Dan Aristead, is a psychologist with an office in Palo Alto. Les uses our birth name, O'Shea, at work, and occasionally Aristead when she's with Dan.

"When Max stole your purse in Amsterdam, did it contain your sister's name and address?" Sergeant Helickson asks.

"No, I haven't had an address book for years and he didn't get my phone."

"What about online, if he somehow got into your Facebook or LinkedIn accounts?"

"Facebook, Twitter, LinkedIn, Instagram or whatever, my privacy isn't for sale to corporate America. I don't do any of it."

"What about your friends or work colleagues, do any of them know your sister?" Lieutenant Ramsey asks.

"You mean if Max somehow tried to trick one of them into identifying her?"

"Something like that."

"A couple of my colleagues at Bay have met Les and I guess several of my friends have too, but they would have no idea of her address and she doesn't have a landline. Jen, my one friend who does know Les pretty well, is on vacation in Thailand."

"What about you Ed? Do you have information about Amy's sister someplace where it could possibly be found?"

"Nope. We've met at a couple of Bay author events, but I don't have her number or address. And I'm not sure she even knows Amy and I are a couple."

"C'mon Mom, there are like what, seven or eight million people in the Bay Area, meaning that my risk of being bitten by a rabid squirrel must be greater than Max finding me at Les's."

"Nice try, but you're not the one whose opinion I want. Just because you're having a FOMO moment doesn't mean that…"

"Amy," Sergeant Helickson interrupts, "while we were talking I checked your name on the White Pages and the other sites that often list family members and your sister doesn't appear. In short, I think I'm speaking for both of us when I say that although nothing is guaranteed, it's hard to see why Tamiko would be at significant risk in Palo Alto for the next few days. But as for FOMO, I think someone better translate."

"Fear of missing out," Lieutenant Ramsey says, looking up from his phone. "But more to the point, as long as we're sure that there are no online bread crumbs leading to Amy's sister and Max doesn't somehow follow Tamiko from Berkeley to Palo Alto, I agree," Lieutenant Ramsey says.

"OK, I surrender," Amy says, flipping up her left palm in capitulation. "I'll call Les and get you invited and to see if she can work from home at least part of the time so you're not alone. And since San Francisco International is half way to Palo Alto, you can come with us that far and take a van the rest of the way. Hopefully all this will be resolved by the

COMING OF AGE IN BERKELEY

weekend and we'll be back in time for your birthday on Monday. If not, you can fly east Sunday after Tsunami's last game, although that may mean missing pizza."

"It'll be fine to delay celebrating my birthday if we have to. I mean it already seems as if I've been fifteen like forever so another day or two won't matter," Tamiko says, drawing out the forever as if it's twenty letters long. "But what about Lec, is he going to be safe here in Berkeley?"

"I have my Organic Chemistry exam Friday and I'm heading back east Sunday to visit my parents for ten days before fall semester starts. I've been seriously cramming and there's no way I'm going to ask for a delayed exam and have to keep studying over my holiday," Alec says as if daring anyone to contradict him.

"Despite what happened earlier you're probably not at the center of Max's target," Lieutenant Ramsey says. "Assuming he shadowed Tamiko while she was on campus last week, he may have seen you, but…"

"Tamiko and I have been meeting after my World Lit lecture outside Evans Hall. Even if Max was on the campus and saw us together, I can't imagine that he knows anything about my afternoon class or where I live."

"Maybe, but we know he's both resourceful and vindictive, so let's not take anything for granted. Where do you live, by the way?" Lieutenant Ramsey asks.

"In a big shared house on Panoramic a few blocks uphill from Memorial Stadium."

"OK, we'll get the details when we are done here and send someone up later with the flyers of Max to circulate to your neighbors. Are you going anyplace in the next few days besides the Cal campus?"

"Not until Saturday when I plan to drive down to Sunnyvale to watch Tamiko play. And, as I said, Sunday morning I fly east."

"I gather you have a car?"

"Access to my buddy Ethan's Nissan Altima, which is parked a couple of blocks from here right now. As you know, Max saw it Sunday when I tried to follow him. But even if he did a better job getting my plate number than I did his, and some-how found the car on the street—which all seems extremely unlikely—it wouldn't help him much since parking is so tight in my neighborhood, I rarely find a space within three blocks. And believe me, after this morning I plan to be very aware of my surroundings."

"Hold that thought. Unless anyone has anything else, I guess that wraps it up. We'll leave an officer out front until the three of you are ready to head to SFO," Lieutenant Ramsey says as he stands.

"That won't be until nine-thirty-ish, since I need to go over to Bay to talk to our employees and close things down for the week," Ed says.

"Fine, we'll also place an officer at Bay Books until you leave," Lieutenant Ramsey says.

After Alec and Tamiko whisper for a minute by the front door and Alec turns to leave, Amy follows him onto the small porch. "Wait a second Alec, I want to thank you again for what you did. I know you were here to protect Tamiko, and in other circumstances I might have something to say about that, but the truth is I'm deeply grateful. When I think of what would have happened to me if Max had gotten into the garage, well…"

"I'm just glad it worked out," Alec interrupts.

· · · · ·

To be sure Max isn't somehow on their tail, an unmarked Berkeley police car follows Amy, Ed and Tamiko as far as the Ashby on-ramp to Interstate 80 just before 9:45 a.m. As her Subaru passes under the Bay Bridge's spiderweb-like east tower Amy says, "We can talk about all this later, but Tami, just so you know I haven't changed my view that Alec is way too old for you. Of course, I'm amazingly grateful for what he did this morning, but still…"

"I'm gonna guess that he's gone up a little in your estimation, though," Tamiko interrupts from the back seat as Ed glances out the window so Amy won't see his grin.

Approaching the terminals on the upper level of San Francisco International airport a few minutes later, Amy pulls next to a van that says Palo Alto on its side. "We land at Dulles about six p.m. West Coast time and I'll call you this evening. In the meantime, don't forget to tell Les and Dan that Sergeant Helickson is bringing the Palo Alto police up to speed and that they shouldn't be surprised if an officer stops by to review safety issues. I know, I know, the chance of Max finding you is extremely remote, but eyes wide open at all times, OK?"

"Got it. But, hey, Mom, Ed, for sure this trip is not what you planned, but you never want to miss a honeymoon because you were thinking of something else."

. . . . .

Twenty minutes after takeoff, Amy closes her eyes and tries to doze. But her mind's eye immediately zeroes in on Max's leering face as she imagines what would likely have happened if he had captured her. Folding her arms tightly across her chest in an effort to avoid shaking, she's grateful when Ed squeezes her elbow and asks, "Are you OK?"

"I was thinking where I might be right now if Alec hadn't been there this morning."

"Fortunately he was."

"Very fortunately for me. So in addition to feeling traumatized, I feel ungrateful and petty for continuing to insist that Tamiko's too young to date him. I mean logically, it's apples and oranges—the fact that he risked his life to stop Max from abducting me shouldn't have anything to do with whether he's appropriate for Tamiko, right?"

"If that's your conclusion."

"Which isn't the same as your saying 'I agree,' is it?"

"Amy, when it comes to your daughter I support you whenever, wherever and forever. Why don't we leave it at that?"

"But you think Alec is a good guy?"

"Don't you?"

. . . . .

Tamiko arrives at her aunt's and uncle's house in Palo Alto's Garden District a few minutes past 1:00 p.m. Just as Les has explained, she finds the key under the stone deer in the backyard. Leaving her sports bag on the covered back porch she scrounges peanut butter and bread in the kitchen and then, backpack over her shoulder, heads upstairs to the attic guest room. After stretching out for forty-five minutes, Tamiko strips off her clothes, steps into the small adjacent bathroom and turns the shower knob to just short of scalding. Squeezing drops from the small bottle of shampoo Les has obviously nicked from a Doubletree hotel over her thick, wet mane she lets her mind drift. Yesterday her yearning for Lec had been so strong she could think of little else, only to have it swept away by the events of this morning. With everyone now safe, her thoughts veer back to Lec standing in the sun at Codornices Park with his shirt raised. Immediately feeling a surge of pleasure she crumples the bottle so that the last few beads of shampoo trickle onto the fingers of her right hand. Placing the longest two between her legs she leans against the wall of the stall as she moves them in small circles as she imagines Lec taking off the rest of his clothes.

"Tami, I'm home," Tamiko hears her auntie's surprisingly loud voice penetrate the nimbus of her delight. Realizing that Les is just outside the bathroom door, Tamiko quickly turns the shower lever to cold as she yells, "I'll be right out. Do you have a hair dryer?"

. . . . .

When Alec gets back to Panoramic Way at four-thirty, after his final class, Sergeant Helickson is in the living room talking with several of his housemates. As Alec perches on the threadbare end of an oversized brown velvet couch, the officer explains how early that morning Alec had interrupted an attempt to assault and abduct his girlfriend's mother.

"Has Alec been to Korea and back as fast as that?" asks Margo, a pleasantly ample young woman whose pretty moon-shaped face is topped by a mop of black curls.

"No, it all happened right here in Berkeley," Sergeant Helickson replies, as if Margo has asked a serious question.

"That's even more amazing, isn't it? I mean, within less than forty-eight hours of one girlfriend leaving, Alec is going to war to protect the next one."

Pausing for the slow, silent count to five she uses when domestic spats threatened to catch fire, Sergeant Helickson replies, "Sticking to the point, I'm here because we believe that the suspect in question, a very large white man in his forties who is known as Max, is extremely dangerous. By intervening and preventing Max from his goal of abduction, Alec may now be a target. We have no information that Max, who's about six feet four inches tall, weighs upwards of 260 pounds and speaks with a pronounced European accent, knows where Alec lives. Just to be on the safe side, I'm here to urge you to take sensible precautions. This obviously includes keeping doors and windows locked and being on the lookout for any big man who looks even a little like this sketch," the Sergeant concludes, nodding towards the flyers on the table.

· · · · ·

In his room a few minutes after Sergeant Helickson has left, Alec hears a tentative knock, followed by Margo's voice asking, "Alec, can I come in for a moment?"

Opening the door to find the busty young woman holding a plate containing two large brownies, Alec says, "Sure, but I'm pretty paranoid about cramming for my final."

"I'll be quick, I wanted to apologize for my bitchy moment downstairs," Margo says, putting the plate on the desk. "It's just that I knew Teri was leaving and well, you know, my friend André has already gone back to France, so, well, I just thought that maybe you and I might, you know, well get together I guess. It's just…"

"I met Tamiko, the girl Sergeant Helickson mentioned, on campus early last week, although the word 'met' hardly does it justice since it really felt more like being hit by a bus."

"You haven't brought her over so I didn't…"

"It was awkward since Teri was still here…"

"You wanted to finish with one before you started with another."

"Once Teri moved up her departure, it worked out that way. But also, I've promised Tamiko's mother that I won't be alone with her," Alec replies, breaking off a large hunk of brownie.

"Her mother?"

"She'll be sixteen in a few days."

"Really Alec, you have a mad crush on a high school kid? For sure I can see why her mother is being…but wait a minute, is this the same woman whose life you just saved?"

"Yes."

"Are you on a crusade to make your life complicated?"

"I don't think I'm trying, but …"

"Oops! Sorry, I came to apologize, not rag on you."

"All is forgiven, or at least it will be by the time I inhale the second brownie."

. . . . .

Dressed in her now-favorite yoga pants and a sleeveless red top, Tamiko comes downstairs ten minutes after stepping out of the shower, her hair still damp. Her aunt, who is waiting with a cup of tea and a big hug exclaims, "Wow! Missy, you've grown up two years in the few months since I last saw you. Come sit here at the kitchen table and tell me what's going on. Even though Amy's call this morning had to be one of the most dramatic I've ever received, I was on my way into my annual performance review with both my boss and her boss so I had no time to find out the details. So, again, what's up? But first, are you hungry? I can do yogurt, guac and chips or a grilled cheese sandwich?"

"All three please if it's not too much bother," Tamiko replies, as she joins her aunt at the kitchen table. "So much happened today, I've hardly eaten."

"Eating like an elephant with the body of a gazelle. I'm not sure how you pull that one off, but c'mon, talk."

"I should start by saying that I never heard a word about anything I'm going to tell you until yesterday. And then there's the fact that I don't want Mom to think I'm tattling."

"Got it, but in my experience, like a kitten, once a family secret is out of the bag, it's not going back in."

As Tamiko tells the story of her mother's ill-fated visit to Amsterdam capped with Max's sudden and violent appearance in Berkeley, she is struck by how little her light-skinned, freckle-dusted auntie, now busying herself slicing cheese, looks like her older sister. With the same Japanese mother and Irish father, it's as if each parent got one daughter.

"Wow, that's one traumatic story, I had no idea," Les says, turning on the burner under an iron skillet when Tamiko finishes. "OK, for now you're off the hook on everything but your boyfriend. I'm not leaving this kitchen until you show and tell."

"Among other things he's an athlete—which explains how he stopped Max with a stick of wood," Tamiko says, holding out her phone."

"I'm gonna guess he's not in your class at Berkeley High," Les says.

"This fall he'll be a senior at Cal, but he took off a year and half to travel."

"Which would make him what?"

"Twenty-two."

"Why do I guess my sister isn't over the moon about that?" Les wonders, as she drops the buttered bread into the sizzling pan.

"When Mom found out we'd met all she could say was that if he comes near me he's going to end up breaking rocks in a striped suit."

"And this is the same guy who just saved her life?"

"Cliché ironic, huh?"

"Does she like him any better now?" Les asks.

"Lec and I are allowed to be in the same room as long as we keep our hands in our pockets."

"But what about you, Tami? You've always been this, how shall I put it, tomboy, I guess. I mean, have you even had time for guys?" Les asks, placing the sandwich on a plate and the plate in front of Tamiko, who she sees has already polished off everything else.

"Not till now," Tamiko says, reaching back to fluff her still damp hair with one hand as she grabs the sandwich with the other. "As usual, I seem to be trying to skip a few grades."

"But this Alec, did I get that right? I mean Tami, not to be a downer, but why is a guy this attractive willing to put up with my big sister on the warpath when presumably he can…?"

"Actually, I call him Lec and he calls me Tamiko, which is the name I use now."

"Tamiko it is," Les says with a chuckle as she pours more tea, "but only if you'll drop the Auntie and call me Les. But Tamiko, I hope you won't get upset if I point out that your big crush comes right on the heels of Amy finding Ed. Are you sure you're not just…"

"Reacting to feeling left out?" Tamiko interrupts. "Maybe I am a little, or like Mom says, maybe I'm a lost kid looking for a dad substitute. I don't think so, but, I mean, everyone else seems to have a load of drama in their lives, so why not me?"

"Sorry, I didn't mean to push any sensitive buttons."

"No worries, really. Compared to Mom, you're a pussycat."

"OK, then, but how is this relationship possibly going to work, given that you still live at home and Alec, or Lec, is an adult?"

"Love conquers all."

"Just so you know, most people say that ironically. Hey, there goes the garage door so Dan's home early."

"I texted him to see if he had time to go out with me for an hour of pitching practice after work. He texted back that his late afternoon appointment had cancelled, so no problem."

"He was a catcher on his high school team so I'm guessing that if the patient hadn't cancelled, Dan would have done it himself."

. . . . .

After a fun hour pitching and catching in the corner of a nearby soccer field using a chain-link fence as a backstop, Tamiko and Dan head towards California Street to meet Les for Japanese food at Jin Sho. As Tamiko slurps tempura udon from a thick bowl under a ceiling full of multicolored balloons, her phone vibrates. A minute later, it vibrates again. Checking as unobtrusively as possible, Tamiko sees that the first call was from Vera, and the second Lec. Back at the Aristeads' by 7:30

and knowing it's getting late in Connecticut, Tamiko returns Vera's call first. When her grandmother picks up saying, "Your turn," Tamiko replies, "*If goodness has causes, it is not goodness; if it has effects or rewards, it is not goodness either. So goodness is outside the chain of cause and effect.*"

"*Milaya moya*, do you believe now I am so old that you must feed me an easy line from *Anna Karenina*, in chapter ten I think?"

"Chapter twelve, but close enough. But listen Vera, I gave you a freebie because I need to talk to you about real things."

"Every word Tolstoy wrote is real. And just so you know, your mom called a little earlier to tell me the whole story."

"Everything? Really?" Tamiko asks, wondering what kind of spin her mother has put on Lec saving her life.

"Even about baby, so I think, yes. So sad. I've even been crying and as you know I'm not much for that. But at same time, Amy is safe, a small miracle to be thankful for. So, tell me how you are doing?"

"Fine, or at least I think so. Things have obviously been pretty crazy with this scary Max guy and the police and all, so…"

"And then there is your pretty boy," Vera interrupts.

"Yes," Tamiko says, stopping herself from talking about how brave Lec was that morning.

"Being in love, especially for the first time, is crazy experience all by itself."

"Vera, I want to ask you one important thing. Could it happen that Lec and I are so, so perfect for each other, that we can somehow get through all of the stuff trying to separate us and be together in a good happy way…"

"Are you asking me whether this is likely, just maybe possible or not completely impossible?" Vera's kind voice asks.

"Listening to Mom, Ruth, Auntie Les, my friend Jazz and I guess, even you, I already know the answer to whether it's likely, so let's focus on the other two," Tamiko says, her voice quavering just a little.

"What do you believe?"

"I have this big, joyous feeling for Lec that fills my heart so full it's like I'm overflowing with it," Tamiko replies. As she listens to her own words she gains confidence and adds, "And I can see in his eyes that he feels the same. So I believe that if we just hang tight, sooner or later, things will work out for us."

"Then I believe this too."

"Truly?"

"*No matter how thick the wilderness, love can make it's own path.*"

"Some Russian must have written that, but for once you have me stumped," Tamiko says with a laugh.

"Vera Gashkin, that is who."

"Thanks Vera, you're the best."

. . . . .

When Tamiko doesn't pick up at 6:15, Alec assumes she's switched off at dinner and leaves a cheerful message. An hour later when she still hasn't called back, and the hands of his watch have long since begun to look as if they're turning through molasses, he calls again. By seven forty-five, after leaving another worried voicemail, he considers driving to Palo Alto when Miles Davis finally begins playing in his pocket.

"Here I am loving you," Tamiko says when Alec picks up. "Sorry for the slow return, but it's been a blur here. Ten minutes ago when I was finally free to call, Mom called me first. Did I already tell you how much I love you?"

"Never enough, especially after this morning. The funny thing is I don't even have anything much to say except that I love you right back. I just needed to hear your voice to be sure you're safe."

"Lec, I probably shouldn't tell you, but in the shower earlier I began to think about you and, well…"

"If this going to be our first phone sex, maybe I better lie down," Alec interrupts with a laugh.

"Don't tease."

"Give me a second to try to recall who began this subject," Alec says, pretending to be serious.

"You're impossible. But listen, I want to ask you something, and I don't want you to laugh."

"No laughing. No teasing, cross my heart," Alec replies.

"I'm curious about whether when, you know, you actually do it with a real person, is it even..." Tamiko breaks off, fearful she's sounding exactly like a fifteen-year-old.

"Do you mean is it better than self-help?" Alec asks, not sure he's followed her meaning.

"Yes."

"With the right person you can multiply by a large number."

"Like, ten?" Tamiko replies, doing her best to keep the excitement out of her voice, but not succeeding.

"Double that at least,"

"You're at it again."

"Hopefully we'll both get to find out before forever."

THURSDAY 2

AT 8:15 A.M. ALEC PEEKS AT HIS CLOCK. Deciding to doze for fifteen more minutes he pulls the black T-shirt he keeps by his bed over his eyes. When he hears the ping that tells him a text has arrived, he thinks, ready or not, August 25 is under way. Reaching for his phone, he sees to his surprise that the message is from his uncle, "*Are you awake? Big sweet news. Call me when you can.*"

"*Eyes wide open now. Give me ten to caffeinate,*" Alec texts back as he steps out of his sleeping pants and into some briefs and slate blue jeans, both of which he has conveniently dropped next to his bed the night before. Padding barefoot to the bathroom for a teeth-clean and piss, he continues down the two flights of steps to the kitchen where Margo, bless her heart, has made a pot of Peet's coffee recently enough that it still smells yummy. Filling a mug, he unlocks the kitchen door, moves a green plastic chair into the sun, and calls his uncle.

"Lec, I apologize for the dawn shout, I hope I didn't wake you."

"No worries. What's this exciting news?" Alec asks.

"Emiko is flying to JFK."

"As in, now? Really?"

"Yup! and Yup!"

"But Friday you told me she'd turned down your invitation to come to the U.S.?"

"Turns out she didn't want to appear before my friends until her English was competent. Remember I told you that at first we mostly spoke Japanese, but recently she's surprised me with how fast she's been picking up English."

"She's been studying?"

"All-day classes, six days a week almost since we met. Yesterday morning, after she aced a proficiency test, she called and asked in Japanese if she was still welcome. When I said of course, she replied in perfect English, 'OK Mr. Charlie, pick me up tomorrow at JFK twelve forty-five p.m. at Japan Airlines. And don't dare be late.'"

"That's cool, you must be excited."

"I feel like I did when I was a sophomore at Dartmouth waiting for my girlfriend to come for Ice Carnival Weekend."

"Does this challenge any of the assumptions you've made about the future of your relationship?" Alec asks, belatedly taking a sip of his coffee.

"I'm going to let the future unwind in its own time."

"Sounds right, but you must have made plans for the next few days."

"We'll stay in Manhattan tomorrow and Saturday to let Emiko catch up on her sleep and get a taste of the Big Apple and then Sunday, we'll fly to Nantucket. But Lec, if I remember correctly, you're coming east on Sunday so I'm hoping you will come up to the Island next week."

"For sure I'd like to meet her. I'll have to stay around home for a couple of days to keep the parental peace. Count on me after that. How long is Emiko staying?"

"When I asked her she just laughed and said, 'Let's see how long it is you want me.' But Lec, how are you doing with your lovely young maiden and her ever watchful mother?"

"If I try to tell you everything that's happened since Tuesday you'll be an hour late getting to JFK. The abbreviated version is that Tamiko's mom, Amy, was attacked Tuesday morning by a very scary guy she met briefly in Amsterdam three springs ago. Then, before dawn Wednesday morning when he tried to kidnap her, I stopped him."

"How? Stopped him, how?"

"By poking him in the gut with a two-by-four before he could take me out with an iron bar. Unfortunately, he ran off before the cops appeared," Alec replies, deciding the details can wait until next week.

"Truly? I mean, I know you don't exaggerate, but…"

"Truly."

"Are you OK?"

Finishing off the now lukewarm coffee in a gulp, Alec replies, "Definitely except for being borderline paranoid about tomorrow's Organic Chemistry exam."

"Got it. Go lean on your books while I pick up Emi."

. . . . .

Tamiko has breakfast with Les a few minutes before 8:00 a.m., her uncle having hit the gym an hour before. When her aunt leaves for work a few minutes later saying that she'll be back for lunch and work from home in the afternoon, Tamiko begins grazing the floor-to-ceiling bookshelves that line the long wall of the rectangular living room. As she pulls out F. Scott Fitzgerald's *Tender Is the Night*, a title she started, but never finished, her phone begins playing Adele's "Hello".

"Hey Mom, what's up? Was your big dinner at the White House fun?"

"The President and First Lady were devastated that we got in too late to meet the Premier of France. But I'm calling to find out what's going on with you."

"It's great fun to spend time with Les and Dan. Dan was even kind enough to catch me yesterday and he's going to take me to Tsunami's practice later and hang out until I'm done. In the meantime I plan to find out what happens to Dick Diver in the second half of *Tender Is The Night*."

"If memory serves, he comes to a squeaky end."

"That's an almost universal problem with famous novels isn't it? No one takes a story seriously when things work out."

"Fair point, which is one of several reasons your dad loved the novels of Anthony Trollope. He thought fictional characters should have at least a fifty-fifty chance to live an OK life. But Sweetie, I need your help with *Death at the Golden Gate*. I just got the final proofs back from the printer and I don't have time to check them. I know Les and Dan have a fast printer so I'm hoping you can save Fitzgerald for another day and get on it. Remember, this isn't a final run-through like you did on *Slide Zone*, just the printer's proof where your job is to check for correct pagination, backwards pages, egregious typos, and anything else truly embarrassing."

"Can I start by changing the title? I mean, Golden Gate Bridge-mongering, really? How about calling it *Murder on Banal Bridge*?"

"Almost funny, but given how broke Bay is, you can be sure that the world's favorite bridge will stay on the cover."

"Got it, but if I'm even halfway careful checking for typos, this is going to take at least all day."

"I don't need to get it back to the printer until early tomorrow, so go all night if you need to."

"Hmm. Perhaps overtime might be involved? I mean, sacrificing *Tender Is the Night* is a pretty…"

"Well, perhaps you're a lucky fifteen-year-old to even have a job, but I'll run the idea past Ed. Changing the subject, is everything good with you? I mean the last couple of days have been full of a load of difficult stuff for you to take in, and well…"

"You mean like absorbing what happened to you in Europe and with the baby? I'm fine, Mom, really. When Dad was killed it was like the Titanic sank in our living room. Compared to that, your telling me about Amsterdam three years ago amounts to a pail of water in the bottom of a rowboat. I mean, I'm sorry about the baby and everything that went down with Max, but it's a new day, right."

"I hope so," Amy replies, as if her determination will make it so."

"Mom, you're the very best and always have been. Now send me the galleys so I can get started."

Adding milk, but no sugar to a large mug of coffee, Tamiko makes her way to the sun-dappled deck. Using her right foot to nudge a lattice-backed chair a few feet to the right she sits in the sun while placing the manuscript on the patio table in the shade of the large yellow umbrella. Ninety minutes later, after proofing seventy-five pages, she stands and stretches. Then, to overcome feeling bleary-eyed, she squats on the postage stamp lawn, cradles her head on her hands and kicks into a headstand.

When her red T-shirt falls to reveal a wide band of toned torso, she thinks, too bad Lec isn't here. Chuckling, she rolls down and places her phone on the grass in front of her before kicking back up. But try as she might, every time she attempts to extend her right arm far enough to activate the camera, she unbalances and tumbles over.

As she sips the last of her now-cold coffee Tamiko considers her options. Bending over so that her hair cascades waterfall-like to the grass hopefully disguising the fact that her head doesn't quite touch the ground, she spreads her legs wide. With her long left arm now extended around and behind her left leg, she angles her phone up as she snaps a picture designed to display her bare midriff at the same time it gives the illusion she's standing on her head. Then, sitting on the grass, her long legs splayed, she sends it to Lec along with a text that says, *"Bet you can't stand on your head and take a selfie at the same time."*

"Fibber—despite being blinded by your way cute belly button I can see under all that hair that your head isn't quite touching the lawn, not to mention the fact that your skinny legs are nowhere waving in the breeze."

"Busted, but don't you think it's even more amazing that I can stand on my head in mid-air? And as to who has skinny legs, well..."

"Ha!"

"Lec, hope you're OK with silly girl moments..."

"Who laughed at your dog joke?"

. . . . .

At 11:30 a.m., Ed's meeting at the Smithsonian wraps up. He has lunch scheduled with an exhibit curator he will work with in January, but in the meantime he borrows a cubicle and calls Amy. "I've been thinking of afternoon delights," Ed says, when she picks up.

"Are you talking about me or an apple tart with cool cherry cream?"

"Although George Harrison singing 'Savoy Truffle' has always made my mouth water, I'm pretty sure that nibbling you will be more fun. In fact, I'm imagining you lying naked on a king-sized bed under a crispy white sheet. You are easing the sheet down just enough so I can see your eager right…"

"Is this a boy fantasy or do I get to play?"

"Need you ask?"

"OK," Amy says with mock seriousness. "You're standing at the foot of the bed with a towel wrapped loosely around your waist. Hold on! I can see now that it's beginning to slip…"

"Sounds promising, but how about we freeze things right there until I can get back after lunch," Ed says, lowering his voice as he belatedly realizes that the young woman in the next cubicle is less than five feet away.

"How fast can you eat?"

"When you're on offer for dessert, we're talking nano seconds," Ed whispers. "But I doubt my colleague will feel the same sense of urgency so it will probably be two-thirty or a little later."

"No rush really," Amy says with a chuckle. "I'm betting once you get here you're going to show a girl a good time."

"Count on it. But in the meantime, any news from the Left Coast? Have you talked to Dana or Melvin?"

"Dana, a few minutes ago. Remember, it's not quite nine in Berkeley."

"And…"

"There's nothing significant to report, except that the Oakland police have found the motel Max stayed in through Sunday night. It's a low-end place on International Boulevard in East Oakland popular with hookers. Apparently he and the elderly Ford showed up there a week ago. But there have been no sightings since Monday even though similar motels from Fairfield to San Jose are being checked."

"So, the shrink was right."

"Malcolm Frank, yes, but in fairness, even without a PhD, Melvin and Dana came to pretty much the same conclusion."

"What about fingerprints in the motel room that could be checked against some sort of European data base, like Interpol or something?" Ed asks, trailing off as he realizes he has little idea what he's talking about.

"Apparently, even the Tip Top Inn wipes down its rooms now and then, not to mention that Room 27 was used on an almost hourly basis on Monday and Tuesday. But on to a subject I actually know something about. Tami, Tamiko that is—and before you say anything, I mostly am doing better—is checking the page proofs on *Death at the Golden Gate* as we speak. I've been able to track down Phyllis at her holiday place in Mexico and she's agreed to change the two surnames in *Dizzy Moon* our lawyer objected to and I'm all over Acme Printing to get *Dragon Little* on the press by next Tuesday."

"I'm still amazed you talked me into publishing that one," Ed says with a vehemence that tells Amy he's about to vent.

"Haven't we beaten this argument stone cold dead?" she interrupts. "It's the kind of Young Adult title that can easily cross over into the adult market in a big way. If I'm right and it does, Bay won't have to worry about paying the electricity bill for a few years."

"A talking dragon who has vampire fantasies and, oh, by the way, is afraid to fly. I mean, really…"

"Flying dragons are beyond banal as Tamiko likes to say. By contrast, an earth-bound dragon is unexpected and so, interesting. And remember, if *Dragon Little* tops our fall list, I get an extra week's vacation."

"Only if you use it to visit me in D.C. for immoral purposes."

"Let's see how it goes this afternoon, big guy."

· · · · ·

With two covers and the fall list catalog to finalize, Amy cajoles several Bay employees to work from home despite Ed's having magisterially granted everyone the rest of the week off. A little before two o'clock she walks a couple of blocks to a chain drugstore where she buys an apple, a box of Cheez-Its, and a bottle of jasmine massage oil. Back in the room by two-twenty, she crawls under the crispy white sheet. Realizing that Ed may be held up for reasons beyond his control she tries to curb her excitement with the always delicious prospect of a mini-nap. But no sooner has she rolled onto her stomach than her phone sounds with its old-fashioned ring.

"Amy, Dana Helickson here."

"Anything new?" Amy asks as she squirms her thin body up and against the headboard with two pillows behind her.

"I'm on your front porch checking on things."

"It would be a huge help if you can bring in the mail and newspaper, which doesn't go on hold until tomorrow. I assume you have the key I gave Melvin," Amy says.

"I have all three in my hand, but there's also a FedEx envelope here with an unreadable return address. Are you expecting something?"

"No, I frequently get overnight deliveries at Bay, but not at home."

"I have an unpleasant hunch. Is it OK if I open it?"

"Please do," Amy says, pulling the spread over her breasts and up to her neck.

"I'm inside now, so give me a second," Dana says. And then after a longish pause, she continues, "I'm going to start by suggesting you to take a deep breath."

"Max?" Amy asks angrily, as she swings her feet to the floor and reaches for her white top lying on a nearby chair.

"Yes, and it's extremely unpleasant."

"Why am I not surprised?" Amy says, pulling the top over her head and reaching for her pants.

"Here goes, minus the many misspellings:

"Amy, I sad if I hurt you. I here to make you happy. So happy like Amsterdam on first night. Remember, you so excited you come back for more. We are such good friends really. I think all time of your pretty pink cunty. I think of my hard big boy inside. Just meet me, make me happy, and I kiss you goodbye forever. Time is short and big daughter so pretty. You come to Montgomery Street BART station by tickets machine near A1 stairs at ten tomorrow morning. We go to nice hotel, have glass of wine, and I make you so happy. I already thinking about sucking your tiny titties. Never hurt you, but I be mad if you not come. Skinny guy with stick not always be there. Max"

"If he had just referred to my breasts as small, he might have had a chance," Amy says dryly.

"I'm delighted you still have your sense of humor."

"It helps to be three thousand miles away. But Dana, when you get back to the station, can you shoot me a copy of the note so I can show it to Ed?" Amy asks, now pacing from door to window and back in the largish room.

"Sure, and in the meantime we'll ask the SFPD to check and recheck hotels over there, even the better ones since Max obviously has a wallet full of your money. And of course we'll be at Montgomery Street BART tomorrow morning. Apparently Max hasn't tumbled to the fact that you're out of town."

"Dana, I'm still worried about Tamiko. For the life of me I can't think of any way Max can find her, but now that we know for sure he's still on the prowl, she's just too darn close to Berkeley for my…"

"As we've found out the hard way looking for Max, the Bay Area is not a bad place to hide," Dana says reassuringly.

"Unless somehow he traces my sister."

"Amy, are we maybe going around in circles here?"

"No doubt, sorry—it's just that I can't seem to escape my anxiety," Amy replies, as she flops back on the bed.

. . . . .

A little before three Ed comes through the door singing "Dessert time." Seeing Amy standing fully clothed with her fists clenched in the middle of the room, he stops short. "I'm guessing something's up at home," he says as he steps forward to wrap her in his arms.

"That disgusting man FedExed me a message that basically says if I don't fuck him tomorrow in San Francisco, he'll hurt me, and/or Tami. There's other nasty stuff too, but that's the gist."

"Was the FedEx sent to Francisco Street?"

"Yes, Dana found it when she stopped by to check the house."

"I guess the good news is that Max must be lying so low he hasn't figured out we've left town, but I wonder why he didn't just call you?"

"Dana thinks he may be between phones, but I'm guessing he actually believes that a few of what he considers to be sweet words will work to get me into his bed," Amy says, wrinkling her nose in disgust. "But Ed, don't you see that the point is no matter how many cops look for him, he's still out there waiting to pounce."

"Even Max isn't capable of a transcontinental pounce," Ed says in his most reassuring tone.

"To land on Tamiko he doesn't need to be. And no need to give me another pep talk about how safe she is, since Dana just finished."

"Did she convince you?"

"I don't know, sort of, but with Max it's hard not to be paranoid so I called Les. I needed to be sure that from now on she's working from home or taking Tami with her to SRI. Listen, I'm sorry but all of this has made me too damn angry to get back into our fantasy, even though…"

"Ever had pissed-off sex?"

"At this point I'm willing to try anything," Amy says, taking a step towards Ed.

"No foreplay. We just fuck on the floor like the world is going to end in three minutes."

"My pants are already half off," Amy replies, as her actions mirror her words.

$\cdots\cdots$

At 4:00 p.m. Tamiko puts down the proofs, blows a kiss at Les who's on a conference call in the dining room, and heads to the kitchen where earlier she'd spotted half of a lemon cake. Mouth now full of tangy crumble she continues up to her attic room to change into her Tsunami shorts and a green T-shirt that says *Don't send a boy to do a girl's job* in white letters across the chest. With only fifty pages to complete and having already found two howler typos—"coach" instead of "couch" and "discrete" to mistakenly describe a woman's effort to keep a dalliance private—she's feeling pleased. With Dan still nowhere in evidence she takes a moment to examine herself in the medicine cabinet mirror. Not remotely satisfied that the person looking back is interesting enough to hold a beautiful older guy's attention, she reaches back with her left hand and gathers her mass of honey-colored hair behind her neck. Puckering her lips, she turns almost ninety degrees, looks back over her shoulder and widens her almond shaped blue eyes. Damn it, she thinks, the girl in the mirror still looks like she goes to high school. When neither grinning nor pouting improves things, she sticks out her tongue as she mumbles, "Good thing you're not the only mirror in the world."

. . . . .

By 4:30 p.m., Tamiko is in the passenger seat of her Uncle Dan's new Ford Fusion, stuck in seriously constipated traffic on the Dumbarton Bridge. "Dan, I'm sorry to put you through this. Except for wanting to show Coach that I've been working on my pitching I could have skipped today."

"Not a problem. I'm looking forward to watching you ladies practice. I've heard that's what you call yourselves, right?"

"Sort of, I guess. 'Ladies' is like a weird historical holdover from the 1920's or whenever women played slowpitch softball in dresses or bloomers or whatever. We never refer to ourselves that way, but coaches love to. Like, I mean, if I had a dollar for every time Coach has yelled, 'C'mon ladies, get the lead out!' I'd be one rich lady,"

"Funny. But if I'm not invading your privacy too much, Les told me that you have a controversial boyfriend."

"Depends who you ask I guess, although I'm betting even Mom likes him a little better since he saved her yesterday."

"I guess you could argue that Alec wouldn't have been guarding your house in the middle of the night if he didn't honestly care about you."

"A point I've tried to make, but hey, you better get over to the right lane pretty soon."

"Got it, thanks," Dan says as he checks his mirror, flicks his turn signal and tucks in just ahead of a green van. "For the record, I think people often make too much of age differences, especially relatively small ones."

"Lec is six years older so I'm trying to cut Mom some slack, at least until she has a chance to get used to the idea. Also, well, the truth is, I have no idea if I can be what Lec wants. In the nine days since I've met him it's like my life has gone from a stroll to a run, but still I started miles behind," Tamiko says.

"But if you were twenty-one and he was twenty-eight, it wouldn't be nearly as big a deal. And if you two were in your thirties or older, no one would notice. Case in point, Ed is almost eight years older than your mom, right?"

"Sure, but…"

"My point is Amy's objection has to be more about her thinking you're too young to be in a serious relationship, not the age gap per se."

"Interesting. Do you agree with her by the way?"

"Not necessarily. I don't know your new friend, so this isn't an endorsement of him, but with all you've had to handle in life and how well you've coped, I'm guessing you're far enough up Fool's Hill to make a good decision."

"Fool's Hill?"

"My grandmother says that no matter how much wisdom mankind accumulates over time, each of us has to struggle up our own mountain of ignorance—Fool's Hill, she calls it—to hopefully see over the top before we die."

"You must have an interesting grandma."

"I do, but of more importance now is whether you're mature enough to cope with disappointment if your friend moves on. I'm pretty sure that's what Amy's really worried about. But enough of that. How about giving me a quick overview of what I'm going to see this afternoon?"

"Turn left at the second light. Eighteen years ago, Coach Rodriguez volunteered to help with his daughter's team and fell in love with fastpitch. When she got too old to play, he kept going. Gradually over the years he's made Tsunami into a mini-dynasty, always one of the top summer club teams in NorCal and sometimes, like this year, in the state."

"Because the team is consistently good, it allows your coach to recruit excellent players like you?"

"Coach does everything a little differently including recruiting. Most coaches at the eighteen and under level almost automatically pick athletes who have been top players at the younger ages. But Coach thinks too many kids who have known early success aren't hungry enough, so he searches out girls with talent who, for some reason, others overlook."

"Like you, perhaps?"

"Well, like my friend Jazz for sure, who's barely five feet tall but a hella good second baseman. I was in a different category since I wasn't quite fourteen when Coach, who was checking out a pitcher at Berkeley High, passed on her, and recruited me. His toughest job was talking Mom into agreeing since, as I said, Tsunami is an eighteen-and-under team."

"Given Amy's protective instincts he must be a convincing guy. In fact, you might ask him to coach Alec."

"Ha, now there's a thought," Tamiko says, again impressed by Dan's unusual ideas. "Coach R is unique for sure. Not only is he almost as wide as he is tall, but he shaves his head, wears a Zapata 'stashe and has one of those way fat Harleys. Years ago he was in the Phillies farm system for a couple of years, and then the military. Now he drives a truck, coaches softball, and teaches pitching. Turn left again at the corner and we're there."

As they coast to a stop in the parking lot behind San Leandro High, Tamiko, who has already changed from flip-flops to cleats, sprints to the field in an attempt to show Coach she's contrite about being late. Perhaps because it's the summer's last practice for his best-ever team, he limits himself to a sarcastic, "Glad you could join us B" instead of his usual diatribe:

Early is on time
On time is late
Late is in trouble.

Alternating at short with Ashley Beck, Tsunami's Jill-of-all-positions backup infielder, Tamiko quickly settles into the rhythm of Coach's brisk infield practice. Standing at home plate the rotund, bald man scalds balls in all directions as he booms out game situations, *"two outs—runner on second, one out—runners on first and third, bases loaded—leadoff hitter who bunts and slaps."*

When he is finally satisfied, Coach calls in the outfielders who have been sprinting after balls hit high and deep over their heads by Roxy's dad. With Amber and Char alternating on the rubber, the girls divide themselves into impromptu teams with scoring based on a well-understood, but impossible to explain system involving the number, distance, and arc of hard-hit balls.

With things running smoothly, Coach motions Tamiko to the pitcher's warm up cage where Juan Gonzalez, Amber's dad, is waiting mask in hand. As soon as Tamiko throws a dozen mostly accurate fastballs, she makes a fist with her pinky sticking up, to tell Juan she plans to throw a screwball. But before she can swing into her windup, Coach, who is standing just outside the cage growls, "Let's look at your riser first." Having long experience with Coach's control needs, Tamiko nods as she again raises her fist, this time with both pinky and forefinger extended. Ten minutes and twenty pitches later Coach, ever the perfectionist, is still fussing with her release point as he says for the fifth time, "Tamiko, unless you lean back further as you drive forward with your legs and spin your wrist, you're gonna throw uphill fastballs with no hop and I think you know where even a half-good hitter will deposit those."

A year earlier, still intimidated by her Coach's formidable reputation and gruff manner, Tamiko would have said nothing. Now, after a summer in which she's proven herself to be one of the best players in Northern California, she replies, "I'm hard on it Coach, but to be fair, isn't my ball jumping? I mean, ask Coach Gonzalez."

Scowling as he turns toward Amber's dad, who's now standing to stretch his legs, Coach says with mock formality, "So tell me Coach Gonzalez, whose risers hop more, Amber's, Charlene's, or the ones this athlete here has been throwing?"

"For sure Char's," Juan replies with a smile. "It's her best pitch."

"Who's second?"

"Amber, no doubt, but to be fair to the athlete standing next to you, otherwise known as B," Jim says, "her riser is starting to hop like a medium-sized rabbit."

"OK, OK," Tamiko says, "Point taken, let's keep working. It's just that I'd hoped to show you that my screwball is…"

"What are you waiting for then?" Coach says with a scowl, his hands resting on the shelf made by his protruding belly.

Knowing better than to reply, Tamiko raises her fist, pinky extended. After another ten minutes during which Coach seems at least somewhat impressed by Tamiko's ability to move the ball up and in towards right-handed batters, he says, "Enough, I need to talk to the team for a minute and it's getting late."

"But Coach, you haven't even looked at my two-seam fastball, I think I'm beginning to get my finger pressure right, but I could use some…"

"I'll see it Saturday, B," Coach Rodriguez interrupts. "The ball will be in your shoe for the third game."

"Really? Wow! Coach, this means a lot to me."

"You're welcome, but remember, I don't do favors for my athletes—you've earned a start and you've got it. But listen B, another college recruiter called about you. This time some assistant coach at the University of Florida who was obviously born someplace else because he never got that accent talking to a gator. Anyway, when he said you were their number one West Coast prospect, I replied like I always do—you're still fifteen and under NCAA rules you are too young to be contacted directly. But especially if this is going to be your senior year in high school, I guess maybe that's not true anymore. Anyway, he says he plans to be at Twin Creeks Saturday so we need to figure out what's what. Obviously B, within the rules I want to do everything I can to help you get a full ride at a top softball school."

"Forget it, Coach. I registered with the NCAA like you told me to, but like I've been trying to explain, I have no interest in going to school in Florida, Texas, or Southern California. I want to go to a top academic school in the Northeast where hopefully I'll have a chance to pitch if I can improve a lot in the next year."

"B, I've been doing this for close on twenty years and you're one of the top two or three hitters I've coached. With your arm you can play shortstop at almost any school you choose, and maybe even make the National team when college is done."

"Thanks Coach, but it's more fun to pitch."

"I'm just another fool who dropped out of high school so I know diddly nada about the Ivy League, but if that's your dream my job is to help you achieve it."

. . . . .

On their way back to Palo Alto a few minutes after seven o'clock, Dan says, "I was impressed by your coach. Not only is he a superb teacher, he's just intimidating enough that everyone busts their butts to please him. Now that I've seen how good your team is I'm really looking forward to seeing you play on Saturday. But why was everyone calling you 'B'?"

"Most of the players on Tsunami come from working-class backgrounds, in part because lots of blue-collar families dream of getting their kids athletic scholarships, which might be the only way they'll get near a four-year school."

"Sorry to be dense, but I'm still not following."

"Yo dude, give me a chance," Tamiko says, as if she's still joking with one of her teammates. The thing is that players from affluent places like Berkeley and Palo Alto, where parents often want their kids to miss tournaments for extended family vacations—maybe even to Europe—are looked down on as being soft by kids who have hardly been out of the Bay Area. So, when Coach brought me in as a skinny, almost fourteen-year-old shortstop, to push aside a popular seventeen-year-old from Hayward, everyone called me 'Berkeley' as if it was dengue fever."

"How did you handle that?"

"Kept my mouth shut until one day at practice when a third girl in a row slid in too high and too hard, I tagged her on the face. This led to some pushing and shoving and even though the other kid outweighed me by twenty pounds I didn't back down. Mercifully Coach stepped in before I got pancaked. In our first tournament the next Saturday after I hit two home runs Coach yelled, 'Way to rock it B," and Jazz and a few others picked it up."

"So Berkeley became B and an insult became a term of affection?"

"More or less, although when a few of them get in a ghetto mood they still yell, 'Yo Berkeley, did Jeeves polish your silver spoon this morning?' But guess what? Coach said I'll pitch the third game."

"So the pitching practice went well. I couldn't tell."

"It's not always easy to read Coach, even for me. I'm guessing he's still doubtful about whether I can succeed at this level, but he wants my bat on the team next year so he'll give me every chance. And then there is the fact that we really are kind of buddies. By the way, he said there will be at least one college scout at the tournament, some guy from Florida with a funny accent, who's coming just to see me."

"I would have guessed most softball coaches are women."

"It's slowly trending that way, but at the most competitive schools there are still plenty of men."

"Did you mention the Florida coach because you're worried about a stranger with a funny accent? If so, we can call your mom and..."

"Oh god no! Really, Dan, if Mom hears a whisper I'll be on the next plane to D.C. Anyway, I'm positive it's just routine. Coaches are always checking out Tsunami players because so many do well at Division One schools. And ever since I got featured by this softball website I'm on a lot of lists."

· · · · ·

Amy's phone rings as she comes down the front steps of the Jefferson Memorial where she's enjoyed reading the great man's words. She and Ed have been trying to escape their worries by playing tourist for an hour, but with her display showing 'Dana' she knows it's back to Max-filled angst.

Hesitating for only a moment, she asks, "Dana, what's up?"

"I'm in a meeting with Lieutenant Ramsey and Officer Sofi from the SFPD here at headquarters. I'm putting you on speaker."

"Got it, Melvin, Officer Sofi, nice to meet you."

"Todd, please."

"Dana, Melvin, Todd, I'm putting you guys on speaker too since Ed is here."

"Amy, Ed, we're discussing the best way to handle tomorrow morning short of Amy flying back to be our tethered goat," Lieutenant Ramsey says.

"I hope that was a joke," Ed says abruptly.

"A poor attempt obviously," Sergeant Helickson replies, not bothering to mask her annoyance.

"I didn't mean to offend," Lieutenant Ramsey says in a tone that makes it clear that he thinks no apology is really needed. "But to get back to the point, our best guess is that Max won't risk being any where near the Montgomery Street BART station tomorrow, but will call and ask you to go someplace else."

"Makes sense, but I don't see how I can help from here?" Amy says, as she nudges Ed towards a sunny bench.

"Maybe not, but let's try," Lieutenant Ramsey replies. "We want you to call us on Ed's phone ten minutes before ten West Coast time and keep the line open. Then, assuming Max calls you at ten, you'll pretend you're in the BART station all the while holding Ed's phone next to yours so we can hear and hopefully react in real time. But don't use your speaker since it obviously changes the sound."

"Let me get this straight," Amy says, looking at Ed and rolling her eyes. "I'm to pretend I'm at Montgomery Street BART next to the ticket machine hoping to have sex with this monster. I mean really Melvin, how believable is that? And, what if he doesn't call but shows up?"

"Officer Wu from the SFPD will be in the station facing the ticket machines so that Max, in the unlikely event he appears, will only be able to see her from the back," Sergeant Helickson says. "Wu's about your age with shortish hair,".

"All Asians look alike?"

"Of course not, but it's the best we can do and as I said we're not expecting Max to show. For example, if he pays someone to give the attractive Asian woman by the ticket machines a note, Wu will probably do."

"Assuming he calls, what do I say?" Amy asks, genuinely at a loss to understand what she's being asked to do.

"You'll have to go with the flow," Sergeant Helickson says. "Perhaps your best approach will be to act worried about Tamiko's safety and make Max promise not to hurt her in exchange for your meeting him. But Amy, the details aren't as important as keeping him talking."

"I'm just a humble book publisher," Ed says, "but I am pretty doubtful Max is going to believe that Amy will voluntarily put herself in his clutches. I mean, if he thinks that why would he have tried to abduct her?"

"Point taken," Sergeant Helickson says. "But we've learned more than once to be cautious about jumping to seemingly logical conclusions when we're dealing with people who may not be entirely sane. So if Max does call, Amy, your job is to keep his hope up so with luck we'll glean something that'll lead us to him. And remember, although he is obviously expert at self-protection, he's just as obviously obsessed with you or we wouldn't even be having this conversation. Malcolm Frank, who I just talked to again, agrees that there is a decent possibility that if you appear receptive to his advances, he'll believe you because some part of him desperately wants to."

"Thrilling."

"Amy, if you don't want to do this we can…"

"Sorry. I'm in, of course, since no one wants to catch Max more than I do. I guess my approach could be something like, 'Max, I had an amazing time with you that first night in Amsterdam, which is why I went back to find you at the Hollywood, but then, you were so angry with me I'm worried that I can't trust you not to hurt me.'"

"Excellent," Sergeant Helickson says, "sound interested, maybe even attracted, but scared. Hang back and let him talk you into it."

"Into what? I'm three thousand miles away."

"But Officer Wu will be there. So for example, if he tells you to take BART to a different station we'll relay the message to Wu and have her catch the next train while SFPD scrambles a bunch of folks over there."

"I'll try of course, but despite being half Irish, I've never been a good bullshitter. And what about tracing his call? Can you do that if I keep him talking?"

"We'll get a court order and try," Lieutenant Ramsey replies, "but he'll almost certainly use a cheap throwaway phone without GPS, which means that the best we can do is to locate the general area where the cell carrier picked up the call. But hold on a second Amy, we have a call from the Piedmont PD that relates to Max."

After less than thirty seconds the Lieutenant is back saying, "To save time I'm putting Officer Michael Soto from the Piedmont force on the large speaker here in the conference room. Hopefully you'll be able to hear what he has to say. Go ahead, Mike."

"Thanks, Lieutenant, and Mr. Crane, I'm sorry to report that your house was vandalized last night, or very early this morning. The teenage neighbor you tasked with bringing in the paper and mail alerted us about an hour ago."

"What did they take?" Ed asks, unable to keep the annoyance out of his voice.

"Nothing as far as we can see, but of course, only you can say for sure. There isn't any obvious sign of a break-in so we're guessing that the perpetrator found a key, or possibly stole your garage door opener from your car which I gather from my Berkeley colleagues, is parked at Bay Books. But Mr. Crane, I'm sorry to tell you that there's considerable damage inside the house, almost as if the perpetrator was angry. For example, the big-screen TV in the nook by the kitchen and the Mac computer in the office have been smashed as have a lot of items in the kitchen. One thing that stands out is a large photo of a Caucasian man and an Asian female was torn into pieces and left on the floor in a pile of broken glass."

"Anything else?" Ed asks, his voice tight and his fists balled.

"Sorry to keep giving you distressing news, but the perpetrator defecated on the bed in the master suite upstairs. In addition, all the drawers in the office desk were pulled out with the contents tossed helter-skelter."

"We obviously have to assume this was Max," Sergeant Helickson says. "Ed, was there anything in those drawers that could have told Max where you are now, or more important, where Tamiko is?"

"No, as I said Wednesday I've barely met Amy's sister and don't have any of her contact info. And as for where we're staying, I made the reservation by phone from the airport."

"What about your computer? Would the hotel have sent an email confirmation?" Officer Sofi asks.

"Damn it. I'm sure they did since they asked for my email. And since my computer isn't password-protected it's sitting right there in my Gmail, which displays on the menu bar."

"So, anyone with minimal computer savvy could easily have found your reservation confirmation. But even if Max got that far he couldn't be sure that Amy is with you. Also there's the fact that you two really are three thousand miles away. Put it all together and I'm guessing that the chances you are in danger are minuscule," Lieutenant Ramsey says reassuringly.

"Sounds right, but as we've already learned, when dealing with Max it's hard to be too paranoid," Amy says, sliding down the bench a couple of feet so as to be in the shade.

"I can't argue with that," Lieutenant Ramsey agrees, "but remember we'll know more by tomorrow morning, since Max will only call if he believes Amy is still in the Bay Area."

. . . . .

Arriving at Clyde's in the Georgetown section of Washington D.C. half an hour early for their dinner reservation, Ed takes Amy's arm and guides her to a stool at the L-shaped wooden bar. "I badly need a single malt Scotch, or maybe three. What about you?"

"As you know, I don't usually finish a glass of white wine, but today I'm all about having a real drink."

"How about a margarita? Sweet, salty, and altogether delicious. In fact, I think I just talked myself into one, too."

"Sounds perfect, but first I need to wash up and take a couple Pepcid AC's," Amy says, sliding off the stool.

"Tummy ache?"

"No, it coats the stomach which means when I drink the tequila I won't turn quite so pink."

"Who said pink isn't my favorite color?"

"If it was, I'm guessing you'd be chasing the woman by the door," Amy says nodding towards a blonde Nordic type who has obviously spent too much time in the sun. "And, if I'm going to drink tequila I'll also need something to eat prontoish."

When Amy returns, Ed is sitting in one of the booths across from the long side of the bar. "Appetizers are on the way, and the blonde was so dazzled by your beauty, she slunk off to buy sunblock," he says lifting one of the salt-rimmed glasses. Waiting for Amy to do the same Ed says, "To peace in the valley." Then, as they clink glasses he asks, "So how do you feel?"

"Did you ever wake from a dream where you were running through an airport or train station, but instead of arriving at your destination, you hit more and more obstacles, dead ends, and even the occasional abyss? The longer the dream lasts the scarier it becomes."

"Sure, but in mine clocks with no hands play a big part, sort of like that Ingmar Bergman movie whose name I can't remember."

"Wild Strawberries—with the old man in the city of the dead. And, yes, that feeling of menace is exactly what I mean. It's as if every time we think we may be free of Max, here he comes again, relentless, scary, and demonic."

"You should have been a poet, but hey, are you going to drink that thing?"

Smiling, despite herself, Amy asks, "OK if we retoast?" Seeing Ed's nod she again touches her glass to his as she says, "You and me, now and forever, one and inseparable."

When the waiter arrives with fried calamari and a plate of olives, Ed takes a couple of bites before pulling out his phone. "Excuse me for a second while I step outside for a quick call," he says, as he slides out of the booth. Before Amy has consumed her third bite of the golden brown squid, Ed is back with a wide grin on his face. "I just made us a reservation at the Willard as Mr. and Mrs. Wickersham."

"But our stuff is at the Holiday Inn." Amy says, genuinely surprised.

"How about we inhale these appetizers and take an Uber over there and pack up. Then we can check into the Willard as George and Edna Wickersham, before ordering the best dinner room service has on offer."

"Oh Ed, you are a sweet man. I know you're doing this to humor me in case Max somehow got into your computer, but…"

"You can kiss me in the cab."

"Depending how long the ride is I'll happily to do more than that," Amy says, taking a big swallow of her drink.

"Let's save the fireworks for later. My thought is that the Wickershams are checking into a posh hotel precisely because it makes them feel horny."

"Perhaps the Wickershams would prefer to say 'concupiscent' or 'libidinous.'"

"Indubitably."

FRIDAY 2

ALEC OPENS HIS EYES AT 6:58, to see he has a text from Tamiko.

"Rise, shine and knock 'em dead! It won't be long until you're free at last."

Sadly not free to do what I have most in mind, he thinks as he texts back *"Looking forward to seeing you tomorrow and maybe even shaking hands. LOL."*

"One can always hope that Mom will emancipate me on my 16th b-day with no need for a civil war," Tamiko immediately fires back, as if she's read his mind.

. . . . .

At 12:30 p.m. East Coast time, with a half-hour to go before Amy's supposed meetup with Max at the Montgomery Street BART station, Amy and Ed sit by the window of their hotel room discussing strategy with the team of officers gathered in Berkeley. For the most part the plan they developed the day before stays in place despite some interdepartmental drama the previous evening. Officer Wu apparently insisted that, despite the opinions of several male supervisors, her flip looked nothing like the picture she was shown of Amy's sleek A-line bob and so refused to participate until the department agreed to pay for her hair to be restyled.

At 12:45 Sergeant Helickson says, "Amy, we think it's best if you and Ed go down to the lobby, or even out on the street in front of the hotel. We don't want Max to become suspicious because there's no background noise."

"When do you want me to call you on my phone?" Ed asks.

"In five minutes, in case Max is ahead of schedule."

. . . . .

As she stands about twenty-five feet to the left of the Willard's front desk Amy's phone rings at 1:01 p.m. indicating a number she doesn't recognize. Moving the green answer icon, she does her best to sound plaintive as she says, "I'm here at Montgomery Street BART, but I don't see you anywhere. Also, Max, I'm feeling a little afraid."

"I know when you get chance to think about it, you come. You remember Amsterdam and want me. No worry, I be gentle, so gentle and strong like you want. Tell me where you are?"

"I just told you, at Montgomery Street BART by the ticket machines near the A1 stairs as you said. But I can't see you anywhere and I'm getting..."

"No worry, you see me very soon. I need you now go upstairs to Market Street and get cab to nice hotel."

"I don't know if I can trust you. I'm worried that..."

"No, no, everything is very nice. Remember how we are such good friends in Amsterdam. This be just like that. You come to fancy hotel where everything is beautiful."

"But where do I tell the cab to go?"

"First get cab, then I tell. No worry, everything safe and happy."

"What did you say? It's so noisy here I can't hear you."

"Go up to Market Street and get cab," Max yells so loud that Sergeant Helickson winces.

"OK, I'm going to the stairs, but this will take a minute since there are a lot of people, so hold on." Then counting slowly to twenty Amy exits the Willard onto Pennsylvania Avenue as she says, "OK, I'm almost at the top now."

"Go outside and get cab on same side of street going west," Max again shouts, excitement thickening his accent.

"Wait, wait a second," Amy peremptorily replies. Counting to ten and pretending to be out of breath she adds, "Sorry, this big guy ran ahead of me and got the only cab. But hold on, here's another one coming. He sees me. Wait a second. Then, after again pausing for five seconds, she gasps,

"Yes, I have it. Hold on while I get in."

"Let me talk to driver."

"What did you say? I can't hear you," Amy says as she steps to the curb and extends her phone towards the sound of a police siren.

"The driver, let me talk to him," Max again shouts.

"He's wearing a turban. I'm not sure he speaks English. Can't you just tell me?"

"Indians all speak English, give him phone."

"Hold on," Amy says as she steps over to one of the Willard's stone pillars and holding the phone a few inches away smacks the pillar twice with her open left hand to simulate banging on a partition. "Mr. Singh, Mr Singh," she says as if reading his name off his license card, "can you take my phone so this man can tell you where to go?" Then handing the phone to Ed she mouths, "Do your best."

"Must go now, sir. Please to tell me where, sir?" Ed says in his best attempt at an Indian accent.

"The Marriott on Post and Mason. It's called JW Marriott. One block from Union Square."

"Yes sir, OK sir, right away. But traffic slow. Take a little moment, sir."

Beads of perspiration standing on his forehead, Ed hands the phone back to Amy. Extending her arm towards Pennsylvania Avenue as if she's taking a selfie, Amy smiles when several Washington D.C. cabs obligingly honk and a siren wails in the distance. Taking several steps in the opposite direction, Ed says into his phone, "Did you guys get all that?"

"Clear as a bell, but Ed, I don't think you have much of a future as a Sikh cab driver," Sergeant Helickson chuckles, "but where's Amy?"

"In front of the hotel pretending she's in the cab. I'll catch her up in a second."

"Do that. In the meantime, the SFPD is scrambling people to the Marriott so obviously the longer Amy can string him along, the better."

"Where you are? Where you are now?" Max is asking Amy when Ed again holds his phone next to hers.

"Stopped at a light on Market. Sorry, I can't see the sign. Wait, wait, the streetcar is moving now. It's Fifth Street and our light just changed so it's only a few more blocks although there's an ambulance parked half a block ahead trying to pick up someone. But Max I'm still scared you'll hurt me. I'm thinking maybe I should go home."

"No, like I say I very nice. I never hurt you. I sorry about putting hands on you before. I upset then, not happy like now. And I make you so happy too. But where is cab? And what color? You should be here."

"Red, it's red like a cherry, very bright. You can't miss it. I think it says 'Flywheel' on the side," Amy says. "We're moving now, but not very fast because of some delivery truck double parked. OK, good, we just squeezed past the truck and the light is green. Which side of the hotel are you on?"

"I'm in hotel drive by entrance at corner of Mason and Post, but I don't see red cab."

"Sorry, sorry, traffic is stopped again," Amy says, trying to sound convincing, even as she fears she's invented one delay too many.

"This big lie, I think. Traffic is fine here and I not see red cab so I leave now."

"Wait Max, wait. I'm just around the corner. The driver is letting me out here to save time. Hold on, I can see the hotel sign now so I'm almost there." Turning to Ed, Amy covers her phone as she says, "Damn, I think we lost him."

"Keep talking. Don't give up, he may still be checking out the street."

"Which I'm not on, obviously," Amy says as she steps out of the way of half a dozen shopping bag-laden Chinese tourists.

"Let's get inside where we can hear better," Ed says when he catches up with Amy. Then, as they enter the lobby he says into his phone, "Dana, are we right in guessing Max got away?"

"Remember we're in Berkeley so give us a minute to catch up with what's happening on the ground. We'll get back to you when we know something,"

Five minutes later when, back in their room, Ed answers his phone at its first sound he puts it on speaker. Sergeant Helickson says, "All we really know so far, is that two SFPD cars arrived at the Marriott barely a minute after a shiny black Cadillac SUV pulled away. The San Francisco officers are talking to the doorman as we speak, and there is an alert out for the vehicle. In the meantime Amy, what can I say, but that you were magnificent."

"I don't mean to be critical, or maybe I do," Ed says, "but didn't the San Francisco police have plenty of time to get someone to that hotel?"

. . . . .

Thanks to his almost maniacal preparation, Alec finishes his exam feeling elated, sure he's aced it. Pulling out his phone, he taps Tamiko's number.

"At the GONG it will be vacation time," she sings by way of answering.

"Already four minutes into it."

"I hope your delay in calling isn't a statement."

"Just taking a moment to think about how lovely you are. What's up?"

"I'm just back from lunch and birthday shopping with Auntie Les. I'll give you a hint, there's not much to my present."

"Assuming it's something you wear, color me enthusiastic."

"Lec, my games are at eight, twelve and four tomorrow and there's a rumor I might pitch a few innings in the last one."

"Yo, girl, I'm already looking forward to seeing your riser hop. But I might not make the first game since one of my housemates is having a party to celebrate the end of the summer session. Actually, party is an overstatement, more of a low key kick-it since most summer session people are already done and gone. But big or small, I have to pick up a couple of jugs and some munchies and then hang out for a while to make up for bringing the blue meanies down on our house. And even if I sneak upstairs to my room early, there'll be no sleeping until everyone leaves and the music is turned off."

When Tamiko doesn't reply, Alec asks, "Hey, you still there?"

"Sorry, I was having a scared moment," Tamiko replies in a small voice.

"Huh? About what?" Alec asks as he heads towards Bancroft Way on the path next to Kroeber Hall.

"Lec, it's just that I've never even been to a party. Well, the kind of party you're talking about anyway. For a minute there I was thinking that maybe Mom's right about my being way over my head."

"College parties are nothing special, just for when you want to let off a little steam or maybe meet someone."

"You're not making me feel better."

"I already met someone, and thanks to my little tiff with Max the other night I've let off plenty of steam."

"For real? I mean the part about your already having met someone, even if that someone is just out of diapers."

"Ha! I'm guessing your shopping trip Friday wasn't to a diaper store."

"Hold on to that thought at your party later. But hey, back to softball. When you get to Twin Creeks you'll find a super confusing scene. There are ten softball diamonds all with bleachers, warm up areas for pitchers and hitters, and even a restaurant at the center of the complex. Games will be under way on all the fields with teams in age brackets from like eight to eighteen. And for every team playing there'll be several waiting, all in bright uniforms, with an entourage of parents, grandparents and siblings. In short, an X-chromosomed zoo. To find the field for our noon game, check the notice board by the café building. Coach is death on electronic gear on game day so I'll leave my phone in Palo Alto."

"Got it, I plan to be there at eleven-thirty, or maybe a bit earlier."

"I usually get a snack after the first game and then find a tree over by the parking lot where I can stretch out. At about eleven-fifteen Coach will pull us all together to make us run sprints. He believes that most games are decided in the first two innings, with the winner being the team that's widest awake."

"Makes sense. Are your aunt and uncle going to be there?"

"Only for the 4:00 p.m. game. But don't worry. Dan, at least, doesn't think that my having an elderly boyfriend is akin to catching ebola."

"But what about your mom's personal monster? Is there any news?" Alec asks as he glances over his shoulder.

"I'm checking in with Mom next. If I hear anything new I'll let you know. Until then, fingers crossed that there won't be any heart-faced Koreans at your party."

. . . . .

With Ed again off to the Smithsonian, Amy goes for a long, calming walk around the Mall. Back at the Willard at two o'clock, she's no sooner burrowed into the big bed's soft pillowtop when her phone rings. "Hi, Dana," she says in a disappointed voice, adding a heavy sigh in case her feelings aren't clear.

"Hey Amy, I'm here at headquarters with Melvin and Todd Sofi from the SFPD whom you talked to yesterday."

"Hi Melvin, Todd—anything new?" Amy inquires, sitting up and doing her best to sound more collegial.

"First thing Amy, I want to tell you what an amazing performance you put on earlier," Lieutenant Ramsey says. "You strung Max along way past what we thought was possible. If a seventeen-year-old nutcase armed with a water pistol hadn't tried to hold up a bank a few blocks away just before you 'got into the cab' Max would surely be in custody. As it is, the first S.F. car missed him by less than a minute."

"If they were so close, how did he get away?"

"He was driving a late-model black SUV in a neighborhood full of them. He abandoned the car about fifteen blocks away in a bus zone where the SFPD found it fifteen minutes later. We immediately alerted BART and Muni but…"

"Any luck? Have you been able to trace him?" Amy asks, interested despite herself.

"The BART station agent at Twenty-fourth Street, which is only a block away, says she saw a huge man wearing a black suit coat enter the station about the right time, but has no idea which way he went. We're guessing south towards Daly City where he presumably stashed the Toyota near where the Escalade was reported stolen, but we've turned up nothing to confirm that."

"So even given this morning's drama, it doesn't seem as if you're any closer to catching Max now than you were yesterday or the day before," Amy says trying not to sound judgmental, even as she realizes she isn't succeeding.

"We would like to think we've made progress, but only time will tell," Lieutenant Ramsey says. "In the meantime, Dana's been talking to Doctor Frank."

"And?"

"He guesses that Max is more and more caught, or maybe torn is a better word, between his obsession with you, and his desire to flee, which Dr. Frank refers to as Max's self preservation urge," Sergeant Helickson answers.

"With respect to Malcolm, isn't that pretty much psychobabble?" Amy asks, not about to let go of her conviction that better policing, not a psychologist's thoughts, are what's really needed.

"Well, that's Dr. Frank's opinion," Lieutenant Ramsey says in a tone that indicates that he, too, is losing patience with psychological theory.

"Does Malcolm—or for that matter, any of you—believe Max came all the way from Europe just to try to have sex with me? I mean, c'mon, Amsterdam was over three years ago. And if he was so hot for me, why did he ruin his own plan by extorting the five thousand?"

"Amy, not to be impolite, but as you well know, we've all been asking these questions all week, and are no closer to a good answer. For all, or part, of the three-year gap Max might have been in custody, married to the Queen of Denmark, or according to one of Dr. Frank's theories, simply embarrassed about hurting you. After all, even King Kong tried to protect Fay Wray. But one thing seems clear, his interest in you spiked these last few days, maybe—and this is another of Dr. Frank's theories—because he interpreted the fact that you promptly handed over the cash as proof you still desired him. Of course we know that you reacted as you did because of his threats to Tamiko, but Dr. Frank thinks Max may equate it to your returning to the Hollywood Bar the second night."

"Surely after this morning, he has to realize that I'm not going to tumble into his bed," Amy interrupts.

"Which is why Dr. Frank thinks he may be about to bolt for home, wherever that is. But listen Amy, have you and Ed set a date to return to the Bay Area?"

"And walk into that monster's den with no protection? You have got to be kidding. As of now the plan is still for Tamiko to take a red-eye Sunday evening to be here for her sixteenth birthday on Monday. And assuming she does, I'll stay for a couple of days to show her around. At some point Ed may need to fly home to deal with work, but we haven't decided anything yet. Sorry if that's not much help."

"On the contrary, it's a real gift to know we have a couple of days to look for Max with no need to also worry about protecting all of you," Lieutenant Ramsey says.

. . . . .

Finishing a panini at Café Strada, an open-air coffee shop on the corner of College Avenue and Bancroft Way, Alec texts his uncle, "*How goes the international love story?*"

"*Somewhere between brilliant and awesome. Are you done with your exam? Would this be a good time to call,*" Charlie texts right back.

"*Great news, and yes.*"

When a few seconds later his phone vibrates, Alec answers by saying, "Are you guys at the top of the Empire State building or maybe clip-clopping around Central Park in a buggy pulled by Old Dobbin?"

"Good guesses, since Emiko wants to do both. But for now we're on the upper deck of the Staten Island Ferry just passing the Statue of Liberty. It's eighty degrees with a light breeze and I'm happier than anyone has a right to be."

"Shades of William Holden and Nancy Kwan on the Star Ferry in Hong Kong Harbor at the beginning of *The World of Suzie Wong*. How about sending me a pic?"

"I'll recruit a photographer in a minute, but in the meantime here's Emiko to sing New York, New York."

"Charlie always make jokes," a lightly accented contralto voice says with a chuckle. "Alec, I not ready for being Frank Sinatra yet, but I happy to say Hi! Charlie tell me so much about you and I hoping to meet you next week at Charlie's island, I can't say Indian name of."

Grinning, Alec almost replies that he had also heard a lot about her, but, catching himself, says, "I'm looking forward to meeting you on Nantucket next week."

"My English better every day. Maybe pretty soon Charlie teach me native people's language too. You talk to him now."

"I'm forbidden to speak Japanese," Charlie says with a laugh, "Every time I try Emiko says, 'Shut up Mr. Charlie, this be America now.'"

"Sweet."

"It's early days, but yes, Emiko's determination to make our relationship work is contagious. How about your coming to Nantucket on Wednesday? I plan to call Ellen and Ted to invite them for the weekend, but it may be easier for Emiko if you come up first to break the family ice."

"Sure. My parents will be excited to see me Sunday and will probably both take off Monday to hang out. But knowing them, they'll each have five reasons why they need to get back to work on Tuesday. So by midweek, for sure, I should be free."

"OK, let's stay in touch. Anything new with Mad Max?"

"I got a call from Sergeant Helickson, Dana, who is the number-two investigator looking for Max, and, for what it's worth, one more attractive woman involved in this drama."

"Lucky you."

"She reports that Max broke into Ed's house in Piedmont and has been calling Amy to try to coax her to meet him."

"But Amy's in D.C., right? And anyway, how can he possibly think she would agree to an assignation after everything that's…"

"Amy answered his call on her cell, pretending to be in the Bay Area. Then she agreed to meet him in the hope that the cops would be in position to grab him."

"No luck, I gather."

"A close call this morning. Deep down it seems that Max has deluded himself into the idea that Amy must be as obsessed with him as he is with her."

"Bizarre. But why is it so difficult to catch a 260 pound sociopath with a strong accent who doesn't know the area?"

"I asked the same question, and the answer seems to be that there's a heavy guy with an accent in every Burger King."

"Got it. But with Max still on the loose, I'll be relieved when you're on the plane Sunday."

"I'll be relieved when Tamiko is."

. . . . .

When Ed gets back to the Willard at four o'clock Friday, Amy is lying in the king-sized bed with the plush white duvet pulled up to her chin listening to Barbara Kingsolver's novel *Flight Behavior* via a little speaker synched to her iPad.

"Do you have any clothes on under there?" Ed asks.

"What do you think?"

"You mean what do I hope?"

"Either way, you would be right."

"My mirror neurons are already shouting 'Yes,' but let me take a moment to degrime."

"No dawdling," Amy replies sticking out her tongue and touching it to her upper lip.

"No worries," Ed says, mimicking her.

Hardly four minutes later, Ed walks across the room wrapped in a towel so huge its bottom edge grazes the floor.

"What's under the tent I wonder?" Amy says propping herself against a couple of pillows so that the duvet slides down below her navel.

"I thought you might enjoy searching for the pole."

"Great plan," Amy says, crossing her legs before tipping forward and crawling towards the foot of the bed. As Ed's hip wiggle causes the towel to drop to the floor, she adds, "Did you know your cock bends slightly to the left?"

"Probably why I ended up in Berkeley, not Kansas City," Ed says as he feels Amy's warm soft mouth envelop him.

After a blissful couple of minutes during which the frontal lobes of Ed's brain light up so vividly they begin to pulsate, the thought that he's being selfish peeks out from a far corner of his mind. Reaching down he grabs Amy's shoulders, pushes her back onto the bed and leans forward, tongue at the ready. "Maybe save that for dessert," she says, pulling him urgently on top of her as she grabs his cock and thrusts it into her warm, slippery tunnel. Moaning as she adjusts her pelvis so that it locks with his like a mated jigsaw piece, Amy begins to rotate her hips as she emits a sound somewhere between a purr and a groan.

"Open your eyes," Ed whispers."

"Here I am, all of me."

"Funny, that's the part of you I love the most."

"Ed, I love you too—oh god, I do. But please, for now, can you just shut up and fuck me until I scream?"

"Born to serve," Ed murmurs as he levers himself up onto his elbows and doubles the speed of his stroke.

When a few minutes later Ed opens his eyes after a brief post-coital mini-doze he sees Amy strutting towards the bathroom grinning like a tuna-stuffed kitten. Amazed as always that this small, almost scrawny woman can explode with hurricane force, he thinks about suggesting she change her name to Katrina. Deciding this is a joke best kept to himself, he rolls over and pulls a pillow over his head.

· · · · ·

When Dan arrives home at 5:45, Tamiko asks, "Do you have enough energy to catch a few balls?"

"Sure, but didn't you tell me your coach said not to practice today so you won't come out flat tomorrow?"

"Yes, but he tells that to all his pitchers before every tournament and I don't believe any rule makes sense all the time. This year I've only thrown parts of a couple of high school games against mostly second banana opponents, so I'm a lot more concerned about my control than I am about over throwing."

"Is this another way of saying you're a tad worried about tomorrow?"

"I had a dream last night that when I pitched, the ball went in every direction except over the plate."

"So the idea is to throw enough strikes to exorcise your dream hangover?"

"Exactly. And since to cope with Mom's anxieties I need to tag along with you and Les to the symphony later, we can keep it super-short."

"I'll be good to go in ten minutes."

. . . . .

Because of a ten-year-olds' game in progress on the closest diamond, Tamiko and Dan set up in deepest center field, far beyond where the mightiest tyke could hit the ball. Once Dan, shin guards and mask in place, is sitting on a bucket with his back to a tall fence, Tamiko pumps in pitch after pitch. Although a couple of riseballs fly over Dan's head and several dropballs hit the grass well short of the rubber plate, most go more or less as directed.

"Enough," Tamiko says as she empties the third bucket.

"Are you sure? We have another fifteen minutes."

"Thanks, but my head is clear and my control is as good as it's going to get so maybe Coach is right about leaving some gas in the tank."

. . . . .

As Alec suspects, Margo's party has less energy than an elderly car battery on a subzero morning. With most summer session students having left town in search of August's last carefree days, only those too broke or too unimaginative show up. At its height, perhaps twenty-five people cluster drinking beer out of the bottle, or cheap red wine out of even cheaper plastic glasses, hardly pretending they aren't as bored as they look. Alec, who had planned to make a late appearance, has somehow gotten sucked into helping with the preparations. Returning from a second booze run, he does his best to act polite, even as he wishes everyone would disappear. Retreating to a deserted corner of the front room, he's followed by a thin girl whose spiky white blonde hair looks as if it has been styled by a lawn mower. Fortunately, the music is so loud Alec can't hear a word she is saying, something she never seems to notice. After ten minutes, pleading a headache, he retreats to the third floor where, earplugs in place, he stretches out on his bed.

Waking with a start a few hours later, Alec feels cold, cramped, and dry-mouthed. Although he doesn't experience anything like the strong sense of foreboding that had pushed him over to the Gashkins' backyard early Wednesday morning, he nevertheless feels uneasy. With the house now quiet he decides to be sure his housemates have followed police instructions to lock up tight. Hearing male laughter as he passes Margo's second-floor door he thinks that at the very least, the party had been a success for its hostess.

Predictably, Alec sees that the living room, dining room, and kitchen are littered with pizza boxes, beer bottles and an ashtray with a half smoked joint. More to the point, several casement windows are cracked open and the kitchen door is ajar. As he pulls it shut, Alec thinks he sees a pinprick of light in the backyard. After waiting for a long minute and just as he decides that his imagination has run away with itself, the light flares again—this time staying on for a few seconds. Alarmed, Alec flips the patio light switch. When nothing happens, he remembers that it'd been his task to replace the dead bulb. Pressing his face to the window Alec is pretty sure someone is moving about twenty-five feet from the house. Thinking he should stay where he is and call the Berkeley Police, he instead grabs a bread knife from the counter and opens the door. In a slight crouch with the lethal-looking, but decidedly dull knife in his right hand, Alec takes two steps onto the patio where he waits for his eyes to adjust. Before they do, the light flashes on and off three times before staying on. Dropping the knife on the table, Alec strides forward. Huddled on the grass, the thin blonde girl is trying to light the wrong end of a filter cigarette with the lighter wand from the barbecue.

Seeing that she's as drunk as she is confused, Alec grabs the lighter as he says, "Let's get you up." When after a couple of feeble efforts it's clear she isn't going to manage on her own, Alec picks her up and heads to the house, doing his best to avoid her sloppy efforts to kiss the side of his chin. "Behave yourself, or I'm going to drop you right here," he says as he nevertheless carries her to the living room, where after peeling off her encircling arms, he deposits her on the couch.

SATURDAY 2

DAN TAPS ON TAMIKO'S DOOR a couple of minutes before her phone alarm is set to sound. An early riser, he has eggs, toast and bacon on the table when she comes into the kitchen a few minutes later dressed in her wine and black Tsunami uniform. "I have a text from Coach," Tamiko exclaims excitedly, holding out her phone, "The ball's in your shoe for Game 1."

"Does that somehow mean you're pitching at eight? I was planning to drop you at seven, but if you're starting the first game I'll hang out."

"Shock and awe is Coach's raison d'etre."

"Maybe he decided that the team you're playing at eight a.m. is a better match up for you."

"Chaos instead of Sting, there's not much difference. Both are tough with players who have been together for years, not just a bunch of rookies playing their first summer of A-ball."

"Has Chaos beaten you?"

"Not yet, but a few games were close. They have a take-no-prisoners pitcher, Jo Mulligan—who's sure to pitch the first game, but their defense is a little suspect."

"I don't get it, why does your coach want you to pitch against her? Why not wait for Sting's third best pitcher in the last game this afternoon?"

"Because softball isn't like baseball where a pitcher lies down for five days between starts. Sting, like many top teams, uses a two-pitcher rotation meaning that either Madison or Hailey, whoever starts the first game will be back for the third. In short, whatever time I pitch I'm going to be up against someone who's basically better than I am. But, c'mon Ed, we'd better get moving so I'm grinning at Coach in the parking lot before he has a chance to change his mind."

. . . . .

Pulling onto the lightly trafficked Highway 101 on their way to the Twin Creeks Softball Complex in Sunnyvale, Dan jokes that California's ever booming economy means that 6:15 a.m. Saturday morning is one of the few times when the freeways are actually free. As they enter the Twin Creeks parking area thirty-five minutes later, Tamiko points to where the huge red Chevy Suburban Coach bought surplus from a fire department, sits just to the right of the gate. By the time she hops out to help Jazz unload equipment, Amber and LaTasha pull up in Amber's dad's green Ram pick-up with Gonzalez Plumbing printed prominently on the doors. At 6:58, with all but one Tsunami player present, the group begins moving towards the entrance. Seeing Dan hesitate, Coach hands him two pails full of balls as he says, "I hereby appoint you assistant coach in charge of moving equipment. You'll have to pay a few bucks, but they'll stamp you so you can come in and out."

"I'm not sure that'll do you much good," Tamiko says. "Since I'm pitching now, you probably won't want to come back to pick me up until after the third game."

"You're kidding—your aunt has planned the whole day around seeing your four o'clock game in which I assume you'll be back at shortstop."

"But Les isn't remotely interested in softball, or any sport for that matter."

"Who said anything about sports? It's your elderly boyfriend she wants to check out."

By 7:03 a.m., Coach has the team running sprints followed by twenty minutes of calisthenics during which, by tradition, the girls mercilessly rag on each other to be sure everyone's minds are as awake as their bodies. Then, after talking briefly to Amber, Coach signals to Tamiko to start warming up behind the first base dugout.

After Tamiko tosses ten pitches to Roxy White, who will catch the first game, she glances across the empty diamond to where Jo Mulligan is also warming up. Guessing that Jo will be both surprised and pleased to see that Tamiko, not Amber or Charlene, will start for Tsunami, Tamiko mouths, "Be careful what you wish for."

Since Tsunami is the home team, Tamiko delivers the game's first pitch at 8:01 a.m., a ball outside. And despite the fact that Roxy keeps raising one finger to call for fastballs, Tamiko walks the small left-handed batter on four pitches. Willing herself to stop aiming the ball, Tamiko again puts both feet on the slab. Batter two, another quick leftie whose one idea is to slap the ball into the ground towards short or third and outrun the throw, confidently slashes her bat back and forth. Again Roxy signals a fastball. Realizing that she's relaying Coach's signal from the dugout and well knowing he hates to be contradicted, Tamiko nevertheless shakes her head. After reluctantly looking at Coach to get another sign, Roxy holds up her right fist with both the forefinger and pinky extended, the sign for a rise ball. Tamiko again shakes her head, careful not to look in the dugout. When, after a long, almost embarrassed hesitation Roxy again puts up her fist, this time extending only her wiggling pinky, Tamiko nods, finds her grip and rocks into her motion. Coming out of her hand as if it's going to be a belt-high fastball, the screwball instead veers towards the outside edge of the plate and at least two inches beyond the end of the swinging bat. "Strike," shouts the small, buff, blue-clad Asian woman crouching behind Roxy.

Seeing that with the batter trying to get a running start to first base, her bat can't cover the outside of the plate, Coach signals for the same pitch. The result is another swing and miss, although this time the umpire adds "batter offered" to her strike call to indicate that if the hitter hadn't swung, the pitch would have been outside. Reasoning that the Chaos shortstop is probably berating herself for going after a ball out of the zone, Tamiko almost smiles when Jackie sets up on the outside corner and calls for a fastball. Sure enough, when Tamiko pours the string straight ball into the mitt, the batter, expecting it to veer outside, takes strike three. Risking a quick glance at the dugout, Tamiko sees that Coach is doing his best to maintain a poker face. Bringing her concentration back to the job at hand, Tamiko somehow coaxes the over eager number three batter to pop to short on a change-up before the cleanup hitter scorches a hanging drop ball into Jazz's glove.

Jo Mulligan, a strongly-built redhead, with an arms length pony tail and a round pleasant face that tends to flush as the game progresses, is her normal effective self. Mixing a 60-plus mph fastball with a killer change, and a high-hopping riser, she's ahead of every hitter. Although LaTasha hits a medium loud line drive at the left fielder, Tsunami doesn't manage a base runner through the first three innings. Tamiko walks a batter in the second and gives up a two-out single in the third, but she too is unscored upon.

In the fourth with one out Tamiko gives up back-to-back singles before La Tasha, the fastest player on Tsunami, sprints into the right center gap to snag a fence-bound rocket. Turning and throwing a bullet to first, she doubles up the amazed Chaos runner. Then, in the bottom half of the inning, after Jazz beats out a bunt and Leah Li lifts a humpbacked single over third, it's Tamiko's turn. Walking to the plate, she recalls how Jo has pitched her in that summer's three previous encounters. In addition there's the fact that in her first at-bat today Jo fooled her into grounding out on a sloppy drop, a pitch Tamiko hadn't even known Jo possessed.

As Tamiko takes her slightly open stance, her front foot angled towards third, she guesses Jo will start her with a screw. Apparently not trusting her ability to control it in the first inning, Jo has been throwing it confidently and often in the second and third. And sure enough, when the ball leaves Jo's hand it starts boring up and in towards Tamiko's chin. Leaning back slightly, Tamiko hears the umpire say, "ball."

Now what Tamiko thinks? If Jo goes by the book, she'll come back with something low and away, but then there's also the fact the rise ball is Jo's best pitch. But will Jo remember that Tamiko hit it hard in July? Concerned that she's in danger of outthinking herself, Tamiko decides to sit fastball and take anything else—which in this case turns out to be a poorly executed drop that hits the ground a few feet in front of the plate. Surprised that Jo would try to fool her a second time with a marginal pitch, Tamiko glances over at the Chaos dugout to see that their regular coach is absent and a woman she doesn't recognize is signaling the pitches.

With the count now in her favor and a base open, Tamiko fears she'll be intentionally walked. But seeing Jo, pink and determined, shake off one sign, and then a second, Tamiko realizes that the Coach is now irrelevant and it's game on between the two of them. Jo will never give in and throw a center cut fastball, Tamiko knows, but beyond that, well…. Guessing she'll finally see the riseball, Tamiko is surprised and impressed when Jo paints the inside corner with a screwball Tamiko guesses is close to 65 mph. Knowing that Jo's unlikely to throw consecutive pitches in the same place, Tamiko, who's still ahead in the count, again decides to sit riseball. As Jo swings into her windup, Tamiko slides her feet forward to the front of the batter's box and raises her arms so the nub of the bat is chin high. Guessing right this time, Tamiko is able to tomahawk the pitch just as it begins its lethal hop. The result is a rope that scorches its way down the left field line to where it clears the ten-foot wire fence by no more than eighteen inches. With the only question being fair or foul, players and coaches freeze as they look at the two women dressed in blue. Having the best angle, the diminutive home plate umpire steps forward holding up her hands a foot apart. Obviously enjoying the drama she waits a few beats before extending her right arm towards fair territory as she calls "count three."

Back in the dugout after circling the bases and exchanging a dozen high-fives and fist bumps, Tamiko takes a seat next to Jazz towards the end of the bench. When, seemingly in her ear, a fastball explodes into a catcher's mitt, Tamiko glances through the wire mesh separating the dugout from the pitcher's warmup area to see that Amber is up and throwing. Uh oh, she thinks as she looks over to where Coach always sits on an overturned plastic pail by the entrance to the dugout to see he's on his feet and lumbering her way. Jazz and Leah Li, who realize what's up, stand, and scoot out of the way.

Exhaling a deep sigh, Coach lowers his bulk into the space vacated by the two players and says, "Nice job, but Amber will be taking it the rest of the way with you back at short."

Biting her lower lip to stop herself from questioning Coach in front of her teammates, Tamiko nevertheless feels her face begin to flush as she thinks, 'this is my game and I should be allowed to finish it.'

Letting the silence stretch out while he watches Rachel, the Tsunami center fielder, take a ball outside, Coach finally says, "I have a question for you."

"OK."

"What was the purpose of your pitching this morning for the first time all summer against a top-level team?"

"So I could show you I can succeed at this level."

"What else?"

Thinking for a minute, Tamiko eventually replies. "Well, I guess so you could show me that you'd give me a chance to pitch if I earn it and stick with Tsunami."

"How did we both do?" Coach asks, grinning as he turns towards Tamiko and makes eye contact.

"Pretty good by me," Tamiko replies as she feels herself relax.

"Pretty good by me too," Coach replies. "And now maybe give a thought to Amber who I had to sit down on her last weekend in front of about seventeen family members to give you your chance."

Chagrined as she realizes how close she's come to acting like an entitled brat, Tamiko takes a breath and says, "Got it. I'll thank her after the game. In the meantime, I really am good."

"You really are," Coach says as he pushes himself up and off the bench. Then before lumbering back to his bucket he adds, "And you'll get better fast if you really can corral a practice catcher."

After the game ends 4-0 and the girls from both teams line up and slap hands, Tamiko helps gather the equipment so a group of excited twelve-year-olds in red Devils uniforms can pile into the dugout. As she helps Jazz move the heavy water canister onto the red wagon Coach uses to drag it from field to field, Tamiko hears a shrill whistle. Glancing over her shoulder, she sees Dan standing on the bottom step of the bleachers with both thumbs up and a wide grin on his face. Then waving his car keys, he heads towards the exit.

As always, a ten minute team meeting at the end of the bleachers is next on the agenda. After Coach is finally finished listing areas that need improvement, Tamiko jokes for a few minutes with Jazz and Ashley Beck, her other best buddy. During breaks between games the three usually hang out, often in a shady spot under a tree or, when it is unbearably hot, at the nearest air-conditioned fast food restaurant. But today, Jazz and Ashley have family they need to attend to, meaning there will be no opportunity for girl bonding. Not wanting to be impolite, Tamiko accepts Jazz's invitation to accompany her to the restaurant to say hi to her parents and Hector, her eleven-year-old brother. Spotting Amber at a water cooler, she makes a short detour. As the older girl stands and wipes her mouth Tamiko says, "I know that should have been your start, so thanks."

"I have to admit that when Coach first laid out his plan my freckles started to catch fire, but when he explained it wasn't hard to understand. With what happened to your Dad and all I'm real glad you've found a way to get back to pitching."

"Thanks, and you can be sure I'll be rooting for you at Oregon next year," Tamiko replies as she steps aside so a ten-year-old in an orange uniform with Crush written across the chest can bustle to the fountain.

Continuing through the door to the snack bar, Tamiko glances at the wall clock to see it's 10:10. Pulling a small woven purse from her bat length sports bag, she orders a berry shake at the counter before joining Jazz and her family at a table by the window. After challenging Hector to several games of hangman and much to the little guy's delight, contriving to lose all of them, Tamiko pleads the need for twenty minutes shut-eye. Gathering her belongings she leaves the snack bar at 10:30. Because she knows that on summer weekends, all of Twin Creek's tightly clustered diamonds will be in use with teams waiting for later games crowding the spaces in between, she heads out the gate to the parking area. Turning right towards the west end of the football field-sized lot, which by now is packed with virtually every model of SUV, pickup, and van sold in the U.S. since the Reagan administration, she pauses to banter for a few minutes with a couple of acquaintances on the Stockton Blitz. Because the restaurant is comparatively expensive the Blitz, along with many other teams, are tailgating for their post game snack. Finally reaching the small, almost secluded grassy area at the end of the lot at 10:45, Tamiko pulls a battered copy of Gogol's short stories from her sports bag. Planning to search for a tricky quote in preparation for her next call with Vera, she instead reaches back into the bag for her sweatshirt. Placing the book under her head and the heavy red cloth over her eyes, Tamiko tenses every muscle in her body before exhaling all the morning's tension.

· · · · ·

When Alec rolls over to look at his clock Saturday morning it is 9:37. Crap, what happened to the nine o'clock alarm, he thinks as, already out of bed, he tries to pull on his jeans while hopping towards the bathroom. Downstairs, a few minutes later, he glances into the living room to be sure the thin girl is gone. Pleased to see that the mess of the night before had been cleaned up, he lifts a piece of paper with his name on it from the coffee table.

"*Thanks Alec. Anyone can have a bad night—maybe you'll give me another chance. Sabrina 526-1751.*"

Crumpling the note before tossing it in the trash, Alec slathers peanut butter and jam on a piece of slightly stale French bread, before pouring himself an evil looking cup of lukewarm coffee. On his way out the front door, Alec stops short as he realizes he's forgotten the name of the softball complex. Phone in hand to call Tamiko, he remembers that she won't have hers. Beginning to perspire as he imagines Tamiko searching in vain for him in the bleachers, Alec tells himself to get a grip. Surely, if he can remember where he was when Tamiko told him the tournament's location, he will also remember what she said. But wait, doesn't everyone have a website these days, even club softball teams? And come to that, doesn't it say .com under Tsunami on her maroon sweatshirt? Phone in hand as he walks up Panoramic Street towards Ethan's Altima, Alec quickly locates Tsunami's website and with it, their schedule. Twin Creeks, in Sunnyvale, he sees under August 27-28 as he climbs into the battered blue car just after ten o'clock. The last two bites of bread still bulging his cheeks, Alec threads his way through robust Saturday morning traffic finally reaching the freeway on-ramp under the BART tracks at Adeline and 51st Street at 10:15 a.m. From here he should reach Twin Creeks in about fifty minutes, possibly even early enough to say hi to Tamiko before Tsunami begins their pregame routine for the 12:00 game.

A few minutes later, as heavy traffic next to the Oakland Coliseum complex causes him to slow to 20 mph, a thought begins tugging at the corner of Alec's mind. Even though he'd blanked on the name of the softball complex, it took him only seconds to find it based on information printed on Tamiko's maroon sweatshirt. And if he's registered this despite his focus having been on the girl under the shirt, what about Max, who must have been observing Tamiko before she underwent her wardrobe makeover? Feeling sweaty for the second time in a half-hour, Alec reaches for his phone. Without a hands-free device he knows he risks a fine twice the size of his bank balance, but he nevertheless scrolls through his directory with his left hand before tapping "Dana H." Answering on the second ring, Sergeant Helickson asks, "Alec, is everything good?"

"Maybe not, I'm worried about Tamiko."

"Tell me."

"Despite what we thought, there's a depressingly easy way for Max to know where she is right now. The oversized red team sweatshirt she practically lived in until the last few days says Tsunami.com on the back."

"Crap! Let me guess that Tsunami is the softball team she's playing for this weekend and their schedule is on their website?"

"Yes, the Twin Creeks Sports Complex in Sunnyvale. I'm already on I-880 heading down there for Tamiko's noon game."

"You're thinking that Max might know all this?"

"He hasn't missed much. I mean, even if Max doesn't have a clue as to what Tsunami is all about, he only had to check the site."

"Tell me you've already called Tamiko to warn her."

"The penny just dropped twenty minutes ago when I realized I'd forgotten the name 'Twin Creeks,' but was able to find it in a few seconds. But here's the thing, Dana: Tamiko doesn't bring her phone to games because electronic devices make her Coach spit fire."

"What's her schedule down there?"

"Her uncle would have driven her over there by seven a.m. to prepare for an eight o'clock start. Game two is at noon and the last one is at four p.m. Softball games are apparently seven innings or ninety minutes, whichever comes first, so Tsunami will be on break now. For what it's worth, Tamiko told me that because of the long day and early start, she usually retreats under a tree to close her eyes for a few minutes between games. Her coach pulls the team back together forty-five minutes before the next one."

"That would be eleven-fifteen. Where are you now?"

"Past the Oakland airport turnoff, just coming up on Davis Street in San Leandro, or in other words, not even to Hayward."

"Hopefully you'll be there in half an hour or so."

"That's optimistic, since traffic is so heavy I'm not even going forty."

"Do your best. In the meantime I'll call the Sunnyvale Police to request that they run a car over there and I'll also try to get a hold of someone at the sports complex. They must have some type of security on a tournament weekend. Did you say the name of the place is Twin Creeks?"

"Yes."

"OK, I'll be back in touch as soon as I know anything. In the meantime let's hope Max is far away and all is well."

Traffic speeds up to 60 mph through San Lorenzo but slows again approaching Jackson Street in Hayward, where a long line of cars are backed up trying to exit towards the San Mateo Bridge. Bullying his way into the fast lane just as a dozen other cars do the same, Alec again drops to 20 mph as sweat begins to drench his already clammy T-shirt. Five minutes later as he approaches the Industrial Parkway exit, now going 45, his phone sounds. Hoping that somehow, magically, it's Tamiko, he sees instead that it is Sergeant Helickson. "Dana, tell me you have good news," he all but barks.

"Anything but, I'm afraid. Turns out a scary fire in the South Bay kicked off about an hour ago with an explosion at a biotech company. It's not in Sunnyvale, but a few miles west in Mountain View. Since chemicals are involved, it's a big deal with fire companies from Milpitas, Santa Clara and Mountain View trying to contain the blaze. In the meantime, police from half a dozen departments are scrambling to close roads and evacuate hundreds of nearby houses and businesses. In short, Sunnyvale has no one to send to Twin Creeks."

"Shit."

"I can't argue with that. But Alec, there is hope since Sunnyvale just asked for help from San Jose under their joint powers agreement and, of course, those guys have loads of resources. I'm trying to insert myself into the bureaucratic process to get one of their cars diverted to Twin Creeks, but Alec, you may be our best bet. Where are you now?"

"Newark, just past Fremont, so I'm maybe ten miles from Highway 237, at which point I'll have another five miles to go. But unfortunately, I'm poking along at forty-five miles per hour. Has someone been in touch with Tamiko's uncle?"

"Dan Aristead. Yes, he'd just gotten home when one of my colleagues talked to him. Apparently he watched the first game in which, incidentally, Tamiko pitched well and Tsunami won. He left about nine thirty-five or forty as the girls gathered for a team meeting. Because a load of players had family there, he's guessing Tamiko was occupied being social for at least a few minutes."

"Dana, it's eight minutes to eleven, so you're talking about events that happened over an hour ago," Alec says impatiently. "I mean, none of this has anything to do with Tamiko being safe now. Have you gotten through to Twin Creeks? And what about the evacuation? Does that affect the games?"

"Alec, calm down. The fire is a few miles away and with the wind blowing in the other direction, Twin Creeks isn't affected. And, no, so far we haven't contacted anyone since no one is picking up in their office. In the meantime I have an officer scrambling to find the cell numbers of people who are down there today. Oops, Alec, sorry I have to go…"

Still holding the dead phone to his ear, Alec zigs into the right-hand lane in an effort to get around a dawdling VW van displaying bumper sticker that says "I'll believe corporations are people when Texas executes one." But even after zagging back into the center lane in front of the opinionated van, Alec moves little faster so it's 11:01 a.m. before he turns west on Highway 237, skirting the southern margin of San Francisco Bay. With the traffic now moving at the limit he guesses he'll arrive at the sports complex in seven or eight minutes, even including the last short stretch on city streets. Then, as if God suddenly places his pinky on the freeway, the traffic stops.

. . . . .

Tamiko, who has shut her eyes for barely fifteen minutes as she imagines telling Lec a new dog joke, is brought out of her reverie when she feels something hard press just above her right ear. "Lec," she murmurs happily as she begins to sit up.

"No talk, no move," a throaty, heavily-accented voice whispers as a big hand catches Tamiko's right shoulder and presses her painfully back onto the grass. "This be gun," the man says, pushing the metal object into her head so hard she thinks it might hurt less to be shot.

"You can't get away with …"

"Shut up. I talk, not you. This simple. When I say 'do this, do that' you do, first time, no questions. You no do, I hurt you. We behind car where no one can see, so you no try silly thing. Now, very slow, reach up both hands and tie sleeves of shirt around back of head. Do it now, or I shoot you now."

Having read somewhere that the best time to escape a kidnapper is before he's established full control, Tamiko thinks about trying to leap to her feet and run. But with the gun still pressing against her head the odds of success seem so tiny she finds herself following instructions.

As if Max senses an infinitesimal tightening of Tamiko's muscles, he grabs a handful of her thick hair and twists it painfully. "Now, very slow, stand up," his low, grating voice demands. "Try to run and you dead," he adds, doing something to the firearm that which produces an ominous clicking sound.

Rolling slowly to her right into a fetal position, Tamiko places her left hand on the ground and levers herself up to her knees. Putting her right foot forward she leans into it as she stands, careful not to take a step. Keeping the gun pressed against Tamiko's head, Max grabs her left shoulder, his fingers digging into her trapezius so hard it almost causes her to forget the pressure behind her right ear. Then roughly turning her to the right, Max says, "Now take very slow steps straight ahead." With the searing pain in her shoulder now bringing tears to her eyes, Tamiko nevertheless counts ten steps before she feels something hard hit her thigh just above her knees. "Now lean forward," the voice orders.

As Tamiko starts to bend from the waist, the pressure on her head and shoulder ceases. Free of pain, she starts to turn to her right with the idea of running towards the busy part of the parking lot only to feel Max's massive hand grab and lift her butt. Tumbling forward into a space that smells slightly of fish, Tamiko thinks incongruously that the owner of the white Toyota must be an angler. As her head hits something hard, she feels Max lift her legs and push them into the trunk behind her. Then growling, "Make noise and I shoot you through trunk," he slams the lid.

A few seconds later, when Tamiko feels the car begin to move, she pulls the sweatshirt off her head and begins to scream, "Help, Kidnap, Rape—Help, Kidnap, Rape!" True, she thinks, this risks the possibility that Max might fire through the back seat and into the trunk, but she hopes he won't dare while he's negotiating the parking lot full of players, parents, and coaches. Yelling even louder she reasons her best hope to survive is that someone calls 911 so that the police can issue an AMBER Alert. When she pauses for breath, Tamiko hears a woman's voice yell, "It's coming from that white car, the trunk I think." Encouraged, Tamiko again screams, "Help, Rape, Kidnap!" But her hope is almost immediately dashed when she feels the Toyota begin to accelerate, presumably as it now heads towards the exit and the open road beyond.

. . . . .

At 11:04 a.m., frustrated beyond caring about consequences, Alec honks his way from the middle lane to the shoulder of the still-constipated Highway 237. Accelerating to 25 mph on the off limits pavement, which fortunately is only a little narrower than a standard freeway lane, he flashes past a long parade of sedans, SUV's, as well as a mattress delivery truck and a BMW convertible. Now high on the rush of his law-be-damned dash, Alec presses his foot down, bringing the Nissan's speed up to 40. Unfortunately after less than a quarter-mile he has to slow to a crawl to squeeze past a black van intruding into what he has come to regard as his shoulder. As he accelerates on the other side, several passengers in stopped vehicles give him the finger and honk their horns. As the howl of frustration spreads virus-like up and down the freeway, Alec keeps his foot on the gas and so covers three miles in little more than five minutes. He is just thinking he may make it all the way to the Caribbean Street exit unimpeded, when a late model SUV pulls squarely into the middle of the shoulder a few hundred feet ahead of him. Leaning on his horn as he prays that somehow the driver will distinguish its sound from all the others and pull back onto the freeway, Alec maintains his speed. But when the front passenger door of the big SUV opens and a boy of perhaps eight begins to get out, presumably to pee in the ditch, Alec has no choice but to slow, his hope of reaching Tamiko leaking out of him like air from a punctured tire. And if things aren't dire enough, above the wall of noise, Alec hears a siren. Glancing in his mirror he sees a motorcycle cop approaching rapidly.

As Alec steps on the brake he shouts, "Fuck, Fuck, Fuck." Perhaps God hears his cry and decides to lend a hand. Or more likely, the driver of the SUV fearing he's the cop's target yanks the boy inside as he swerves back into the still empty freeway spot. Either way the pavement in front of Alec is suddenly empty. Stomping on the accelerator, Alec grins as he realizes that not only is he going to make it to Twin Creeks, but he'll have a police escort.

It's 11:12 a.m. when Alec reaches the Caribbean Street off-ramp. Following his iPhone's turn-by-turn instructions, he flies through a stop sign with the cop now hugging his bumper using her microphone to demand he stop. Making the turn into the Twin Creeks Sports Complex, Alec slows to get his bearings. Seeing a white Japanese sedan accelerating towards him, he squints against the glare of the sunny morning in an attempt to see whether there is tape on the right headlight. Not sure, Alec raises his gaze to see that a huge arm complete with an oversized watch rests on the open window frame. Screaming "Tamiko!" he swings the wheel hard left so the Altima fishtails across the path of the white car. Taking the heart-stopping hit just behind the passenger side door, Alec feels the Nissan lift and roll, first onto its side and then, emitting a sound remarkably like a groan, all the way onto its top, back wheels spinning.

. . . . .

Less than ten seconds after the Toyota begins to accelerate, Tamiko hears Lec shout her name. As Max curses and hits the brakes she slides hard against the front end of the trunk, her puny efforts to brace herself overwhelmed by an impact so strong she feels as if she's been dropped from a three-story building. Experiencing searing pain in her right shoulder, chest, and all the way down her right side, Tamiko fights to stay conscious as she groggily tries to assess whether she is more or less OK, or in the process of taking her last breath. Before she can reach a conclusion or even focus on the will-o-the-wisp thought that instructs her to shout Lec's name, she's surprised to feel the Toyota, its engine straining, shift into reverse. After metal grinds on metal for a few seconds the Toyota leaps backwards, before Max again stomps on the brake. For the third time Tamiko crunches against the front panel of the trunk this time the impact multiplying her pain by a number she cannot calculate. Now fully conscious, Tamiko begins yelling "Lec, Lec, I'm here, I'm here!" as she feels the car turn left and strain to accelerate, its engine roaring so loudly she doubts anyone will hear her.

. . . . .

Momentarily so stunned by the crash that he doesn't know where, or for that matter, who he is, Alec returns to himself sufficiently to realize he's hanging upside down from his seat belt with something warm and salty running into his eyes. Too muddled to come up with even the beginning of a plan to free himself, Alec closes his eyes to avoid being blinded by his own blood. Thinking how comforting it would be if he believed in God, he hangs like that until it comes to him that since he doesn't, he better get on with the job of helping himself. So, with his eyes still shut, Alec tries to reach up to find the seat belt catch.

"Don't move, son. Trust us to get you out. When I need you to do something I'll tell you," a man's voice says in a tone so authoritative that for a moment Alec thinks a higher power really has intervened.

"I don't think you should move him until the medics get here," Alec hears another voice say, this time a woman's, high-pitched and strident.

"Stand back, Officer, and keep everyone else back as well," the first voice orders, as if it's used to being obeyed. "Tom and I are off-duty Fremont firefighters. Fuel is pouring out of this old puppy meaning we absolutely need to get this guy out now."

Feeling a hand on his left shoulder, Alec hears the voice say, "Son, I'm going to release the seat belt in a few seconds, but before I do, I need you to reach towards me with your arms extended as if you had just spotted your girlfriend after a month's absence. Since the door is jammed, we need to take you out through the window. My partner has the door open behind you and he'll do his best to lift and push. Now, can you extend your arms towards me?"

Hanging, as he is, upside down, Alec is still trying to figure out where his arms are and which way he is supposed to move them, when he feels a strong hand pull his right wrist towards the window. Reasoning that if he is going to reach Tamiko, his left arm should go the same way, he extends it across his torso, doing his best to lean his body in the same direction.

"Good job. Now try to twist even more towards me as if you want to dive out the window to grab hold of her."

As his desire to hold Tamiko fills his mind, Alec stretches his arms towards the God-like voice just as he feels someone grab his butt from behind to almost throw him forward. In just a few more painful seconds he is out of the Nissan and being carried rapidly away in arms so strong he feels entirely secure. Then as he is placed gently on the ground, backside down, he begins to choke on his own blood. Gasping and spluttering he feels himself being lifted and flipped so he is now able to cough, spit, and to his huge relief, clear his throat. Just before losing consciousness he hears a whoosh and feels a surge of heat as the familiar voice says, "It doesn't get a lot closer than that."

· · · · ·

Amy, who turned her phone to mute while she and Ed toured the National Picture Gallery early Saturday afternoon, returns Sergeant Helickson's call at 2:27 p.m. East Coast time, palms sweating. "I listened to your message about Max maybe having a way to find Twin Creeks," she snaps, "have you guys gotten hold of Tamiko? Is everything OK?"

"Amy, I'm terribly sorry but Max did indeed show up at Twin Creeks. I honestly don't know the details but, apparently he's driving off with Tamiko as we speak."

"No! No! That can't be. Oh my god, Dana, you have to be kidding. Goddamn it! I knew it was a mistake to let her stay in…"

"Amy, berating yourself or anyone else, isn't helpful and I don't have time to listen, so let me tell you quickly what I know—all of which I've gotten second-hand and piece-meal since I'm caught in traffic on I-880 in Hayward, still a long way from Twin Creeks. Roughly ten minutes ago there was a car crash by the Twin Creeks entrance. Apparently Max was trying to kidnap Tamiko when Alec got there and deliberately crashed into Max's car. Alec is hurt, maybe critically, I don't know."

"Tamiko, where is she? How is she?"

"Amy, again, I simply don't know, but my best guess is that she's still in the white Toyota with Max who I'm told is still trying to escape. If you even briefly glance at the news you'll see that all this is happening at the same time as a large fire at a nearby biotech company, which apparently has a stock of dangerous chemicals, so there is a major evacuation happening a few miles away with every cop within thirty miles on hand. But listen, since that's absolutely all I know I'm going to hang up and try to catch up with events. Good or bad, I'll call you the second I know anything more, anything at all."

When Amy realizes she is holding a dead phone, she lets it clatter to the floor of the museum's lobby. Turning to Ed, she pushes her head against his chest and begins to sob.

. . . . .

As the Toyota crabs it's way along at what she guesses is only 25 mph, Tamiko, who has stopped yelling, takes an inventory of her physical condition. This includes a large and painful bump on her head, which, although slippery with blood, isn't gushing, and a stabbing pain across her chest and down her right side. Attempting to squirm her way to a more comfortable position, she feels as if a bread knife is twisting under her right breast so opts to remain still, something that becomes impossible as the car turns hard right. The bumpy pavement now smooth and the damaged engine roaring as Max tries to accelerate, Tamiko guesses they have reached Highway 237. Trying to think if there is something, anything, she can do to try to escape, her thoughts are hijacked by her worries about Lec. Is he OK? Is he injured? Is he…? Scared by the direction of her thoughts, Tamiko yanks her mind back to the present and with fingers crossed, beseeches the universe to produce a police siren. Instead she feels the Toyota slow and veer right, possibly, she guesses, to exit the freeway. When, after a few hundred yards, the car almost stops before turning left, Tamiko again begins to yell "Help, Rape, Kid…"

The crack of the pistol shot combined with a scorching pain in her left arm shuts Tamiko up mid word. Since the car is still lurching forward, albeit now making a grinding metal-on-metal sound, Tamiko guesses Max has extended his arm directly behind him to shoot blindly through the back seat. The fact that she is still curled in a fetal position on the passenger side of the trunk has probably saved her life. Panicked that Max may fire again, Tamiko ignores the blood streaming down her left side as she redoubles her effort to make herself small. Suddenly, the car jerks to a halt and a moment later Tamiko hears a door open. As Max grunts and mutters something in a language she doesn't recognize, the car sways and rises slightly, telling her that he's now outside. Imagining Max standing by the trunk, gun in hand, preparing to empty all the bullets into her, Tamiko squeezes her eyes shut and imagines Lec stepping in front of the huge man, stick sword extended. Now, almost sure she hears receding footsteps, she counts slowly to thirty before again beginning to yell. She has been at it for less than a minute when she hears the trunk latch click. As the lid slowly opens above and Tamiko squints against the bright light, she is vastly relieved to see two dark complected Asian faces staring down, eyes wide as if they've found a rattlesnake on the doormat.

"Please call 911, I've been kidnapped and shot. I really, really need your help."

"We saw him, the big man driving this car," the middle-aged woman says in an accent Tamiko can't identify. "He's bleeding also and trying to get away..."

"Please call 911 now, please," Tamiko interrupts, trying to push herself up from the bed of the trunk before sinking back, overwhelmed by pain.

· · · · ·

"Stay with me—stay awake," Alec hears a distant voice say. Feeling a fresh blast of pain, this time from his left ear, Alec tries to lift his hand to swat it away.

"Open your eyes, sir. Soon as you do I'll stop pinching your ear," the voice insists in an accent that Alec guesses is Jamaican.

Anxious to stop the pain Alec opens one eye to see a dark-skinned face looking down at him. Knowing that he must ask a crucial question, Alec is overwhelmed by his attempt to put it into words and so again shuts his eyes.

Again feeling the sharp pain in his ear Alec demands, "Are you allowed to do that?"

"Don't know sir, but my job is to try to keep you awake until this wagon gets us to the E.R., and it seems to be working pretty good."

"Where's Tamiko? Where's my friend?" Alec asks as he tries to sit up, only to realize straps prevent it. "Goddamn it, tell me what's going on."

"Sir, I have no clue. But right now we can't worry about anything except your answering my questions. First, sir, I need you to tell me where you feel pain, in addition to your head and your lip."

"Not counting my ear, I guess?"

"I'm going to take sarcasm as a good sign, but please sir, answer my question."

"My back hurts like hell and feels sticky so I guess it's bleeding."

"We're going to roll you over in a minute, but first, can you move your toes and your fingers?"

"I think so," Alec replies, obediently doing just that. "But why the hell can't you find out about Tamiko—that's Tamiko Gashkin. She's…"

"Now, how about your neck? Can you move it?"

"My head hurts," Alec says as he rolls his neck side to side as if signaling no. "But what about my friend?"

"I'll try to check as soon as I know you're stabilized."

A woman's voice outside of Alec's field of vision says, "Wilbur, his lip and head injuries are bloody, but probably no big deal. Since his spine seems to be OK, we need to flip him so we can check his back. I'll unclip the restraints."

"Right, I've got his arms so if you take his legs we can roll him right on my count of three."

After Alec feels himself being lifted slightly and turned over, he hears a ripping sound, which he guesses is his shirt being cut open.

"So far good news, sir," the lilting Caribbean voice says. "You have three nasty gashes on the middle of your back, probably from broken window glass when the fire guys pulled you out of the car, but none of them is life threatening."

. . . . .

When help in the form of an ambulance led by a California Highway Patrol cruiser arrives at 11:50, Tamiko sits legs splayed on the asphalt between the patiently squatting Aquinos and half a dozen others attracted by the drama. Loudly demanding to know what has happened to her friend Alec Burns, Tamiko refuses to move when the San Jose police officer says she doesn't know and doesn't have the time to find out. "Listen Miss, we can stay here all day, or you can get in the ambulance and we'll take you to the same hospital he's at," the senior medical tech, a thin, Latino man in his forties assures her kindly. Fearing bad news is being deliberately withheld, Tamiko still refuses to cooperate.

In an effort to defuse the standoff, Mrs. Aquino brushes past the hovering paramedic to look into Tamiko's frightened blue eyes with her kind brown ones. "C'mon now, dear, God has watched over you so far," she says as she gently, but firmly clasps Tamiko's good arm and leads her to the back of the red truck, where the EMT takes over. Siren blaring its familiar high-pitched *oogah-oogah* to clear a path through the still heavy traffic, they arrive at the emergency room entrance just past noon. Tamiko, who has been coaxed with some difficulty to lie on the gurney, is wheeled down the metal ramp, through a short corridor, and into the emergency room, all the while asking everyone in sight about Alec Burns. When no one pays attention, she tries to unbuckle the restraining straps in an effort to stand. Unceremoniously thwarted by the paramedics, she reluctantly lies back, pain shooting down her left side. Tears of frustration now welling in the corners of her eyes she shouts "Alec Burns, are you here?" Before Tamiko can gather the breath necessary for a second effort, a heavyset young woman in a lab coat, whose name tag identifies her as Yolanda, puts a firm hand on Tamiko's undamaged shoulder as she says, "Keep that up and I'll have to sedate you. But if you'll be a little patient I'll find out what's going on with Mr. Burns, who I know we admitted about fifteen minutes ago."

"Promise me you'll come right back," Tamiko replies, her tears now mingling with perspiration to give her face an oily sheen.

"Count on it," Yolanda replies, more gently as she wipes Tamiko's brow with a towel.

. . . . .

"We have her, injured but safe," Sergeant Helickson says when Amy, hand trembling, finally manages to slide open the answer bar on her phone.

"Really safe? Injured how? What…"

"Give me a chance to tell you," Sergeant Helickson interrupts. "Tamiko is in an ambulance on the way to the E.R. As far as I know she was shot in the upper left arm apparently superficially, has a big bump on her head and maybe some internal injuries."

"What kind of…"

"The EMT says she likely has cracked or possibly broken ribs. But so far all of her vital signs are good and there don't seem to be any spinal issues."

"My god, is she conscious?"

"Very much so, in fact it was her yelling that caused some good Samaritans, a Mr. and Mrs. Aquino, to release her from the trunk of the Toyota where Max had stuffed her. All this apparently happened in a shopping center parking lot a few miles east of Twin Creeks. Unfortunately, because of the confusion produced by the fire, it took over fifteen minutes for the CHP and eventually an ambulance to get there, but as I said, Tamiko is on her way to the hospital now."

"But she was shot? Oh my god, Dana."

"Yes, as I just told you, but in the fleshy part of her arm. Apparently she was screaming for help when Max drove off with her in the trunk so my guess is he shot into the trunk to try to shut her up. Her other injuries were probably sustained in the car crash when Alec pulled in front of Max to try to stop the kidnapping. I don't have all the facts sorted out yet Amy, but it's a very good bet Alec's intervention ultimately saved Tamiko's life."

"What about Alec? I'm so upset about Tami, I almost forgot about him."

"All I know is that two off duty firemen pulled him out of an upside-down Nissan just before it caught fire and that among other things he has a nasty head wound. He's already in the E.R. at the same hospital where they're taking Tamiko. I'd be there myself if I had a siren, but since I'm in my own car I'm just another civilian caught in stop-and-go traffic. In the meantime, I'll try to contact the officer who's providing security for Tamiko to see if he'll lend her his phone so she can call you."

"Security? You're kidding. Dana, tell me Max isn't still on the loose?"

"Sorry Amy, no can do. He's hurt, maybe badly, but still out there and obviously still dangerous."

"How did he…?"

"After leaving Twin Creeks he headed east on Highway 237. I'm guessing the Toyota was failing since he only made it a couple of miles before exiting and abandoning the car. Then he assaulted a woman getting out of a KIA Sol, grabbed her keys and took off. Unfortunately, she doesn't remember her own license number so he has a good chance of getting away, especially given that every officer in the South Bay has been scrambled to help with the aftermath of the fire."

"I'm on my way to Dulles right now to fly back. I got talked into abandoning my daughter once, now I need to be there," Amy says, sounding crazed even to herself.

"Amy, take a breath please, or if Ed's there, let me talk to him while you calm down."

"The phone's on speaker."

"OK then, both of you. Please sit tight until I get to the hospital, which should take no more than twenty minutes. In the meantime, Tamiko is well protected. Even if you leave for the airport now and get a flight within a couple of hours, it's going to be something like ten hours before you get here."

"Good point," Ed replies. "We'll give you a few minutes to sort things out before we decide on next steps."

. . . . .

Tamiko sits in an emergency room cubicle wearing a light green hospital gown. The bullet gash in her arm is being rebandaged by a young Pakistani doctor who she suspects is spending more time than necessary feeling under her left breast. Yolanda returns and says, "The good news, if you can call it that, is that Mr. Burns is making an even bigger fuss than you are."

"He's OK then," Tamiko says delightedly as she tries to push the doctor aside to give Yolanda a hug. Hearing Tamiko gasp, the big woman says drily, "Hugging with broken ribs isn't recommended."

"What's wrong with Alec, and when can I see him? Tell me."

"They're doing tests right now. So far it's obvious he's got a bloody gash on his scalp that will need a bunch of stitches, a cut lip, and some nasty glass cuts on his back. At the scene they suspected internal injuries since his mouth was so full of blood he was in danger of choking, but apparently it all came from his scalp and the cut on his lip—which will also require stitches."

"Young woman, you are definitely not authorized to disclose confidential patient information, especially not your opinions," the doctor angrily interrupts.

Realizing that Yolanda has gone far beyond hospital protocol on her behalf and may even be in danger of being disciplined, Tamiko emits a gasp as she reaches for the doctor's hand and places it directly under her breast. "I just felt a jolt of pain right here. I think this is the spot we need to worry about."

Dr. Pasawanda probes gently to be sure her ribs are all where they are supposed to be during which time Yolanda slips out unnoticed. "Except for a precautionary X-ray, that's it for you," the doctor concludes.

"What do you mean 'that's it for me'?" Tamiko asks in a voice hovering between concern and indignation.

"Probably two, and possibly three, of your ribs are cracked, but they are all in place so aside from your having to take it easy for at least a few weeks there is no more to be done. As I already said, the bullet wound on your arm is only a graze, so that's not going to be an issue. I'll prescribe some Tylenol with codeine, which you may need for a couple of nights, but otherwise, you're ready to go home.

"What about my head? Don't I have a concussion?"

"When you were asked who the president was in the ambulance I'm told that you not only said, 'Barack Obama', but you named his wife, his children, his dog, and started on the cabinet."

"I had to guess the Secretary of Agriculture."

Twenty minutes later, a chest X-ray having confirmed Dr. Pasawanda's diagnosis, Tamiko is wheeled into the waiting room where Sergeant Helickson stands and kisses her on the cheek as she extends her phone. "Tamiko, you're the first crime survivor I've ever kissed, which should tell you how happy I am to know that you're OK, but you need to call your mom pronto or she'll fly out here without a plane."

"Dana, where's Alec? I absolutely need to see him first. I really do."

"All I know is that he's still being treated, but is not listed as critical. Apparently you both were amazingly lucky."

Looking over Sergeant Helickson's shoulder Tamiko sees a young woman in scrubs heading for the same locked door she has just been ushered out of. Undoing her waist strap Tamiko stands. When her balance seems fine, she pivots around Sergeant Helickson, and treading as silently as she can, follows the woman back into the long treatment area corridor. Seeing that the first two rooms are empty, Tamiko opens the third door to find an elderly man hooked to a tangle of tubes. Retreating quickly, she stands irresolutely in the empty corridor, caught between her determination to find Alec and her fear of disturbing the critically ill. That's when Yolanda, exiting room number seven, spots Tamiko and gives her a 'not you again' scowl before pointing towards the waiting room. Then, as if deciding that on a day when she has already broken a week's worth of rules, one more won't matter, Yolanda holds up her right hand, palm open and her left fist with two fingers extended. Turning on her heel she walks away.

Guessing that at some point Yolanda must have been a catcher,

Tamiko takes three steps along the hall and cracks open the door of room seven. Although her view is blocked by a white-coated figure bending over the person lying on the examination table, Tamiko grins widely as she recognizes Lec's long, jeans-clad legs and battered Mexican sandals. Hearing something behind her, the elf-like doctor glances over her shoulder as she says, "Miss Gaskin, I presume."

"Gashkin, actually," Tamiko says, stepping to her right so she has a clear view of Alec, whose puffy lower lip is in the process of being sewn up. "Oh my god Lec, you look like you just lost a battle with a weed whacker." Then, as if fearing this sounded insensitive, she adds, "But, I do love all of you, especially the broken parts."

Turning back to her task, the doctor cautions Alec, "Don't even think of saying anything until I finish sewing you up."

"Is this where the knight who rode to the damsel's rescue gets the kiss that makes everything better?" Alec manages to croak, when the small physician in the white coat finally steps aside to make room for Tamiko.

"How about on the cheek for now," Doctor Stone suggests, still holding the suturing needle.

"Thank you," Tamiko says simply as she leans over Alec, her tangled sweat-encrusted caramel mane falling over their faces like a bedraggled tent. Content to feel her cheek on his until the end of time, Tamiko nevertheless reluctantly stands when she hears the doctor cough for the third time. "How long will Alec have to stay in the hospital?" she asks.

"This is 2016 my dear. People visit hospitals but are rarely invited to stay."

"What Dr. Stone is saying is that since my brain scan is OK, I'm good to go," Alec says. "But tell me, how did the pitching go?"

"Four shut out innings thanks to some wizard defense," Tamiko reports proudly. Then realizing the doctor has no clue as to what she's talking about, she adds, "I play softball, fastpitch. I had a game this morning."

"I kind of guessed your uniform wasn't for bowling. But as far as Romeo here goes, we'll want to keep an eye on him for a few hours just to be sure no concussion issues surface. And now, please get out of my treatment room so I can finish."

Mouthing 'I love you,' Tamiko does as ordered.

. . . . .

"Tami, oh sweetie, I've been so scared," Amy says when, back in the waiting area Sergeant Helickson hands Tamiko her phone. "But where have you been? Dana said you were out of the E.R. ten minutes ago."

"I needed to see Lec to be sure he's OK. Amazingly, given everything that went down, he more or less is. He needed fifteen stitches to close this long gash on his head and a bunch more for his lip, and his back is full of glass cuts, but, Mom, he's been super lucky. I mean his car exploded about twenty seconds after the firemen pulled him out."

"I gather he's not the only lucky one."

"True, but Mom, he's the reason my luck had a chance to kick in," Tamiko says in a rush. Then in a quieter voice adds, "For sure Mom, Lec saved my life."

"Tami, Tamiko, listen sweetie, I blame myself. How could I have left you alone in the Bay Area with that crazy man on the loose? I'm still shaking all over…"

"Mom, nothing that happened is remotely your fault. No one, not even the police, made the Tsunami connection."

"No one except Alec."

"Mom, I haven't even had time to get Dana to catch me up with the back story so you probably know more about that than I do."

"I can't believe that, even with Alec broadsiding him, Max still got away and shot you in the process. How is your arm, by the way?"

"Truly, Mom, it felt like a wasp sting. I'm hoping for a scar, but…"

"Tami, none of this is even a little bit funny."

"Sorry. And full disclosure—especially high up under my right breast I feel like I've been stabbed and I have a fried egg-size bump on my head, but my arm really is OK. And just so you know, I'm giving you a pass on calling me Tami today, but still hoping for better."

"Are there plenty of police there in the hospital in case Max tries to come after you again?"

"Mom, he's badly hurt and on the run. But, yes, two more officers just came in, making four counting Dana."

"Listen, sweetie, when I found out you were OK I called the airline and changed your ticket to this afternoon at ten minutes after five. Les is on her way over there with your clothes and will drive you to SFO."

"You want me to fly out in, like, three hours? No way, Mom, I can't just leave Lec. You're truly overreacting."

"Alec has his flight to New York in the morning and Dana says the word is that he should be released in a few hours. Les and Dan will invite him to their house tonight and take him to SFO tomorrow."

"But…"

"Tamiko, please don't argue. I need you to be here. I just do."

"Well, sure, of course I want to be with you too. It's just that Lec is…"

"I don't know if this will help you feel any better about getting on the plane, but I want you to know that I'm good with you and Alec seeing each other."

"Did I hear you right? Dating? Really? Do you mean like…"

"I do. As Ed says, a man willing to risk his life for you twice in a week, is a man worth respecting, and I agree."

"But what about the 'I'm way too young issue'?"

"Of course you are, but now it's up to you and Alec to cope with that."

"Thanks, Mom, I'll be on the plane for sure. And, well, it's like, just amazing that you're trusting me. Both of us I guess. But…"

"I thought you were going cold turkey on the word 'like'?"

"Like you are with 'Tami' I guess."

"I love you, Tamiko."

"I love you too, Mom. See you later and give Ed a big hug. That guy has my back."

· · · · ·

At 2:30 p.m., Alec's head and lip stitched and back bandaged, Yolanda wheels his bed into a long room with half a dozen others that the hospital calls its recovery area. "We'll keep an eye on you until five o'clock and if you can still pass our short concussion protocol, you'll be released. And, oh yes, I have two notes for you. Do you want me to read them?"

"Please."

"The first is from a Berkeley police sergeant named Dana Helickson and says,

"*Dan Aristead, Tamiko's uncle, will pick you up at 5:00 p.m. and take you back to his place in Palo Alto and then to the airport in the morning. In the meantime, if there is any word about Max, I'll be in touch pronto.*"

"What about the second?"

"You mean the one from the world's most fetching softball player?"

"Maybe I should read it myself."

"Possibly, but then, I've already read it."

"Nosey of you."

"There's not much romance in this job, so I grab it when I can."

"Go ahead, then."

"*Lec, I'm bummed to have to run out on you, but Mom is going to vaporize if I'm not in D.C. tonight. But here's the big news. Assuming you are still good with it, we are now approved for adult snuggling. That's right. According to Amy Gashkin, this oversized, underage virgin, complete with Medusa hair, broken ribs and a chunk out of her arm, is all yours. I really do hope you are as excited as I am. Talk later. XOXO, T.*"

"I could explain the context."

"Why not close your eyes and fantasize."

"Good idea."

. . . . .

By three o'clock Tamiko has changed into the black pants and red T-shirt Les has brought from Palo Alto and given a statement to Sergeant Helickson, and an officer from the Sunnyvale force. Now, in her aunt's car on the way to San Francisco International Airport she busies herself inspecting every car on the freeway. "When you crane around to look behind us like that your ribs must hurt like they were stuck with a hot fork," Les says. "Just so you know, I'm keeping a close eye on the rearview mirror so there's no need."

"Do you know what a KIA Sol looks like?"

"No, so I'm watching out for any and all small blue cars even though your Sergeant friend says that Max is so banged up that it's unlikely he'll be a danger anytime soon."

"Since everyone but Lec has been underestimating him all week, I've decided being in a little pain is better than being dead."

"After what you've been through today, I would be silly to argue."

. . . . .

At 4:45 Alec, who has also given a statement to the police, has his vital signs checked for the last time. After telling the nurse that he still knows who he is, why he's in the hospital, and that on August 27, 2016, Barack Obama is president of the United States, he is wheeled to the curb, where he introduces himself to a slim, medium tall man with slightly receding sandy hair who is standing next to a white Ford Fusion and says, "It's kind of you to pick me up. I don't know how I would have gotten home without a car."

"The Berkeley police sergeant, sorry, I forgot her name, offered to drive you, but it seemed easier, and maybe safer to have you stay with us since I'm told it's remotely possible that Max knows where you live. I guess he's badly injured, so it's highly unlikely that…"

"Say no more, that man is harder to stop than lava running downhill," Alec interrupts with a rueful chuckle. "I'm all for staying as far away from him as possible," he adds, as he gingerly settles into the front seat just as Miles Davis begins to play. Fumbling his phone out of his pocket he says, "Is that really you?".

"*C'est moi, je t'aime.*"

Hesitating, Alec is about to confess his ignorance of French, when Dan, who has overheard mouths "*Moi aussi.*"

"*Moi aussi.*"

"I thought you took Spanish in high school? *J'espère que vous pas pratiqué avec les jeunes filles.*"

Giving Dan a 'sometimes you can't win' shrug, Alec asks, "What's this with French anyway, I'm looking forward to my true love teaching me to flirt in Russian."

"*Ya lyublu tebya tak sil'no.*"

"Nice, but before you translate, maybe I should remind you that I'm in the car with your uncle."

"The one who knows French, probably."

"Probably."

"Oops, they're boarding my plane. You're still flying East tomorrow, right?"

"Absolutely. No matter how crap I feel now I'll only need to think of how great it will be to get three thousand miles away from Max to get to the airport two hours early."

"Did Mom talk to you?"

"Not yet, although I see she called several times when my phone was in lock up. But I read your note with the fantastic news that she has lifted the bundling board separating us."

"Definitely. So, maybe we can even meet this week. I mean D.C. is, like, only a few hours from New York, right? But…"

"I can't think of anything I'd rather do."

"*Moi aussi.*"

. . . . .

When they arrive in Palo Alto, Alec redoubles his vigilance, even asking Dan to drive slowly around a couple of blocks to be sure they aren't being followed. With no small blue cars in sight, Dan turns from busy University Avenue onto Maple Street, two blocks from his home. Then, as Alec is telling Dan how he violated 101 traffic laws to get to Twin Creeks in time to intercept Max, Alec's phone sounds. Seeing it's Tamiko again, he answers saying, "I thought you were…"

"Lec, where are you?"

"Just getting to Dan's."

"Stop, stop—Max is there. Stop!" Tamiko all but screams.

Just as Dan turns into the driveway and pushes the garage door button on the sun visor, he hears Tamiko's desperate shout. Hitting the brakes, he brings the Ford to a juddering stop thirty five feet from the garage. As Dan frantically tries to fumble the gear lever into reverse the garage door rolls up to reveal Max sitting in a chair holding a long-barreled black handgun, arms extended.

"Down!" Alec yells, as he reaches up and stabs the garage door button a half-second before the windshield explodes. Two more shots immediately ring out. The first buries itself in the engine compartment while the other flies over their heads to explode the rear window as the Ford lurches backwards across Maple Street. Jolting over the curb and bouncing through a low hedge, the car comes to rest in a bed of lavender a few feet from a two story brick house when Dan finally remembers to take his foot off the gas. Launching himself out of the passenger door, Alec tries to make himself as small as possible as he runs the half-dozen steps to relative safety behind the trunk of a massive Monterrey cypress. Peeking out, he sees that Dan's garage door is now closed with Max nowhere to be seen. His phone still in his right hand, Alec ignores Tamiko's hysterical voice as he ends the call and presses 911. As he starts to give the address of the shooting, the dispatcher interrupts saying this is the third call they've received and the police are already in motion.

"Are you OK?" Dan's tremulous voice enquires from the car.

"I think so, you?"

"I've got some glass cuts on my face and my eyelid is bleeding, but I can see OK so I'm hoping it's not serious. Do you see anyone moving?"

"Nada. But I'm delighted that those sirens mean the posse is almost here." Then hearing his phone and seeing that it's Tamiko again, Alec answers saying, "It was your turn to save my life. Dan's too for that matter."

"Oh my god Lec, tell me."

"Dan managed to reverse the car while we were still at the street end of the driveway. We—that is Dan, the Ford, and yours truly—are now in the yard across the street and the cops are pulling up"

"I heard shots."

"Max was waiting in the garage. But instead of shooting us like kittens in a basket, he had to fire from maybe forty feet. He blew out the Fusion's windshields, front and back, but not us—although Dan has a face full of glass. But how did you know..."

"My plane got delayed to check some kind of caution light. I was thinking over what happened today for about the ninety-ninth time, like you know, whatever we do Max manages to outsmart us. That's when I remembered that when I flopped down to take a nap, my little red Indian purse where I keep my I.D. and a few dollars was lying on the grass next to me. I had taken it out of my sports bag in the Twin Creeks Café, but somehow never put it back. And since Max never misses anything I just knew he'd grabbed it."

"I don't follow."

"On the way to the airport Mom wrote a bunch of contact numbers, including Les and Dan's address and phone numbers on a piece of note paper, which I put in the purse."

"But you have a Velcro memory."

"Mom doesn't, so sometimes she forgets. And remember, she was more than a little freaked about leaving me. Oops, they just cleared us for take off and a cabin attendant is heading my way so I really do have to get off."

"There are now four cop cars here so things are very much under control."

"Maybe the plane has Wi-Fi so you can email me."

"I'll try, but otherwise call me the second you land."

. . . . .

"Les just called to confirm that Tamiko's plane has left the gate," Ed says when Amy comes into their hotel room holding two Diet Cokes. "Let's take a long walk, get a drink or three and maybe even go to a movie. Tamiko won't arrive at Dulles until well after two a.m."

"I'm so tense I can't think straight, but sure, as soon as I take a shower.

All the anxiety has me wet all over."

"I thought Asians hardly perspire."

"My Irish half appears to be sweating enough for both," Amy replies as she quickly steps into the bathroom, closing the door behind her.

A few seconds after Ed hears the shower start, Amy's phone rings. "Gashkin's Answering Service," he intones on picking up.

"Hey Ed, it's Dana. Is Amy with you?"

"In the shower."

"Can you pull her out? I have big news—news that starts out ugly, but ends brilliantly. So toss her a towel 'cause she's going to want to hear this right now."

"OK, hold on," Ed replies as he makes his way to the bathroom and opens the door to the shower.

"Oh, goody, you're coming in," Amy says with a wide grin.

"No such luck, and I'm afraid you need to come out. Dana's on the phone with news so big she only wants to say it once—worry not, she says it ends well."

Shaking her wet head like a Labrador walking out of a lake, Amy steps into the large bath towel Ed holds out for her.

"OK Dana, go for it, the phone's on speaker."

"The headline is that Max is dead and Alec and Dan are OK, although Dan's at the hospital with some nasty glass cuts on his face."

"Max attacked Alec and Dan?" Amy asks incredulously. "Given everything that already happened today, how could that be fucking possible? I mean Dana, are you guys good for anything?"

"Apparently Tamiko had the Aristead's address in her purse, which Max grabbed when he abducted her, a possibility we all missed," Sergeant Helickson says patiently. "After he stole the car at the shopping center he somehow got to their house and was waiting in the garage with a large-caliber hand gun when Dan and Alec arrived. When the automatic door rolled up he shot into Dan's wind-shield a couple of times, but mercifully missed them. Then, either Alec or Dan hit the garage door controller again, because the door started to close while Max was still firing. One of his shots hit the heavy metal bar at the bottom of the garage door, ricocheted back and caught him in the eye. It was a one-in-a-million kind of thing, but that doesn't make him any less dead."

"Really?" Amy asks. "I mean, Dana, have you actually kicked his body?"

"I promise you, he's stone cold dead. I can forward a picture if it'll convince you."

"But what kind of garage door has such a heavy metal frame?" Ed asks, as if somehow this is relevant.

"Apparently this one has been there fifty years and was built to last. But again, the point is that when half a dozen Palo Alto officers rushed the garage they found Max in a chair with a hole in his face."

"He was sitting in a chair?" Ed asks, surprised as he reaches for a second towel to wipe up the puddle Amy's made.

"He broke his leg in the car crash."

"Does Tamiko know all this?" Amy asks, remembering that her daughter is nowhere near Palo Alto.

"The important parts anyway. It was her last-second call that very probably saved Alec and Dan."

"You said Dan was hurt?"

"His face got cut by flying glass, but his eyes are fine. Your sister is at the emergency room with him now and I guess he'll be released shortly. I'm at the Palo Alto P.D. where they're finishing taking Alec's statement."

"Is he there? Can I talk to him?" Amy asks. "It's unbelievable what that guy has survived today."

"In another room giving a statement, sorry. As soon as he's done I'll take him to the Garden Court Hotel where your sister made a reservation for all three of them under the name Brown. Her idea is to kind of lie low for a day or two to avoid as much media as possible."

"Will that work?" Ed asks skeptically.

"Maybe for a while. The fire and evacuation, which has now been lifted, are a huge story out here. Also remember, since newspapers have only a few local reporters these days and it's Saturday night, so..."

"But a killing in an upscale Palo Alto neighborhood has to be news," Ed interrupts.

"I just helped write a bland statement that suggests it was a home invasion gone wrong. By Monday, reporters will undoubtedly connect the dots back to the violence at Twin Creeks and begin to dig out at least some of the back story. But with all of you out of the Bay Area and presumably not taking media calls, they may move on to something else by the time you return. Eventually, you'll likely be cornered and quizzed, but in the meantime you'll have time to think of how best to respond."

. . . . .

At 6:40 p.m. Sergeant Helickson pulls her car near the back entrance of the Palo Alto Police Department as Alec emerges. As they drive away she says, "Sorry for the cloak and dagger, but we had a couple of calls from San Jose media outlets and you never know whether a TV crew will show up."

"Thanks Dana, you've been a friend," Alec replies as he tries to find a position that doesn't tweak his raw back.

"Since I wasn't a bit of help catching Max, I'm trying to make up for it. More to the point, I'm thinking you better call your parents. It may seem unlikely that a reporter who learns your name will locate them, but in the Internet age you never know, especially since there must be a load of articles about your sports exploits out there. Anyway, since your head bandage makes you look like you were just evacuated from Afghanistan, it makes sense to alert them as to what to expect at the airport tomorrow."

"Good point, and yes, it's top of my list as soon as I figure a way to prevent Dad from turning it into a two-hour inquisition. Also, if I can stay awake long enough, I need to call my Uncle Charlie in New York. I've been closer to him lately and he's been following what's going on day-to-day."

"If it will make things easier I can call him," Dana says, turning left onto Cowper Street.

"That would be great, especially if you can do it in a way that won't freak him out. I mean getting a call from the police late Saturday evening and all."

"Hi, this is Dana Helickson calling at the request of your nephew Alec to report that both he and Tamiko Gashkin are safe and well and to tell you that…"

"Brilliant," Alec interrupts with a laugh. "By the time you tell him you're a cop he'll be relaxed."

"Actually, if for some reason I don't get hold of him until tomorrow morning, I won't be," Dana says, pulling alongside the Hotel a little short of the entrance.

"Huh? Won't be what?" Alec asks, twisting slightly to face the tall, fair-skinned sergeant.

"A cop, which is my awkward way of telling you this was my last case and I'm off to grad school in St. Louis, Missouri as soon as I can pack. I'd planned to leave Thursday but I just had to see this case through."

"You're leaving, really? But I thought you liked the action that goes with being a detective."

"Occasionally, between all the boring bits, work can be exciting but it's time for my next adventure."

"Do you want a PhD to teach?"

"Maybe, but I'm also interested in law enforcement policy so maybe I can combine the two. It's no secret that policing in America is typically old-fashioned and inefficient, and in low-income areas, often brutal. It will be fun to try to improve things. In addition, I recently broke up with my longtime boyfriend so…"

"So this is goodbye," Alec says as he unlatches his seatbelt. "But listen, after all we've been through this week, I hope we can stay in touch."

"I'm counting on it. Years from now when I recount my most exciting case, all my students will want to know what happened after Romeo and Juliet galloped into the sunset."

"What's your guess?" Alec asks as he cracks open the door.

"When I first saw you and Tamiko come into the station last week looking as if you'd both been ripped from a romance movie I guessed your relationship would last about as long as a Kardashian marriage."

"And now?"

"Alec, really, I have no clue as to whether gorgeous people can ever be content, but if it's possible, I'm betting on you two," Sergeant Helickson says as she extends her hand to firmly shake Alec's.

. . . . .

When Alec checks into the Garden Court at seven o'clock, Les and Dan haven't arrived so he heads up to their two-bedroom suite feeling uncharacteristically light-headed. Worried that he could be experiencing concussion symptoms, he realizes that save for a few crackers and a small box of grape juice in the recovery room, he hasn't eaten since the hunk of peanut butter-smeared bread that morning. Picking up the hotel phone, he orders a cheeseburger and two beers. When he's told the cheeseburger will take twenty minutes, he asks for the beer to be brought up first along with a couple of soft rolls. Ten minutes later, half of the Corona already making him feel slightly flushed, Alec taps his dad's cell. "Dad, I'm fine, I really am, so no worries," Alec blurts when his father picks up. "I'm looking forward to seeing you and Mom tomorrow," he adds more calmly as he explains he's been a nasty car accident but is basically OK and will be on the plane tomorrow as scheduled.

"Hold on Alec, your mother is going to boil me in tar if I don't get her in on this."

"Where are you injured?" his mother asks, her voice telling him she's grabbed the phone and put it on speaker even as she adopts the no-nonsense tone of her medical practice.

"Fourteen stitches on my scalp and six or eight more on the right side of my lower lip, plus gashes on my back from when the fireman pulled me out of the car before it caught fire. They did a CT scan, but there's no concussion."

"But how did the accident happen? Were you drinking?" his dad persists in a voice so loud it's obvious he's reclaimed the phone.

"Mom, Dad, as maybe you can imagine, I'm pretty beat right now, so why don't I tell you the whole story tomorrow? But I want to alert you that bits and pieces of the story may already be online."

"Fine, but Alec, if you were just involved in a simple traffic accident, why would the story be on the Internet?" his dad asks in the excruciatingly reasonable tone he has perfected over many years as a trial lawyer.

"This guy was trying to kidnap my girlfriend who was in the trunk of his car. I cut him off which resulted in my car being hit and rolling over."

"The Korean girl you've been dating this summer?" his mother asks.

"No, not Teri, who is back in Korea. This was my new friend, Tamiko Gashkin."

"What kind of name is that?" his father asks. "Have you ever considered dating an American girl?"

"Tamiko was born in Amherst, Massachusetts."

"Is she OK?" his mother asks.

"She was shot in the arm, just a nick really. In addition she has some cracked ribs and a bump on her head, but basically she'll be fine. Mom, Dad, please can we save the details until…"

"Is Gashkin spelled like the famous Russian dancers from thirty or maybe forty years ago?" his dad interrupts.

"Ted, stop cross-examining him. How would Alec know if the girl's name is spelled like those Bolshoi dancers who defected years before he was born?"

"Actually, Mom, Tamiko is their granddaughter. But listen guys, if I don't hang up this conversation will last forever so I'm doing it now."

. . . . .

As Alec finishes eating his burger by inserting small bites into the undamaged side of his mouth, Dan and Les arrive. Handing his second beer to Dan, whose puffy face is decorated by half a dozen small circular Band-Aids, the men review what happened and how lucky they are to be alive. Then, as Les calls room service to order more food, Alec excuses himself and goes to his room where he texts Tamiko.

"*Put a big, happy smile on your face because all really is well. The headline is that Max is dead and thanks to you, Dan and I are safe. I know that Dana has told the whole story to your mom and Ed so I'll trust them to explain the details as soon as you're off the plane. In the meantime—not to mention all the rest of the time—I love you and good night."*

SUNDAY 2

PULLING HER AUNT'S BLACK ROLLER BAG, Tamiko comes past security at Dulles at 2:15 a.m. Spotting her mom, she lets go of the handle and runs forward, only to pull up short as her hand flies to her chest. Ed, who grabs the abandoned bag, turns to see the tall girl crouch slightly as her much smaller mother steps forward arms outstretched. Clearing his throat after a long minute he says, "If you two keep that up I'll have to mop up the puddle."

Belatedly realizing she's in danger of being impolite, Tamiko reaches out an arm and pulls Ed into the embrace saying, "Three-way hug—let's make a really big puddle."

In a taxi on the way to the Willard a few minutes later, Tamiko says, "I know from Lec's message that Max is dead and no one else is badly hurt, but I don't have any idea as to what happened in Palo Alto. Did you talk to Lec?"

"No, I guess he crashed soon after getting to the hotel. But Dana filled us in and we also talked to Les, and very briefly to Dan."

"I want to hear it all, but first can we talk more about Lec and me? You know Mom, about what you said this afternoon?"

"I'm not thinking about backtracking if that's what you're worried about. If it's still what you both want, we plan to welcome Alec to be—I'm not even sure what word to use…"

"Part of our extended household," Ed says helpfully, "which means sleepovers are part of the deal."

"Wow! All of a sudden I feel shy. I knew you guys would get to like Lec once you knew him, but …"

"I hope so, but Tamiko, I want you to understand that my decision has far more to do with you than with Alec, or any other guy you might date. With Ed's help I've come to see that you are mature enough to make your own decisions."

"Mom, to be sure I make good ones I'll still need your help, and yours too, Ed."

"No need to rush into anything," Amy says so quickly it's obvious she's been rehearsing the words.

"If you mean Lec and me getting together, Mom, I kind of think that countdown has already begun. Well, that is, if he still, well, you know, if he's still…"

"On the launch pad?" Ed interrupts with a chuckle. "Somehow I don't think you have to worry about that."

· · · · ·

Alec awakes at 3:30 a.m. feeling anxious and achy. Getting up to take a couple of the Vicodins they gave him at the hospital, he sees to his delight that he has a text from Tamiko.

"*Mom really has pulled down the red flag so I'm all yours. How about meeting at the top of the Empire State building a la Sleepless in Seattle?*"

Sitting on the edge of the hotel bed in the dim, green glow produced by the digital clock, Alec replies,

"*Wherever, whenever, and however, I can't wait to get my hands on the loveliest young woman on the planet (any planet).*"

Then, rolling onto his stomach he reaches back with his right hand to pull up the duvet before falling into a deep sleep.

· · · · ·

Les holds out an extra-large Oakland A's hat and a small backpack when Alec emerges from his room at 7:30 Sunday morning, "I hope I'm not hurting your feelings, but your bandage looks so scary that unless you cover it they may not let you on the plane."

"Thanks, and I'm glad you're a fan of the right Bay Area team," Alec says as he gingerly maneuvers the hat over his bandage. "But what's the pack about?"

"A pillow, lightweight blanket and sweater, and a pill bottle with a couple of Ambien Dan uses when he travels. I figure you're going to feel like shit today so you'll want to sleep as much as you can. And, well, I'm always cold on planes so I thought…"

"Thanks, I get chilly too."

"OK then, let's move. There's a cup of Peet's and two scones for you in the car."

"But I need to check out and pay my share of the bill."

"Don't be silly."

"Really, I…"

"Need to shut up and get a move on. You volunteered to save both my sister and niece, so I guess I can volunteer to pay your hotel bill."

A few minutes later in Les's middle-aged Toyota Camry on the way to the airport, Alec removes the plastic top from his coffee. As he takes an appreciative gulp, Les says, "Alec, I hope you're going to treat my niece well. She's a particular favorite of mine."

"I think of little else."

"Is that supposed to be reassuring?"

"What did you think about when you fell for Dan?"

"Fair point I guess, but full disclosure, when Amy told me that Tamiko wanted to go out with a guy six years older, I was just as upset, OK, make that appalled, as she was. I mean, you're almost as close to my age as you are to Tamiko's."

"You're taken."

"Ha! I guess I deserved that. But what I mean is that it's a huge experience canyon for someone her age to cross, especially for a tomboy kid whose never even had a boyfriend."

"Her tomboy stage seems to be done and dusted."

"I was getting to that. After hanging out with Tami for a couple of days, I can see that my mental picture of her is way out of date. Or, as Dan put it—Wow! And then, of course, there are the facts that in between proofreading a book for Bay, and practicing pitching for what I gather is a super elite softball team, she amused herself by reading F. Scott

Fitzgerald. In short, I went from worrying about whether she was in over her head with an older guy, to worrying how she could ever find a guy to keep up with her."

"Does that mean you might be ready to approve of me?"

"Only if you turn out to be as sweet as she is."

Alec is about to reply when his phone pings to announce a text from Tamiko saying,

"*What's up? U OK?*"

"*Les is driving me to the airport,*" Alec immediately replies. "*But since we're almost there, how about I call you when I'm through security?*"

A couple of minutes later when Les pulls the car to the curb in front of Terminal One, Alec climbs out slowly, mindful of how much his back screams every time he tweaks the scabs. Les, who is already standing on the curb, holds out a paperback copy of *War and Peace*.

"What's this?"

"Tamiko, and especially her Gashkin grandparents, take everything Russian super seriously."

"So to measure up, I'd better brush up? Really Les, I don't know how to…"

"Just be good to my niece."

. . . . .

After breezing through the short Sunday morning security line, Alec is trying to scrunch his feet back into his sandals without sitting down to manipulate the heel strap, when Miles Davis begins to play. Thinking that it's Tamiko, he hobbles quickly to the nearest bench only to see that it's Charlie. "Hey, what's going on?"

"Given what's happened in the last twenty-four hours I'm pretty sure you're the one who's supposed to answer that question," Charlie replies.

"Stiff, sore and kinda slammed, but very grateful to be alive. Hopefully I'll sleep on the plane and feel better by the time I get to Westchester."

"I talked to Dana Helickson last night so I don't need to quiz you as to what happened, or at least not until later. But Lec, how's the head?"

"At the moment it's the one part of me that doesn't hurt. And with a baseball hat over the bandage I can pass for normal except for my lip, which looks like I tried to kiss a chain saw."

"And your back?"

"Fine, if I don't move."

"After your mom gets her hands on you this afternoon you'll feel a lot better.

"But Lec, did I understand the good Sergeant correctly when she said that Tamiko's mom—her name is Amy, right?—that Amy is now OK with your seeing her daughter?"

"The one good thing that's come out of this appalling week. But enough about me, how are you and Emiko doing?"

"Amazingly. Although I never thought it could be possible, I seem to have remembered how to be happy. It's not that I don't miss Claire every ten minutes, it's that now it doesn't cancel out everything else. When you meet Emiko in a few days I hope you'll understand. But listen, since I know you have a plane to catch, here's my idea. We're up here in Nantucket hanging out, but after a few days I'll want to show Emi Boston—walk the Freedom Trail, ride in a duck boat, tour Harvard, and maybe even go to a Sox game. So why don't you invite Tamiko up here Tuesday or Wednesday and have the place to yourselves for a couple of days? That's assuming, of course, you two will be up to traveling and it's OK with Amy?"

"Really? Wow! For sure, I'll be OK-ish in a couple of days and I doubt Amy will change her mind. But Charlie, I don't want you and Emiko to give up Shangri-La just so…"

"It's her idea to share this with you two. Also, she's excited about inhaling as much of America as she can so Boston looms as another cool adventure. We'll come back Thursday evening so Emi can get comfortable with both of you before your parents show up late Friday. I invited them last night, which I hope works for you."

"Charlie, it all sounds perfect. Again, I don't know how to thank you."

"No need. Oh, and one more thing, check at the podium before you board."

Seeing that boarding has been delayed fifteen minutes, Alec steps into the men's room to dab cold water on his lip and then to Peet's to order a decaf latte. Arriving at the gate area, he is just about to call Tamiko when he hears his name being called.

"Sir, you've been upgraded to Business Class," the heavyset African American woman behind the counter tells him with a wide grin when he produces his I.D.

"How did that happen?"

"Fairy godmother maybe," the woman says with a throaty chuckle that makes Alec think of a cheerful cement mixer.

"But I didn't…"

"Sir, the way you look I'd just shut up, get on, and not try to talk me out of it. In fact, we're boarding Business Class now."

Once in his seat, Alec immediately taps Tamiko's number.

"I love you," Tamiko says by way of answer.

"Charlie called just as I cleared security. In addition to upgrading me to Business Class, which is a huge gift given how raw my back feels, he's invited us to use his place on Nantucket Island for a couple of days starting Tuesday or Wednesday."

"Just us?"

"Just us until Thursday evening when he and Emiko return from Boston."

"Yes, yes, yes—oh my god Lec, but are you going to be up to it?"

"Fortunately, that's one of the few parts of my body that's still working," Alec replies with a chuckle. "But what about your ribs?"

"What's a little pain when you're having fun? But, hey, really, I'm good to go although maybe at half speed."

"And your mom?"

"I hope she's not invited. But, seriously, no need to worry. The red flag is not only down, but buried. Mom even started me on birth control pills last night."

"I'm a little worried that maybe Nantucket by ourselves might seem like too much of…"

"Just tell me how to get there, dummy."

"I think you fly to Boston and take a small plane to the Island. I'll check with Charlie when I get to my parents. In the meantime I'm going to just sit here, think of you and hopefully nod off."

. . . . .

At 10:00 a.m. Ed leaves the hotel for a longish ramble, guessing that Amy and Tamiko will have plenty of mother-daughter bonding to catch up on. Two hours later when Washington's oppressive August heat gets the better of him, he heads back to the Willard where he finds Amy and Tamiko giggling over the remains of their room service breakfast.

"I'm off to Nantucket to meet Lec, hopefully on Tuesday," Tamiko says even before Ed snags a chair.

Glancing at Amy to register her almost imperceptible nod, Ed does his best to act as if this is routine news, not something that would have been beyond contemplation a few days before. Then looking for a way to change the subject he says, "With Max finally out of the picture, I need to get back to Berkeley. Assuming I can grab a redeye tonight it will allow us to drop the second room which will save a few bucks."

"I hope you won't mind if Mom and I stay until Tuesday, especially if we move my birthday dinner up to today. I mean, if from now on I'm going to be your over-grown daughter, you absolutely need to be there."

Seeing that Tamiko's almond-shaped eyes are damp at the corners, Ed feels his heart speed up as he says, "I wouldn't miss it. After all, celebrating a new daughter who comes without diapers is not an everyday occurrence."

. . . . .

Alec dozes most of the way to Chicago, where he tries without success to read the first chapter of *War and Peace* before boarding a second plane to Westchester County Airport in White Plains, New York, less than twenty minutes from his parents' house in leafy Chappaqua. Coming past the security gate an hour and a half later, he's surprised to see both his mom and dad. Awkwardly hugging them in an effort to protect his back, he says, "Wow, Ted and Ellen Burns both picking me up. I hope you're not disappointed that I left my backup singers in California."

"We both wanted to be sure that you really are in one piece," Ellen says. Then giving Alec another quick hug she asks, "Are you in pain now?"

"Only when you do that," Alec says remembering too late that it's a bad idea to smile. "But for sure, sitting on planes all day hasn't done my back any favors. My head has never hurt much and my lip is mostly OK except when I eat, so early warning, I'm hoping to have dinner through a straw."

In the passenger seat of his dad's Audi S4 five minutes later, Alec asks, "Did you two talk to Charlie last night?"

"Yes," his mother replies from the back seat. "Although sadly I missed the first and most interesting part of the call when he told Ted about his new Japanese girlfriend. To say the least, this has been a weekend of surprises."

Letting that one sail by, Alec says, "I'm sure Charlie filled you in on everything that's happened to me in the last two weeks. I know he talked to Dana Helickson, that's Sergeant Helickson of the Berkeley Police, after I fell asleep. So at this point, you may even know more about what happened yesterday than I do."

"Lec, I think there must have been a misprint online about your new girlfriend's age," Ted says so matter-of-factly that Alec knows from long experience he's about to be taken to the woodshed.

"Dad, please no bullshit. I'm too beat to play games. As you've obviously figured out, Tamiko is going to be sixteen tomorrow."

"OK, then, if you want me to give it to you straight, I find it bizarre that you apparently risked your life at least twice for a fifteen-year-old, who, in case you haven't noticed, it's illegal for you to even date. In fact, it's so strange it almost makes Charlie turning up with a Japanese girlfriend almost twenty years younger seem normal."

"Ted, please stop it," Ellen says, her voice raised in annoyance.

Sitting in the corner of the cheerful white and yellow laundry room in the basement of his parents' substantial two-story Colonial-style house, Alec tries not to grimace as his mom unwraps the bandages around his torso. When she says nothing, he asks a little anxiously, "How does it look?"

"You'll live, but it's going to be ouchy for a week or so."

"Right now it's my lip that hurts most. And sorry, it doesn't help to talk."

"Lips heal fast so you'll be fine in a few days. But if you're thinking about meeting your young lady on Tuesday, I don't think you'll be much of a kisser."

"Charlie told you he invited us up to his place?"

"He did, although he wasn't sure if it would be OK with Tamiko's mother."

"It is, and Mom, don't worry about the kissing, we can wait a few more days if we have to."

"Are you saying you haven't kissed this girl?" his mother asks, peering carefully at his head wound to make sure it's not infected.

"Nothing beyond a couple of pecks."

"Alec, I hate to channel your dad, but…"

"Mom, I really am beat. How about finishing with this, heating me a can of soup, and letting me crash. After I sleep in my own bed for fourteen hours where I'm pretty sure no one is going to try to kill me, I'll be happy to talk about anything and everything. But, Mom, before I go upstairs, take a look," Alec says, holding out his phone with Tamiko's grinning picture.

"That girl looks happy enough to burst."

"That's my Tamiko. Let me text you her mother's cell number. Maybe it will ease your mind if you give Amy a call."

"Won't that be awkward?"

"With your bedside manner, c'mon."

. . . . .

At five o'clock Sunday afternoon, Amy pulls open the drapes saying, "Rise and shine, you've slept all afternoon. In fact, you've now slept almost thirteen of the seventeen hours you've been in Washington, D.C."

"Kinda like what I've read about Ronald Reagan. But do I get jelly beans?"

"Dinner is at six-thirty and it will take fifteen minutes to get there. Ed is on a flight at eleven so he'll leave from the restaurant. How do you feel?"

"My ribs are tweaky, but let me take a few ibuprofen and I'll be good to go. No way I'm going to miss my birthday dinner."

"You sure you'll be up to going to Nantucket Tuesday?"

"Mom, I just want to be with Lec—the two of us, happy and safe. It's like, if rubbing noses is the most we're capable of, that's beyond OK."

Gingerly swinging her feet to the floor, Tamiko glances at her phone to see that she has three messages from Lec so calls him back.

"Finally," Alec says. "For a while there I thought you might have run off with the doorman."

"I doubt the words 'Tamiko' and 'run' will belong in the same sentence for a few weeks yet. I woke up at eleven-fifteen, ate a huge room service brunch and was back asleep by one. The good news is that I'm finally feeling a little less slammed. How about you?"

"As we speak Mom's making me some soup and salad cut in bits. Then I'll crash. Hopefully I'll feel a lot better *mañana*."

"Your head, your back, your lip? Tell me, are you really OK?"

"Mom's been doctoring me."

"She knows how to do that?" Tamiko asks, making her way into the bathroom.

"It probably helps that she's a physician."

"Really? Cool. Isn't it interesting how little we know about each other? Are your parents fine with your leaving again right away?"

"Not really, but they're also both superbusy, so it's not like we would be bonding over mahjong. Anyway, as you'll remember, I'm old enough not to need their permission."

"It's still nice to have," Tamiko says, turning slightly so she can see to brush her hair in the mirror.

"Sure, and I think I can get Mom on board. However, Dad may be beyond reaching. He checked your age online and is channeling Amy, circa twelve days ago."

"Lec, I'm sorry," Tamiko replies, forgetting about her hair. "Maybe I need to save your life a few more times."

"Charlie invited them up to Nantucket next weekend so you'll have a chance to demonstrate that you're toilet trained."

"Or I could just meet them wearing a diaper and nothing else," Tamiko says, grinning at herself in the mirror.

"That would get Dad's attention for sure. But hey, Mom's calling me from downstairs. How about we touch bases first thing tomorrow to figure out logistics. What are you doing now, by the way?"

"Naked on the bath mat about to put on the obligatory bra as part of dressing for my birthday dinner. It got moved up a day since Ed needs to fly home later this evening."

"Wish I was there."

"Hold that thought for Tuesday."

. . . . .

In the cab on the way to the Hay-Adams Hotel, Tamiko's phone rings. Seeing it's Jazz she answers, "So how'd we do?"

"We're all out eating pizza, celebrating."

"You won the tournament without me?"

"We won it for you. In fact we were losing the second game yesterday five-zip when we heard you were OK. From that moment we rocked and socked."

"What was the final?"

"Fourteen to five. And the most exciting part of it was that the littlest player on our team hit her first home run ever."

"Which would be you," Tamiko replies as she mouths, "We won the tournament" for her mom's and Ed's benefit.

"It would, but hey, hold on while we sing for your birthday. Then Coach wants to talk to you."

When the familiar song comes to an enthusiastic conclusion, Coach Rodriguez's gruff voice asks, "You're really OK?"

"Couple of dicey ribs, but otherwise good to go."

"Hold on a second while I walk outside. So, OK B, I need to tell you that a couple of reporters showed up today to question me about what happened. I think they're trying to find a hook to turn this into a big story."

"I've been sweating that. What did you say?"

"That I had no clue as to what happened yesterday or why, and that I was pretty sure you had left the Bay Area to be with your mom."

"Tell me they went away?"

"Well, they tried to talk to several of our players until I called security. And I also told everybody your cell number should be treated like a state secret."

"Thanks, Coach. Just so you know, this guy who tried to kidnap me was someone Mom once knew who had become mentally deranged. He shot himself, so it really is all over. And listen, I'll be back in a week or ten days and we can start work on grips and spins. My ribs are a little banged-up so it may be a bit longer before I can go flat out, but we can make a start."

"Good, since I plan to enter us in three or four fall tournaments, but not until the end of September."

"I'll be ready."

"I know you will."

. . . . .

Sitting at dinner a few minutes later at the Lafayette Restaurant in the Hay-Adams Hotel, Tamiko says, "Ed, this is awesome, thank you. I can hardly believe we're celebrating my birthday at a hotel whose slogan is 'Where nothing is overlooked except the White House'."

"It's a treat for me too. Since we're just across the street from 1600 Pennsylvania Avenue, it's a fair bet every President since the 1920's has been in here. But enough history," Ed says as he pours a few sips of red wine into

Tamiko's glass. Then raising his, he toasts, "To Tamiko, a remarkable young woman on her birthday, and to Yuri and Amy, who made her so. Cheers!"

. . . . .

After seeing Ed into an Uber to Dulles, Amy and Tamiko take a second one back to the Willard. "How about we check out the movie archive on TV and find the sappiest one?" Amy suggests.

"They probably won't have *Love Actually*, *Princess Bride*, or *Four Weddings and a Funeral*."

"If they don't, perhaps we can add a new favorite to our list."

"It's a tough club. So, why don't we cuddle close and stream one of them on my iPad. My ribs definitely need a break."

"You might remember that on Tuesday."

"I hope this is the start of a Sex 101 talk. I mean, like Mom, Lec is slim and all, but he's still maybe, like 180 pounds, so I'm a little worried," Tamiko replies, blushing slightly.

"Why don't we postpone the rest of this conversation until we get upstairs?"

When mother and daughter close their door, Amy says, "When it comes to Tuesday I wouldn't worry, sweetie. Go slow and your body will let you know what will work. And I don't mean to annoy you, but Alec surely has plenty of experience."

"That part is great, isn't it? I mean, traveling all over the world he must have learned lots of things that will come in handy. But you know me Mom, I like to know things too. And except for a porn video or two, I'm pretty clueless."

"Well, I hate to disappoint, but there's no way I'm going to draw stick figures on a hotel notepad."

"C'mon, if you're not going to coach me, who will? I mean I could call Jazz, but…"

"Wait a second, I've got an idea. Your dad's roommate at Cal had this embarrassing poster called, if I remember right, Hump of the Week, hanging over his bed. It showed fifty-two small drawings of people having sex, each in a different position. The guys in the dorm thought it was way cool while all the girls pretended to be disgusted while leaning in for a closer look. Hold on, I bet like everything else, it's online." After a few key strokes on her iPad, Amy adds, "Aha, got it," as she hands the tablet to Tamiko.

"Wow! Mom, you're the best. For sure, this is exactly what I need."

"I'd say don't bother memorizing them, except I know you already have. But I will say that for most people, most of the time, half a dozen are more than plenty."

"Really?"

"Really. Remember, it's what happens in your brain—all those amazing chemicals getting released—that gets you high and they're the same whether you share sex lying on your back or standing on your head. But listen sweetie, have you taken your second birth control pill?"

"Yes, before we went to dinner. But I'm sure Alec plans to use a condom since I just started."

"I hope he does, but just so you know, the population of the world would probably be half what it is if guys always did what they were supposed to. Anyway, I called my gynecologist and she said that since you just ended your period Friday, all should be well even though you just started taking the pill. But to be safe you should also use the morning-after pill for a few days. And you should also make sure Alec has been checked for STDs recently."

"Got it."

"Ready for the movie?"

"Totally!"

. . . . .

In bed a few minutes before eight with a full stomach, Alec taps his uncle's number.

"I hope you're calling to report that you're feeling better."

"Still kinda slammed to tell you the truth, but thanks to you and that roomy plane seat, I'm a lot better than I could be."

"What's your mom say?"

"Everything is healing fine. By tomorrow she predicts I'll feel like I was hit by an SUV instead of a dump truck."

"And Tamiko?"

"She reports that all is good as long as she moves like a zombie who never coughs, sneezes, laughs, or poops."

"Are you two feeling well enough to come up Tuesday, or do you need another day or two?"

"Tuesday, definitely."

"I hate to mention this, but a little earlier I got an email from your dad chewing me out for inviting you and Tamiko up here. I was just thinking of how best to reply to that one when he switched to lecturing me on dating Asian women half my age."

"Ouch! So how did you respond?"

"Deleted the message and gave Emiko a hug. There's never been any point arguing with Ted when he's convinced he's right."

MONDAY 3

WHEN TAMIKO OPENS HER EYES AT 7:00 A.M., she sees that she has an email from Alec's uncle cordially inviting her to Nantucket and providing a suggested travel plan. Borrowing her mom's credit card she quickly makes a reservation scheduling her arrival at 3:15 Tuesday. She then forwards the details to Lec noting that she plans to leave for Connecticut early Friday to visit her grandparents. Saying she'll call him later, Tamiko adds that she's engaged in an important research project on how to snuggle while at the same time minimizing pain from broken ribs and battered backs and attaches the Hump of the Week poster.

A few minutes later, waiting for their room service breakfast, Tamiko calls her grandmother. "Hi Babushka, it's your birthday girl. Sorry, I had my phone turned off last night when you and Stepan called."

"Are you ready for a tough one?" Vera asks, the change in the sound of her voice alerting Tamiko that her grandmother has put the phone on speaker.

"On my birthday?"

"When better?"

"Go for it."

"For every beauty there is an eye somewhere to see it. For every truth there is an ear somewhere to hear it. For every love there is a heart somewhere to receive it."

"You're cheating a little."

"Me? Never."

"Ivan Panin emigrated from Russia and wrote that in the U.S."

"You can take the man out of Russian, but never Russia out of the man."

"Ha, I know Mom's updated you guys on what's been happening, but…"

"You are alive and well, which is answer to my prayers," Stepan says.

"But Dedushka, I thought you didn't believe in God?"

"I believe in prayer. God is a detail."

"Maybe we can continue the discussion Friday, if it's OK for me to come visit."

"Always, but we thought…"

"Lec's parents are coming to Nantucket Friday and I'm getting the vibe his dad disapproves of baby-doll girlfriends. So I'm thinking it will be more fun to hang with you two. Mom says I can take Amtrak from Boston to somewhere in Connecticut not too far from your place so…"

"We'll check and explain exactly," Vera says. "How long can you be here?"

"Maybe until Monday. I'm thinking Lec will be back at his parents in Chappaqua by then so he can drive over and take me to the airport."

"Since we are not prudish Americans, he is welcome to stay overnight in the guesthouse with you," Vera says.

"Thanks, but I should probably take things a step at a time. Who knows, Lec may be tired of me by next week."

"Tired of my most beautiful girl, I think very doubtful," Stepan says gallantly. "More likely, he'll be on knee."

"Tamiko is way too young for that. This Alec might be sweet boy, but she must live more before she settles down," Vera says in a voice so firm Tamiko realizes she's trying to chisel it onto her psyche.

"You've been wanting to say that, haven't you, Vera?" Tamiko responds.

"Yes, and you smart to listen."

"But if I remember right, you two have been together since you were barely seventeen."

"Russians have no good sense when it comes to love," Vera replies seriously.

"Ha," Stepan adds.

· · · · ·

After sleeping thirteen delicious hours Alec wakes to read Tamiko's text and texts back, "*Happy B-day! I love you. As for your sophomoric poster, I had*

*hoped we could begin at week fifty-three. But hey, let me know when you're
ready for a stupid dog joke."*

Ten minutes later, coming into the kitchen he finds his dad sitting at
the table reading the *Wall Street Journal*.

"I thought I'd make us waffles and bacon. Grab a chair and I'll pour
you some coffee."

"Sounds perfect, Dad," Alec replies, taking the chair on the corner
that was his as a kid.

"You feeling a little better?"

"Better than yesterday anyway."

Placing the plates on the table in record time, Ted says, "Lec, I want
to say that at times I know I've been too opinionated—bossy might even
be a better word—when it comes to your life. And that includes more
than a few rants about your decision to go to college at UC Berkeley
instead of Yale and quitting the Modern Pentathlon before trying for the
Olympics. It's as if for a few years there I didn't quite understand that you
weren't fifteen anymore. But when it comes to Tamiko Gashkin, I really
do think she's far too young for you. But just so you know, I'll be civil this
weekend."

"Whoa, Dad, that's a truckload. But as far as Tamiko goes, there are
no worries. She just emailed me that she's off to visit her grandparents
in Greenwich on Friday. She's close to them and I'm sure with what
happened this last week, they're anxious to give her a big hug."

"Is this about what I said yesterday?"

"I did caution her that you're in the disbelief stage about our
relationship."

"I hope this won't be one more nail in my coffin as far as Ellen is
concerned."

"If you don't mind me saying so, you and Mom didn't seem to be too
pleased with each other yesterday."

"We've been going through a brambly patch. I've been pretending it's
normal empty-nester angst, but I guess I need to accept it's more of an
existential crisis."

"Really? Why? About what?"

"How to create an interesting new life, if that doesn't sound too pretentious."

"I noticed Mom looks super fit."

"She's been biking, hiking, and doing yoga with friends."

"What about you, Dad?"

"I've had a busy year at the office so not so much," his father replies, glancing down at his slightly protruding belly. "But the larger point is that Ellen wants to move to the city and change her medical practice to a more holistic model and in her words 'become a more interesting person.'"

"Whoa! How are you coping with all that?"

"Truth be told, not that well. I like Chappaqua, my law practice, and my golf buddies. I have no desire to turn my life upside down because of Ellen's midlife crisis."

"Perhaps a compromise might make sense."

"This seems to be a conversation where we give each other relationship advice which neither of us wants to hear," Ted says as he reaches over to refill Alec's coffee. "Had enough to eat?"

"Yes, fabulous, by the way. But, hey, Dad, do you still have the old pickup parked on the other side of the garage?"

"Sure, there's no quit in Dump Run Betsy."

"I'd like to borrow her to go shopping."

"Of course. While you're out I'll nip into the office for a few hours. Ellen is planning to be back with lunch by twelve-thirty."

. . . . .

Alec drives the familiar route to downtown Chappaqua turning onto King Street and marvels at how little the posh suburb has changed since he was a kid. Parking the faded green GMC with rusted door panels between a black Mercedes C class and a white Tesla S, he heads for an old-fashioned jewelry store he guesses must mainly survive by replacing watch batteries. This isn't the ideal place to shop for Tamiko, Alec thinks, but seeing no alternative goes in. Studying the small selection of rings he's dismayed that most are too fussy, too expensive, too ugly, or all three. But just as he turns to leave, he spots a thin gold band with a tiny red stone, in the far corner of the display case. Bending over for a closer look he's delighted that it's offered for a price he can actually afford.

Back home a few minutes later he makes his plane reservations for the next day and is about to call Tamiko when his phone rings. "Hey birthday girl," he says by way of answer.

"Young woman, please."

"Of course, how silly of me."

"So tell."

"Huh?"

"One stupid dog joke."

"OK, but remember, since I'm new at this you need to cut me some slack."

"No excuses."

"So a dog walks into a bar and asks the bartender for a job. The bartender says, 'the circus is in town, why don't you try there?' The dog says, 'Why would they need a bartender?'"

"Sweet. I knew there was a good reason I fell for you. But hey, I've got one that's even better."

"Like the elephant said to the giraffe, I'm all ears."

"I'm saving it for tomorrow in case I feel embarrassed during the taking off my clothes part. But more to the point now, your mom just talked to my mom for twenty minutes."

"I suggested it so I hope it turned out to be a good idea."

"Mom was laughing, so I'm guessing some positive bonding took place. But I don't really know since an oath of confidentiality was front and center."

"My mom just pulled into the garage, so maybe I can coax her to share."

"If you don't mind me sharing a little first, I'm like, beyond excited about our trip."

"You mean the one that's twenty-six hours and seventeen minutes away?"

"God I love you."

. . . . .

"I brought egg salad and soft rolls," Ellen says as she comes through the kitchen door. "What have you been up to?"

"Talked to Dad for a while and then went to town to get Tamiko a present."

"Dare I ask what?"

"Just some jewelry," Alec replies. Then, seeing that his mom isn't going to move until he shows her, he pulls a small velvet box from his pocket and hands it over.

"Ruby with gold, simple and lovely," Ellen says when she pushes back the hinged lid with her forefinger. Then holding the little ring up to the light she adds, "You must have inherited your good taste from your mother. But Lec, for your information, a ring is never jewelry."

"I don't follow."

"Earrings, bracelets, and under some circumstances a necklace qualify as jewelry, but a ring always means something special."

"I guess I got it right then," Alec says, clicking the little box shut and slipping it back into his pocket.

"Following your suggestion I talked to Amy Gashkin this morning and she told me that although it was akin to moving Mount Everest, she now believes that Tamiko is mature enough to make her own dating decisions. Still, like your dad, I worry that you're getting too serious too fast with someone who is too young. To say the least, you're assuming a huge responsibility."

"Mom, if I didn't make it clear last night, it's not a matter of choice. I picked up her book, looked into her eyes and the deal was done. I'm only grateful she had the same reaction. But out of curiosity, what else did you and Amy talk about?"

"That was for our ears only."

"Truth be told, I'm a lot more interested in Amy having given us the green light than why she decided to do it."

"Even with my limited experience I've noticed that when it comes to sex, guys are almost always more interested in results than process," Ellen says with a slight frown as she puts the chicken salad and baguette on the table and sits across from Alec.

"So Mom, are you going to tell me what's going on with you? Since I saw you at Christmas it seems like you've lost ten pounds and ten years," Alec asks as he cuts a pickle in half, examines the pieces, and eats the slightly smaller one.

"I've decided to make some changes to my life. The prospect of sitting in a suburb with a boring job, and a man who's in a deeper rut than I am, for the next thirty years became too depressing."

"But you're a wonderful doctor. I thought you loved it," Alec says, letting his concern show.

"I guess it came to a head after I got involved with yoga, biking—and Lec, I know this is going to sound like I'm just another menopausal ditz—but also meditation. To vastly oversimplify, as I began to feel a lot better I finally confronted something that's been increasingly bothering me for several years—which is that many, if not most, of my patients cling to lifestyles almost guaranteed to make them feel crappy. The result is that they come to me to beg for pills to fix them up—including antidepressants, anti-anxiety medications like Xanax, painkillers—some of which are highly addictive, and so on. And, oh yes, I'm also expected to routinely order up a bunch of mostly irrelevant tests both by my patients and the insurance company that handles our malpractice coverage."

"So I'm guessing that you're working harder to get people to change their habits."

"Exactly. But I also have a chance to join a friend from medical school in a holistic practice in the city where we would be helping people willing to invest time and energy in their health."

"And Dad says you also want to move to the city?"

"The leaf blowers of Chappaqua or the symphonies of New York, which sound track would you pick for your life?" Ellen replies seriously, depositing half of her sandwich on Alec's plate.

"What about Dad? I'm not sensing he's ready to make big changes."

"Or any changes as it turns out. Even though you and Caitlin are grown, the house is paid for, and we've saved a bundle, Ted can't imagine living in a different way. But listen, like you and your new love, Dad and I are going to figure this out on our own or not," Ellen says as she stands and reaches for his plate. Then, halfway to the sink she turns and says, "Lec, I want to say that, although I obviously didn't know about the danger you were in until after it was over, I've been shaking inside ever since. It's as if I can't stop beseeching the universe to keep you safe, even though you're right here in front of me."

"Thanks Mom, I love you too. And for what it's worth, I think you're on the right path and I hope Dad signs on."

· · · · ·

When the sound of a siren breaks into Tamiko's two-hour nap, she starts to stretch before being painfully reminded this is a bad idea. Alerted by her daughter's slight gasp, Amy, who is reading on the other side of the king sized bed says, "Do you have the energy for another expedition? I heard the Newseum is very cool—a history of the U.S. through media. But if we're going to do it we need to get a move on to allow time get to the lingerie shop before it closes."

Gingerly levering herself off the bed and padding into the bathroom Tamiko looks over her shoulder as she replies, "Mom, we did plenty of cool shopping last week."

"But Vera texted me about an exclusive European style lingerie shop called Jar Yan on Wisconsin Avenue," Amy says, climbing out of the big bed and reaching for her black pants.

"Don't tell me this is also about buying something for yourself?"

"You're not the only one with a boyfriend. And since I've never even set foot in that type of store, I thought maybe…."

"Got it. But how about we both wait until Boston in a few weeks and go with Vera, who actually knows something about the subject?"

"But it's still your birthday and you're going to a house with a pool…"

"Um, Mom," Tamiko says, putting her head out of the bathroom, "I didn't want to upset any family apple carts by mentioning it before, but Auntie Les already got me a birthday bikini."

"She did what? My little sister…"

"Droit de Auntie, she said. It's like Grandma Vera with the sexy underwear—they're just having fun. And how can you get mad at Les when you're only a few days behind with the same plan?" Tamiko says, deciding it's best not to mention that her mom would probably have pushed for a more modest suit.

"Ever diplomatic," Amy says with a rueful laugh as she pulls a pair of comfortable shoes from her roller bag.

"Mom, my new wardrobe, this trip, the amazing dinner last night, has all been fabulous. Let's go to the Newseum and not worry about shopping," Tamiko says as she comes out of the bathroom fully dressed.

"C'mon, you're only sixteen once," Amy protests. "Getting you something special is nonnegotiable."

"OK then, if you don't mind your new young woman having a last fling at being a kid, I'd love to have a pair of cowboy boots—the shorty ones with square toes and a harness strap in back."

"You're kidding, right? Aren't you the one who has always obsessed about being too tall?"

"There's nothing like a tall boyfriend to help me get over it. Lec is six-three so a couple more inches just makes kissing him easier," Tamiko says, sitting on the bed to put on a pair of blue and gold running shoes.

"But we're in Washington, D.C. not Cheyenne, Wyoming. There can't be many western stores around here."

"All I need is the Frye boot store on Wisconsin Avenue in Georgetown, which, just in case you're wondering, is open until eight on Mondays."

"And you're the one who doesn't want to go shopping?"

TUESDAY 3

AT 6:01 A.M., TAMIKO OPENS AN EYE TO PEEK at the digital clock. Seeing it is still way early she tries to turn over to grab a few more winks, but succeeds only in tweaking her ribs, which brings her fully awake. Slipping silently out of the king-sized bed so as not to disturb her mom, she runs a scalding bath before lying back in the spacious tub and closing her eyes. Dozing for twenty minutes she twists the hot tap on again with her foot as she begins daydreaming about Lec slowly undressing just as her mom cracks the door open and says, "I'm going for a run before breakfast. I ordered you a bagel with cream cheese, orange juice, and coffee with hot milk and a king-sized bowl of sugar to arrive at eight."

"I told you, I've graduated from sugar."

"I was joking, or trying to."

"I wish I could run with you. I'm twisted tighter than our Christmas lights after a year in the attic."

"Walk around a few blocks. And remember, since Alec is even more beaten up than you, this might be a day to take things slow."

"Ha, like just how slow will you and Ed take things when you get home tonight?"

"Fair point, I guess."

. . . . .

After following her mother's advice and walking over to the Mall and back, Tamiko stands in the middle of the hotel room in nothing but a pair of low-cut cherry red panties as she surveys the clothes she's laid out on the bed. Feeling momentarily nostalgic for the days when she would have unthinkingly climbed into her baggy jeans and extra-large Tsunami sweatshirt, she tries to focus. Tempted by her new yellow dress, which with its flared skirt and tiny pattern of white cranes, felt so perfect at the Hay-Adams, Tamiko remembers reading that the worst social faux pas is to be over-dressed. So instead she slips into her new black bra, teal tank with spaghetti straps, straight leg jeans and, of course, her new black harness strap boots.

"You look super," Amy says, coming through the door a few minutes before eight. "But planes can be chilly, so you better put something with long sleeves in your purse."

"Nice to see you're still on mom patrol."

. . . . .

Soon after Alec appears at 7:15, his mom has him in her laundry room clinic. "Your lip looks a lot better. Take it easy on nuzzling from the right side and it will be healed by the end of the week."

"What about the stitches?"

"They're the dissolving kind. Your head wound is also healing fine but it's still a work in progress so you need to keep it dry. Keep your hat on and you'll look fine until I take those stitches out next weekend."

"My back is still pretty tender."

"That's because when you move you tweak the scabs that are trying to close your gashes. I'll rebandage it now and once you get to Charlie's your best bet will be to remove them and let the air dry things out. I'll give you plenty of fresh bandages and antibiotic cream for when you need to cover up."

. . . . .

An hour later as his father drives him to Westchester Airport, Alec says, "Dad, when I was getting ready for bed last night I overheard you talking on the phone—was that to Charlie?"

"Yes, partially inspired by our talk yesterday. I apologized for anything impolite I said about Emiko earlier."

"Chill Dad. What did Charlie…"

"He just laughed and put Emiko on the phone to say hi."

"And?"

"She seemed sweet."

"Hold that thought."

"I'll try. And Lec, I hope you know that I wish nothing but good things for you and your new young friend. It's just that…"

"Thanks Dad, I appreciate it and who knows, maybe you'll visit Berkeley one of these days and I'll introduce you."

. . . . .

Hugging her mom goodbye outside the security gate for Amy's 10:50 a.m. flight to Chicago connecting to Oakland, Tamiko sees that her eyes are wet. "Mom, I could never have made it to today without you, but now I really am good to go," Tamiko says, crossing her fingers behind her back in hopes that she's right.

"I know sweetie, I really do, it's just that…"

"Give Ed a hug for me," Tamiko says, turning away so that her mom can't see that she, too, is blinking rapidly.

. . . . .

Alec's flight lands at Boston's Logan Airport at 11:20 and he's back in the air a few minutes past noon. When the nine passenger Cessna 402S rolls to a stop outside Nantucket Memorial Airport a few minutes before 1:00 p.m., Alec collects his black roller bag from the small pile on the tarmac. Coming through the terminal door, he immediately sees Charlie standing with his long left arm draped around the shoulder of a tallish, surprisingly busty Asian woman, whose wide grin splits her oval sun-reddened face. With both of them wearing black T-shirts, faded jeans, and sandals, Alec thinks they could be models for a Tourist Board poster entitled "Happy International Couples Vacation Here." Hoping he's reading the situation correctly, Alec steps forward bracing slightly for his uncle's bear hug. But remembering Alec's injured back, Charlie pulls up short, sticks out his hand, and says, "Lec, it's just so damn good to see you in one piece. Let me introduce Emiko. Where did she go, anyway?"

"I right here," Emiko says, stepping around Charlie to give Alec a pretty little bow. Then extending a surprisingly cool, long-fingered hand to firmly grip his, she adds, "I hope we be good friends."

"Count on it," Alec replies, impressed by Emiko's lack of artifice.

"C'mon you two," Charlie says. "We've got barely two hours before we need to be back here so Emiko and I can check in for the same plane Tamiko is arriving on. I reserved a deck table at the Straight Wharf for one-fifteen, after which I want to run you to the house for a mini-tour."

A few minutes later, seated on a deck overlooking the harbor, they sip Arnold Palmers and wait for their burgers. Reaching into her striped canvas tote, Emiko fishes out a woven cobalt bag secured by a magenta drawstring and hands it to Alec.

"For me?"

"Sort of. You open."

"Emiko, this bag is so beautiful it's already a present."

"You have just received two lessons on how the Japanese mind works," Charlie says, beaming at Emiko.

"I don't follow."

"In Japanese culture, presents are the elixir of social interaction. When chosen with care, as they almost always are, they make everything flow more harmoniously."

"Makes sense, but what's lesson two?"

"Two is more of a footnote."

"Which is?"

"Every present comes wrapped in another present, sometimes two."

"Which, of course only makes sensible," Emiko says seriously. "One word for 'present' is *omiyage*. Other words also, but depend on, uh…," she adds, fluttering her hands in the air to make it clear that she can't come up with the needed word.

"What Emiko's trying to say is that like the fifty or so Eskimo words to describe different types of snow, Japanese has lots of words for present depending on the social context."

By now Alec has opened the blue bag to extract a black T-shirt with

"I ♡ Tamiko" printed across the front in bold red calligraphy.

"It was all I could do to stop Emi from adding a 'Hello Kitty' face," Charlie says deadpan.

"Probably big mistake, since that very lucky kitty," Emiko replies seriously.

"Thanks Emiko, I'll wear it to the airport this afternoon," Alec says, an unusually big grin lighting up his angular face as he makes eye contact with Emiko to emphasize his gratitude.

"You be sweet to young Japanese girl, yes?"

"She's only one-quarter Japanese."

"You still be nice to all of her. Now show me picture."

When Alec hands her his phone, Emiko exclaims, "She's beautiful… and look happy too. Nice for you all together in one person. She even tall like me I think, which good for you since tall girl always grateful, very loyal."

"I hope so," interjects Charlie with a full throated laugh.

"When tall girl is little she still be tall. Other girls think 'I glad this not me' and guys laugh and tease. Tall girl always remember this and not happy until she have man who make her feel right size."

"None of this could be autobiographical, could it?" Charlie inquires.

"Only thing I understand about that big word is that you laugh at me," Emiko replies, pretending to pout. "Better you be happy you be first big guy I meet."

At 1:30 with their burgers and fries before them, conversation gives way to chewing. A few minutes later, with most of his lunch consumed, Charlie asks, "Lec, are you up for a riveting story?"

"With a set up like that, how can I say no?" Alec replies, starting to lean back so as to push his chair up on its hind legs when his back reminds him this is a poor idea.

"You can't, especially since you're the only one besides the two of us who will ever hear it," Charlie says, placing a Bank of Tokyo check for $32,000 on the table in front of Alec.

Not knowing what's expected, Alec says slowly, "OK, I see that Emiko has written you a check for a lot of money, but I don't quite…"

"This is the exact amount of money I've paid her to be my, my…"

"I too tall for Geisha and play no music so I guess you call me escort—you know, woman who take money for sex," Emiko says as she laughs so heartily a blade-thin blonde woman at the next table looks over her shoulder.

"Maybe I'm a little above my pay grade here," Alec says, feeling his face start to flush.

"I try to explain," Emiko says quietly. "I first see Charlie at company party in summer 2013. My husband, Tash, how you say, 'esective'?"

"Executive," Charlie put in, "Tash was a vice-president of a company that makes bio ceramics used for things like heart stents, which was, and is, one of my important clients."

"As usual Tash in back room drinking with friends—my husband always drink too much—so I by myself," Emiko continues. "This is when I see Charlie by sushi bar talking and laughing with many people. I want to go over, but too shy. That night, next day, next week I keep thinking of this beautiful American Charlie guy. Story stop now until maybe year and half later in January 2015 when I see Charlie at same kind of business party. But now all smiling is gone and he look sad. When I ask my friend Miya what is happening she say, 'Wife die last year, very sad'. Then, month later, my husband Tash kills his self at train when boss say he drunk too much and probably lose job. I sad for him, but also happy not to have to live with man who always drink and not even like to stand next to too tall wife."

"I'm sorry," Alec says, realizing that he isn't sure what he's sorry for.

"Anyway," Emiko continues determinedly, "my friend Miya, who is wife of big…esecutive at this company, try to cheer me by bringing me to company party next September. I fine, really, but living with parents and two children, not very, um, not very…"

"Exciting," Charlie offers.

"Yes, so I go to party at golf club and see Charlie standing by cherry tree, still look tired and sad. Since no one by him I watch until he get food and then stand close behind and make small noise. When he turns, we bump and I drop paper plate. Charlie help me clean up and we talk, just little bit. Later, at home, I feel excitement for first time since I can remember. I sorry I don't know how to describe…"

"You had a crush on Charlie," Alec says, grinning.

"Thank you. Yes, big crush, so lots of time I don't think of other things, just have head full of Charlie. This new feeling for me. I know all this silly for grown-up person to say, but I know parent love for child and child love for parent, but this first time for me for woman-man love."

"Whoa! What happens next?" Alec asks.

"Now get to exciting part," Emiko says. "Miya knows Charlie partner Phil from sitting next to at dinner party, so she call him to explain about me. In few days Phil invite us to lunch. At first I like teenager and not want to go. But I keep thinking of Charlie so tell Miya OK. At lunch Phil explain how much Charlie love Claire, really love her so much he not able to think of other woman since she die. But then Phil also say after party in September Charlie ask him who is beautiful tall woman who he help pick up food."

"Ah, so there's hope," Alec interjects, munching his last fry.

"Little bit I think. But Phil also say that in New York when people try to introduce Charlie to nice woman, he not interested. So Phil pretty sure Charlie not ready to go on date right now."

"When was this?"

"November, last year. But Charlie is now back in U.S. until after New Year so Phil says he will think about this and let me know. I pretty sad because I see whole thing as big fantastic."

"Fantasy," Charlie corrects gently as he picks up Emiko's still-almost-full basket of fries, and divides them between Alec and himself.

"So I surprised when at beginning of February I get call from Phil," Emiko continues. "He say Charlie is come to Tokyo next week and will meet with me. I excited but Phil say 'Wait, Emiko, this not so simple.' Then he explain that he tell Charlie that I widow with two children and little money so he must pay to see me."

"So Phil told Charlie you were a courtesan."

"I ready to hang up phone now but Phil explain Charlie still not ready for real date so this be only way. He say he tell Charlie I not really professional woman, just need money for kids so sometimes…"

Charlie interrupts with a loud laugh as he says, "Knowing Phil as I do, I should have seen through the whole charade, but of course I knew all about Tash's suicide so his tale about Tash's cash-strapped widow almost made sense. And then there were the facts that I'd been attracted to Emiko at the party and hadn't been with a woman since Claire died so I was hardly in a mood to…"

"Are you trying to say the part of your body with which you were doing your thinking wasn't your head?" Alec says with a grin as he shakes a large dollop of ketchup on his purloined fries. Then realizing that his remark was in doubtful taste, he glances at Emiko hoping she hasn't understood. "Emiko—I gather you weren't impressed by Phil's plan," he says.

"I tell Phil I not escort—I not going to sell self even if it pretend. I have little business translating scientific and technical materials from Hindi to Japanese and back, plus live with parents and have little pension from Tash's company so whole idea silly. Phil listen politely but say same thing as before. Charlie think too much about Claire to go on real date, so Emiko, this be your only chance to get to know him. Since this be all too crazy, I tell Phil 'no.' Then I call Miya to explain. She laugh and ask me how much I think about Charlie and what we do in thoughts. So I ask her, 'Do you think it stupid to say no to what I want just because Charlie pay me?' Miya not answer, just wait for me to think about this. Finally I say 'OK I call Phil back and say yes.' He say buy pretty dinner dress for next week."

"Were you excited or scared?" Alec asks.

"Little nervous, but excited, pretty much. Sometimes I think I change mind, not because of Charlie pay me, but because I not have experience with men and well…. But even more than being shy about what to do, I want to see if real man woman thing can happen for me. So, I call Miya and she help me find black dress with little bit low top and high shoes that show red toes. Then Phil call and say Charlie expecting me at Les Saisons

Restaurant at the Imperial Hotel next day at seven-thirty p.m. When I get to restaurant Charlie looks tired, but also happy to see me and very polite, like real date. He speaks good Japanese and tells funny stories so I relax, little bit."

"Just so you know Lec, now that I've officially entered this drama, I'm tempted to add my perspective, but I'm keeping my mouth shut."

"Good thing since this my story now. So, anyway, we have nice dinner, but I too nervous to eat much except amazing crème brulée which is so good it make us laugh. But now I see Charlie not sure what to do next and I scared maybe evening about to be over. So I put my hand on his and say 'I'm having nice time.' For little minute Charlie say nothing. Then he squeeze my hand and say, 'Let's find the elevator.' So very soon we in room and nice dress on floor. For me everything that happens now is amazing but then, well, I don't..."

"I'm guessing Lec gets the idea," Charlie says his eyes twinkling. "But time is short and we need to move."

"Wait, this story needs an ending," Alec says, almost indignantly.

"Since I want to show you the house, Emiko will have to wrap it up on the way," Charlie says with a chuckle as he signs the credit card receipt.

Five minutes later as Charlie pulls out of the parking area, Alec says, "C'mon Emiko, out with the rest of the story, the suspense is killing me."

"OK, so when I leave hotel in the morning, I don't know if Charlie want to see me again, or if check he give me is like he say 'Sayonara'. You understand this..."

"Goodbye?"

"But no need to worry since by the time I get home, Charlie is already calling me to invite for weekend in Kyoto, which is very beautiful two days—temples and gardens, like magic. But the next week Charlie is back to New York and I not hear for six days. So hard to wait, but then magic happen again and Charlie is flying right back to Japan for very important business. I hope now I be little important too because Charlie ask me to stay with him in hotel."

"This was March?"

"Yes, and after that Charlie comes back to Tokyo late April and again we be together in this beautiful way. I feel like Cinderella except when Charlie leave instead of glass slipper, I have big check. Since that part bother me I call Phil and say I want to give back money and tell Charlie truth."

"I'm guessing he said not to," Alec says, now so caught up in the story he wants Emiko to tell it faster.

"Phil say that he worry if Charlie not pay me, he still think of Claire too much and everything be over. But he also say he knows Charlie very happy with me so not worry. Then next day Charlie call from New York and ask me to come there. I now so confused I make excuse about kids, how they need me. Then I worry I make big mistake, but no want to go to New York as sex girl. Well, sex part fine," Emiko adds after a pause, "just not be paid."

"I understand," Alec says, turning slightly in his seat to take the pressure off his back.

"Also I am now taking English lessons like crazy person everyday Charlie not in Japan, so I can speak so Charlie proud of me. But Charlie seem disappointed that I don't fly to New York and not come back to Japan until almost July so now I pretty scared. Then we go visit Buddhist temples in Shikoku. Very beautiful and I so in love with Charlie I decide next time he ask I go anyplace. But he not ask. So now I worry he decide I only good for sex girl in Japan. Maybe time to not feel shy I tell self over and over. So last week I buy air ticket, take bus to Narita Airport, and call Charlie to say I on way."

"Wow!"

"Yes, I so excited on plane, not possible even watch movies. Charlie meet me with limo. I think we make driver very embarrass, but can't stop kissing in back seat. We barely through door of apartment when Charlie say, 'I have something for you.' But I say this my trip so I go first and give him check and tell him story."

"Is that when he gave you the ring on your left hand?" Alec asks.

"Lec, you too smart. I try to hide it so not spoil story."

Hard to hide something you're that delighted with, Alec thinks as Charlie turns into a long driveway and says, "We're here."

Quickly scrambling out of the back seat, Emiko opens Alec's door holding her ring finger up to the light. "And best thing Lec, Charlie buy it for me when he still think I sex girl."

"Who says I didn't like you better bought and paid for?" Charlie says, coming around the car and putting his arm around Emiko with a conviction that makes it clear he doesn't plan to let go. "But Emi, Lec has a plane to meet so let's hustle through the house tour. I'm going to guess he's more interested in his own love story than in ours."

When Charlie leads the way into a bright white-walled living room whose tall casement windows face the sea, Alec spots what appears to be a shrine at the far end. Walking the length of the long room he sees that Claire's picture is bracketed by a candle and the polished wooden Buddha she always loved. Placed in front of the picture, on a deep purple cloth are both Claire's and Charlie's wedding rings.

"Emiko set it up yesterday," Charlie says as he moves over next to Alec.

Seeing the two men standing together when she enters the room, Emiko says, "Claire always Charlie's first big love. It good to remember this every day."

. . . . .

When Tamiko's Cessna rolls to a stop in front of the Nantucket terminal at 3:26 p.m., the cabin attendant struggles to open the door. Sitting in row three, Tamiko takes a deep, slow breath as she successfully resists the urge to scoot forward to help. However, once she is finally on the ground and reunited with her bag, she forgets her resolution to be patient and comes through the terminal door at a pace just short of a sprint. Now, half a dozen steps into the building she looks expectantly for Lec but sees only a lone taxi driver. Just as Tamiko's grin begins to fade and her ribs began barking their dissatisfaction, she hears a low wolf whistle. Turning she sees Lec standing immediately to the right of the door she has just charged through wearing a black shirt with 'I ♡ Tamiko' written across the chest.

"You look so damn beautiful," Tamiko says, locking her eyes on his.

"Not half as beautiful as you," Alec replies, stepping forward to gently wrap her in his arms. "Just so you know," he whispers, "if your ribs were OK, I'd squeeze the breath right out of you."

"Just so you know, if your lip was OK, I'd kiss you until tomorrow," Tamiko whispers back.

"Let's very gently try a little of both," Alec says as he presses his body closer to Tamiko's.

"You're on," she murmurs as she touches her lips to his.

Eventually pulling back from the dizzying pleasure of touching one another, Alec says, "I love your amazing yellow dress, especially the white birds. And with those boots…"

"They're cranes—very Japanese, and very romantic. And Lec, it's my first dress since I was maybe five. Actually, this morning I started out in jeans and a tank, but in Boston it just came to me to, well, go for broke, as Grandpa Takahashi likes to say."

"I'm flattered."

"You'll probably be even more flattered if I tell you how many times in the last few hours I've imagined you unzipping it."

"What's the rush? Let's take our time, stop for something to eat, drive around the island, and maybe shop for some souvenirs."

"You'd better be teasing."

In Charlie's car Alec and Tamiko take turns going over every moment of the previous Saturday's drama, especially Alec's and Dan's close call in the Aristead's driveway—which Tamiko has only heard about secondhand. "The whole day, all the things that could have gone wrong all the times we could have ended up dead—it's almost enough to make you believe in divine providence," Alec says without a shred of sarcasm.

"I'll settle for the power of love," Tamiko replies with a happy chuckle. "Hey, Lec, Nantucket is sweet and all, but how far are we from your uncle's?"

"A couple more turns. It's a big place with four bedrooms. Charlie wanted us to use the master suite, but I chose the smaller room over the garage, which kind of sticks out from the house. It only has a partial view of the ocean, but I thought that…"

"It would be like our own little nest," Tamiko interrupts happily.

"Yup," Alec replies as he wheels the venerable BMW into Charlie's long, slightly up-sloped driveway. Stopping the car on the pavement instead of pulling into the open garage, Alec plans to enter the rambling gray shingled house through the front door as part of giving Tamiko a tour. But before he can find the button to undo his seat belt, she is out of the car and heading up the wooden steps.

"This must be our place up here," she says excitedly from the landing as Alec clambers out of the car and prepares to follow. "Wait Lec, I've been fantasizing about meeting you in the pool. How about I put on my bathing suit and then find you?"

"I'm never going to say no to that kind of offer," Alec replies with a laugh, "but you don't have your bag."

"It's not the kind of bathing suit that needs wheels," Tamiko says, pointing at her shoulder purse.

"When you're ready, come down the inside stairs, and find the kitchen. The pool is ten steps outside the sliding glass door."

When Tamiko enters the surprisingly large white room complete with gabled ceiling and dormer windows, she tosses her bag on a Shaker style black rocker and moves to the east-facing windows. Craning her neck slightly to the right she looks across a field of waist-high grass to where the calm gray-blue summer sea spreads to the horizon. Turning back to inspect the room she spies two navy blue yukatas lying on the red bedspread next to a wicker basket. Picking up one of the thin Japanese robes, she smiles to see Hokusai's iconic white wave cresting on the back. Turning her attention to the basket, Tamiko sees a card with a hand drawn yellow butterfly perched on a purple peony over the printed words, "*Dearest Tamiko, I wish you much joy and happiness at this lovely house. ♡ Emiko.*" Below she finds artisan soap, shampoo, and a tall, elegant blue bottle, which on inspection turns out to be massage oil. "Perfect," Tamiko thinks as she fishes a fat white envelope from the bottom of the basket with, "*very good you be careful*" printed on the front. Grinning as she opens the flap to find foil-wrapped condoms, she flushes slightly when she shakes out nine.

Not wanting her dawdling to turn her entrance into an anti-climax, Tamiko unzips her yellow dress before lifting it gingerly over her head. Then freeing herself from her bra with an audible sigh, she steps out of her panties, fishes the bikini pieces from her purse and goes into the bathroom, reaching up to try to corral her fly-away hair as she passes a full-length mirror. Stepping into the maroon bikini bottoms with the thin black band around the top, she pauses before pulling the top over her head and adjusting the small triangles of fabric so that they more or less cover her breasts without being so tight they zap her ribs. Feeling more than a little shy as she examines her long body in the tiny bathing suit, she mumbles, "It's probably a good thing I don't plan to wear you long."

. . . . .

Sure that Tamiko will need a few minutes to perfect her presentation, Alec wanders around the rambling house. After spending a moment in Charlie's bright, spare, sea-facing office, one whole wall of which consists of an overflowing floor-to-ceiling bookcase, he moves on to Claire's shrine at the southeast corner of the living room. Holding his hands prayer-like in front of his chest, Alec bows slightly and wishes her well. He then continues into the bright white and yellow kitchen with its glass wall overlooking the pool, where he spots a plate of chocolate cookies on the granite counter next to a note that says, "*Eat Me—that's an order.*" Standing at attention, he salutes with his right hand as he grabs two with his left. A minute later, out on the pool deck tucked behind an eight-foot weathered board fence, Alec finds himself in a pocket of sun-soaked warmth, free of the ubiquitous Nantucket breezes. Picking up a long-handled rake he fishes out two yellow maple leaves that have somehow wafted over the fence to announce that summer is well past its prime. Satisfied that all is pristine, Alec slips off his cargo shorts to reveal a black Speedo racing suit. Momentarily fantasizing about how nice it would be to take off his shirt and baseball hat and dive in, he instead sits in one of the two sun-faded blue canvas director's chairs at the far end of the pool. Resting his eyes for what seems like only a few seconds, he comes fully awake when Tamiko calls, "Hey Sleepyhead, what do you think?"

Seeing her standing just outside the kitchen in a wine-red bikini, the sun lighting her cascades of hair as if they are spun gold, Alec feels a quickening between his legs. Scrambling to his feet he says, "Where did you leave your scallop shell?"

"I think Aphrodite was also supposed to be a porpoise," Tamiko replies as she descends the wide pool steps, slides into the water and rolls over on her back.

Towel held in front of his groin with what he hopes is nonchalance, Alec walks the length of the pool and follows Tamiko down the steps and into the water. "You were born to wear that bikini," he says admiringly.

Taking a few kicks towards the deep end, Tamiko treads water just beyond where Alec can stand and still keep his back dry as she replies, "And I'm kinda hoping you were born to take it off."

"If you don't come over here and give me a chance, I'll have to catch you," Alec says, pulling his T-shirt over his head and tossing it onto the pool deck.

"What happened to your bandages?" Tamiko asks in surprise.

"Mom says my back will heal faster in the open air."

"But Lec, really, you're absolutely not supposed to put your head in the water."

"True, but that doesn't mean I can't catch you," he replies as he begins swimming towards her in an awkward, but surprisingly fast dog paddle.

Startled, Tamiko turns and takes a couple of quick strokes towards the northeast corner of the pool, with the idea that once she gets enough separation she can scoot along the side wall and so slip past Alec. But seemingly without effort, Alec not only closes the gap between them, but anticipating her plan, moves to his right to frustrate it. Trapped now in the corner of the pool, Tamiko feels Alec's fingers graze her leg as knife-like she dives to the bottom. Kicking several times she surfaces fifteen feet behind him in waist-deep water, her hair now plastered against her head like a tawny helmet.

"You maybe forgot the porpoise part," she says, her laugh cut short by a grimace.

"Sweet move," Alec says admiringly. "but it fried your ribs, didn't it?"

"Maybe a little, but showing off was definitely worth it."

"If I could put my head in the water, I could catch you, no problem."

"Maybe yes, or maybe no, but I'm thinking it's a moot question as Mom's lawyer friend Miriam likes to say."

"I don't quite follow..."

"Since I don't plan to move, catching me isn't going to be a problem."

"Promise?"

"I do."

Paddling a couple of strokes to where he can put his feet down, Alec begins slowly walking up the pool's sloping bottom, water sluicing off his slim, slightly sloping shoulders. Then seeing Tamiko lift her bikini cups over her breasts so that in an instant the bright cloth is floating on the water, he stops, stunned.

"I've always hated bras," Tamiko says matter-of-factly.

"I've never liked them much myself," Alec replies huskily as he steps to within a few inches of Tamiko, the slope of the pool all but eliminating the difference in their heights. Not wanting to spear her with his erection, Alec leans his head forward. Not wanting to spear him with her super-erect nipples, Tamiko does the same. In an instant their tongues find each other and begin the age-old dance of exploration and discovery.

"Finally," Tamiko whispers when momentarily she takes a breath.

"Finally," Alec agrees as he edges up the pool's incline so that his body now presses firmly against hers.

"Gad, sir, is that a pole?" Tamiko says as she begins moving her pelvis in small circles. "I hope I'm doing this right," she says as she leans in.

"Since pole dancing doesn't work as well as you might think in water, it may be time to think of getting warm and dry," Alec replies.

"This little bird is already heading towards her nest," Tamiko says over her shoulder as she climbs the steps at the shallow end of the pool. Following her up-turned bum, Alec notices that the bikini top is still floating in the water and pauses as he considers how best to retrieve it. Tamiko, who's wrapping herself in one of the elephant-sized white towels she's retrieved from a pile by the door, chuckles as she says, "No need, really, since I'm guessing I won't need it for a few days."

Trailing the tall girl's damp footprints through the kitchen Alec pauses to extract a carton of milk from the fridge before grabbing the plate of cookies. By the time he enters the bedroom Tamiko is already in the large stall shower rubbing shampoo into her thick mass of hair. Seeing Lec through the glass door she opens it a foot and tosses him a turquoise shower cap.

Catching it reflexively, Alec protests, "No way I'm wearing this dumb thing."

"I brought it all the way from Washington for your poor battered noggin," Tamiko says, sounding disappointed.

"Still."

"I thought you'd want to soap my back and whatever else comes to mind."

"Well, put that way."

Stepping to one side so the bulk of the falling water warms Alec, Tamiko looks down, surprised by the unaccustomed sensitivity of her erect nipples. Maneuvering her body so she's back to front with Alec, she is delighted when, taking the hint, he reaches around to cup her breasts. After a few minutes standing almost chastely like this under the cascade of warm water, Tamiko slowly turns 180 degrees. Holding Alec's long cock in her strong right hand she asks, "Is all this going into me?"

"That's the plan."

"Will it fit?"

"Count on it."

"OK if I play with it?"

"I thought you'd never ask. But slippery feels best, so put a little shampoo on your fingers."

"How's that?" she said wrapping the long soapy fingers of her right hand around his surprisingly hard shaft.

"Great start. Now move your fingers up and down as if you were stroking a puppy," Alec murmurs as he reaches the first two fingers of his left hand between Tamiko's legs as if to show as well as tell.

"Oh Lec, oh my god that just feels so good, so-o-o good…"

"Trust me, we're both about to feel even better," Alec says as he turns off the water. Stepping onto the mat, he grabs a fresh towel and spreads it wide for Tamiko to walk into. "Yikes, you shaved your pussy," he says in surprise.

"Mostly just the sides so hair wouldn't stick out of my bikini. I saw from the history on our desktop at home that Mom forgot to delete that she'd been researching the subject so I thought, like mother, like daughter. I hope it's OK," she adds, blushing as she wraps herself in the towel so his view is cut off.

"I love it," Alec says grabbing a second towel. "And why should I be surprised that you're always a step ahead."

"Amazingly precocious, to the point of being borderline obnoxious, I once overheard a teacher describe me," Tamiko says, using a second towel to rub her hair.

"Amazingly lovely, to the point of being the most beautiful creature on earth, I once heard your boyfriend describe you. But, hey, can I dry you?" Alec asks, leaning over to give Tamiko a light kiss.

"Isn't it faster if we each dry ourselves?"

"You in a hurry?"

"You promised to stop teasing," Tamiko replies as she drops her towel and takes several long strides towards the bed. Pausing as if preparing to leap the last several feet, her right hand flies to her ribs as a pulse of pain reminds her this is a poor plan.

"Easy does it," Alec says, as he sees her flinch.

"I'm too excited to care," Tamiko replies, pulling down the spread and lying on her left side to face Alec, who has deftly mirrored her movements.

Eyes locked, but otherwise not touching, Alec says, "We could stay like this forever or I could kiss you."

"Or I could kiss you first," Tamiko says, scrunching forward to lightly touch her lips to his. Immediately feeling heat surge from lips to tongue, to heart, to every cell in her body, she reaches down and takes Alec's erect shaft in her right hand as she mumbles, "Is this where I get on top?"

"Soon, but hold on until I put this little rubber thingy on. Then I'll move on top for a minute but since I'll brace most of my weight on my elbows I won't crush your ribs."

"Forget about the condom, I'm full of pills, with more in my bag for tomorrow morning. So as long as you're disease-free I'm good to go."

"I got tested after my trip so…"

"OK then, so shut up and help this clueless virgin get over it."

"At your service," Alec says with a chuckle at his own unintended pun. Moving on top of Tamiko as he balances most of his weight on his left elbow he reaches between her legs with his right hand. "You're dripping," Alec whispers as he massages her clit until her breath comes in quick shallow gasps.

"Oh god Lec, I am so ready, can you please get on with it?"

"Music to my ears," Alec murmurs as he guides his cock into the mouth of her vagina. Pushing firmly against her body's wall of resistance he slowly increases the pressure. Worried that he must be hurting her he's about to back off when…

. . . . .

God, I'm being invaded, Tamiko thinks as she feels the pressure steadily increase. Excited as she had been by their foreplay, Tamiko is shocked at how awkward and strained this feels. Too embarrassed to admit she hurts and too shy to ask Lec to tone down the pressure she shifts slightly to one side in an effort to get away from what is now real pain. Then, suddenly and to her infinite relief, Alec's cock is all the way inside her and the pain is gone. As her vagina immediately opens to receive it, Tamiko is as surprised as she is delighted that with no practice apparently needed, her body has begun moving in sync with Lec's.

"Oh my god," Tamiko gasps.

"You OK? Did that hurt?"

"A bit, but I'm good now. Whatever you're doing, don't stop."

Almost immediately Tamiko's mind's chatter is swept away by mounting waves of delight, a feeling soon so immediate she quickly loses track of the physical details of what's happening. Conscious only that her eager body is straining for some kind of release, she is suddenly hit by an explosion of pleasure so intense her only recourse is to howl.

. . . . .

"My god Lec, that was beyond amazing," Tamiko whispers a few seconds after Alec pulls out and rolls onto his back. "I had no idea…I really didn't. I mean it was like my bones turned to liquid and flowed into you…" she trails off with a long breath that ends in a sigh.

His mind too blown to respond for a couple of minutes, Alec finally rouses himself to ask, "How are your ribs? I'm guessing an orgasm as awesome as that must have kicked off major pain."

"I guess, but not enough to stop me from wanting to do it again. Like, it's beyond weird but I feel absolutely content and yet I can't wait to…"

"I get it, my bones melted too. But hey, grab a cookie while I recharge," Alec says with a chuckle. "And no worries, we'll have plenty of opportunity for repeats. But first I need to hang the bloody sheets out the window."

"You're teasing again."

"Absolutely not, it's what one does when the virgin princess is finally bedded in the tower."

"Whoa, did all that blood come out of me?" Tamiko asks, sitting up and moving towards the pristine edge of the bed.

"Most of it's probably from my back. When you reached your arms around and dug in your fingers the scabs got knocked off."

"Oh Lec, I'm so sorry. For a minute I forgot pretty much everything. Let me have a look," Tamiko says sitting up. "Poor baby," she adds when

Alec rolls over. "Especially under your left shoulder blade it looks kinda like raw hamburger."

"Mom sent along bandages and tape, so maybe you can wipe me off with soap and water, apply antibiotic salve, and wrap me up."

. . . . .

When Tamiko and Alec have cleaned up, changed the sheets, and Tamiko has run her hair under the dryer, Alec stands naked by the foot of the king-sized bed, the white tape around his torso making him look like an escapee from a mummy movie. Looking at Tamiko lying half-propped against an oversized yellow pillow, her blue yukata open far enough that he can see both the insistent swelling of her breasts and the neat stripe of clipped hair on her pubic mound, he says, "Sorry to go all cliché on you, but your breasts look like big ripe peaches, or maybe the world's sweetest pair of cantaloupes."

"I hope you like fruit."

"Nothing better, but since my back may need a bit more time to recover, is it OK if we just nuzzle," Alec says as he lies down next to Tamiko.

"My ribs aren't going to take much more pounding either," Tamiko replies twitching her shoulders back so that her yukata falls fully open. Gripping Alec's right hand and placing it between her legs she adds, "But maybe we can try deep nuzzling."

"Or do you want to try being on top for a really deep nuzzle?" Alec asks.

"*Chick in charge*' it's called in the poster world," Tamiko murmurs. "But isn't it going to hurt your back?"

"Now that it's protected I'm sure it smarts less than your ribs."

"What ribs?" Tamiko says, pushing up to her knees before moving gingerly to straddle Alec. Then taking his hyper erect shaft in her left hand she confidently slots it into her wet center as she murmurs, "I've always been a fast learner."

After a few minutes realizing that Tamiko has not achieved her former state of bliss, Alec inclines his pelvis allowing his pubic bone to increase the pressure on her clit as he asks, "How's this feel?"

"Like lightning."

"Find your rhythm and the thunder will follow."

"Like this?" Tamiko gasps as she begins rotating her pelvis in slow circles around Alec's pole.

"Waltzing is lovely," Alec says after a minute, "but there's also salsa."

Increasing her speed and intensity Tamiko almost immediately begins chanting, "Oh my god, Lec, oh my god…please don't stop, please…"

Waiting a few beats until he feels Tamiko's body swell as if to burst, Alec thrusts his cock powerfully upward once, twice, and then lifting Tamiko into the air a final time to bring them home together.

Still slumped on Alec's chest a few minutes later, Tamiko lifts her head and says, "Open your eyes."

"Got it."

"What do you see?"

"Your soul looking back at mine?"

"True enough, but it's also a soul hungry enough to eat a pillow."

"Charlie left the number for Vincent's, his favorite restaurant. He alerted them we would call twenty minutes before we arrive."

"Guess you better make that call," Tamiko says, climbing gingerly off the bed and reaching for her dress. "Howling ribs and all, I'm going to be in the car in four minutes and twenty seconds."

Alec, who's already standing by the foot of the bed, cell phone in hand replies, "Race you." A minute later, wearing his 'I ♡ Tamiko' T-shirt and underpants, Alec is stepping into his jeans when he hears Tamiko clear her throat. Glancing up, he sees her standing by the door, looking almost impossibly lovely in her yellow dress and harness boots, her still damp hair sticking out wildly. "How did you do that so fast?" he asks.

"Is underwear required?" Tamiko replies as she sticks out her tongue.

"Maybe not, if you don't mind the possibility of bleeding on the chair."

"Ugh! You sound like Mom," Tamiko says, blushing slightly as she steps into the bathroom to retrieve her underpants.

"How about you also wear one of my long-sleeved shirts? Otherwise you'll have half the guys in the restaurant banging their spoons on the table."

"Done, I'll take the soft silver one with the black buttons. But fair warning, I plan to keep it forever. My friend Jazz says half the reason to have a boyfriend is to get free shirts."

. . . . .

In the car on the way to Vincent's, Tamiko says quietly, "Lec, I'm sure you know that what just happened, blew my mind. Or maybe I should say, lifted the top of my head off."

"Ditto."

"I mean, despite all the books and movies or even fooling around on my own, I, well, I simply had no idea."

"I get it. Being with you—being together like that—was epic."

"I don't mean to be possessive, or obsessive or whatever, but it's like I know you've had this same experience with lots of women."

"Nope."

"But…"

"Feeling ecstatic comes with being in love…not just ejaculating."

"Don't bullshit me."

"I just told you the truth, the whole truth and nothing but the truth. I promise that my bones don't turn to water with just anyone."

"Sorry to be so needy. But except for a couple of your uncle's cookies and a bag of Cheez-Its at the airport in Boston, I haven't eaten since seven a.m. So, maybe it's just lack of calories that's all of a sudden making me feel, I don't know, a little drained, maybe."

"Are you worried about anything else?"

"I guess I can't help wondering whether any of this with you is for real, or if somehow I've stumbled into, well, like a parallel universe, maybe. You know, like a cliché fairy tale where a princess meets an impossibly beautiful prince who beds her after slaying the fiercest dragon. Sorry, I don't even know what I'm trying to say except I want this to be about a real me and a real you, not something out of…"

"No doubt there's been something borderline fantastical about the last sixteen days, but I don't see how you can question what just happened."

"It's just that two weeks ago I was a kid in a dumb sweatshirt fantasizing about saying yes to her first date and now…"

"Suppose I agree that your story could have been ripped out of a fairy tale. As if one August morning walking across campus you fantasized about a shiny new life complete with a guy a little like me. And boom, your fairy godmother waved her wand and it happened. But how does any of this compute unless I also fantasized you, which I'm pretty sure I didn't. In fact, the last thing I was looking for that Monday morning was a girlfriend."

"Leaving aside the little detail of who followed whom down the path, your fantasies have to be your business, I guess. But maybe by this summer you were getting jaded by your worldwide parade of exotic beauties. And so, with Teri scheduled to leave in a few weeks, your subconscious ordered up a teenage virgin who could restore your sense of innocence."

"Yikes! We really do need to eat. But assuming, for the purpose of discussion, I buy even a little of that, what difference does it make? From the instant you turned around to face me on the path in front of the library—girl or woman, princess or peasant, fairy tale or not, I was poleaxed. And the more I've hung out with you, the more poleaxed has turned into gobsmacked."

"At the very least I've caught a prince with a silver tongue," Tamiko says with a chuckle.

"Ready to get out of this car and eat the menu?"

"Totally."

. . . . .

A large, balding man in his late forties wearing black pants and a white shirt with sleeves pushed up to his elbows, grabs Alec's right hand in both of his warm meaty ones as soon as Tamiko and Alec push through the glass door of Vincent's. Booming, "Welcome to my humble corner of Sicily, you look so much like Charlie I would recognize you in Logan Airport." Vincent glances at Tamiko before adding, "And just like Charlie you are with a gorgeous woman. Would you two like me to evict someone so you can sit by a window, or will you trust me to show you to our most romantic table at the back?"

"I bet you can guess we're all about romantic," Tamiko says, taking Alec's hand and squeezing it.

"Long may this be true, my friends," Vincent says as he shambles between the tables of the noisy, crowded dining room towards the back right corner, where, for reasons lost to history, an L-shaped nook is cantilevered over the parking lot. Although open to the restaurant on two sides, it feels as if Alec and Tamiko are entering a room of their own.

Seating Tamiko with a flourish, Vincent says, "Of course Charlie insists that everything go on his tab. To start, may I suggest the delightful, extra dry French champagne that is the star of our cellar?"

"Sounds great," Alec says thinking that if Vincent isn't going to worry about Tamiko's age, there is no reason they should. "And maybe also something to nibble since we're..."

"Charlie predicted you would be ready to 'mangiare tutto'. How about some calamari *fritti* and bruschetta while you look at the menu? Or if you wish, I can speed things up by starting a lobster and a medium rare steak with baked potatoes and a big salad so as to have them here almost before you finish your squid."

Seeing Tamiko nod, Alec replies, "Sold, as long as someone also brings two baskets of rolls and a pile of butter."

Moments later, a slim young waitress whose name tag identifies her as 'Amanda,' places a heaping bread basket on the table before deftly pouring each of them a glass of champagne. Lifting her flute so that the candle lights its dancing bubbles, Tamiko says, "I guess this princess is ready to stop pouting and propose her first grown-up toast."

"Go for it."

"If I have this right we hold up our glasses while I do my best to say something profound, followed by a silly word like, 'Prost' or 'Salute'?"

"That's it, but you'll want to switch the glass to your left hand since it's closer to your heart."

"*Perfectamento*," Tamiko replies, making the adjustment. Then, pausing for a few seconds as if scanning her encyclopedic memory for the perfect lines, she locks her eyes on Alec's and says, "True love."

"True love," Alec echoes, touching his glass to hers.

Saying "*Cin cin*," as she places the calamari and bruschetta on the table, Amanda adds, "Ain't love lovely," before spinning and heading back into the dining room.

So intent on eating that neither speaks for a couple of minutes, Alec swallows the last hunk of calamari dripping with aioli and says, "OK, so back to my taking your worries seriously that somehow we're not entirely free agents, but…"

"I'm over it, like totally. Promise me I won't lose my glass slipper anytime soon and I'm ready to move on to how we're going to deal with real, day-to-day stuff back in Berkeley."

"Not so fast. Before we leave the fantasy world entirely, I have something for you," Alec says with a grin as he places a tiny blue velvet box on the table.

"Wow!" Tamiko says delightedly. "But hold on a second," she adds as she rummages in her bag and pulls out a small, square tin box tied with a red ribbon.

"I hate interrupting another precious moment," Amanda says, "but I also come with presents and mine are hot."

"Eat first, open second?" Tamiko asks.

"Eat first," Alec concurs as he moves the boxes out of Amanda's way.

"Thank you. And I hope it's OK that I divided the steak and lobster and gave you each a baked potato with the salad here in one bowl," Amanda says, placing the plates on the table.

After inhaling her steak and taking a few appreciative bites of lobster, Tamiko asks, "Do you plan to eat the rest of your potato?"

"You mean the one dripping with butter and sour cream?" Alec asks, picking up his fork.

"Exactly."

Cutting the last hunk of potato in half and forking one portion onto Tamiko's plate, Alec grins as she says, "I'm all for my princess keeping her strength up."

As Amanda clears the plates, she asks about coffee and dessert, adding that everything is sold out except the Tiramisu and chocolate budino. "I could also put together an affogato, that's vanilla ice cream with espresso."

"OK," Tamiko says.

"OK to which?" Amanda asks in surprise, as if, perhaps, Tamiko hasn't registered the entire list.

"OK to all three, plus two cappuccinos."

"That's gonna be a lot of caffeine."

"We're not planning on going to sleep for a while," Alec says.

"Optimistic aren't we," Amanda replies with a grin as she turns and marches off.

"Finally time to open presents?" Tamiko asks

"Mine was on the table first," Alec says seriously as he slides the blue box in front of her.

Thumbing back the top, Tamiko sits so still Alec worries she doesn't like it. Then, picking the thin gold ring from its nest of cream satin and holding it next to the candle so that the tiny red stone glows, she says, "Really Lec, I'm blown away. It's beyond perfect, even though it totally keeps us in the fairy tale."

Grinning now that he sees his gift is a success, Alec says, "You can give it back."

"Never," Tamiko replies, closing her right fist around it.

"Which finger are you going to put it on?"

By way of answer, Tamiko opens her hand and slips the thin gold band on the ring finger of her left hand.

"Just so you know, when it comes to rings, that's your most serious finger," Alec says, making eye contact.

"Even tall tomboys in cowboy boots know that much," Tamiko replies seriously. "But now it's your turn to open."

Sliding the thin red ribbon off the square tin box, Alec pulls off the lid to find a woven copper bracelet. Fingering it with obvious delight, he slips his watch off his left wrist and replaces it with the bracelet. "Just like making a toast, I want this bracelet on the side closest to my heart," he says seriously.

"Here I come, interrupting yet another special moment," Amanda says as she places the desserts and coffee on the table. "But since Tiramisu is the Italian cake of love, I'm guessing my timing is about right."

"Spot on," Tamiko says, as she picks up her fork, breaks off a generous chunk and holds it up to the slim young woman. Glancing over her shoulder to be sure she's unobserved, Amanda opens her mouth wide and snags the whole piece in one bite. "Thanks," she says, "it's sweet to be included in your special night."

"Your turn," Alec says as he cuts a second piece and stuffs it in Tamiko's open mouth. "So back to the meaning of the ring and the bracelet," he continues as she licks her lips. "What do you want them to signify?"

"Oh my god Lec, this is our first big joint decision. Do you want to go first. I mean, for once I've run out of words. For sure don't let me have another sip of champagne."

"No question things are moving at warp speed so if you prefer we can leave our serious conversation until tomorrow and talk instead…of shoes and ships and sealing wax and cabbages and the king…"

"Kings," Tamiko says with a grin. "The Walrus in *Through the Looking Glass* says 'Kings,' not 'the King.' But I'm betting you knew that and were just giving me a moment to chill."

"My lips are sealed," Alec says, taking the last bite of Tiramisu.

"Ha! OK then, what I think is this. Although I'm head over heels in love with you—in the real world I'm barely sixteen, live with my worried mom, play a bunch of high school sports, and still need to choose a college. By contrast you're like this borderline adult who, at least this fall, has to study like crazy and prepare for the GMATs and whatever else. So, while I want nothing more than for us to be a real couple, the kind that eats bagels together on a sunny morning and feels glad, I have no clue how we're going to pull it off."

"You never run out of words for long," Alec says.

"Just a motor mouth princess, I guess," she replies before eating the last bite of budino.

"Is it my turn?" Alec asks.

"Go for it."

"For starters I'm all in on the couple idea, so it just comes down to a matter of logistics. I mean, we only live ten minutes apart so how hard can it be now that Amy's on board?"

"But I can't just move into your house with a bunch of college seniors, and grad students, can I? And no matter how reasonable Mom has become I don't think she's going to move over to Piedmont full time and give you our house key."

"Suppose we settle for being a couple half the week. For example, maybe you and your mom go along like always on Sunday and Monday nights, but on Tuesday and maybe, now and then, Thursday Amy stays over with Ed while I hang with you at Francisco Street. On the weekends we can be at my place where house rules allow guests two days a week. And maybe on school breaks we can take off someplace with our sleeping bags. As I remember, you said something about wanting to learn to surf."

"I knew there was a reason I fell for a wise old dude. The ring and bracelet mean our hearts and souls are committed to each other for the next year but without needing to be together every second."

"Put the word 'absolutely' before 'committed' and I'm all the way in."

"Which it turns out is exactly where I want you to be."

THE END

ACKNOWLEDGMENTS

Toni Ihara deserves a paragraph all to herself. Not only did Toni help me develop the underlying plot, but during the editing process suggested dozens of improvements and caught a boatload of mistakes. And, as if that wasn't enough, she also contributed countless hours of data entry. In short, without Toni, *Coming of Age in Berkeley* would still be coming.

I'm also very grateful to my wise volunteer editors, Ilene Gordon and Heather Merriam. Each gave me the gifts of close attention, creativity and conviction. Thank you my friends.

Thanks too to Andy Ross, who brought much needed "keep it simple and kill the sub-plots" advice to an early draft. And to Irene Barnard, who not only proofread my shaggy manuscript, but made a number of deft editorial suggestions.

Gregg Mayer, Ken Armistead and Mai Hagimoto contributed many ideas and insights concerning the Japanese aspects of my story. Thanks to all three and to Susan McConnell, Peter Beren and Michael Gordon for their valuable help.

And thank you to Jaleh Doane and Susan Putney, who literally made this book. Working together again after many years is a great pleasure. And the same is true for Jackie Mancuso, the multi-talented artist and children's book author (*Paris Chien: Adventures of an Ex-Pat Dog*) who designed and created the cover art.

And finally, to get this independently published book out into the world, I'm thankful for the good advice of Jaleh Doane, Jackie Thompson, Whitney Vosburgh and Helena Brantley of Oakland's Red Pencil Publicity.

JAKE WARNER is the author of *Murder on the Air* (with Ihara) as well as a number of popular children's stories including *Sheriff Daisy and Deputy Bud*, *The Tibbodnock Stories*, and *Clem, the Detective Dog*. He is also the co-founder and longtime publisher (now retired) of Nolo, America's leading source of consumer law information. Among his many non-fiction titles is the bestselling *Get a Life: You Don't Need a Million to Retire Well*. Warner lives in Berkeley, California with his wife Toni Ihara.

CPSIA information can be obtained
at www.ICGtesting.com
Printed in the USA
LVHW041739111218
600075LV00002B/189/P